THE INVASIVE

MICHAEL HODGES

SEVERED PRESS
HOBART TASMANIA

THE INVASIVE

For Pam, the strongest woman I have ever known. This story would not be possible without you.

The Invasive would not be possible without my agent, Laura Wood. I'd also like to thank Sarah, Debbie, and Charlie for their help. And to the numerous campers across the state of Montana who wondered why a guy was writing on his laptop on picnic tables at U.S. Forest Service campgrounds: this is why.

THE INVASIVE

Something wasn't right. At least that's how Bishop felt as he walked onto the deck with the cake he'd bought to surprise Angela for their fifth anniversary. A certain odor clung to the air, and he couldn't help but feel there was a darkness to the Montana forest that went beyond the night, even as he held the candlelit cake out in front of him. With each step, the candles hissed and the flames shifted. Far off in the woods, something popped like fireworks. Maybe kids.

Bishop pushed away the negative thoughts and focused on the positive. For one, he was damn happy to be here. The Apex Valley was his home, even though he lived in Chicago. This was where he wanted to be, and for three days, he and Angela hadn't even gotten in their rental car. Just pure relaxation at their cabin rental. The valley had gotten into his blood thanks to his father, who'd taught him how to fish and camp in these woods a long time ago. His father often met him on trips out here, but not this year. Cancer made sure of that. The last thing he ever told Bishop was that Bishop was a mountain man at heart, and a mountain man is a homeless man in Chicago, roof or no roof.

The candlelight cut through the night and illuminated Angela's beautiful face, giving her cheeks a warm glow. Her eyes pooled with moisture and she smiled.

"Happy anniversary," Bishop said.

"Bishop, you didn't have to—"

"Yes, I did," he said.

Bishop placed the cake onto the table and sat down next to Angela.

"You get to blow it out," he said.

"From Brownies Bakery?" Angela asked.

Bishop nodded, and Angela leaned into the cake, her skin radiating from the candlelight. She pursed her lips, and the candles rippled and fluttered, then went dark.

Something screamed from the woods.

Angela turned and stared into the leafy darkness.

"Just an animal," Bishop said as the candle smoke wafted around them. "It always takes us a bit to get used to the change." Bishop cut a piece of cake for Angela and placed it onto a pink paper plate.

"Delicious," Angela said, licking frosting from her upper lip.

A screech ripped through the forest, and Bishop rose to his feet.

"OK, that one scared me," Angela said, putting her fork down and looking into the night.

Bishop had heard similar sounds before, but he couldn't be sure if these were a match. He'd heard mountain lions attacking deer, and that was sort of similar. Owls were also an excellent source of weird noises.

"Probably nothing," he said. Bishop cut a piece of cake for himself and wondered why he couldn't shake the uncomfortable feelings. This was supposed to be a happy time for them, but his thoughts were tinged with melancholy. He looked at Angela and the sadness faded. She had a way of doing that. He still wasn't sure what the heck she'd seen in him all this time. Either way, he wasn't going to press his luck.

"Five years married, five years coming to Apex Valley," Angela said. "Coincidence?"

"Maybe," Bishop said, grinning.

"I think this will be our best trip yet," she said, forking her cake.

A moth buzzed against the porch light and was swallowed by an even bigger insect.

Angela put down her fork and reached for something under the table.

"Close your eyes and hold out your hands," she said.

Bishop did.

Angela placed the object in his palms and he opened his eyes. He smiled when he saw a tiny gift-wrapped box. He untied the silver bow and ripped open the paper. Inside was a fire flint.

"You talked about how much you wanted one," Angela said. "Finally, you have your damn fire flint."

Bishop laughed and kissed her on the cheek. "Thanks," he said. Then he bit her on the neck.

Angela tilted her head back and laughed. "Ouch."

Bishop stood and headed towards the cabin door.

"Where are you going?" Angela asked.

"Forgot something," he said. He'd also purchased a bottle of wine for their celebration, and had kept it hidden in his backpack. Sometimes, Angela would look at him like he was crazy. He lived in Illinois full time, yet he traveled with a hiking backpack as if he would head into the mountains on any given day. Angela had told him it was wishful thinking. He thought she was sweet.

When he opened the door, the smell he'd noticed earlier had become a stench.

"Honey, what is that?" Angela asked, waving her hand in front of her face.

Bishop shrugged.

He went into their rental cabin and took the bottle of wine from his backpack. Halfway across the kitchen, Angela screamed, and through the window, he saw her stand and point in the orange porch light, framed by darkness. Bishop dropped the bottle and ran outside. Two steps onto the porch the screeching started, seeming to come from things much smaller than humans, as if thousands of worms had obtained the ability to shriek with almost comprehensible inflection. His vision sharpened, but what he could make out didn't seem real. For a moment, he saw a chubby mammal-like creature peeking up between the slats in the deck. Its oversized eyes contained three silver pupils. A rectangular tag on its neck pulsated with a reddish color, like a stop light. He looked up from the strange creature and saw Angela leaning over the deck railing, shouting that she could see unknown figures at the forest's edge. She pointed to the woods with a shaking finger, and then looked back at Bishop with wild eyes. He reached for her, but Angela was not quite Angela. As she turned, he noticed a peculiar leaf clinging to the right side of her face. As he swiped the rotten leaf away, it made a shrill squeak. This seemed to agitate something in the forest, which came alive with unsettling hoof stomps and grunts.

Bishop grabbed Angela and pulled her to the cabin door.

"You OK?" he asked.

Angela nodded but did not speak.

They entered the cabin and locked the door. Angela slumped against the wall and slid to the floor.

Bishop kneeled and met her eyes. "Are you OK?" he asked again. Angela looked at him and nodded. He embraced her and pulled her up.

"What is going on?" she asked, her voice uneven.

"I don't know, baby."

Bishop paced the cabin and ran his hands through his hair. More of the leaf creatures appeared on the deck, and his first thought was how to stop the things from coming inside.

"What are they?" Angela asked.

"They aren't native," Bishop said. "I know that much."

"Did you...see things too?" she asked.

Bishop nodded.

"And the smell, Bishop..."

He nodded again and squeezed her shoulder. Then Bishop took a big piece of plywood from behind the wood pile and dragged it to the fireplace.

"Take the other end," he said.

Angela picked up her end and dropped it. She flailed as it fell. "I'm sorry."

The fireplace shook and the cabin lights went black. They wanted to run, but the last thing they should do was go outside. Bishop reached for Angela in the murky light, wrapped his arms around her and pulled her close. He felt her trembling as she sobbed.

"Shhh...don't make a sound," he whispered.

They looked towards the moonlit hearth, the soft glow streaming in from the dual skylights.

From deep inside the fireplace, they heard a noise, like a pressurized can releasing its contents. They retreated to the far wall and stared at the firebox with jittery, wide eyes.

Something peered out at them.

An ominous pair of almond-shaped eyes scanned the room, the eyeballs touching each other with no separation, unlike human eyes. Each eye contained three silver pupils. The creature extended from the fireplace and peered up at the moon through the skylights. Its complete form revealed an elongated, sinewy piece of meat with staggered fins on the top and bottom. Surrounding the bones and meat was a gaseous exterior. There were no hands or feet of any kind, and it propelled through the air by undulating its eel-like body. The mouth resembled that of a moray eel, but with more menacing teeth. The creature skulked its way to the kitchen, remained silent for several seconds, then emitted a pressurized hiss.

They cowered in the corner, Bishop holding her tight, keeping her from trembling so hard that she might make their presence known. He felt her, he loved her. She was beautiful, and he always reveled in the shampoo fragrance of her blonde hair, even now, even as this thing slunk in the cabin, searching for whatever such things search for.

Bishop put his mouth on Angela's head and kissed it, but his lips were dry and the kiss was too loud. The creature spun around, eyed their corner, then hovered in their direction. Bishop clutched her, offering his body as a shield. The organism inched closer, eyes searching, the six pupils moving independently for maximum coverage. It stalked within three feet of their position and all six pupils locked onto Angela. Bishop leaped at the intruder and screamed.

"Run!"

The creature twisted past him and struck Angela, wrapping the sinew and fins around her neck and cinching. It let out another pressurized hiss and a croaking, sandy call which seemed like mocking laughter.

Bishop reached out to grab the creature. The boney fins sliced into his flesh like an errant paring knife. A flash of powerful electricity stunned him, but he held on, discombobulated from the shock. The creature shrieked and yanked free of Bishop's bloody grip. Bishop adjusted and seized Angela as the creature wrapped itself around her neck. As he clutched her, the electric shock floored him again, forcing him to release his desperate grip.

"Hang on!" he shouted.

The thing dragged Angela to the glass doors and jerked her through. It never hesitated, not even once. Spikes of glass tore into her back and calves. The last thing Bishop saw was her moonlit blonde hair disappearing over the railing like the luxurious tale of some wild animal. From the woods came unspeakable noises—a grotesque clicking of jaws and repetitive shrieks. The noises echoed in his mind as the world dimmed.

*

A stench woke him, and he scrambled to his feet, panic bouncing off the walls of his skull. When he saw the bloodstained glass, his bearings righted themselves, and the panic receded to determination. He gazed upon the pink-streaked sky, and the reality of what happened last night began trickling in, each piece of the puzzle infuriating him. He gripped the rug, uttering things no one could ever understand and vomited—the retching attracting something in the forest. A hostile utterance emitted from behind a row of ponderosa pines, and the disquieting tone was held for thirty seconds for maximum effect. Bishop remained quiet, a thick string of drool hanging from his chin. He wiped it away and stood. In a moment of clarity, he pictured Angela's pretty face, and soon clarity morphed into rage. Bishop raced into the kitchen and seized a meat cleaver from the knife rack. He took his cell phone from the counter. No reception. He opened the cabinet below the sink and stretched on a pair of rubber gloves.

Taunting whispers floated from the woods.

Go ahead and mock me, he thought. *I've got a little present for you.*

Bishop ransacked the closet, taking a daypack, first-aid kit, and lighter fluid. He loaded the pack, grabbed the fire poker near the hearth, and set out to the deck. When he reached the jagged glass, he realized the deck was seething with the rotten leaves. Bishop took the lighter fluid from the pack and moved carefully, raising his feet high with every step so the rotten leaves couldn't latch on. He held out the bottle of lighter fluid, splashing it onto the glistening, pockmarked backs of the chittering creatures. Satisfied with the level of saturation, he reached the steps and struck the fire flint, careful to turn his face away. The flames purred and rose into the air behind him, in harmony with the squealing of burning creatures.

Bishop ran towards the deep woods, his back warming from the heat. At the edge of the forest, he stumbled to the ground and rolled onto his back. A rotten leaf bit into his knee and chortled. Bishop grasped the thing with his right hand and closed his fist. The creature shrieked and bit his palm. He squeezed harder, felt it crunch, and the cries went silent. Bishop opened his fist. The rotten leaf was flaccid. He checked the forest and gasped as the thing jumped at his left eye. Bishop swatted with his left hand and sent it flying into the understory.

Stop wasting your time, he thought. *Angela is out there somewhere.*

He stood and dusted himself off, checking for more of the creatures.

A tremendous roar shook the woods. Bishop placed his hands over his ears and grimaced. Not more than five hundred feet above, two A10 Thunderbolt jets flew, their powerful engines kicking up a roiling storm of forest litter. For a moment, he thought he saw one of the dark-helmeted pilots craning his neck and scanning the ground.

The jet engines faded, and the unfamiliar noises returned.

Heart pounding, Bishop walked the edge of the lawn where it met the ponderosa pine forest, looking for any sign of blood. He found a slick patch on a fern and his heart sank. There was simply too much. Then he noticed a flattened trail of sweet grass and bracken fern and followed it. As he entered the forest, his chest tightened, and his heart popped out of rhythm—what his doctor called atrial fibrillation. He pounded his chest and coughed simultaneously, and his heart settled back into a normal rhythm.

Peculiar animal vocalizations mocked him from shady nooks, mixing with rustling leaves and snapping branches just out of sight. He didn't care. His concern was for Angela, her blood trail pointing the way. He didn't want the creatures to have her, even if she was dead. He'd provide for her a proper burial. And when he finished that, he'd find the eel thing and tear it to shreds.

Another splash of blood on a fern.

When Bishop's gaze left the fern, six aligned pupils met his own, followed by hissing. The eel floated before him, its eyes narrow and fiery. He dropped to his knees and the creature darted past him. Bishop jumped and swung the fire poker down upon its tailbone. The eel buckled and shrieked. It recovered and faced him again, tail end sagging. Bishop heard a faint charging sound, like a muffled hairdryer starting. The eel struck, although this time its speed was lessened without proper propulsion from the tail. The creature went for Bishop's knees, expecting his head to be there after the last dodge. Instead, Bishop leaped into the air, and the eel darted under his feet. Bishop twisted around and brought the fire poker down, creating a flash of sparks and a throbbing buzz which forced him to drop the poker. He fell to his knees as the shocking sensation faded. The rubber gloves had done their job. The retreating eel rode through the understory like a frenzied seahorse, its bony, tapered end slithering between a pair of aspen trees.

Then Bishop heard the groaning.

"Angela?"

The groans became louder, responding to his call.

"I'm coming. Keep making noise, sweetheart. Please keep making noise."

The groans came to him again, and he was able to ascertain their location. He sprinted through the brush, coming upon a small depression with two large tree roots forming a V-shape. In the depression lay his injured wife, bleeding from her legs and torso. To her right lay several dead animals—a small white-tailed deer and a six-limbed furry animal he'd never seen before. *A food cache*, he thought.

"Hey...you're going to be OK," he said, dropping to her side. But deep down internal alarms flashed as he examined her.

She was in bad shape.

Bishop took off his pack, retrieved the first-aid kit, and applied hydrogen peroxide to her wounds, focusing on the heart-sinking calf wounds first. Her torn pants were stained and glistening, and he realized she may have nicked a vein. He took off his flannel and cut it into strips with the meat cleaver, then wrapped the strips around each leg below the knee, pulling tight. Then he rolled her over.

"Angela, look at me, honey," he said. "You're going to be alright, I promise you."

Angela opened her eyelids part way, her striking, blue eyes twitching in his direction. Her face was pale.

"Bishop...thank...I love y-you...I never thought..." she groaned, grasping at his right arm.

Bishop washed his hands in peroxide and prodded into her back and calf wounds. Angela grunted and shook, but too weak to scream. He pulled out an inch-long shard from her left calf and dressed the wound. The right calf was free of glass, and he wrapped that as well. Bishop reached into his pack and brought a bottle of water to Angela's lips, tipping her head towards it with his left hand. She drank some of the fluid, and he sighed with relief. Then Bishop laid her head back upon the soft ground.

"That better?" he asked.

Angela nodded, clinging with what little strength she had to his forearm.

Mosquitoes stung Bishop's shirtless back. These particular bites were nastier than usual. He swatted at his sweaty, pale back, feeling one of the things crumple under his fingers. Bishop brought his hand back and examined the squashed bug, only to find that it wasn't a mosquito at all, but rather a peculiar specimen with two oversized, round eyes—each with three silver pupils. The bug featured a saw for a snout and wings that were leathery rather than the fragile see-through membrane of a mosquito. The wings were supported by a fleshy tendril that tapered to a four-pronged end. And it wasn't dead. It buzzed its wings in an effort to fly. Unfortunately, flight was not the only thing on its mind as it jabbed its saw-snout into Bishop's hand. It buzzed and seethed, its eyes mirrors of rage, trying with everything it had to jerk the saw into his flesh. Bishop closed his fist and squeezed, listening to the leathery wings crumple, feeling the reservoir of gunk in its plump sack squirt onto his skin. He squeezed harder, and the foul organism gushed between his fingers. One of the eyeballs squeezed out, and as it dripped down his fist and onto the forest floor, the pupils fetched onto him in a psychotic gaze.

Two more bites on his back.

"Motherfuckers," he said, reaching behind but missing the insects. They sawed into him, leathery wings fluttering against his flesh. Bishop rolled onto his back and moved in an up and down motion, smashing the pests into the ground.

He curled up next to Angela and held her. He grabbed her wrist and caressed it, checking her pulse in a way that would not alarm her.

Fifty beats per minute.

It was OK. Not good, but OK. He rested his head against the tree, his nose filling with the scent of that certain shampoo she used. He felt the slow rise and fall of her breathing, this precious being who'd sworn to spend the rest of her life with him.

They lay in the forest, hearing unidentifiable grunts, clicks, and hisses. The enchanting forest he'd known since childhood was now a freak show beyond description. *What happened? How did these creatures get here?* It didn't matter. He needed to find immediate medical treatment for Angela.

Bishop gently placed Angela over his shoulder and rose to his feet. He was never into weight lifting, and now he wished he wouldn't have poked fun at the overstuffed gym rats at the office health club. But he *was* a runner, and at least years of cardio training would help. Bishop grunted and stumbled through the forest, using the fire poker for support. He worked his way east to the only paved road in the area, Highway 18.

He busted through bracken ferns, white spiraea, and sweet grass, sometimes hearing chortling and deep grunts. What he wished to hear were common forest sounds, but these were hopes with no realization. The forest was vacant of such welcoming and familiar noises, perhaps the most frightening thing of all—even more so than witnessing the eel yank his wife through the glass doors as if her life held no value.

He'd gotten even with that son of a bitch, though, hadn't he?

In the maddening landscape, Bishop cracked a smile. He scrambled down a steep hill, careful not to smash Angela's head against the ground as he put his feet forward. The more he perspired, the more difficult Angela became to hold.

At last, he reached Highway 18, the dim ribbon of asphalt a spectral slice through the greenery. He prepared to step onto the embankment, and an ominous sensation pricked his skin. Bishop pulled back into the trees and placed Angela on the ground as she moaned. He turned to the road, chest heaving, mouth sucking air, eyes darting. The faint hum of a car engine drew near, and Bishop's heart thumped. But there was something off about the approaching vehicle's cadence. Bishop hunkered down in the bushes next to Angela. Part of his mind urged him to run onto the road while the more salient portion froze him in place. The car appeared over the ridge, and Bishop could see the hood and headlights as it descended into their little valley. His chest tightened when he noticed the yellow Subaru hatchback was not traveling at highway speed. The rear driver's side tire shot sparks as the rim ground into the road. The elderly man driving the vehicle jerked the steering wheel and repeatedly checked the rearview mirror. The car swerved across both lanes, skittering onto the embankment and just missing the trunk of a ponderosa pine.

His hope at the sound of the car had become caution. He was learning to trust his instincts. So far, he'd remained relatively unscathed in this changing forest.

The car swerved closer, and Bishop noticed a hairy, branch-like object on the hatchback. The man's face came into view, all grimace and furrowed brow, his mouth forming a half-scream. With each growing engine putter, the object dialed into focus, now appearing to be a leg with a sharp claw, maybe a hoof. The driver swerved to the right, allowing Bishop to get a better view. What he saw he did not care to see, for the back of the yellow Subaru was covered by a creature with spider-like legs—two gripping the roof rack, and two gripping under the rear bumper. The long, hairy legs led to a midsection that resembled a flounder. A bulbous eye protruded from the center of the organism, sometimes covered by a rubbery eyelid that glistened with fluid. The eye contained three silver pupils. As the creature adjusted its vice-grip on the car, muscle strain caused the eye to bulge and then relax.

As the car passed Bishop, the creature's roaming eye never paused. The left rear leg snaked under the car to the tire and stabbed into the shredded rubber. Between each jab of claw, a sandy croaking emanated from the beast, as if it celebrated each stab with great delight.

Bishop let the ferns swish back into place.

The last thing he needed was to be seen by that eye. Perhaps this creature could alert others to his presence.

The Subaru swerved on the hill leading up the valley and crunched into a red cedar. Smoke billowed from under the hood. The passenger did not move. The spider-like creature clawed along the driver's side of the vehicle, each hairy, moist leg groping, the eye not looking forward but backward to protect itself from ambush. Bishop ran towards the car, then stopped. He retreated back into the woods and kneeled beside the woman he loved.

Bishop watched from behind the ferns as the foul creature smashed into the driver's side glass, clearing any jagged spikes with a hoof-claw. The midsection of the thing lay flat against the driver's door, the eye gazing behind it as it groped inside the car like a kid into a box of Cracker Jacks looking for the elusive prize. The creature found its prize and pulled it through the window opening. The unconscious man's body balanced on the window frame, then flopped to the ground. One leg remained vertical, hanging on the window frame by a single, white sneaker.

It's almost like a crab and a spider, Bishop thought, studying it. A word shot to the tip of his tongue: *Secapod*.

The secapod grunted and covered the man's head with its fleshy midsection. Bishop turned away.

"Bishop..." Angela said weakly.

He leaned towards her lips.

"I'm right here, sweetheart," he said.

"Bishop...what...what was that noise?" she asked.

"Someone hit a tree," he said.

Bishop turned and watched the secapod grope under the car. Seconds later, it emerged in-between the car and the tree line. It clawed its way up the rough bark of a cedar and disappeared behind the sweeping branches and green needles.

He placed the water bottle to Angela's lips and she sipped, some of the fluid escaping out the corners of her mouth. He needed to get her medical attention, needed to find more water.

Bishop caressed his pretty wife's face, feeling the slight curve of her nose and brushing along her cheek. Her face had lost color. He thumbed under her wrist and checked the pulse—a normal rhythm and sixty beats per minute.

Bishop listened, hoping for the familiar sounds of this Rocky Mountain forest—a place he'd visited for years. He based his entire year in Chicago on the couple of weeks he could take off and come west. The insurance office was an impossible place to escape, and he spent much of his time gazing out the window across the artificial chasm towards the pigeons and other birds that perched on the precipice. Once, he had seen a peregrine falcon blaze down from the sky, punching through the typical Chicago winter inversion. It had bulleted a group of pigeons, talons outstretched and wings back, avoiding the pecking beaks of the scattering birds. The flock of pigeons had dispersed, and the falcon's talons were empty. It had roosted on a skyscraper, and Bishop had thought it was staring at him, urging him on with cries of *freedom, freedom!* When the bird had flown off, he thought perhaps it headed west. Or maybe it had been hearty, instead choosing to live in the land of steel towers, and for that, Bishop respected the hell out of the thing even more. He wished he was as brave. Instead, he spent all his thoughts on Montana, living for two weeks out of fifty-two.

And then there was his father. This was the first trip to Apex Valley without him, and Bishop swore he felt his spirit in these mountains, in the vast forests and alpine meadows. It was here where they bonded, fly fishing for cutthroat trout in pristine rivers and enjoying photography.

Bishop surveyed the woods, thumbed a dead fern in his fingers, then rolled it up into a little ball.

A powerful engine rumbled through the valley, this time exhibiting a normal cadence. Bishop emerged from their hiding place and sprinted onto the road, waving his sweaty arms. The black SUV raced down the hill, then gradually reduced speed. Bishop could not see the driver through the tinted windshield. He waved his arms frantically and then relaxed for fear of looking like a nutjob. The SUV rolled to a stop, the hefty V8 rumbling with latent power. Bishop approached the vehicle. The driver shifted into reverse and backed away.

Bishop stopped.

They stared each other down on the road, Bishop pointing back to tree line, his head whipping to check Angela, then the truck.

The vehicle door cracked open, and a tall man stepped out. His grey hair was neatly combed back and he wore tinted shooting glasses. In his hand was a sawed-off shotgun, pointed to the ground.

"You seen any of them?" the man asked.

"Yes...my wife, they attacked her real bad—"

"What kind?" the man asked.

"I don't know. Look, we're wasting time here. My wife...she's in trouble. Can you help us? We need to find a hospital—"

"What *kind*, I said?" the man asked, re-gripping the sawed-off shotgun.

"It looked like an eel, shocked the hell out of me."

"Yup. I seen them too. But they're no match for Justine."

"Justine?" Bishop asked. He got the feeling this character didn't do so well with questions.

"You're looking at her," the man said, holding up the hacked shotgun.

"Sir, can you please take us to—?"

"Let's go get her," the man said, waving him on as if Bishop was dillydallying the whole time.

Bishop felt a hundred pounds lighter. The man followed him to the tree line.

"Sir, can you take her legs?" Bishop asked.

"Name's Colbrick."

The two men stood over Angela and shook hands, then reached down and lifted her. She moaned and fluttered her eyelids. Bishop's heart sank.

Soon, their footfalls pattered across the road. Colbrick's eyes scanned the forest around them in controlled but intense movements. They laid Angela upon the road, and Bishop kneeled, holding her head off the pavement. Colbrick pulled the rear door lever, and they placed Angela inside the vehicle in-between coolers and backpacks. Bishop crawled inside and sat next to her in what was now an unofficial ambulance.

Colbrick went to shut the door, and Bishop caught movement from the tree line eighty yards behind them. At first, he thought it might be a black bear, but its hide was much too smooth, and the facial features were alien to him.

"Colbrick, behind you!"

Colbrick spun around, snatched his shotgun off the road and aimed it at the charging creature.

A sense of disbelief overcame Bishop when he understood just how far off he was, for this organism was far from any black bear.

Colbrick slammed the hatch and hurried to the driver's door. The creature scuttled towards them on six limbs. A thick, slug-like appendage trailed out behind it, leading to a saw-like tail of some hard material. A dull, ceaseless cry emitted from its mouth and Bishop covered his ears. Then Bishop's left eyeball twitched and pulled itself up to the corner of his face, the left side of his mouth following suit. He tried to speak, but nonsensical words stumbled out. The creature was twenty feet behind them now, and Bishop noticed four of the limbs led to webbed feet with small claws poking out of the webbing. The two remaining limbs were high on its chest and contained multiple claws with deep curves. Its jiggling neck was similar to that of a sea lion. Upon its blubbering, brown chest were horizontal streaks of lighter brown which grew shorter in length towards its feet. How this creature could see Bishop had no idea, for it had no visible eyes. The bizarre creature's mouth stretched wide and deep across its smooth head, suggesting a permanent smile like a dolphin. The mouth opened and closed as it called out, revealing no teeth, but rather abrasive textures meant for scrubbing and scrapping. A visible streak of slime trailed behind it and glinted in the sun. Its saw tail jerked side to side, and Bishop realized it was gaining speed.

"Go, Colbrick! Go!" Bishop mumbled out the corner of his mouth, his left eyeball and lips twitching to the top of his head. Colbrick shifted out of park and slammed the gas. As they put distance between themselves and the creature, the twitching faded. They climbed out of the valley, and the image Bishop saw of his once favorite pocket of nature was the seal-like beast opening and closing that repulsive mouth.

THE WIND DANCER

Angela and Bishop walked hand in hand along the lakefront, admiring the water as it contrasted with the pearl white sailboats. Seagulls soared above them, hoping for a handout from the bag of popcorn they shared.

Bishop stared into the water. He thought of Lake Gallatin, how he and his father used to fish it when he was younger. In reality, the contrast couldn't have been more distinct. Here, Lake Michigan was bordered by a massive metropolis of ten million people. A person could drive for hours to the west and not escape the houses and sprawl. There were a few cabins on Lake Gallatin, but it was close to a huge wilderness complex. Another difference was the zebra mussels. Lake Gallatin didn't have those. Bishop gazed at them, sunlight creating broken light patterns across their siphons. The zebra mussels had come to Lake Michigan via the ballast water of vessels that had traveled the ocean. It was only a matter of time before they'd carpeted great swaths of lakebed. They'd become so numerous and grew so dense they sometimes clogged pipelines and water intakes. Besides pushing out other freshwater mussels, the zebra mussel was also responsible for cases of avian botulism, killing thousands of Great Lakes birds. The seagulls above them didn't seem to mind, at least for the time being.

"What are you thinking about?" Angela asked, reaching for a handful of popcorn.

"The valley," he said.

"One of these days I'd like to go," Angela said, flashing her eyes at him.

Bishop couldn't resist. He was a sucker.

"Now that you mention it, I have some dates lined up if you're interested."

Angela turned to him, surprised. "So I'm finally going to see the vaunted Apex Valley? Hold on, Bishop. Let me mark this down in my planner. This is a historic occasion."

"Smart ass," Bishop said, shaking his head.

"I try my best."

Bishop laughed and tossed a piece of popcorn at her. It missed, and a daring seagull swooped in behind them and plucked the morsel.

"So are you going to tell me where we're going?" she asked.

"I told you, it's a surprise."

Bishop stopped, and so did Angela. "You were one of those kids who peeked at their Christmas presents early, weren't you?" he asked.

Angela blushed. "Maybe—"

"Aha," Bishop said. "I always had a hunch. I'm afraid you're going to have to wait on this one. Well, at least for the next few minutes."

Lake Michigan sloshed against the concrete retainer wall. Up ahead was a series of piers with moored sailboats. The piers were fenced off from the sidewalk, and the entrance was guarded by a huge man wearing blue slacks and a sweatshirt.

"Bishop, party of two," he said to the guard.

The guard checked Bishop's driver's license and ushered them through the fence gate.

Bishop and Angela held hands and descended the wooden steps to the main pier. Her hand trembled in his. He looked at her, and she smiled and exhaled unevenly. Maybe she knew what was coming.

The sailboat captain greeted them and assisted them into the boat. It was a modest vessel of forty-two feet, as much as Bishop could afford.

"Welcome aboard the Wind Dancer!" the captain said.

"Thank you," Angela said, taking a seat on a bench inside the cockpit.

On a checkered tablecloth, still fresh and steaming, was a meal of grilled corn on the cob, baked beans, and turkey burgers from Angela's favorite restaurant, *Vendottis*.

"Bishop, what's going on here?" Angela asked, trying to hide her trembling hands on the other side of her lap.

"In case you haven't noticed, we're going on a little sunset sail."

"What's the occasion?" she asked.

Bishop met her eyes, a smirk on his face. He was loving every second of this. "Does there always have to be an occasion?" he asked.

"You're playing me," she said. "You're enjoying this, aren't you?"

Bishop grinned. "Sorry. I thought you'd enjoy a nice evening on the lake. It's something different, right?"

"Oh...OK, for sure. Yeah, this is great," she said, a tinge of disappointment in her voice.

The captain unmoored the Wind Dancer and motored into the open lake. A gust of wind finessed between the skyscrapers and tousled their hair. A few seagulls followed them out to deeper water.

When they were a couple hundred yards out, the captain unfurled the main sail, and the Wind Dancer cut across the water, leaving the seagulls behind. Many of the buildings in the impressive steel and glass skyline began to turn on their lights, creating an uneven lightshow. As beautiful as it was, Bishop knew he'd be sucked back into the corporate world tomorrow, back up to his hi-rise office where he'd gaze out across the city like he was serving a term of self-imposed imprisonment. He shook off the negative thought and focused on the matter at hand—the one thing in Chicago that made him happy.

"Beautiful night," Bishop said.

Angela nodded, unable to speak thanks to the gourmet burger.

"Good. I'm glad you're enjoying this."

Angela stared at the skyline, the wind blowing her hair across her face. She brushed it away and took another bite.

"When I was younger, my father used to tell me a lot of things," Bishop said. "Some of them stuck, others did not. Well, this one stuck. We were out fishing a stream in the Apex Valley, and I was tired. I mean, I could barely cast my fly rod. It had been a long day, and I was sunburned and dehydrated. My father realized I was beat and told me to call it an evening, that my best shot was to try the next day after rest and hydration. So I did, and he was right. That was my best shot. You've got to know when you're ready to do something, so you can do it right."

Angela met his eyes, and Bishop knew she was wondering what he was going on about. *Good*, he thought.

"And Angela, you're my best shot, and I hope I'm yours. I love you so much, and I want to do this right." Bishop reached into his pants pocket and took out a small felt box. He opened it, revealing a diamond engagement ring.

Angela gazed at him with watering eyes. All was silent except for the wind in the mainsail.

"Will you marry me?" Bishop asked.

THE SEARCH FOR SAFETY

The thick metal truck frame provided a sense of security. At least for now.

Bishop sat next to Angela and examined the backpacks and coolers. They were filled with aluminum pouches that hikers used as self-contained meals. Bishop unzipped a backpack as Colbrick watched him in the rearview mirror.

"What are you doing?" Colbrick asked.

"Uh...just looking at your gear. You don't mind, do you?"

"Would you mind if I poked around your stuff?" Colbrick asked.

"In this situation, I wouldn't care at all," Bishop said.

Colbrick grimaced. "Go ahead and take a look. I got nothing to hide."

"Thanks," Bishop said. "You know where Spargus Hospital is, right?"

"Of course I do. I live in these parts. Where do you think I'm going right now?"

"Sorry," Bishop said, squeezing Angela's hand. He caressed her with a single finger and she whispered to him.

"Water," she said.

Bishop held the water bottle to her lips, then took a drink for himself.

"There's plenty more," Colbrick said, watching them through dark sunglasses in the rearview mirror. "And these ain't no wimpy Evian bottles. I got full gallon jugs in the coolers."

Bishop opened one of the plastic coolers, lifted a hefty jug, ripped the cap off and gulped the water.

"Hey Colbrick, you got a shirt I can borrow?" Bishop asked.

Colbrick nodded. "The blue backpack."

Bishop took a red-checkered flannel from the impressive pack.

"Good," Colbrick said. "I was getting tired of looking at your sweaty ass crack."

And I'm getting tired of your fake cowboy attitude, Bishop thought. Even so, Bishop thanked him with a forced smile. He wasn't sure what to think of Colbrick. He felt a sense of protection with another pair of eyes, but at the same time, the guy seemed like a classic prick. Since protection was the priority, any dislike would have to be jettisoned if they were to survive.

"So Colbrick, how long have you been in this area?"

"Much longer than you."

"That's not really specific."

"There was no call to be, so there you go."

Bishop clenched his teeth and squeezed Angela's hand a little too hard.

"Any reason why you're being so difficult?"

"Any reason why you ask so many God damned questions, city boy?"

"I've been coming here since I was a kid. Please don't classify me as some touron."

"What city you from?" Colbrick asked.

"Now who's asking questions?" Bishop said.

"Has to be somewhere out east. You sure as hell ain't from the west."

"That makes me less of a person, doesn't it?" Bishop said. "And thanks. I like being insulted while my wife lays here injured."

Colbrick didn't respond, and they drove on in silence. Bishop checked his phone again—no bars. Not unusual for the Apex Valley. He tried to call 911 anyway, but the phone only produced beeps, crackling static, and a sweeping frequency.

"Have you checked the radio?" Bishop asked.

"Yup. We get two stations out here, and neither are coming in."

Verdant cedar and spruce blurred by, and no other cars were seen. Pine-covered mountains surrounded the highway as it cut through the valley, stretching on for ninety miles. This area was one of the most remote in the lower forty-eight—the main reason Bishop's father became attracted to it many years ago.

Spargus Memorial was still a good fifty miles away. Bishop stared out the window at familiar and well-loved sites. He kicked a backpack when he thought of what was happening to his favorite place in the world, a place with snowy peaks, rare grizzly bears, and tumbling rivers with trout and the diving water ouzel. *What are those things doing to this place?* His stomach heaved, but he managed to stop the acidic soup from rising.

Colbrick mumbled and jerked the steering wheel, causing the truck to swerve.

"What are you doing?" Bishop asked.

"Something ain't right," Colbrick said, slowing down.

Bishop looked through the windshield and saw what one would expect to see—more asphalt with a lane marker, rows of spruce and pine, and a narrow embankment. But far ahead of the familiar scene, Bishop noticed haze across the road.

Tons of it.

Colbrick slowed the truck as they peered through the windshield. Mangled trees emerged from the top of the haze, some with upended roots dangling in the air.

"Looks like downed trees," Colbrick said. "And I don't have my chainsaw."

Bishop concentrated on the hazy obstruction as it grew larger. What Colbrick said was correct. They were trees. The problem was it was a pile of them, or at least had to be as the silty air obscured the bottom two-thirds.

"What the—?" Colbrick asked, inching the truck forward for a better look.

"Maybe we should turn around," Bishop said, although the thought of delaying treatment for Angela made him clench his fists.

"Hold on a damn second, we could learn something here," Colbrick said, craning forward.

Below the hazy, massive obstruction water pooled, and their truck made a small wake as they entered the flood periphery.

Bishop and Colbrick stared ahead, mouths agape. The imposing presence loomed thirty feet above the highway. Worse than that, a combination of gnarled vegetation and haze seemed to stretch into the forest on either side of the road as if whatever freak of nature had built the thing had done so deep into the wilderness. The air boiled with thick dust, and Bishop swore it was getting darker by the second.

From deep in the trees came frenetic buzzing and clattering.

"What is this?" Bishop asked, eyes wide.

"How the hell am I supposed to know?" Colbrick said.

"I thought you knew everything since you lived here," Bishop said.

"Punk."

"Did you drive us into a dead end, Colbrick?" Bishop said, grinning. He thought he may have even heard a weak chuckle from Angela.

Colbrick coughed as bits of dust blew into the interior. The scent of moist wood and vegetation permeated the cab.

"I'm going closer," Colbrick said. "Maybe there's a way around."

"Are we seeing the same thing?" Bishop asked.

Colbrick tapped the gas pedal and shot into the standing water. Spray flew up around the truck and splattered on the windows.

"Do you want to get to the hospital or not, slick?" he said. "There might be a way through it, and this water ain't deep."

Colbrick shifted the truck into four wheel drive. The sky darkened as they drew closer. Bits of sawdust and pungent soil clouded their vision. Colbrick flicked a switch and the headlights cut through the haze, reflecting off the roiling water that surged away from the truck.

At the base of the vegetation wall, Colbrick put the truck in park and let the engine idle.

They remained in the truck, the headlights illuminating the back end of a Honda and a tangle of aspen and spruce. The Honda's plates were personalized, reading: 2fast4u. The glow of the instrument panel turned Colbrick's serious face a tint of green.

The truck began to shake.

"Damn engine's dying," Colbrick said. "Water must have flooded the intake."

"You can't be serious," Bishop said.

Bishop felt the truck shake again, and when he looked at the RPM gauge, the needle lay still. Colbrick tried to start the engine but it wouldn't turn, so he hammered his fist onto the dashboard. A faint trickling of fluid whispered in the haze, and a raspy breeze entered the cracks in the windows.

Dim buzzing came from deep within the forest.

Bishop sighed when he realized the water they were stuck in was Cooke's Creek, a place he and his father had fished for cutthroat trout many times. As depressing as that was, it wasn't as bad as Angela's condition.

"You OK?" Bishop asked her, placing his fingers on her forehead, checking for fever. She moaned. Bishop's stomach churned when he realized they wouldn't be getting to the hospital as fast as he thought.

Colbrick pocketed his shades, reached into the glove box, and pulled out a headband. He placed it on his head and pressed a switch, and a bright beam of light shone on the dashboard. It was one of those newfangled headlamps Bishop's father was always telling him to get. *It sure beats the hell out of sticking a flashlight in your mouth while you work*, his father had told him.

"There's more of these in the front pockets of the backpacks," Colbrick said, his voice swallowed by a cloud of dust.

Bishop fumbled around, unzipped a pocket, and grasped one of the elastic headbands. He stretched it around his head and felt for the plastic switch. Bishop adjusted the headband so it centered on his forehead and pressed the convex switch, illuminating the cargo area of the truck. He turned to Angela, and she winced from the bright light.

"Sorry, honey," he said.

The buzzing grew louder from both sides of the road.

Bishop peered into the haze.

"I'm getting out of here," Colbrick said. He opened the door, then disappeared as he slipped and fell on his ass.

"Colbrick, you OK?"

"Yeah...I'm OK," Colbrick grunted. "But I got some kind of God damn slime all over me. It stinks like shit too."

A few seconds later, Colbrick opened the rear door and Bishop got out.

"Careful here, this is slick as can be," Colbrick said.

Bishop planted his feet, and cold water numbed his ankles. He examined the giant wall of vegetation and noticed water seeping from it, not unlike the tiny, cliff-bordering spring creeks he and his father used to fish in certain sections of the Apex Mountains.

Bishop turned, and his headlamp beam caught something that raised the hair on his neck. He returned the beam across the eastern portion of the vegetation wall, revealing the object once more.

"Holy hell," Bishop said.

Colbrick followed his lead, and they shone their dual beams upon the distant object.

"It's a tail light to another car," Colbrick said.

A spike of adrenaline tweaked Bishop's heart, and a little voice in his head told him to run.

"Fuck this, Colbrick. We need to leave."

"Hold up there, city slicker," Colbrick said. "We ain't gonna abandon all the gear I've got." Colbrick took a backpack from the hatch and leaned into it, then secured the heavy-duty hip and chest straps. "This is good quality shit here. These packs are full of food, clothes, and ammunition."

"Ammunition for what?" Bishop asked.

"For Justine and the .357 in the other pack," Colbrick said.

Bishop grinned. He'd never been a gun person, but he was born again. He took a backpack, grunting as he hoisted it onto his frame. Once set, they reached into the cargo area and carefully lifted Angela—Bishop taking her arms and Colbrick her legs.

"Where'd you get all this stuff?" Bishop asked.

"Here and there. I like to be prepared," Colbrick said.

"I'd say so," Bishop said. Although Colbrick was an asshole, at least he was on their side, and sometimes you need an asshole on your team.

They carried Angela towards the reflecting tail light, each step bringing a bigger piece of the car. Much of the vehicle was covered with dripping vegetation. Their headlamps shone into the broken windows, revealing plush seatbacks with map pockets.

With the next sweep of beam, Bishop's worst fears were realized; in the front seats slumped two motionless humans.

A shiny, black stain streaked down the shattered passenger side window, reminding Bishop of oil.

They inched closer, their headlamps shifting the once murky details into high-definition. It was surreal to be fixated on the trashed interior of the Honda and the unkempt, front-lit hair of the dead passengers. Bishop was glad he couldn't see their eyes.

"I'm not going any closer," he said.

"Nah. We might learn something here," Colbrick said. "If they're dead, I want to see how they got it so I can make sure that don't happen to me."

"OK...you have a point," Bishop said. "But please mind Angela."

"I've been minding her since we met. I ain't going to stop now."

Bishop's shoulders eased. Despite the abrasive nature of the man, he was glad to have found him.

They stopped a foot from the passenger side and peered in. An obese woman slumped pale-faced in the driver's seat with her mouth agape. To her right slouched a younger, slender woman—perhaps her daughter. She was hunched over, her dirty brown hair obscuring portions of her defined cheekbones. Both women's jaws thrust outward in a peculiar fashion. From each mouth corner hung icicles a good eight inches long. The tips of these odd structures dripped fluid—not as clear as pure water but more translucent than oil. Bishop flashed his lamp onto the right ear of the driver, noticing more crystals hanging from the lobe. His eyes followed them down six to eight inches to their tips, and he froze.

At first, Bishop wondered if he'd lost his mind, if he'd taken a bad fall at their anniversary cabin and the hospital had pumped him full of meds. He waited a moment for a sign, for some kind of clue, but it never came so he shook it off.

At the bottom of the icicle, a tiny primate-like creature suckled on the tip as if a colt to a mare. Its thin lips quivered, its abnormal crimson eyes with Revlon lashes blinking as it received fluid from the icicle. Each eyeball contained three silver pupils, and it alternately grasped the icicle with six hairy limbs. Bishop exhaled, his breath glazing the shattered glass and disrupting the feeding organism. He watched with morbid curiosity as the tiny creature fluttered and shrieked. Its cries rose in a steady, fevered pitch.

What the hell? Bishop thought.

The creature's jagged cries lost their peaks and troughs and became alarm-like, consistent in tone and tenor.

"What in God's creation?" Colbrick asked.

"I don't think this has anything to do with God, if he/she even exits," Bishop said. He glanced to the dashboard again, this time noticing the broken heater vents...the thin plastic slats pushed outward.

Something had come into the vehicle from the ventilation system as well as the windows.

Whoever was inside this poor Honda had decided to wait things out. *Bad idea*, Bishop thought.

The creature's shrieks grew louder and more annoying.

"OK, lesson learned," Bishop said. "Let's get out of here."

The primate-like creature wailed as it trembled and thumped the seatback. Bishop wondered if its eyeballs would pop from the pressure.

From either side of the road came manic buzzing and shuffling. Bishop didn't care for the inconsistent tone which implied multiple sources.

"Where to, all-knowing cowboy?" Bishop asked.

"The hell out of here," Colbrick said. "But unlike the city, you can't just step on a subway to cart your lazy ass around."

"The subway beats your driving," Bishop said.

"I had no problems driving before I found you two," Colbrick said.

"Shut...up," Angela moaned. "Get...get us out of here."

Bishop looked down at her and she winced, the headlamp blinding her again.

"Sorry, sweetheart," Bishop said.

They left the death Honda behind and waded through the shallow water that had been Cooke's Creek. The cries of the primate creature faded, replaced with the hyper-buzzing that came from both sides of the highway.

"Let's move a little faster, eh?" Colbrick asked.

"I'm trying man, I'm trying. This pack is heavy."

"These packs will save our lives, city boy. You need to get stronger."

"Yes, sir," Bishop said, rolling his eyes.

They trudged through the floodwater away from the vegetation wall, their lamps illuminating the dark pavement underneath. Behind them in the haze something scraped against one of the vehicles, and the distinct tone of ripping flesh carried towards them. The buzzing grew louder, and Bishop thought he could discern shrieks of derision and the clicking of small, bony parts.

"Colbrick—"

"Shhh. Not wise to make noise," Colbrick whispered.

A shriek erupted from behind them.

Creatures were honing in on their voices and footfalls. Dozens of limbs pattered and splashed behind them in the murk.

Splish splash.

The light changed ahead of them, as if they were in a dark movie theater with a malfunctioning projector and a dim screen. Colbrick increased his pace, almost yanking Angela out of Bishop's hands. Bishop's legs throbbed and he gasped for air. *So much for cardio*, he thought. *I guess it doesn't matter when you're carrying your wife and a fifty-pound pack.*

The light bloomed as the debris haze dissipated. Ten more steps and they entered the penumbra, and seconds later, they glimpsed the blurry outline of trees and highway. Behind them, the unseen army clamored and splashed, and Bishop swore he felt his eyelid twitch.

They exited the debris cloud and stepped onto dry land. Bishop looked down at Angela and saw her crack a thin smile.

"Holy shit do I love you," he told her.

"Keep going," Colbrick said. "And don't look back. It'll slow us down. Keep on!"

Bishop lost his balance and stumbled to the ground. He managed to put a hand under Angela's head, stopping her from hitting the pavement. In doing so he hit his chin, forcing stars and swirls. He gawked in a stupor, not knowing his name.

A shotgun blasted his ears, adding to the confusion.

Bam! Bam! Bam!

Bishop's stomach heaved.

Bam!

The fir trees spun, swirling in a wild pattern. Bloody drool slathered down Bishops' split chin.

Bam! Bam! Bam!

"I don't think so, sons a' bitches!" Colbrick shouted, his words mangled by firearm reverberation.

Bam!

Bishop's ears rang from the blasts, which mixed with the noisome scurrying of creatures and tearing of flesh. The smell of gunpowder permeated the air. Out of the corner of his eye, Bishop saw Colbrick stumble.

Bishop clutched Angela in the chaos.

"Get up!" Colbrick said, reaching out a hand to Bishop. "Get up now or you're gonna die!"

Bishop wobbled to his feet, half-deaf and still dizzy. He grabbed Angela's arms and Colbrick took her feet. They stumbled down the valley road, away from the massive structure. Bishop glanced behind and saw the appendages of a dozen of the primate creatures, their little limbs separated from their bodies and their strong jaws with tiny rows of teeth jutting open, their lifeless eyes staring at the dusty sky.

"Keep going!" Colbrick shouted. "Keep on!"

Bishop tapped into a surprising reservoir of energy, and they pulled away from the structure. When they reached what felt to be a safe distance, they looked back up the road.

Angela cried out.

"What in the hell?" Bishop said, mouth agape.

Far away, at the top of the road dam, numerous seal-like creatures scurried, placing vegetation where they could. Some traveled in groups, using this strength advantage to carry logs and small trees.

"God damn," Colbrick said. "Impossible."

"Bishop...get us out of here, please," Angela said, clutching his left arm.

"Don't move," Colbrick said. "Let's wait until they clear the barrier. Our movement may trigger an attack. Prey is best unseen."

The seal-like creatures groped and scurried atop the road dam. Bishop noticed several of them had the blinking, red devices he'd seen earlier on the mammal creature under the deck. He estimated the pulsing at thirty beats per minute.

Bishop wanted to cry when he tried to picture Cooke's Creek, the place he and his father had enjoyed fishing. Trickles of silted water spread downhill towards them like fingers reaching for help.

"Motherfucker," Bishop said. "I'm glad Dad isn't around to see this."

"I used to fish that one too," Colbrick said, spitting onto a fern and gripping his shotgun tighter.

The horde of seal creatures finally scurried off the enormous vegetative dam. As they did, a gust of wind blew the particulate air in Bishop's direction.

Angela coughed and Bishop took her hand.

"You alright, baby?" he asked.

"A little better," she said. "Can you find me a place to rest?"

"Of course."

Colbrick got the message and took her feet.

"Alright, let's do this," Colbrick said. "I know a hunting trail on this side of the road that leads to Big J Outfitters. It may take us a day to get there, but I don't see no other choice."

"A day?" Bishop asked.

"Yep. Unless you have other ideas, slick."

Bishop looked at Angela and she nodded. It was settled.

Silhouettes appeared in the silted clouds and haze, from the direction of the road dam.

"Wait a second," Bishop said.

"What's the holdup?" Colbrick asked.

"Thought I saw something," Bishop said.

They waited for several seconds, unable to see much of anything except for dust clouds. Frenetic scrapping and slapping came from the haze below the dam, followed by the shapes of unknown beings.

Bishop shivered when he realized the things were bigger versions of the tiny primates, their eyes the same shade of crimson and their teeth larger. The creatures—seven or eight in total—shambled towards them using six limbs, each with a worn knuckle. Although they were not blazing fast, the monkey-like things were speedy enough. The creatures headed straight for them, mouths gnawing at the air.

"Go," Bishop said. "Into the woods!"

They hustled into the trees. Figures appeared on the road below them and shambled across the blacktop on bloody, worn knuckles.

Makes sense, Bishop thought. Why wouldn't there be creatures which preyed upon those unlucky enough to be corralled by the barrier? The ambushers would pick off whatever they could, like remoras attached to a shark.

Bishop and Colbrick darted through the forest as much as two people carrying an injured person could. Angela's head bore the brunt of slapping branches—some thicker than Bishop liked. Dust clouds filtered between the trees, giving an otherworldly luminance to the understory. Bishop coughed and tried to shake it off.

"Who knows what's in this stuff," Colbrick said between coughs.

They pushed through huckleberry bushes and bracken fern, slamming into the trunks of cedar and aspen. Their faces poured sweat, and Bishop's slick hands made it harder to grasp Angela.

"Hold up a second," Bishop said, chest heaving. His flatlander cardiovascular system was not cooperating as he'd like.

"Come on, slick," Colbrick said. "Those things could be on our tail. Get a movin'."

Bishop lowered Angela, placed his hands on his hips and gasped at the sky. He turned when he thought he heard slapping vegetation behind them.

Colbrick put a finger to his lips, then gestured to Bishop with his other hand towards the unbroken forest. Bishop hoisted Angela and they proceeded west, the forest floor rising, many of the trees replaced with car-sized boulders and slippery green moss logs. The forest floor was not reliable, and each time they passed over an ancient fallen cedar, they weren't sure how far they'd sink into the spongy moss.

"Why are we going higher?" Bishop asked.

"You ever go hunting?" Colbrick asked.

"I was always more of a fisherman," Bishop said.

"Deer and bear like to walk the easy routes, too. That ain't a trait unique to us humans. The way I see it, those things will follow the lower, easier trails. In other words, I'm trying to lose our tail."

"Makes sense," Bishop said. For the first time since meeting Colbrick, he felt a sense of gratitude. After all, who else would be helping him carry Angela? He shuddered at the thought of not having any help, and although he was out of breath and sore amongst these new arrivals, he was glad to be alive.

They worked upslope, shifting between patches of shade and afternoon sun rays. The incline steepened, and they hiked in switchbacks, the many fallen cedars making it difficult.

"I need a break," Bishop said, looking down to Angela, making sure she was OK.

"Yes, please take one," Angela whispered.

They set her gently upon the spongy moss.

Bishop unbuckled his pack and the air cooled his backside. Colbrick kept his on and squatted, observing the lower valley from which they had climbed.

"There's water in your pack," Colbrick said.

Bishop reached into the pack and took a bottle. "We're going to need more," he said.

"Plenty of streams 'round here. The question is do we trust it after these God damned things sloshed around in it? Those monkeys and dam builders—I imagine they have to shit and piss somewhere," Colbrick said.

"So what do we do about it?" Bishop asked.

"Go into the bottom of that first pocket," Colbrick said.

Bishop did and pulled out a device with a hose attached to a small pump.

"Nice," Bishop said. "A water filter."

"Yup. I got one too. We're good to go. These will catch any germs which might be swimming around."

"You really are prepared, aren't you?"

"No man can prepare for this, slick. I just like to collect things."

Bishop brought the water bottle to Angela's mouth, and this time, she squeezed the sides to get more water.

"How much farther to Big J?" Bishop asked.

"A few hours," Colbrick said.

Colbrick turned, stared downhill, and put a finger to his pursed lips. Below them, far down mountain and emerging then disappearing between gnarled pines, was a line of the monkey-like creatures. Colbrick reached into his pack and pulled out a pair of binoculars. Bishop dug into his pack and found another pair. As Bishop glassed the line of creatures, he realized some of them had russet fur as well as black. They reminded him of huge Guatemalan black howler monkeys, or *Alouatta pigra* as they were known in the scientific community. His heart thrummed when he heard a faint bleating and then a mad scramble and shrieking as the line of pigras peeled to a central location. They reached into the pile's center with lanky limbs and bloody, worn knuckles, their backsides covered with shaggy hair, some of them shitting as they grunted and screeched over what was in the center.

The bleating stopped, and a delicate, light-colored limb emerged from the gang of pigras. The leg of a deer fawn. The pigras shrieked, some of the more perturbed individuals slamming a lone claw into the others, and those stabbed fell to the ground and howled in pain.

Angela let out a harsh cough as water went down the wrong pipe.

The pigras ceased all vocalizations, and their heads slowly turned side to side while gazing at the forest. They lifted their moist snouts into the air, their triplicate-pupil crimson eyes shifting as they sniffed and gawked.

Uh-oh, Bishop thought.

Angela put a hand to her mouth. Her face reddened as she tried to hold back another cough.

Colbrick took the butt of his shotgun and cracked her in the head, knocking her out.

Bishop shook as rage boiled within him. He formed a fist and spun around, then stopped his fist in midair. He wanted to kill Colbrick more than anything, but after rapid thoughts of appropriate responses shuttered through his mind, he knew Colbrick was right. Angela would've revealed their location, getting them all killed. He felt horrible. His stomach churned, and his eyes moistened when he looked at her, at how peaceful she was. *I'm sorry, sweetheart,* he thought. *But you'll be awake soon. And alive. And that's better than the alternative.*

Bishop and Colbrick observed the pigras as they returned to their line, fresh blood staining some of the faces and soiled tangles of fur. Soon, the pigras lurched northeast, away from them. Bishop sighed. He watched until the last one disappeared behind a patch of ferns.

"You know anyone in that direction?" Bishop whispered.

"I knew a few people, "Colbrick said. "But I couldn't do anything for 'em."

Bishop placed the binoculars back into the pack and clenched his fists.

"Come on," Colbrick said. "Let's get to Big J."

Colbrick faced away from Bishop, bent down, and held Angela's feet in the crooks of his arms. Then he led them in a westerly direction.

They crested the rugged mountain, only to find even higher mountains awaiting them. These mountains were not the highest in Montana, but they attained such a height that the trees on the upper slopes grew stunted and windblown—their branches all facing east from years of violent gusts.

"How much farther?" Bishop asked.

"You sound like a kid in the backseat," Colbrick said.

"Yeah, I guess I do. But that doesn't change the question."

"You see those mountains?" Colbrick asked.

"You mean the Apex Mountains?" Bishop said.

Colbrick turned his head and raised an eyebrow. "Very good. I didn't think too many of you slicks knew what the ranges were up here."

"I've been coming here all my life," Bishop said. "I'm not your average Main Street touron."

"We'll see about that," Colbrick said. "You see that flat piece of land in front of the Apex's there?"

"Yes."

"That's Big J."

"Shit. That's at least several miles away."

"You got a better idea?"

"Hell no. Just venting."

"Ain't nothing wrong with that. A man's gotta vent somehow." Colbrick looked down to his shirt pocket. "Son of a bitch," he said.

"What's wrong?" Bishop asked.

"I must have lost my shades."

Bishop held back a snicker.

They proceeded down the mountain. This was more difficult than climbing, for placing your foot in a downward position on the slick moss and moist rocks was far more treacherous.

"Careful," Bishop said as they sent sticks and rocks tumbling. Bishop paused and glanced down at Angela to make sure she was OK.

Angela stirred as her bottom scraped against boulders and fallen timber. A chunk of rock tumble down slope. Bishop glanced at Colbrick's feet to see how it was displaced, but Colbrick was standing on moss. Colbrick crouched and pointed to a pile of rocks thirty yards ahead. Bishop kneeled, keeping Angela's head off the moss while following Colbrick's finger.

Something flashed behind the rocks.

A creature blinked back with eyeballs the size of doorknobs. It had a sharp, yellow beak and a thin neck which led to whatever lay hidden behind the rocks. Its pupils were tiny, leaving way too much white. Above the eyes grew a tuft of brown feathers. The bird ducked below the rocks and they remained still, only to see the weird bird peek out again, its oversized eyeballs elevating like two unusual sunrises.

"What the heck is that?" Bishop whispered.

"How the hell am I supposed to know?" Colbrick asked.

The bird let out an energetic chirp, starting low and calm then escalating into an ear-piercing ring that reverberated across the mountain. The tuft of feathers on its head quivered with each call.

Angela blinked.

"Bishop, what...*is* that thing?" she asked.

"I don't know, sweetheart." Bishop wanted to blurt it all out, to tell her everything they'd encountered. He had to be honest with her. She was going to find out soon enough. A protective instinct wanted to shield her from the things he saw, but it wasn't fair. Bishop cleared his throat and met her eyes. "I do know these mountains are infected with many new species—kinds we've never seen before. Do you remember the thing that dragged you away at the cabin?"

"Yes."

"While you were out I saw more things, and so has Colbrick. But we're going to get out of this, do you understand?"

"I don't need a pep talk, Bishop. I'm a big girl."

Bishop turned away, embarrassed.

"I'm sorry," Angela said. "I didn't mean it like that. I just need a place to rest. Also, I could really use some freaking painkillers, honey. My cuts...they itch so bad."

Colbrick gave them a dirty look while holding a finger to pursed lips. The weird bird disappeared behind the rocks, and they heard stones skittering and feet scratching as it moved down mountain.

"Where did these things come from?" Bishop asked.

"Again, how the hell should I know?" Colbrick said. "But wouldn't it be nice if like in the books and movies we ran into a scientist or some random billion dollar bunker full of expensive lab gear to explain everything?"

Bishop laughed, and even Angela let out a chuckle.

"Shit ain't like that," Colbrick said. "We aren't going to find a God damned scientist, and there's no super fancy bunker with groups of people waiting to explain everything to us. If we're lucky, we might be able to piece together some clues, but I get the feeling that's about it."

"I know a bit about nature," Bishop said. "So does Angela. There's also Great Prairie Air Force Base."

"That's four hundred miles from here," Colbrick said.

"We need to find a car," Bishop said.

"And if we do, what's to stop us from driving right into those dam builders again?" Colbrick asked.

"You mean the frequency seals," Bishop said.

"Glad you took the time to give them a name," Colbrick said.

"Well, that's what they are."

"What's a frequency seal?" Angela asked.

"Trust me, you don't want to know," Bishop said.

"Try me," Angela said.

"Alright. It's a creature with six limbs, a slug tail tipped with a saw-like blade, and it builds enormous earthen barriers. Oh, and they also stun you with some sort of frequency."

"Don't lie to me, Bishop."

"OK, sorry."

Colbrick grinned and took Angela by her feet.

The strange bird rustled ahead of them as they worked down the mountain.

"It's keeping an eye on us," Colbrick said. "If it sticks much longer, I'm going to shoot it. I don't want it giving us away."

"I don't think it's evil," Angela said.

"Every creature we've seen has been," Colbrick said.

"Maybe there are a few good ones," Angela said.

More rustling and scraping from below.

"It's starting to get on my nerves," Colbrick said.

"Honey, he's right. These things aren't friendly, OK?" Bishop said.

"It's not doing anything wrong," Angela said. "Don't you shoot it."

Colbrick grunted and mumbled something under his breath. Bishop pretended he didn't hear it.

They reached the valley floor and encountered a gurgling creek in the shade of an old growth ponderosa pine, its bark ragged and its crown higher than the other trees.

"This feeds the Golden River," Bishop said.

"Yup," Colbrick said.

They stopped beside the stream and filtered the cool water, one tube in the creek, the other tube filling empty bottles. Bishop gazed into the hypnotic water, and his heart filled with joy when he observed a finning cutthroat trout.

"A cutthroat," he said, pointing to a multihued collection of stones on the riverbed.

Colbrick cracked a smile, for even the grump was warmed by the existence of the beloved cutthroat.

"Maybe we still have some natives left," Colbrick said.

Angela was now able to sit up on her own, and she downed the fresh, clean water.

"Only a few more miles," Colbrick said.

"Do you think anyone will be there?" Bishop asked.

"I can tell you the folks up at Big J are as hardcore as they come—big on survival. They got everything up there. The bad news is that they may view us as nothing more than a drain on their supplies."

BIG J

Bishop and Colbrick carried Angela between the aspen and ponderosa pine. Her wounds were growing puffy, so it was better she did not walk, at least for now.

They reached a grassy clearing below the abrupt and forested Apex Mountains. An impressive log ranch sprawled across the other side of the clearing. Sprinkled here and there were fenced enclosures with dirt surfaces and wooden water troughs. To the north of the lodge sat several outbuildings, two of them with metal doors. A majestic stand of Douglas-fir rose behind the structures.

Bishop scanned the property, desperate to see anything, but did not even witness a bird in flight. The enclosures stood empty. Bishop pictured beautiful horses fanning their tails and nodding down to drink water. Where the horses had gone he could only guess. Or maybe he could.

"What the hell we doing?" Colbrick asked, his face scrunched in irritation.

"What do you mean?" Bishop asked.

"Walking right out into the open like this," Colbrick said, gesturing to the meadow. "Come on—let's get back to tree line."

They maneuvered into a patch of bracken fern and aspen, then set Angela down. Bishop and Colbrick took binoculars from their packs and Angela sat up to watch them, her hair tousled, her eyes bloodshot.

"I don't think anyone's here," she said.

"Lay down, honey, you need your rest," Bishop said.

"I'm sick of lying down. Besides, the cuts on my back are itching like crazy."

Infection, Bishop thought as he glassed the outbuildings.

"I don't see a thing," Colbrick said. "This meadow is prime wildlife habitat. We should be seeing birds or deer on the edge here."

Bishop knew from many hikes with his father that there should be *something* stirring or flying away, or even sprinting across the grass. Instead, the place was dead. Colbrick was right.

They moved across the clearing towards the lodge, passing the empty paddocks, the faint scent of manure still clinging to the air. They hunkered near the log wall, checked the meadow for pursuers and stood to peer inside the window. The interior was decorated with various organic themes such as antler chandeliers, wooden fish carvings, Santa Fe style blankets, and iron forgings of cowboys and wildlife. The kitchen was immaculate with marble countertops and silver appliances.

Bishop saw the clock on the microwave and couldn't believe it. "Big J has power," he said.

"What?" Colbrick asked.

"The microwave clock still works."

"Might be a battery," Angela said.

"Yup. Could be," Colbrick said. "No one's home. I'm going in."

"Thank God," Angela said, scratching at her wounds.

They crept to the front of the dark-stained lodge and opened the heavy door that was adorned with a cow skull knocker, and the ambiance of the old lodge spilled out. Sturdy logs rose in unison to the pitched ceiling. The floors were polished wood, and the couches burgundy leather with plush foot rests. A wide, slate fireplace protruded from the southern wall and dominated the living room.

They carefully set Angela upon the largest couch, and Bishop inspected her wounds.

Colbrick went into the kitchen and picked up the cordless phone from the countertop.

"No go," he said, clicking the phone back onto the receiver.

"Nothing at all?"

"Dead as can be."

Colbrick moved with grace—surprising for a man of his size—to the refrigerator and swung the door open. It contained venison steaks, Budweiser, and hunks of Colby-Jack cheese.

"We'll I'll be," Colbrick said.

"You were right," Bishop said.

Bishop walked over to the refrigerator, and Colbrick handed him a hunk of venison.

"For the lady," Colbrick said. "You don't even need to cook it."

"Thanks," Bishop said, taking the meat back to Angela.

She snatched it from his hands and devoured it.

"You have no idea how good this is," she said. She glanced around the lodge, her eyes shimmering with excitement. "I can't believe we found this place."

"Yup," Colbrick said with a mouth full of venison.

Bishop glanced towards a dark hallway and stood. "I'll be right back, honey. I need to find something."

"What?" she asked.

"Antibiotics."

Bishop entered a narrow hallway decorated with tacky pastel paintings of ranch life. Along the east wall were four wooden doors spaced several feet apart. He opened each door slowly. The rooms were similar, each with a skylight, a single window, and made up like a hotel with attention to neatness and efficiency. The largest of the rooms contained an immaculate marble bathroom with a Jacuzzi and walk-in closet. Above the sink was a hinged mirror.

His face had numerous small cuts from branches, and his hair was disheveled. *I'm starting to look like a mountain man*, he thought. Bishop pulled the mirror back to reveal a shallow medicine cabinet. Several yellow-tinted bottles stood on the shelf, and he grasped each one with a shaking hand, reading the labels. The first bottle, Vicodin. *Angela will be pleased*, he thought, pocketing the bottle. And Angela wasn't the only one. He skimmed past bottles of cholesterol pills and blood pressure pills and found a bottle of amoxicillin. He let out a sigh of relief. The expiration date was two months ago, but these would do the trick for Angela's infection.

He closed the mirror and saw his father behind him, all crew cut and black-rimmed glasses.

Bishop's heart popped out of rhythm and he gasped, dropping the bottle of antibiotics onto the tile floor. He closed his eyes, opened them, and his father was gone.

Bishop collected himself along with the pills. *Dad knows I'm going to save Angela. Maybe I can save the valley too,* he thought. The mountain lodge crackled with a presence, giving him an unexpected surge of energy. He paused for a moment and then hurried out of the room.

When he returned to the living room, Colbrick was seated on the couch next to Angela, feasting on venison and cheese.

"Here you go, slick," Colbrick said, sliding a loaded plate along the coffee table.

"Thanks," Bishop said. He sat beside Angela and placed an amoxicillin and a Vicodin in her mouth. "These will help with the infection and pain."

"You knew I had an infection," she said, swallowing the pills.

"Of course," Bishop said. "But I don't want you to worry. The pills will handle it."

"Thank you," Angela said.

His eyes met hers, and Bishop shivered. They had always captivated him, and although she was sick, they didn't waver one ounce in their power.

Bishop rubbed her shoulder and headed into the kitchen. Although the phone was dead, Bishop heard a faint humming which he assumed was a generator. He wanted to find the source, but didn't care to go outside. He checked his cell phone. No reception.

Bishop lifted the faucet handle and the water spat and bubbled. As he stared out the kitchen window, Colbrick strode over, chomping his food. They gazed upon the meadow and the ominous tree line.

"I guess this is the part in the movie where the survivors hole up in some building and a bunch of monsters attack them," Colbrick said. "Except shit ain't like that. Monsters ain't that great at coordinating attacks. If anything, they'll find us by accident."

"Do we stay?" Bishop asked.

"We've got food, water, shelter, and power," Colbrick said. "I like our odds here better than out there."

Bishop looked at Angela who was still enjoying the venison. He wasn't sure what the best course of actions was, but he was certain of one thing—they needed rest, and this was the best possible place. Hell, it was the only place.

A jolt of panic sizzled inside Bishop. He turned and bolted for the living room.

"What the hell you doing?" Colbrick asked.

"The fireplace!" Bishop said.

"Oh my God," Angela said, mouth full of meat. "Jesus, Bishop, what were we thinking?"

Bishop closed the flue so that nothing could descend.

"Colbrick, back at our rental one of those eels attacked us by traveling through the fireplace," Bishop said.

"Yup. We gotta make sure everything is locked up," Colbrick said, nodding.

They checked the lodge for other fireplaces and made sure all the doors were locked. Bishop went into each empty room and checked the windows, holding the levers and counting to five, a relic of obsessive compulsive disorder which sprouted up when he had bad anxiety. Except this time he was just being vigilant, he told himself.

"One, two, three, four, five," he mumbled, releasing the levers.

Bishop approached the master bedroom where he thought he'd seen his father and his heart pounded. He didn't want Colbrick to think he was weak, so he soldiered on. He loved his father so much, and losing him was the hardest experience of his life. A wave of grief flowed through him and his throat tightened. His father had taught him everything, and Bishop could still feel his spirit in these woods. Every grain of sand and every tree branch reminded him of his father. This was his home, and something was trying to take that away.

Bishop reached into his pocket and took the bottle of Vicodin. Once, long ago, these little white wonders had a hold on him. But that was many years ago, of course, and the passage of time had wiped away any of the withdrawal. Of course. Mostly he remembered the wonderful, fuzzy haze and gushes of confidence when the suckers kicked in. He'd become addicted to them to escape his mundane existence back home. There was no need to take them here. The Apex Valley was his natural drug, and taking anything only watered down that buzz. But this wasn't the Valley he'd known, and these were not its animals. And whatever had done that to his wife would do it to him, and anyone else that got in the thing's way. Bishop popped a vicodin into his mouth like it was candy, and shivered in anticipation. *Nothing's going to take this valley away from me.* He felt alive. More alive than he'd felt for years. A long time ago, his college buddy, an anthropology major, told him he only felt alive when he was with the tribes he was documenting. Danger you could see and smell, not some boss to suck up to and a bunch of boring paperwork. Well, he could see those silver-eyed devils, and he was going to take care of them.

Back in the living room, Angela was napping on the couch, and Colbrick was standing in the kitchen with a polished shotgun.

"Looky what I found," Colbrick said, grinning. "A beauty of a side-by-side. There's also a box of shot. Today's your lucky day."

Colbrick handed Bishop the shotgun, and it felt like the first time Jenny Zimmerman let him feel her breasts, way back in high school. Bishop cracked a smile, and Colbrick nodded in a way that inspired confidence.

"Keep that sucker close," Colbrick said. "That's yours now, partner."

"Thanks," Bishop said.

Colbrick handed him the box of red shells and Bishop examined them, thumbing the smooth, plastic grooves and brass caps. Yes indeed, he was born again.

*

The two men sat in uncomfortable, artsy chairs near the glass porch door, watching the meadow for signs of life. Typically, one would see elk feeding along the edges, or perhaps a black bear ambling along. Not this evening. Although not seeing common wildlife was dreadful, it was also a relief to see no movement at all. An empty, lifeless meadow was better than a creature-filled meadow.

Bishop glassed the far tree line, thinking he caught a pair of eyes peering behind swaying vegetation, but it turned out to be nothing.

A gust of wind buffeted the glass door, and Bishop shivered. One of the paddock gates swung freely. He thought of the lone cutthroat in the creek.

"What happened to all the animals?" Bishop asked.

"They left," Colbrick said, tapping his sawed-off, then rubbing a hand through his hair. Although Colbrick lost his shades, it was like he never took them off.

"Where would they go?" Bishop asked.

"Away from these things. Most animals, if you spook 'em enough, will respond by seeking new territory. They're not dumb."

"I know they're not dumb, but you're talking about a mass migration."

"They can sense things we can't. They don't need to see the creatures. They get a funny feeling or scent, and *bam*, they're gone."

"Even the bears?"

"Yup."

"You'd think the bears would stay and fight."

"What the hell is a bear gonna do against all these things?"

"Good point," Bishop said, staring at the ground, defeated. He'd grown up in awe of the mighty grizzly bear, the undisputed king of these woods. But the new arrivals made the grizzly seem like a poodle. "Still, they could be out there, waiting."

"Yeah, they could be. And I could be a genius scientist who'll explain everything."

"Where do we find one of those?" Bishop asked, joking.

Colbrick chuckled. "I think we're gonna have to figure things out for ourselves. You got any brain juice, slick?"

"Some."

"How about your girl? She seems to have her wits about her."

"She's much smarter than me."

"And I guess more so than me," Colbrick said.

Bishop turned and glimpsed a bloody sneaker resting on the couch arm. *Holy hell, she's been through so much*, he thought.

Bishop shifted his attention to the darkening meadow. "She graduated from University of Aberdeen with a masters in philosophy."

"Well, that's sort of useful," Colbrick said, his eyes glinting at the shadowy tree line. "I know a hell of a lot about the Apex Mountains, partner. I've been hunting and fishing them since I could burp. I know every alpine creek, every box canyon, and shady glen. But what I don't know is what the hell happened and how things changed so damn fast."

"Where were you when it happened?" Bishop asked.

"I was in my yard playing horseshoes with Buck Henderson. One of the eels took him into the woods. I tried to chase him, but I smacked into a branch and knocked myself out. I was lucky the bastards didn't find me."

"Wow," Bishop said.

"When I woke, I tried to find a trail but no luck. There wasn't any blood. I just ran through the woods shouting. Wasps—a kind I ain't never seen before—bit the hell out of me, and I went back to the house and grabbed all sort sorts gear I'd collected over the years. Then I got into the truck and drove away. I even left photos of my ma and pops, God rest their souls."

"And that's when you saw us."

"Yup."

Bishop glassed the meadow, then put the binoculars down.

"I'm sorry your parents passed," he said. "I just lost my dad."

Colbrick looked at the ground, his tough man façade fading.

"I never knew my pops," Colbrick said.

"I thought you just said—"

"Yeah, I know. My pops was killed on Guadalcanal. I only know him from pictures."

"I've always had deep respect for World War II vets. I bet your father was a brave man," Bishop said.

"Yeah, I guess maybe he was," Colbrick said. "They even sent a Purple Heart to our house…and then took it back."

"What? How could they take it back?" Bishop asked.

"It was a mistake, meant for another soldier," Colbrick said. "I guess pops was just a regular Joe who caught a stray bullet."

"Hey, don't say that. You don't know the whole story. Only the people on that island know the truth."

"I can still remember my mother's face when they took that heart back," Colbrick said. "She lost all color."

"Unbelievable."

"So I never knew my pops, and then the Marines took away what I thought I knew of him. Kind of a double whammy I guess. But screw my pity-party, Bishop. No good. You said you lost your pops?"

"Yes, to cancer."

"He brought you to Apex Country, didn't he?" Colbrick asked.

"Yes. Good guess. We liked to hike and fish."

"There ain't no finer place to fish for trout in the United States," Colbrick said, gesturing to the meadow and woodlands. "They come from all over the world to fish these waters."

"My father's favorite river was the Golden. We'd always make time for the salmon fly hatch."

"Yup. That's the big one."

"The biggest," Bishop said, kicking at the shiny hardwood floors. He liked the lodge, and if he were a man of means, he would've purchased a place similar to it. He knew his father would have liked it, too.

"Your mother still alive?" Colbrick asked.

"That I know of," Bishop said, twitching his fingers. "She's back in Chicago, which is where I live full-time. I hope she's OK."

"Chicago may be fine," Colbrick said.

"Or it may not be," Bishop said. "If we let our guard down for one moment thinking any place is safe, that's the time we die."

"You're darn right, slick. Best to consider everything shot to hell until proven otherwise."

Colbrick got up, proceeded to the refrigerator, clanked around and then sat back down. He handed a cold Budweiser to Bishop.

"Drink up, partner," Colbrick said.

Although Bishop had outgrown drinking in college and found it to be rather boring (not to mention the old, frightening drunks he encountered when his grandparents would take him on their boozing trips in Minnesota), he accepted the cold beer and twisted the cap off, for now was not a time to refuse drinks, or the hand of a man offering his friendship.

"To survival," Bishop said, tilting his beer to Colbrick's.

"Yup."

As they touched bottles, something moved on the far edge of the meadow—something big. It bounded into the opening, powerful front legs tracing to a massive hump. The beast held a hairy creature in its jaws, and the twisted limbs of the poor thing dragged out behind the lumbering animal.

Colbrick dropped his beer, picked up his gun with one hand and held the binoculars with the other.

"It's a God damn grizzly bear!"

"Yeah!" Bishop shouted, pumping a fist in the air and spilling beer onto his lap.

The bear stopped, having heard Bishop's shout. It stared towards the lodge with the dead thing in its mouth, then bolted for the tree line. Bishop identified the twisted dead thing as one of the pigras which had tracked them from the road dam.

Colbrick and Bishop followed the bear with binoculars, their eyes moistening with pride, for seeing the mighty grizzly bear, an icon of these mountains, was a heartwarming sight. The very presence of this native animal did more for their spirits than any possible speech. Sometimes, no words were needed, and an inspirational image was enough to keep men going. After being trapped and killed off in most of the lower 48, grizzlies found refuge in the remote Apex Mountains. Man had not been kind to the bear, and here in the last of the wilderness the unpredictable grizzlies existed in small populations, high up along the alpine peaks and cold meadows where man did not care to tread. It was in these last wildlands where they raised their cantankerous cubs, far from the eyes and guns of man, along these twisted mountains and in the cold winds sent down from the Arctic as if by vengeful spirits who shunned southern climates. The region celebrated the great bear, naming streets, shops, and sports teams after them. There were tales of bears faster than horses gobbling up running men like trout to a minnow. Locals uttered the name in hushed tones with wild eyes.

The rear end of the muscular bear disappeared behind trunks of aspen, and they set their binoculars down in awe.

"I don't believe it," Bishop said. "They're still here." Tears streamed down his face. and he wiped them away so Colbrick wouldn't see. What Bishop didn't know was that Colbrick did the same thing, although his tears were of course fewer, for mountain men needed water for hydration, not emotion.

"Yup," Colbrick said, his voice uneven. "*Ursus arctos horribilis* still lives."

"Did you see what was in its mouth?" Bishop asked, smiling.

"Yup. And I can tell you I was happy as hell to see it."

Bishop remembered his father telling him about Old Three Toes, an infamous grizzly in these parts. Old Three Toes evaded traps for years, snatching bleating rancher's sheep from the high meadows. A local poacher by the name of Higgins had trapped Old Three Toes in 2006. But the grizzly had covered himself in dirt and leaves at the trap site, and when Higgins showed up clumsily, Old Three Toes leaped upon him and bit his head off, then freed himself from the steel jaws that were clamped on his leg. To Bishop's knowledge, the bear has not been seen since.

The Apex Tribe revered the grizzly too, claiming to see the massive bear in the stars and that this certain northeast constellation, which formed the outline of the grizzly bear, was home to a sister planet which watched over brother earth.

They sat, looking out the glass door, dusk eaten away by the encompassing darkness, the weathered wood of the paddocks eerily glowing.

"Well," Colbrick said, "guess it's time for me to hit the hay. First, we need to set aside some rules."

"Shoot," Bishop said, sipping his beer.

"First, no flipping light switches. I don't want those damn things to see us. We either keep the lights on or off. Which do you and Angela prefer?"

Bishop's thoughts went back to the dark cabin and the gaseous eel that took Angela, and the answer hit him like a fastball that got away.

"Lights on," he said.

"OK. That's done. Now, do we all sleep in the same room, or can I go back into that master bedroom?"

"I don't know. On one hand, if we all sleep in the same room, we can protect each other. However, if we sleep wider apart, maybe one party can tip the other off."

"I want to take that back room on the other side of the lodge. That way I can hear any bastard trying to claw its way in," Colbrick said.

"Alright," Bishop said. "Angela and I will take the couches."

"You know how to use your shotgun?" Colbrick asked.

"Yeah, pretty much. I've shot clay pigeon before."

"Good. That's much more difficult than shooting those monkeys. Also, make sure you don't shoot me. The last thing we want is crossfire in the lodge. If one of those bastards does come in, make sure you have clear lines, OK, slick?"

"No problem."

Colbrick disappeared to his bedroom with a hunk of venison and his sawed-off.

Bishop took two Santa Fe blankets from a wooden shelf beside the fireplace and curled up next to Angela. He held her, growing warm under the thick blankets. The two extra Vicodin he'd taken had started to kick in. They really were little white wonders.

"I love you," he whispered.

She mumbled back something, but he understood.

Dozing off, Bishop pictured the grizzly heading up into the mountains, framed by the stars and peaks.

GALLATIN LAKE

"Over there, next to those lily pads," Bishop's father said, pointing to the aft of the rowboat.

Bishop stood and yanked his fishing line behind him. The fly rod bowed and quivered, sending the fly pattern out into the lily pads. The grasshopper fly pinched a section of water in-between two enormous pads and stared back at him with buggy, lifeless eyes.

"Nice one," his father said, reaching into his flannel pocket for his pipe tobacco and lighter.

Sunlight glinted on the calm, blue waters of Gallatin Lake. On shore, orange butterflies fluttered and landed on a clump of bear stool.

"What time is the flight?" Bishop asked, watching his grasshopper pattern.

"Eight sharp," his father said, pulling from his pipe and exhaling the smoke. "I suppose we have to be up at sunrise."

Bishop nodded.

"You've got your first meet on Friday," his father said. "You'll need time to prepare."

"Nah, I'm good," Bishop said. This wasn't an exaggeration. He'd been running all summer at increased intervals while shrinking his times.

"Nepqua this time?" his father asked.

Bishop nodded. "They've got some strong runners. Coach says we need to not burn ourselves out early on. He says they have a habit of fading at the end."

"Tough school," his father said. "They've got a good football team, too."

"Yeah. Real good."

The red rowboat creaked and groaned as Bishop shifted on his seat. He took his 7up and chugged it, beads of condensation moistening his fingertips.

Bishop's father pointed to shore. "You see that?" he asked.

Bishop tried to follow his pointing hand.

"What? The aspen?"

"No, below them."

Bishop focused on a patch of lanky weeds with orange tops.

"Orange Hawkweed," his father said. "That stuff is taking over the place. I see it everywhere now."

"What's the big deal?"

"It grows in mats and crowds out other species. Animals and plants that depend on the native species also get bumped out of the way."

Bishop watched as his father cast his own fly line to the edge of the lily pads. As soon as his grasshopper pattern nipped the water, it disappeared.

His father set the hook and the fly rod doubled over. Line zipped off the reel and droplets of water gleamed in the sunlight.

Bishop wiped his forehead and grabbed the wooden net.

"Nice one," he said. "Real nice."

"Why thank you," his father said, going into a wide stance and bending his knees. The boat rocked as he moved, and the strong tail of a brown trout splashed the surface and disappeared.

"Brownie!" his father said. "Big one."

Bishop dipped the net into the water and scooped up the hefty brown trout. He didn't remove the net all the way from the water so the trout could breathe and keep cool. He took his forceps and plucked the barbless grasshopper pattern from its jaw.

"Heck of a fish," his father said, pulling on his pipe while staring down at the trout.

The trout fanned its gills and its glassy eyes exhibited indifference. Its spots were like a leopard's, and it had a hooked snout.

"This is one of the biggest we've caught," Bishop said. "I mean, this one is really big."

Bishop's father laughed. "I think you might be right. I also think it's time to put her back."

Bishop sunk the net into the water and nudged the trout from the back of the netting. The trout flipped its tail twice and ghosted into deeper water.

The two of them said nothing as it disappeared. A cool wind rippled the lake and swayed the pines and aspen. The Apex Range loomed to the east, what was left of the glaciers bright and silvery in the sun.

Bishop's father scanned the landscape, and Bishop swore he saw pure admiration and love in his eyes. The valley had a way of making his father happy and confident. And over the years, Bishop noticed it did the same for him. He felt stronger here, more vibrant. Or maybe he was off his rocker. Were teenagers supposed to think about all this spiritual bullshit? He was supposed to be focused on girls and grades and fucking around. But here, on this lake, on this day, for the first time, he sensed something bigger than himself—a sense of place and time beyond his limited daily path.

Bishop shook his head and wondered if he wasn't zoning out. Nope, he was fine. Maybe he was learning, growing.

His father looked at him and smiled, his scrunched cheeks pushing up his black-rimmed glasses a half-inch. It was almost as if his father knew what he was thinking and was pleased.

Nah, couldn't be, Bishop thought.

"You wanna call it quits?" his father asked.

Bishop gazed around the lake, as if the surface and rustling vegetation on shore would give him thumbs up or thumbs down on the current cooperation levels of the trout. Thumbs down it was.

"I think that's going to be the only fish of the day," Bishop said, reeling in his line.

His father patted him on the back and took the oars.

"I got that," Bishop said.

His father waved him off. "I'm not an old man…yet," he said.

Bishop smiled and drank his 7up. The oar hooks creaked in the metal holders. The gentle sound of the wooden oars meeting water lulled Bishop into a meditative state. Everything blurred together, the trees, the lake, the flying insects and the occasional flap of wings from an eagle or osprey. A cut of moon appeared in the darkening, blue sky. This was his world, his time. And steering the ship was his father. A chill coursed down Bishop's limbs as he watched him, and he knew this was love. His dad. This pristine landscape. Forever.

"Shaping up to be a nice evening," his father said, pipe in mouth, oars caressing water, the drops rolling off the splintering wooden edges.

There was no need to say anything.

SPARGUS TEXT FEED

AmyTreat Amy Heartmann
@BrendaSulke Jim's still not home yet. He was doing a cut near Elmore on Forest Service land.

BrendaSulke Brenda Sulke
@AmyTreat It's only nine. I wouldn't worry.

AmyTreat Amy Heartmann
@BrendaSulke He's never late and they don't log after dark.

BrendaSulke Brenda Sulke
@AmyTreat Sorry, maybe he went drinking with the boys.

AmyTreat Amy Heartmann
@BrendaSulke Maybe. If he comes home drunk again I'm going to kill him.

DAWN OF THE MOUNTAINS

Faint, pre-sunrise glow tinted the lodge. As Bishop woke, he felt his left lip quiver and his left eyeball twitch to the upper corner of his face. He tried to turn to Angela, but he was unable to master his own body, and each attempt to raise an arm sent rippling, muscular spasms throughout his limbs. Realizing what was happening, Bishop tried to shout and a feeble oomph of slobbery grunting escaped. He mustered enough power to face Angela, who also was caught in a seizure. She looked at him with one normal eye and a frightened, twitching eye.

Screeching and shadowy movement came from the sliding glass door area. Two gaping, brown mouths battered the glass, scratching and scraping with abrasive action. Smudges of glop stained the glass as the mouths gnawed.

Fucking frequency seals, Bishop thought.

He tried to get off the couch, but could not. They were too far under the spell.

Holy hell, keep yelling, Bishop thought. He reached for his shotgun but could only move his hand a few inches.

The ceaseless cries increased in fervor, and the scraping transformed into pounding. One of the frequency seals spun its saw tail and slammed it into the glass.

The glass cracked.

Come on, move your fucking hand.

The maelstrom of cries and ringing frequencies owned them.

A window pane next to the sliding door broke into pieces, and intolerable wails pierced the room. They succumbed to even worse spasms and convulsed on the couch, waiting for the frequency seals to grab their limbs with scrubbing, ripping mouths.

Another pane broke, and the cry from the second seal assaulted their ears. A scent of fetid cheese entered the lodge, and Bishop went to cover his nose but could not. He tried to speak to Angela, but his speech was garbled. *I love you*, he thought. *And I'm so sorry.*

Angela gathered enough strength to grip Bishop's leg just above the knee, and through the spasms gave a hearty clutch. He was sad to think this is how their partnership would end. Of all the things that lurk, this insanity would be their final path.

The cries ceased in a series of blinding flashes and thunder. Glass pieces blew into the kitchen along with microscopic matter that had belonged to the frequency seals. Thick, soup-like goo stained what was left of the windows and trim. The frequency seals slumped to the stone patio, their blubber flopping and six limbs twitching as fluid sprayed from their headless necks.

"Gotcha!" Colbrick said from behind the smoking sawed-off. He moved his hand off the barrel, wincing. He went to the cracked glass door, reached his hand through the open pane on the right and flipped the lock.

Bishop and Angela stirred on the couch.

"You two alright?" Colbrick asked.

"Yeah... I think we're better," Angela said, sitting up and shivering as the effects faded from her body. The spasms had jostled their minds, and although the frequency seals were not speedy, they were not something you recovered from easily once they got into you.

Bishop sat up and rubbed his temples, then put his arms around Angela.

"That was close," he said. "I love you."

"Love you too," Angela said, her face buried into his neck. She tried to hold back the tears, but it was no use.

"What is happening to us?" she asked. "We don't deserve any of this."

"I don't think anyone really cares what happens to us besides the people we know," Bishop said. "If there was someone up there watching, they sure as hell wouldn't let this happen."

"Thanks," she said, giving him a light slug with her fist. "I feel so much better."

Colbrick watched them, not looking as tough as he usually did.

"Thank you so much, Colbrick," Angela said. "We'd be dead without you."

"How'd you know?" Bishop asked.

"I walked the perimeter this morning," Colbrick said. "Any hunter worth a damn knows that most animal activity is at dawn and dusk. I figured these new arrivals operate in a similar fashion. When I rounded the last corner of meadow, I heard these two bastards knocking against the window, and I ran across the property, then took 'em out from behind."

"Were those the only creatures you saw?" Bishop asked.

"Yup."

Angela wobbled to her feet, limped over to Colbrick, and hugged him. For a moment, Bishop thought he saw Colbrick's shoulders relax just a bit. Colbrick still held the shotgun, so he patted Angela on the back with the other arm.

"You're welcome," he said.

"We need to board that door," Bishop said. "The eels could get through those broken panes."

"I found a tool shed on my walk, but the damn thing is locked," Colbrick said.

"There's a rack of keys in the pantry," Angela said.

"When did you go into the pantry?" Bishop asked.

"Last night while you were sleeping. I ate some crackers. I had a real bad craving for salt."

"Good work," Bishop said. "I bet that's where the shed key is."

Bishop entered the pantry and examined the key rings that hung from wooden pegs along the far wall. He pocketed all three and went back to Angela.

"You OK here?" he asked.

"Yeah, sure, but I'm still really sore. The itching is better now, and I do feel better overall but still not a hundred percent."

Colbrick ruffled through one of the backpacks he and Bishop carried from the highway, and pulled out a shiny object with a polished wooden handle, then handed it to Angela.

It was a pistol.

A big pistol.

"You see anything move that isn't named Bishop or Colbrick, you shoot the hell out of it," Colbrick said. "That there is a .357 Colt Python revolver. She'll pack a punch, remember that. The rounds travel fourteen hundred feet per second. It will maim what it hits. The switch next to the chamber is the safety."

"You know I never liked guns," Angela said, her eyes riveted to the pistol. "But suddenly I'm finding them useful." Her grin was mischievous.

Bishop laughed, and his heart warmed when he realized her sense of humor was returning.

The forest air lingered clean and cool, and golden rays of light tipped over the Apex Mountains as if on a hinge, flooding the meadow and trees. Bishop and Colbrick walked the worn path to what they guessed was the tool shed. Bishop fumbled with the keys as Colbrick stood watch, his gun held in a ready-position. On the eighth key, the silver lock gave a welcoming click, and Bishop yanked the lock back, then slid it out of the clasp.

"Careful," Colbrick said.

"Good point," Bishop said. "You hang left, and I'll crouch on the right. That way I won't be in your line of fire and only one of us would get attacked."

"Unless there are *two* creatures."

"You had to say it."

"Yup."

Bishop lifted the rolling shed door about six inches and listened, his feet and shins vulnerable to whatever might lurk.

"There's nothing in there," Bishop said. As the door rolled up on squeaky wheels, they saw two work benches and a wall of hung tools ranging from screwdrivers to power drills. Paint fumes wafted from the unit.

"Nice," Bishop said.

"Any outfit like this is gonna have the right tools," Colbrick said.

Wide pieces of plywood lay half-hidden behind a sawhorse against the back wall. Bishop took several of them and proceeded to the worktable as Colbrick kept watch. Next, Bishop reached for a red hammer and a white box of roofing nails.

"Nope," Colbrick said. "Nothing that makes noise."

"How are we going to get these in place?"

"Screwdriver."

"That's a pain in the ass," Bishop said.

"Yup."

Bishop took a rattling box of screws and stuck a manual screwdriver in his back pocket. They shut the rolling door and walked to a smaller, nearby outbuilding. A muffled rumbling came from the outhouse-sized structure, and a padlock secured the door latch. Bishop set the plywood against the shed and opened the lock, revealing a five-thousand-watt generator and walls padded with foam insulation. Colbrick switched it off and checked the fuel level.

"About a day left," he said.

"I thought these people were prepared for anything," Bishop said.

"Compared to you, they were the most prepared people in the world."

Bishop looked down, a touch ashamed of his arrogance. "What do you think happened to them?"

"I think they just got up and left. Either that or we're walking on top of them now. People in town talked of a prepper bunker up here. Sometimes you can trust what the town folk say."

"Sure, sure. Everyone makes shit up—doesn't matter what part of the country you're from."

Colbrick popped the generator again.

"Big J ran several Suburbans, and I don't see any of 'em," Colbrick said. "I don't think they're in a bunker. I think they left." Colbrick spit on the ground and stared across the meadow.

"So this place is ours for now," Bishop said, closing the door.

"For now," Colbrick said. "And lock that bastard."

They walked the perimeter of the lodge, checking for weaknesses.

"We should board all these," Colbrick said, pointing to the windows.

"Do you really think we can wait this out?"

"Maybe," Colbrick said. "No vehicle, but we've got food and water."

Bishop studied the ever-present Apex Mountains. "But what if...what if the Apex Mountains are the epicenter of this thing, and if we moved out of that ring, we'll be back to a normal ecosystem?"

Colbrick pointed his sawed-off towards the gravel road that led out of Big J. "There you go. Hit the road and send us a postcard."

"Smart ass."

"Yup."

They passed the lodge and followed an intermittent, graveled drive to a voluminous aluminum garage that contained tools, equestrian gear, a loft, and two parking spots.

A glint in the loft caught Bishop's eye, and he climbed the metal parallel stairs to examine it. He held the object out for Colbrick to see.

"A nail gun," Bishop said.

"You've got a shotgun. You don't need that."

"It's for the windows."

"No noises."

"Yeah see I kind of thought about that, and I think taking all day to screw in the plywood exposes us more than just getting it the fuck over with."

Colbrick looked at his feet, then up at Bishop.

"Yeah, yer right."

Confidence seeped into Bishop—a feeling he grew to like when dealing with clients back in Chicago.

They exited the garage and proceeded to the main lodge, scanning the meadow edges, always wary of the slightest movement. There was nothing—not even pleasant bird chatter. *Maybe Colbrick is right*, Bishop thought. Maybe the animals did migrate. Well, except for one pissed off and hungry grizzly bear.

They boarded up as many windows as they could, saving the last pieces of plywood for the broken kitchen windows.

Thack! Thack! Thack!

Colbrick on watch at his back.

Thack! Thack! Thack!

The racket from the nail gun reverberated across meadow and forest, but the whole process did not take long. No creatures came after them, nor were any spotted. Still, Bishop couldn't help but feel as if they'd just *sort of* gotten away with it, like the time he and his cousin Bobby had lifted Wacky Pages from the local White Hen. Oh, they'd basked in the glory of all those sarcastic product stickers like *Weakies*, *Pieces Crumbled Candy*, *Headhunter Helper*, *Cap'N Crud* and *Ajerx*, and then were called into White Hen the next day to apologize to the owners.

Bishop's heart sunk when he saw Angela sitting at the kitchen table, the no-nonsense looking pistol next to her. The scene was such a contrast with their normal life. She was munching on dry cereal and sipping lemonade. Although he'd been outside a short while, it felt like an eternity away from her.

She stood and clutched him.

"I missed you," she said.

Bishop felt her chest rising and falling against his, her touch providing a much-needed boost. He pulled back and looked into her eyes.

"You look fantastic," he said, putting a hand to her forehead, checking for fever. "How are your cuts?"

"Not that great," she said. "I think I'm going to need stitches."

"Colbrick, did you see a needle and stitching anywhere?" Bishop asked.

"Nope. But I can look," Colbrick said as he left the room.

"We'll find something," Bishop said. "How's the food?"

"As good as dry cereal gets, I suppose."

Bishop jabbed his hand into her cereal, grabbing a fistful and slamming it into his mouth, letting the flakes fall everywhere and chewing like an absolute pig. He stuck his tongue out at her, the mealy fiber coating it grotesquely. The unexpected childish antics forced Angela to laugh, and she coughed up a piece of cereal.

"Gross," she said. "Are you five?"

"I wish," Bishop said.

Colbrick appeared across the living room, holding a fishing rod high for them to see.

"You going fishing?" Angela asked, smirking.

"Be back by dark," Bishop said, imitating a concerned mother.

"You two are real comedians," Colbrick said. He unhooked the lure from one of the guides and pulled the line out, placing a section of it into his mouth and biting it in half. He wound the line around his hand, went into the kitchen, placed it in a bowl and then ran it under the tap water. He opened a cabinet below the sink, shuffled a hand around inside and took out a bottle of dish soap which he squeezed into the bowl of fishing line. Colbrick cut the lure off with his teeth and then jabbed at the rear treble hook with a pair of red pliers he pulled from his pocket. Metal snapped, and he held up one silver hook that curved into a threadable eye.

"She needs stitches, slick," he said.

Colbrick placed the hook into the plier jaws and held it over a stove burner. He twisted a dial and a flame billowed out, lapping at the shiny hook as he twisted it about.

Angela looked on, her eyes a buoyant mix of apprehension and gratitude.

"Thanks, Colbrick," Bishop said. "Honey, let's get you lying face-down on the couch, OK?"

"Turn your eyes away," she said to Colbrick as she took her shirt off, revealing bloodied, puffy flaps of skin on her back. Light green puss seethed at the cut lines. Bishop thought of the gaseous eel, and hoped he'd killed it.

Angela took her pants off and laid face down upon the cold, leather couch, her white bra and underwear contrasting with the streaks of red on her skin and the striking wounds.

Bishop took the warm hook and line and tied them together. Then he examined the wounds, and although they seemed better, they didn't look fantastic.

"This couch is so cold, Bishop."

"It'll warm up. Just give it some time," Bishop said. "Colbrick, could you hand me a towel?"

"Sure thing."

Colbrick reached for a towel that hung from the stove door and rinsed it under tap water. He soaked it in the soapy bowl and rinsed it again, then lathered the towel once more.

"Here you go, slick. Clean those wounds before you stitch her up."

"Colbrick, are you looking at me?" Angela asked.

"Uh...no...uh, not at all. I was handing Bishop a cloth."

"Bishop!" Angela said.

"It's fine. He wasn't looking," Bishop lied. A tickle of a laugh paused on the tip of his tongue. Yeah, so Colbrick was checking her out. Lots of guys do. Except this one just saved their lives. The truth was he now trusted the hell out of Colbrick.

Bishop took the hydrogen peroxide from his original pack and soaked the towel. Next, he dabbed the towel into her wounds. Her back arched at each touch. "Sorry," he said.

Angela winced as the hook pierced each hole, and she added a grimace when Bishop pulled the fishing line through. While he stitched her calves, Bishop couldn't help but think of the white laces of a football, and how they held the rough skin together. Small amounts of green puss bubbled out from the reddened flaps as he tightened them. Bishop watched her back muscles strain as she tensed. Each poke of hook and each pull were as gentle as the most thoughtful surgeon.

"Forty-two," Bishop said.

"Jesus, really?" she asked.

"Jesus isn't here right now, but I can tell you it is indeed forty-two stitches."

"Funny."

"I actually thought it would be much worse," Bishop said.

"Forty-two is a lot. How do they look?"

"Did you take your amoxicillin this morning?"

"Yes."

"That should do the job." Bishop covered her wounds with gauze and band-aids.

Angela sat up and slowly got dressed, wincing all the while. When all was clear, Colbrick came into the living room. In his hands were a candle and a pack of matches.

"You know what today is, don't you?" he asked.

"Today is the day you killed the frequency seals," Bishop said.

"So you're sticking with that pet name? What's next, you going to pick an outfit for 'em?"

"What else are we supposed to call them?" Bishop asked.

"Fine, fine. They're frequency seals. I guess what matters is they're dead as hell."

"If there is a hell," Angela said.

"I think we're looking at it right now," Bishop said.

Colbrick looked at them with the eyes of a man who'd spent a long, long time outdoors. A *touched* look. "This ain't hell, folks. These are the Apex Mountains—God's gift to mankind, and one of the most spectacular places in the world. We're blessed to be standing on this ground. Hell may be stopping by, but I can tell you right now this ain't Hell."

"So what day is it?" Angela asked.

"It's the Fourth of July," Colbrick said. "In addition to the morning's fireworks, we have this nice candle which I'm going to light in honor of those who fought for this great country, my pops included." Colbrick set the white candle on the coffee table and struck a match. The lone flame produced an organic luminance, and their eyes watched it, lulled by the soft movement.

"Happy Fourth," Colbrick said. "Happy God damned Fourth."

THE FOURTH OF JULY

They feasted on Doritos, venison, peanut butter and jelly sandwiches, beer, lemonade, crackers, and whatever else they could find in the pantry. The pig-out provided much-needed energy, and Angela was regaining color with each morsel.

"I want to thank the fine folks at Big J for today's holiday bounty," Colbrick said.

"Ditto," Angela said, the corners of her mouth orange from Doritos.

Silence filled the old lodge as they ate.

Vivid alpine light cut through the meadow, outlining the grass and trees in high-definition and with more vibrancy than at lower altitude. For a moment, it did feel like a holiday. But this did not last long as morose thoughts crept back into their minds like a spider devouring sunlight with its gnawing mouth and gathering arms.

"We can't stay here forever," Angela said.

"I'm glad you're with us," Colbrick said. "We need a fresh set of eyes."

"Colbrick thinks we should ride this out as long as we can," Bishop said.

"Well, that makes sense," Angela said, forcing down a hunk of venison. "Out there, back in the woods, we had no chance. Even though I was out of it, I could still sort of understand what was going on. In here, we have food, water, and shelter. We can make a stand." She looked down at her food, poking at it with a finger. "But...if we do stay here, we'll be in a vacuum. We won't have any idea what's happening. What if we're in the worst of it here? What if a trip to the plains or a city reveals a healthy environment? The truth is, we won't know any of these things if we stay here. Sure, we might be more comfortable, but eventually not knowing will tear at us and dominate our thoughts like what's out in those woods."

Bishop glanced at his plate of food and nodded.

"Hold on," Angela said. "I haven't mentioned what we should do—I just presented the two sides. We go out there, our ability to survive likely decreases, but our knowledge of what is happening may increase. You've heard the saying 'knowledge is power,' and it is. But the risks are high for acquiring information. If we stay here, the chances of survival increase, but we lose the ability to gauge the situation. Normally, acquiring information would increase your chances of survival, but not necessarily in this specific case. The truth is, any knowledge gained could be worthless because of the potential enormity of the situation. In other words, any quest for knowledge may be pointless."

Colbrick eyed Angela, his face as solemn as ever. "So after all that, we flip a damn coin?"

Angela returned the serious expression, her eyes steady. "Yes."

"How 'bout this…you two go on your little suicide hike, and good ole Colbrick stays here and eats the rest of this food. When you find help, come on back to Big J. I'll leave the light on."

Angela turned to Bishop, her eyes flashing intrigue. "That's not a bad idea."

"What? You're not actually entertaining this, are you?" Bishop asked.

"Yes, of course. He makes a great point, although not in a way he thought he was making it. Maybe he stays at Big J, and *we* use it as a base for exploration. We don't have to leave, per say. We can go on day hikes, searching for information and at the same time increase our odds of survival. The food, water, and comfortable place to rest keeps us alive. It's the best of both worlds. When we gather enough information, we can then embark from Big J permanently."

Angela's plan sounded reasonable to Bishop. Hell, it sounded fucking perfect. But deep down, he didn't want to split with Colbrick. He knew what he was doing in these woods and had saved their lives once already—two if you count picking them up on the road. Who knows what sort of creature would've found them had Colbrick not come along in his SUV?

"OK," Bishop said. "You make a compelling case. It doesn't have to be all of us who leave. One day, you and I can hike out, the next Colbrick and I, or vice versa."

"Now you're God damned talking," Colbrick said, cracking a rare grin and then biting into a misshapen venison sandwich. He swallowed the chow with Budweiser and burped.

Bishop watched them eat, satisfied with the plan, elated they were still even alive. Although invasive, unexplained entities now roamed the Apex Mountains, they had managed to find their own castle of safety. How long such a thing would last, no one could know.

*

Sunset came to the meadow, tilting down on a hinge from behind the Apex Range and delivering angled rays of light upon the structures and tree line. Within minutes, the rays diffused into pink and red hues.

They gazed between the plywood slats that now reinforced the living room windows. Bishop and Colbrick held their shotguns, and Angela kept her Colt Python at her feet on the floor.

Angela noticed fluttering in the saturated meadow light.

"Hey, a monarch butterfly," she said.

"Well I'll be," Colbrick said. "That's the first one we've seen."

"Thank God," Angela said. "When you combine this with the grizzly you guys saw, maybe it means things are headed back to normal."

Angela watched the pretty butterfly and thought of those rock concert posters from the sixties and the LSD culture which inspired them. Then a horrible thought crept into her mind.

"What if this is all a hallucination?" she asked.

"What the hell are you talking about?" Colbrick asked. "Impossible. No hallucination would last this long. Why would Big J appear normal? Why isn't the lodge trying to eat us?"

Angela continued to watch the butterfly, fascinated by its erratic but pleasant fluttering in the last mountain light. "You're right. A shared hallucination is more far-fetched than these animals being real. I don't think they're from our planet, so they must have come or been brought here."

"What about a rip in the fabric of space, like a wormhole?" Bishop asked.

Colbrick laughed. "Shit don't work like that. No one came here from some zipper in reality. All those bad movies have poisoned your mind."

"And you know this how?" Bishop asked.

Colbrick waved his sawed-off in the air and paced around the room. "Because this is just air, partner. You can't pull a lever and hop along to other places. Sure would be a neat trick, but I ain't buying it."

"Many top scientists have theorized that exotic matter might be manipulated into doing that," Bishop shot back.

"How many of those scientists have handled exotic matter?" Colbrick asked.

"None," Bishop said.

"That's right. All they're doing is guessin', no more than carp looking out of a pond at the shit above it."

"OK, you've shot down everything like some dick on an internet message board, so please tell us what you think this is," Bishop said.

"I don't know a thing about it," Colbrick said. "But if I had to guess, I'd say these bastards come from aliens who wanted to screw with us. Either that, or the aliens are trying to make this place feel all homey before they settle in. And what the hell were those flashin' tags? Can you say 'pets,' anyone? Someone is tracking them."

"That scenario makes sense. They could've been sent here in some type of vessel. There was a show on The Science Channel about how we are looking for planets like ours. Goldilocks planets with oxygen and water. *We're* looking. Why couldn't someone else be looking, too?" Angela said, still watching the butterfly.

"Then where are they? The people doing the tracking? All we've seen are animals. We drove into a road dam built by things that stun with sonic blasts," Bishop said. "Call me crazy, but I don't think those creatures could build a space ship."

"I only remember pieces of that," Angela said. "I was either sleeping or watching your eyes, and what I saw in them I did not like."

Colbrick turned to them, his face shading red. Angela didn't think it was directed at them, but rather mounted from his inability to comprehend the situation. They were all at a loss. There were no answers yet. All they could do was to sit, watch, and learn.

The last hint of light fought the growing darkness, and the butterfly disappeared.

Angela told it goodbye in her mind, holding onto the vision of fluttering, fanciful wings.

*

Ten p.m. on the Fourth of July usually held fireworks, celebrations, and the heavy scent of black powder. There were no children running with sparklers and no frogs calling from unseen pools in the woods. There were no dogs running for tennis balls or sticks.

But there was something.

It appeared high in the sky to the south—two objects glowing neon green. At first, Bishop thought they might be the lights of a low-flying plane, but there was no red navigation light nor engine noise. Behind the two glowing objects, a shadow randomly blocked the stars which glimmered with subtle intensity.

Wings, Bishop thought.

Up so very high the black wings beat, always led by the two neon green objects.

Eyes, Bishop thought.

Behind the first shadow, four more followed.

And then twelve more.

Bishop turned to Angela who was napping on the couch and then gestured to Colbrick who was sitting at the kitchen island, head slumped between his arms.

"Colbrick," Bishop whispered. "Psssst."

Colbrick grunted, licked his lips and walked over to the living room windows.

"Dear God," he said.

Their mouths hung open in awe as the night sky filled with flapping, soaring creatures. The dark shapes cast a shifting, honeycombed blockage of stars, while green eyes surveyed the land below. Dozens of fliers swarmed the sky, the beating of their wings like rotten instruments of which only low, sour notes could be played.

As the unknown squadron approached, smaller sets of glowing, green eyes plummeted towards the meadow at astonishing speed. Down they came, hundreds of them, filling the horizon like reverse fireworks. Before the smaller fliers reached the ground, they swooped up in mad U-turns, and a freakish knocking emitted from the horde of them. Once reaching a certain height, the small fliers rocketed towards the lodge, aligning side by side in neat rows. Their green eyes illuminated the grass, casting a surreal glow upon the empty paddocks.

The sound of frantic, beating wings reverberated off the lodge windows, and the incessant knocking increased to intolerable levels.

Thack! Thack! Thack!

"What's going on?" Angela asked, sitting up on the couch with bed head.

"Don't come near the windows," Bishop said, raising his shotgun. "Stay back."

"Bishop, I want to see."

"No!"

"Where have we heard that noise before?" Colbrick asked, aiming his sawed-off towards the glass.

"Guys, what's happening?" Angela asked, her eyes wide, her hand gripping the back of the couch.

"Take cover," Bishop said. "Take fucking cover NOW!"

Angela dove behind the couch.

The squadron of fliers thumped into the lodge, their colorful, lit eyes bouncing off the logs and onto the grass like demented fireflies. The second row of fliers which observed the first wave pulled up short, and their leathery wings lashed against the logs and windows. An ear-piercing knocking encircled the lodge, coming from every possible angle, like erratic surround sound.

Thack! Thack! Thack!

One of the fliers smashed into a narrow slot between plywood edges, getting trapped between wood and glass. Its distended midsection puffed against the window as its outstretched wings scraped and folded. The knocking sound wailed from the creature and rattled the glass.

Thack! Thack! Thack!

Colbrick went to shoot it.

"No!" Bishop shouted. "If we shoot the glass, these things will have an entrance. Do not shoot the glass!"

The fluttering, noisome creatures surrounded them. Thousands of intrusive eyes cast the lodge in an eerie, green glow.

Thack! Thack! Thack!

"What the hell is that noise?" Bishop asked.

"I can't believe it," Colbrick said. "It's the nail gun."

"What are you talking about?"

"Listen. Open your God damn ears and listen."

At first, Bishop thought Colbrick had gone senile, but he was right. In each wailing flier, a short loop of the nail gun boarding the windows burst forth. Not an exact replica, but close enough. It was unmistakable.

Bishop peered out the window, only to see an endless stream of glowing eyes racing towards the lodge like artillery tracers. The inside of the lodge became a psychedelic light show, the luminance seeping through the skylights and the openings between plywood.

*

"Jesus, the skylights," Angela said, looking up to see a half dozen of the fliers. They gawked at her as their bloated midsections pulsed and their leathery wings stretched and bundled.

"Keep quiet," Colbrick whispered. "Everyone keep quiet. They're trying to find us."

Angela froze, hoping the monsters in the skylight would fly away.

"Get out of their view," Colbrick said. "Get on the ground. No movement, no sound."

They lay on their backs and stared at the ceiling, weapons clutched across their chests, hearts pounding in their ears.

Thack! Thack! Thack!

"I guess the nail gun wasn't such a good idea after all," Bishop whispered as he flipped over and crawled to Angela.

"Don't," she whispered. "They can see me."

Bishop froze.

"Are you OK?"

"I'm fine. Just don't crawl over here. They're watching me through the skylight."

Something big thumped on the roof.

The small fliers on the skylight scattered.

"Dear God," Colbrick whispered.

"They left the skylight," Angela whispered.

Another massive thump shook the roof, followed by another. Whooshing air buffeted the skylights, followed by scraping.

"Those might be the first ones we saw," Bishop said, staring at the ceiling.

"What are you talking about?" Angela asked.

"Before the small fliers, there were bigger ones—much, much bigger," Bishop said.

"Well folks, I guess if we're gonna go, this is an exciting way." Colbrick turned his head and spit onto the floor, then pressed the safety button on his sawed-off.

Bishop crawled over to Angela, snuggled up to her on his back and held her trembling hand.

"Could you ever imagine this in a million years?" he asked.

"Of course not," Angela whispered, her teeth chattering.

Another thump shook the roof. The looped mimicry of the nail gun relentlessly mocked them.

Thack! Thack! Thack!

Wood and dust particles crumbled to the floor, some of it falling into Angela's mouth, making her spit.

"I think they might be leaving—"

The skylight filled with an intense, green glow. Then Angela heard elephantine breathing, and the powerful beat of an alien heart thudding onto the aluminum roof. The glow focused into a concentrated ray, like someone twisting a flashlight, and the shaft of illumination searched the floor of the lodge in measured movements. The ray disappeared and reappeared, and Angela realized the pause was created by an unseen, blinking eyelid. She adjusted to the skylight glare and saw three huge, silver pupils in a sea of green gasses like spots on a planet. The pupils rotated, scanning her and then Bishop, the shaft of green scaling up their legs and over their chests, revealing floating dust particles. They remained still and held their breath.

The shaft moved onto the couch like a spotlight and onto the wall.

A hostile utterance erupted from immense, unseen lungs, and the green shaft disappeared.

The looped mimicry of the nail gun ceased, and the thing on the roof grunted once more. Uncountable wings fluttered and slapped, and then fell silent. Whooshing air buffeted the roof, followed by scraping and the trickling of fluid. The stout ceiling logs creaked and groaned as the things pushed off, the rhythmic beating of wings blasting the aluminum like wind from the mountains.

Bishop, Colbrick, and Angela ran to the living room windows. They looked out with a strange combination of horror and wonder as massive, flying beasts as long as city busses thundered away from Big J, their scaled backs serving as holding platforms for the smaller fliers which sat backward, their green eyes glaring at the lodge as they swayed like a brood of penguins. The big fliers lacked tails, their back ends tapering like a sea turtle. Chunks of stool and mists of urine leaked down from them.

Soon, the big fliers reached a dizzying altitude, and the glowing eyes of the passenger fliers clicked off as if someone flipped a switch. Darkness swallowed the backs of the flying beasts, and the great wings once again blocked the stars. Gloomy eyes searched the landscape as long necks craned and adjusted.

"Good pick on the nail gun," Colbrick said.

"Hey, you agreed to it," Bishop said.

"Who cares who did what?" Angela asked. "All I care about is what just happened. We didn't die." Her strength was improving. "And you know what? We didn't die because we had shelter. Can you imagine what would've happened if we were outside?"

"Never would've had a chance," Bishop said.

"You still want to play Johnny Hiker?" Colbrick asked.

"I don't think we have a choice," Angela said. "We need to do both."

Thump.

"Dear God, another one," Colbrick said.

Thump Thump.

Bishop aimed his shotgun at the roof, but something wasn't right. The thumping wasn't coming from that direction.

Thump.

"You hear that?" Bishop asked Angela.

"Yes," Angela said, looking at the ground. "I think it's coming from below the living room rug."

Colbrick approached the rug and the thumping stopped. He lifted a corner and then pulled it, coffee table and all. As the rug swept over the floor, a rectangular trap door appeared. A metal handle was folded flush within the surface of the door.

"I knew it," Colbrick said. "They bragged about it in town." He went to reach for the handle.

"Wait," Bishop said. "We don't know what's down there, and you just want to open the door like we're walking into an ice cream shop?"

"That's what Justine is for," Colbrick said, holding up his sawed-off.

Colbrick pulled the trap door open, revealing clinical light and wooden steps.

"Shhh…" Colbrick said, putting a finger to pursed lips. "Something's down there."

*

Bishop listened, and his ears caught faint movement, maybe dragging. His mouth dried and he swallowed. The dragging sound stopped, and then he heard flesh tearing and popping and a smattering of leaking fluid. The scent of loose earth rose from the entrance.

Something clacked and buzzed down below, mixing with the mealy sound of teeth working on flesh.

Angela turned to Bishop with nervous ungulate eyes, her Colt Python shaking as she pointed it towards the bunker entrance.

"Sons a bitches!" Colbrick shouted, running down the steps into the light.

"Colbrick, no!" Angela shouted.

It was too late.

The clacking morphed into a menacing growl, followed by scuffling and shouting.

Like a warning from the pits of hell, deafening shotgun blasts ripped through the room. Muzzle flashes danced on the lodge ceiling, the scent of gunpowder rising to greet them in choking wisps.

Something slumped to the floor below.

A man coughed.

"It's alright. Come on down," Colbrick said. "But Angela, you may not want to."

Bishop crept down the wooden steps. Clinical light revealed a concrete bunker twenty by twenty feet. Along the walls lay cots, heavy duty shelving stacked with canned goods, bags of clothing, and several first-aid kits. In the southeast corner, a gaping hole, three feet wide. Next to the hole lay a puzzling figure with smooth, reddish skin and segmented rings spaced every eight inches down its length. Colbrick stood at its side and kicked it over with his boot. As he did, dozens of reaching, wispy legs folded across the thing's torso—a postmortem reflexive muscular spasm. Before the underbelly had been covered by the folding arms, Bishop observed some kind of armor plating tinted with red.

The head was a different story.

Two black eyes (each with three silver pupils) the size of golf balls were half-covered by protective membranes similar to chain mail shark-proof dive suits. The odd, wide mouth also contained this veil of protection. Two shovel-like appendages that hinted at horse hooves stuck out between the mouth and eyes. The sturdy hooves bore marks from frequent burrowing, yet retained a dangerous sharpness. At the top of the head was a circular patch the size of a plate, and every few seconds, the plate changed color from purple to brown and then to crimson. Bishop thought it might be some sort of skin regeneration system—a must for anything spending all that time burrowing deep into the earth.

Bishop walked over to the hole. He reached for one of the flashlights on the industrial shelf and Colbrick stopped him.

"Uh-uh, partner," Colbrick whispered. "We don't know where that goes. For all we know, there could be more of them bastards waiting just a few yards in. You shine a light down there, they see it and we're beetle juice."

"Then we need to close it," Bishop said.

"You guys alright down there?" Angela asked, her voice shaky.

"Yes. Do us a favor and keep watch OK?"

"Gotcha," Angela said.

"Before we came down here…did you hear flesh ripping?" Colbrick asked, checking the bunker.

"Hell yes I did."

"Yup, so did I. But I don't see no other body here, just this bastard."

Colbrick booted the thing again, and they noticed a small wound on its lower back, where the hind of the creature was protected with an overhanging shell like a beetle.

Green ooze dripped from the gash.

"Was this thing eating itself?" Bishop asked.

"Got me," Colbrick said. "Who knows what these freaks do in their spare time. Maybe old Ringo Starr here got hungry."

Bishop reached for a mattress to lean against the hole, and their world went black.

"There she goes," Colbrick said.

It was nice while it lasted, Bishop thought.

"Guys, I think the generator went out," Angela said.

Colbrick grunted and spit.

"Angela, go in the packs and you'll find headlamps," Bishop shouted.

"I'll try. I can't even see my hand in front of my face."

Bishop reached for the flashlight again and grasped the cold, steel handle. His searching fingers found the rubbery button and pressed it, releasing a slicing beam of light that quartered the bunker.

"Let's get that hole sealed up," Colbrick said.

Bishop turned to the hole with the flashlight.

A pair of blinking, black eyes glared at him from below, and a haunting, multi-clicking rose from deep in the burrow. The creature's shovel appendages rubbed each other as if it was irritated, and its eyes filled with a murky, brown ink, replacing the black.

Before Bishop could discern more facial features, the giant bug's head blew apart. Bishop's ears rang from the blast, and for a second, he thought he saw a legion of black, blinking eyes nestled deep in the burrow, illuminated by the muzzle flash and several pulsing, red tags.

The wounded creature scurried into the bunker, shrieking and smearing its bleeding face against the concrete walls, leaving inconsistent streaks of slime like a confused painter. Bishop tried to follow it with the flashlight, and when the light seeped into the creature's shredded eyes, it panicked even more. Colbrick let loose another blast and the creature collapsed, the wispy legs folding in and protecting the underbelly.

"Bishop!" Angela shouted from above, her voice sounding far away.

"I'm fine," he said, ears ringing. "Did you find the headlamps?"

"Yes. I've got one on now."

"We'll be up in a minute after we plug this hole, OK?"

"What hole? What's going on?"

"Nothing," Bishop said. "We'll be up in a minute."

The ringing in Bishop's ears faded, and he heard movement from within the ominous hole.

The two men grabbed one of the cots and leaned it up against the hole, then stood back and examined their handy work. It didn't look very impressive.

"Screw this," Colbrick said. "Shine a light on that far shelf."

Bishop did, and two reflective cans of liquid stove fuel caught the beam. Colbrick took each one and drained them into the hole. Gas fumes filled the bunker.

"What are you doing?" Bishop asked.

"What does it look like I'm doing? I'm having a beetle barbecue. Maybe we'll get McCartney this time."

The metal fuel cans gurgled as they emptied, the rivulets trickling down into the grim burrow, and who knows what creatures the artificial streams encountered. Without warning, Colbrick struck a match and tossed it into the darkness, igniting a fury of orange hell. Colbrick jerked back as the inferno exploded past his head, and Bishop caught the unpleasant odor of burning human hair.

"You alright, man?" Bishop asked.

Colbrick stood and dusted himself off, checking his hair with both hands. "Never been better."

In the firelight, Bishop noticed Colbrick's face had been penetrated by a few of the shotgun pellets. "Your face...does it hurt?"

"Nah. It's nothing." Colbrick grinned, his face glowing from the flames.

Bishop wondered if the man was crazy.

When the heat subsided, they stuffed mattresses into the hole, even managing to jam one of the cots into it.

"Much better," Colbrick said.

They took as much of the food as they could along with the first-aid kits and went upstairs. Colbrick closed the heavy trap door behind him, and then dragged the rug over it.

"Not good enough," Angela said.

They went into one of the lodge rooms and pushed an antique dresser along the hardwood floor, setting it atop the trap door.

"Yeah, still not good enough," Angela said.

They dragged two more dressers and placed them next to the first.

"Now that's a proper blockade," Angela said.

Bishop looked at Angela, puzzled. "Don't you want to know?"

"No," she said.

"Can't say I blame you," Colbrick said.

"What happened to the quest for information?" Bishop asked.

"The curious cat is beat," she said, collecting her hair in a ponytail and cinching it with a rubber band.

The three of them slumped onto the couch in the dark, two headlamps and a flashlight beaming light shafts here and there on the old logs. Strange how a place you'd never seen could keep you alive. Strange how a place redefined *home*. How long it would last, no one could know.

*

"I'm starting to get pissed," Angela said, blowing upward at a lock of hair covering her eye.

"Maybe—"

"Not now," she said, fuming. "I mean I'm *really* starting to get pissed off."

Bishop said nothing. You do not get in Angela's way when she's in one of her moods.

"How many of these attacks will we survive?" Angela asked. "The next one? The one after that? When does our luck run out?"

"Big J's been our lucky charm," Colbrick said. "We'd be dead otherwise."

"Then why did the owners leave?" Bishop asked.

"They probably saw the freak beetles in their bunker and hit the road," Colbrick said. "Take a look around the property, there ain't a vehicle in sight. They might have seen the beetles first, without seeing any of the other bastards. To us, them beetles ain't shit."

"So they took off," Angela said.

"Yup."

Angela stared at a porcelain figurine of a lassoing rancher on a far shelf. "They panicked and drove into a worse situation," she said.

"Yup."

"I'm not much of a religious person," Angela said. "But God Bless the owners of Big J."

"I couldn't have said it better myself," Colbrick said.

"Oh, and Happy Fourth everyone," Angela said, faking a sense of cheer.

They sat, holding their guns, their headlamps tilting down as they dozed off.

SPARGUS TEXT FEED

JennyGomes Jenny Gomes
@**PaulaW** Trucks pulling into driveway, big spotlights WTF

PaulaW PaulaW Anderson
@**JennyGomes** What are you talking about

JennyGomes Jenny Gomes
@**PaulaW** Knocking on door, shouting, they have dogs, too. Mom won't answer.

PaulaW PaulaW Anderson
@**JennyGomes** OMG

JennyGomes Jenny Gomes
@**PaulaW** Other neighbors too. They're coming upstairs. Soldiers. Need to hide phone. GTFO of Spargus

BRANCHING OUT

Sunlight illuminated the earth like it always has. The warming rays creased back the dark edge, revealing oceans and continents that always seemed to belong to each other. In one small corner of North America, these rays caused the receding glacier atop Kilbrix Peak to shimmer. These are the Apex Mountains, home of the last grizzly bears—a landscape that has survived the onslaught of development—a place that does not give in so easily. And as the sun first glinted upon Big J meadow, a strong, proud man walked, shotgun in hand.

"*It's a small world after all*," Colbrick hummed. His boots glistened from morning dew. His olfactory senses scanned for anything strange. His eyes were wild, yet contained.

Why are you so God damn happy? he asked himself. *Because you saw two deer this morning, you old fool.*

The two deer mattered.

The numerous flier droppings (and some of the small dead ones he kicked around) did not. Even those winged bastards couldn't ruin his vision of the two deer. When he saw them, he'd stopped, and the hyper-alert mammals fled. He hoped that he hadn't pushed them into one of the horrible things in the woods. It made him sick to realize that to the deer, the horrible things in the woods, were no different than himself. Hell, he shot and killed deer. Even ate 'em. How was he any different? The new arrivals were just more things that wanted to kill and eat deer. This was nothing new to them.

Colbrick hung his head, the song coming to a halt as he continued to walk the meadow perimeter. Something flashed in the trees and Colbrick froze. Branches swished and a chittering arose from behind rustling leaves. A brown weasel raced up a tree, its tiny claws scrapping across the rough, twisted bark. It dragged a luxurious tail.

A fisher, he thought. Rare in the Apex Mountains. Seeing one was considered good luck, and it damn sure felt that way today. Colbrick watched the fisher scurry out of sight up the old growth tamarack. Then he moved away, wanting to give it space. It was time to head back to the lodge, anyway.

Bishop and Angela walked out to meet him.

Angela had on a daypack, and Bishop hoisted one of the beefier backpacks.

"What you hauling all that for, slick?"

"Just in case," Bishop said. "I'm taking a lesson from you."

"And what do you have in your hand, Angela?" Colbrick asked.

"You know what it is," she said.

"That's right. Now don't go shootin' yourself with it," Colbrick said.

She raised the Colt Python .357 and studied it with electric eyes, then looked into the sky.

"If those things come back, I'm going Clint Eastwood on them," she said.

Bishop and Colbrick looked up and grimaced, for the sky was no longer a pleasant space gleaming above them. Now it was capable of hurling death via glowing eyes and looping mimicry.

Colbrick reached into his daypack and retrieved two yellow items, then handed one to Bishop.

"Wow…walkie-talkies," Bishop said. "Did you—?"

"—yup. No luck. Empty as a casino in a recession. Nothin' but snap, crackle, and pop. I found 'em this morning in the tool shed inside a coffee can. Go figure. But they'll work just fine if we need to contact each other. Use channel nine and remember they have a range of two miles, max."

Bishop took out his cell phone.

"No bars out here, slick."

Colbrick was right. Again.

Angela moved across the meadow and Bishop stayed back for a moment. Then he leaned into Colbrick and whispered, "If we're not back by dark, don't come looking for us."

Colbrick walked away while nodding, and Bishop jogged over to Angela, who was waiting impatiently at the northeastern tree line.

"We could follow the road," she said.

"Easy walking," Bishop said.

"Or we could follow this horse trail," Angela said, pointing into the woods.

They stared into the dark tunnel of vegetation, turned to each other, and headed for the road.

A moment later, they crept under the Big J compound arch, their nerves tingling. Gravel crunched under their feet, sounding like bullhorns in a monastery. Bishop watched the left side of the road, Angela the right.

"Do you think we're exposed?" Angela asked.

"I don't think so. The road is pretty narrow here."

Angela glanced at Bishop and smirked. "Well aren't you just a badass with that shotgun?" she said. Something about Bishop holding the gun fascinated her—a side of him she'd never seen. Heck, she'd never expected to be holding a gun herself. She grew up in the affluent Hamptons. The scariest things in those backyards were the tennis ball launchers. All her life, her mother had covered her like a war hero protecting a comrade from a grenade. That was before the drunk driver took her from this world. Angela watched her sneakers, and for a moment, she was on those Hampton tennis courts, and instead of a gun in her hand, there was a tennis racket. Birds were chirping, it was humid and her mother stood courtside, drinking iced tea and wiping sweat from her brow with a delicate, white towel.

"Angela?" Bishop asked. "Hey, Angela?"

She snapped hear head up and looked through Bishop, surprised.

"You OK?"

"Yeah, I'm fine. I just spaced out there for a moment I guess. Sorry."

"I need you awake for this, OK?"

Bishop's gaze lingered, driving home the point.

They winded up a hill, and there were so many tire tracks they couldn't follow one set. A climax forest of spruce, tamarack, and aspen bordered the road. The sandy, cut embankment sometimes revealed the roots of an unlucky tree.

They stopped and listened to the woods. Goose bumps rose on Angela's arms, and she cracked a smile.

"Do you hear that?" she asked.

A pleasant call came from the north side of the road.

Wee-ah Wee-ah.

"A gray jay," Angela said.

"You nailed it. That's the first normal bird we've heard since this started," Bishop said.

They watched the gray jay rustle in the vegetation, wings fluttering and head twitching.

"Amazing," Bishop said. He grasped Angela's hand and squeezed.

They followed the road downhill and spilled out onto a meadow a hundred yards wide. Fat bundles of hay lay staggered across the grass, as if waiting for a purpose.

Something moved on one of the haystacks. Bishop halted and yanked Angela to his side.

"Shhh," he whispered.

Then he crouched and Angela followed, watching his eyes the entire time. She'd seen that reaction before and did not care for it, not at all.

Something else moved on the next haystack and glinted in the morning sun.

Angela looked to the haystack and then to Bishop.

A dark wave of dread, like food poisoning or a virus, overcame Bishop as the creatures pulled themselves atop the haystacks and hunkered down. Their hairy legs extended and groped as they placed their flounder-like centers upon the sun-warmed part of the hay. Their lone, bulbous eyes blinked lazily.

"What the heck are those?" Angela asked, her fingers tapping the .357.

"I've been calling them secapods. I've seen them before, back near the rental."

"When I was out of it," she said.

"Yes."

"What aren't you telling me?" she asked.

Bishop sighed, not wanting to tell her, but he didn't want to lie to her either.

"When you were out, I watched a secapod attack a man and kill him."

"Tell me something I don't know," she said. "All of these things attack."

"Well, not all," he said. "Remember the odd bird?"

"Yes, the one I told Colbrick not to shoot."

"That one didn't attack," Bishop said. "You said there might be good ones."

"But not these," she said.

The glistening secapods rested on the haystacks, their fleshy centers rising and falling.

"What do we do?" she asked.

"We leave," Bishop said. "Quietly."

They started to walk the road, hand in hand, trying not to make eye contact with the secapods and trying not to crunch gravel. Halfway across the meadow, Bishop accidentally kicked a smashed aluminum can that had embedded itself in the gravel like a camouflaged flounder. The scrape of aluminum echoed across the meadow, each turn and flip of the can an eternity.

"You did not," Angela said.

Bishop gulped and turned to check the haystacks.

Both creatures held their fleshy centers high above the haystacks, then marched in place as their lone claws poked and prodded the hay.

Bishop thought he glimpsed a mandible underneath their fleshy centers. Perhaps a weak spot.

The creatures bent their front legs so the midsections angled towards the road. At once, the bulbous eyes locked onto Bishop and Angela. Upon realizing their targets, the secapods emitted staccato clicking. One of the secapods had a rectangular, flashing tag under its midsection. Bishop counted the pulses. Forty beats per minute.

"How can they make so much noise?" Angela asked.

"Because there are more than two of them," Bishop said, aiming the shotgun at the first secapod.

More secapods crawled out from behind the haystacks and groped their way towards them, their prickly, glistening legs stabbing into the dewy grass as their eyes rotated.

"Time to bail on this party," Bishop said. "Are you well enough to run?"

Angela was already ahead of him, yanking his hand.

They sprinted down the road, and the secapods, which Bishop initially thought were slow, were not.

The secapods moved with precision, using long strides and pushing off with their claws. Soon, the gap had closed, and when Bishop looked back, he counted four of them—one of which had reached the road and shit a white string of slime. The second secapod paused and flattened its midsection upon the road as it tasted the slime, clicking louder while it pressed itself on the foul juice.

"Angela?"

"Yes?"

"If we do not gain distance in twenty seconds—"

"—we stop and fire."

"Mind reader."

"Shoot, I don't know if I can!" Angela said, her chest heaving.

"Of course you can," Bishop said. "You have to shoot those fucking things for both of us. Do you understand?"

A strange noise came from the tree line.

Two weird eyes below a bad haircut watched them.

"Hey, it's that bird," Angela said, pointing.

Before she could utter another word, the odd, four-foot bird ran from tree line like a crazed ostrich, stumbling and losing balance but never falling. A long, thin neck connected the eyeballs and beak to a plump midsection with saturated emerald and purple plumage. Below this protruded four muscular legs, and powerful claws protruded from three-toed feet. The bird happily joined in the chase, far behind the fast-approaching secapods. Bishop was shocked at the speed of the secapods.

"Keep going, baby!" he shouted. He'd never run with a backpack *and* a gun before.

The weird bird gained on a tailing secapods, and to Bishop's surprise, slammed its beak into the bulbous eye. The stabbing forced the secapod into a seizure, and it wrapped its legs around its midsection, shrieking. The bird let out a mournful wail and maneuvered its beak to its chest plumage. The chest feathers parted, revealing a fleshy straw appendage that slurped the gunk off the bird's beak like an elephant trunk sucking water.

The next secapod paused when it heard the shrieking. The nutty bird took advantage of the hesitation and caught it, and it too was stabbed in the eye, the gooey contents licked from the bird's beak by its own protruding flesh tube.

Angela glanced back and laughed. "Holy freaking cow! Two down, two to go!"

"Keep running!" Bishop shouted.

They reached the end of the meadow and began pulling uphill into the forest. Now only two secapods groped after them, the bird right behind. They chugged up the hill, not needing to turn around when they heard the disgusting splatter of another plunged eye and secapod shrieking. The bird cried out.

"I think it's really fucking hungry," Bishop said.

"I hope it's not hungry for us," Angela said, her forehead peppered with sweat as they slogged uphill.

They stole a glance as the final secapod gained, but the bird was right on top of it, staring at it with a cross-eyed gaze, aiming its beak.

Thwap!

Eeeek Eeeek!

Cheeekooo Cheeekooo!

"Was that the last one?" Angela asked, sucking air and scanning the meadow.

"Yes, yes!" Bishop said.

The flesh tube retreated into the bird's colorful plumage, and the bird paused along the road. So did Bishop and Angela; out of breath and doubled over. The bird gazed at them with an intelligent curiosity.

"Is it going to try and eat us?" Angela asked.

"I don't think so."

The bird lingered, ruffling its feathers and tilting its head.

"I think you were right," Bishop said, grinning at Angela. "It's friendly."

Angela looked at the bird and smiled. Bishop was proud of her. She'd made the right decision back when Colbrick had other plans for it.

The bird let out another warbled call and ran clumsily back to tree line. They wondered if it was going to fall, but it never did. It disappeared into a patch of northern beech fern and aspen, crashing through the brush as it worked upslope. They turned in the direction they came from and saw the secapods scattered along the road, curled up in puddles of goop. Bishop examined the closest secapod and kicked it over. It made an unpleasant sloshing and sure enough there was a sharp, squid-like beak under the midsection. Inside the open beak was a small, coarse tongue. Around the beak were wart growths that released thin streams of white slime from their moist tips. Bishop guessed this was some sort of reproduction mechanism. The thought sent his heart crashing out of rhythm, and he coughed while pounding his chest to snap it back.

"One of those again, huh?" Angela asked. She walked up to him and rubbed his back with her free hand.

"I think they're reproducing," Bishop said. "That means—"

"No, they *were* reproducing," she said. "But not anymore thanks to the bird."

A stench of rotten calamari filled their noses.

Bishop reached down to a secapod and removed the blinking tag. The material was smooth in his hand, like a river-worn stone. How it had attached itself to the secapod, he had no idea. He counted the pulses. Forty-two beats per minute.

"What is it?" Angela asked, examining the device and then their surroundings.

Bishop couldn't help but think of Colbrick. *Someone is tracking them,* he'd said.

The device clicked in his hand and the red light went dark. He thought about putting it in his backpack, but it stank. So instead, he dropped the tag on the gravel road.

"Unreal," Angela said, shaking her head. "I don't even have the strength to ask 'why' anymore."

"There's plenty more where that came from," Bishop said.

The sun hit them harder, their skin soaking in the vitamin D.

Far away, they heard the awkward bird stumbling through the understory as it headed southwest.

"Where do you think it's going?" Angela asked.

"I don't know," Bishop said. "But I hope that wherever it goes, it's OK."

"Me too."

*

Every step, every breath on the narrow, wooded road was a potential disaster. Trees that had once elicited a sense of comfort were now potential ambush locations. Death pervaded everything. They could taste it on their tongues, a metallic toxin.

Bishop unstrapped his pack and took two water bottles he'd filled at Big J. They drank along a sandy embankment in the shade of an aspen. No doubt the tree roots were also trying to drink quietly below them.

Bishop handed Angela a yellow walkie-talkie and thumbed the power switch.

"Where did you get this?" she asked.

"From the nut with the sawed-off."

Angela swept the channels and pressed the transmit button.

"Hello? Is there anybody out there?"

Her voice was met with crackling static, although the changes in cadence were frenetic and agitated—more so than normal.

"Colbrick said he tried this morning. No luck. He's on channel nine if you dare."

Angela thumbed to channel nine. "You there, Colbrick?" she asked into the device, releasing the transmit button and listening to the static.

"Yup. I read you loud and clear," Colbrick said. "What's going on out there?"

"Oh, Macy's is having an awesome sale, and the chicken francese at Maggiano's was divine."

"Smartass," Colbrick said.

"We're two miles out on the ranch road. There's creature activity. Things I've never seen before and that weird bird."

"The one we saw coming down the mountain to Big J?"

"Yes."

"What were the others?"

"Hairy spiders with a big eye in the center. Bishop calls them secapods."

"Yup, yup. I seen those out on Highway 18. Ran one over."

"They're horrible," Angela said. "We're going further up the road. The good news is we haven't seen any fliers, or the monkeys Bishop told me about. We'll contact you soon."

"Good," Colbrick said. "Over and out."

"Over and out, I think…"

They strapped on their packs and headed down the road. Soon, rising temperatures forced them into the shaded embankment. Even animals native to the Apex Mountains sought relief on such warm days—the moose wallowing in bogs and flooded vegetation, the grizzly bears playing in remnant snowfields or lounging in creeks.

In the distance, far down the road, Bishop thought he saw a glint of metal, but he wasn't sure if it was a heat mirage.

"Hold up," he said, raising a pair of binoculars to his eyes. He aimed towards the glint, and the optics revealed the back end of a Chevy Suburban.

"What do you see?" Angela asked.

"A gas guzzler," Bishop said.

"Funny."

"It's an SUV," he said.

"You had me at gas guzzler," she said.

They trotted towards the vehicle, powered by hopeful eagerness, but never let their guard down. Distractions could increase the odds of being nailed by a new arrival. What they found near the road dam had confirmed their suspicions.

Thirty feet out, they approached with extreme caution, guns drawn. The passenger side door was wide open, the paint scratched as if living things had once clung to it. Two bodies slumped in the front seats, the sexes not readily identifiable. The faces were deformed and gouged, the skulls punctured. The necks and arms displayed numerous bites, and flaps of torn flesh revealed white flashes of bone contrasting with red tendon and muscle.

A nostril-offending stench permeated the truck perimeter.

"Jesus," Angela said, coughing.

"I don't know about Jesus," Bishop said, "but the keys are in the ignition."

"I don't believe it."

"Oh you better believe it," Bishop said. "Let's move these bodies."

"I was afraid you'd say that," Angela said.

"Better yet, I'll move the bodies. You get my back."

"Can do."

Bishop set his pack and shotgun down and grabbed a body by the shirt collar, dragging it into the woods. He tried not to breathe, but the nauseating odor filled his nose and lungs. Halfway through dragging the second body, he vomited onto the road.

"You OK?" Angela asked.

"Yeah, no worries."

Bishop regained his composure, stretched his shirt over his mouth, and dragged the last body into a patch of honeysuckle. After all, these might be Big J residents, and the least he could do was not let them rot in the sun for the entire world to see.

When he finished, Bishop wiped his hand on his pants and headed back to the truck. Angela was guarding the vehicle with the intimidating Colt Python revolver.

He did a double take. They had changed, and not just After School Special change, but a complete transition. Angela looked like she was part of a special ops task force. Here they were, exploring a country road, carrying firearms and securing a motor vehicle. The creatures weren't the only dangerous things in these woods now.

Bishop turned the key and the truck roared to life. The gas gage indicated they had half a tank as the windshield wipers fluttered. Bishop guessed the wipers were triggered when the driver tried to fight off the secapods. Maybe the secapods were even waiting when they got into the truck. Bishop checked the backseats and cargo bay again. Nothing.

"Where to?" he asked. "There's beautiful Florida with its many beaches, or the tranquil hill country of Appalachia."

"How about just down the road?" Angela said.

"What about Colbrick?" Bishop asked, fiddling with the radio buttons but getting nothing.

"Let's go a few miles up the road," she said. "But go at a speed where something can't latch onto us without getting hurt real bad."

Bishop stomped the pedal and they flew down the road, dust billowing out behind them, deep forest thinning into another haystack meadow. They crossed over a tumbling creek that flowed through a metal culvert and then raced downhill towards Highway 18. Soon, the ranch road widened like a river mouth as it met the highway. Several colored mailboxes in various states of disrepair decorated the left side.

Bishop tried his cell phone. Nothing. Angela worked one of the walkie-talkies, turning it off when the unit emitted uncomfortable, descending and ascending frequency sweeps. The haunting cadence of the radio lingered in the afternoon stillness.

"Something's not right," Bishop said. "It shouldn't be making noises like that."

Angela examined the road, north to south.

"The highway looks clear."

Bishop raised the binoculars and glassed both directions. To the north, he saw something that tweaked the hairs on his arms and neck. While the view appeared normal to the naked eye, the binoculars revealed haze, and Bishop couldn't help but shudder when he saw gnarled, toppled vegetation protruding through it.

"I think that's a new road dam," Bishop said, the binoculars shaking in his hands.

"What? Where?" Angela asked.

Bishop handed her the binoculars and guided her to the spot.

"See the haze and jumble trees?"

"Yes..."

"Not good," Bishop said. "Our route to the north is blocked."

"So we go south," Angela said.

"South is where the first road dam was."

"Maybe it's gone," Angela said. She pulled away the binoculars and looked at him with pleading, desperate eyes. "Bishop, how big are these things, and what the hell built them?"

"I already told you," he said. "But you didn't believe me."

"I thought you were joking."

She glassed back down the road, looking for a way out. The sky above the road dam swirled with silt. Her upper lip quivered, a tiny drop of sweat forming above it.

"We have no choice but to go south."

"What if it's worse?" Bishop asked. "What if Big J is the safest place?"

"Do you want to find other people?" she asked.

"Are there other people?" Bishop asked.

"There has to be. We aren't the only survivors."

"How do we know?"

"We know by leaving Big J."

"Colbrick will never go for that," Bishop said.

"Then Colbrick can stay behind."

"He's done a lot for us," Bishop said. "Plus, he's good with a gun."

"He'll understand," she said, flashing sympathy eyes at Bishop. "We can't stay at Big J forever, even if that means leaving Colbrick."

Bishop studied the horizon and sighed. "There's one thing I didn't tell you," he said. "When I went looking for you, two Air Force jets flew over. I don't know what it means, but I could see the pilot scanning the ground."

"See, there are people out there, maybe people who know what's going on," Angela said, willing him with her eyes, no longer pleading, but demanding. "We need to go south. Tomorrow."

A sense of dread overcame Bishop, that virus-like seizure of body and mind. Not even Angela's beautiful eyes could dispel the feeling that they should stay on the mountain.

"We should head back and tell Colbrick," he said.

The truck left a plume of dust as it drew into the foothills of the Apex Mountains.

*

When they pulled into the dirt driveway, Colbrick opened the front door, grinning.

"Welcome back, slicks," he said. "And it seems you two found a nice little present out on the road. Fill me in on the rest."

Bishop got out and examined the truck alongside Colbrick, who nodded with approval.

"I hate to interrupt *Truck Time with Colbrick*," Bishop said, "but there's another dam north on the highway."

Colbrick's grin morphed into a frown. "God damned things."

"We're going south," Angela blurted out. "The first dam may be gone."

"What are you on about?" Colbrick asked.

"Are you in, Colbrick?" she asked.

"South is where I came from. I ain't going back that way. I saw more things back there than up here. Something about the lower elevation makes 'em thicker."

"We can't go north, obviously," Angela said.

"Well I ain't going nowhere," Colbrick said.

"OK. Bishop and I are going to take the truck *we* found and head south."

"You're going to leave me here without wheels?"

"What do you need them for? You think Big J is the safest place, so why would you leave?"

"Fine by me. You two go on ahead. Ole' Colbrick will do just fine."

"Colbrick—"

"—Nah. Don't patronize me, slick. You two go on ahead. There's lots more food and the water works fine."

Colbrick grumbled and entered the lodge.

"I knew that wouldn't go well," Bishop said. "Don't you feel bad leaving him here?"

"Of course I do. But he has a choice and he made it. He's more than welcome to come with us, but he doesn't want to. What am I supposed to say?"

"Goodbye, I guess," Bishop said.

*

Angela and Bishop packed what they needed, raiding the closets and the pantry. They took one of Colbrick's backpacks and a duffel bag they found, cramming them with essentials. There was little talk.

A creeping dread overcame Bishop, and he couldn't help but wonder if they were doing the right thing. To the north was Spargus—where they had originally tried to reach when Angela wasn't doing so well. Spargus was a decent-sized town of fifteen thousand. Thirty miles to the south was Elmore, with a population of one thousand in the winter and five thousand during tourist season depending on the economy. There wasn't much in Elmore save for a small downtown district and second homes scattered about the woods. In Elmore, they would still be in the shadow of the Apex Mountains, which ran north to south for one hundred and fifty miles.

Soon, the backpack and duffel bulged, and they could fit no more. Angela filled empty bottles with tap water, including two old milk jugs. Colbrick even agreed to let them have one of the water filters.

Colbrick watched them pack, and each step they made towards completion caused him to blink.

"When are you two slicks leaving?" he asked.

"Tomorrow," Angela said, securing the zipper on the duffel. "You know, it's not too late for you to come with."

"Nah. I told you, Big J is the best place to be."

Bishop had had enough. He stood from the packing and got in Colbrick's face. "Come on, man. Just fucking come with us already. What are you going to do here by yourself? We stand a better chance of surviving together." Bishop felt his eyes watering. He kicked the duffel bag as hard as he could, and it lurched across the living room.

"I got water and I got food," Colbrick said. "What else do we need? Plus, we've only had two visits by them things."

"Sure, if you count that flying army as one thing," Angela said. "And whatever those things are, they know we're here. They might come back."

"Ah let 'em," Colbrick said, turning his back.

"We don't know shit," Bishop said.

"That's why we're leaving," Angela said.

"Curiosity killed the cat," Colbrick mumbled.

"What?"

"Nothing."

"You just used that old cliché, didn't you?" Angela asked

"Yup."

"That's encouraging, Mr. Doom and Gloom."

"Look, sweetheart, I'm not sure we're doing the right thing," Bishop said, his voice shaking.

"The problem here is that nobody knows what the right thing is," Angela said.

Deep down, Bishop knew she was right. No one knew anything. It was awful, but not as awful as dying by the beaks and claws of the new arrivals.

"Let's just go to Elmore and see what we can find," she said. "There's no finality in any of this. If it's bad, we can always come back."

"Fine," Bishop said. "But at the first sign of trouble, we get our asses back here."

"I'm OK with that."

"Then it's a deal?"

"Promise."

*

Bishop met her eyes and Angela understood he was placing an enormous amount of trust on her with bigger stakes than they'd ever seen. Not only was he putting his life in her hands, but Colbrick's too.

She didn't want to be so pushy, but her instincts told her to get this ball rolling. As a child, she'd always been the explorer, always wanting to see new things. And although she appreciated the relative safety of Big J, not knowing a freaking thing gnawed into her not all that differently from the gnashing teeth of the creatures. And it was knowledge of the new creature's patterns and habits which must be known.

Where did the fliers go to?

Where did they come from?

How many are there, and what is their impact?

These questions pummeled her mind.

Something else frequented her mind, something worse. It flashed in threatening black and red, front and center. She tried to ignore it whenever it flashed, but seeing the image knocked the air out of her lungs.

Don't you get him killed, she thought. *Don't you dare get him killed.*

*

Dinner consisted of plain tuna, slices of questionable bread, and graham crackers. Colbrick ate on the couch.

"We need to try one last time," Bishop whispered.

"He's not budging," Angela said, scarfing down the crackers.

Bishop stood and walked over to Colbrick, putting a hand on his shoulder.

"We need you, big fella."

Colbrick looked up from his plate.

"Ah...thanks slick, but I'll do just fine here. I wish I could say the same about you guys."

Bishop leaned into Colbrick and whispered, "You know, I don't feel all that different from you on this. But Angela is no dummy. She's smarter than both of us."

"I hope so," Colbrick said, standing to meet Bishop. "We've been through hell, slick. I'll be sad to see you two go. But what can you do? You've made your choice."

"As have you," Bishop said, walking away.

"Make sure you take the radio," Colbrick said.

"I thought you said the range was only good for two miles?" Bishop asked.

"Yeah, I did. But you never know when we'll be within those two miles, partner. Maybe never again, but you never know."

Colbrick retreated to his room and closed the door.

*

Night fell upon Big J, and there were no glowing-eyed fliers—just the silence of the mountains and the three survivors at last resting, their thoughts and dreams eclipsed in bleakness by the waking world.

INQUISITOR

Dr. Ted Donaldson liked to chew gum. Lots of gum. He didn't wear a white lab coat, but neither did any other field biologist. He had the look of his profession—half scruffy academic, half outdoorsman.

Donaldson passed through the bright cafeteria of Northwestern University and waved at several of his peers in the biology department. They waved back with half-smiles. Sometimes, he got the impression they didn't care for the way he chewed his gum. Or maybe it was something else. Their camaraderie was often laced with competitiveness, more or less friendly.

Donaldson made his way down the tiled corridor to his office. When he opened the door, two men of similar height stood in unison from a pair of chairs. His red-headed secretary, Amber Johansen, stood in front of them.

"These men need to speak with you urgently," Amber said.

Donaldson examined the men, and assumed them military right off the bat thanks to their crew cuts and rigid posture.

"Dr. Donaldson," the first man said, reaching out a hand.

Donaldson shook it. He couldn't help but feel these two men were brothers, or at least related somehow.

"Sorry for the intrusion, but we have something we'd like to discuss with you."

The two men paused and their eyes turned to Amber. One of the men cleared his throat.

"I've got some calls to make," Amber said. She took a stack of papers from Donaldson's cherry wood desk and shuffled out of the room. When she closed the door, Donaldson turned his attention back to the men.

"Are you here about those strange reports?" Donaldson asked. "Everyone's been talking about them. I got a call from a colleague last night."

The first man smiled. "Yes."

Donaldson lifted an eyebrow. "Give me the details."

"We believe the, uh, animals originated in northwest Montana, and we'd like to discuss some of the…shall we say, implications with you," the first man said.

It was clear to Donaldson this was going to go above and beyond his usual processes. "Who do you represent?" Donaldson asked.

"Homeland Security," the first man said.

Donaldson tapped a finger on his desk three times. "What kind of implications?" he asked.

"One right up your alley," the first man said. "Possible invasive species. We're familiar with your distribution model for the spread of invasive species. The link between distribution, physiology, critical thresholds, climate model projections, and spread predictions are very interesting to us, especially in regards to this situation."

The other man nodded.

The first man pulled out a briefcase that had been resting on the carpet. He unlocked it and placed a manila folder on Donaldson's desk.

"We call them Harassers. The others we know as Stunners."

Donaldson sat there, staring at the picture. It showed a bat-like creature unlike any on earth. The next picture showed a six-legged seal-like creature atop a massive pile of trees, obviously taken from a long lens due to the atmospheric haze within the images. His colleague had been examining the remains of one of the aerial predators, but he didn't know about the other animal.

The first man retrieved a tape recorder from his briefcase, and pressed play while setting the device on Donaldson's desk.

The sound of cars and people talking roared from the device's cheap speakers as Donaldson stared at the photos.

"So what's the connection?" Donaldson asked without looking up.

The second man opened his briefcase and placed an iPad on Donaldson's desk.

"We thought you might ask that," the first man said, turning off the cassette player. "Now here's the video."

Donaldson watched as the iPad entered video mode. A cluster of the bat-like animals fluttered across a grey sky over a prairie. The speakers on the iPad blared with the same sound of cars and people, but the problem was there were no cars and people, at least not in view.

"They *mimic*," the first man said in a way that made Donaldson shiver. "Beyond any creature we know of."

Donaldson pulled out a wad of Big League chew from his desk drawer and turned back to the video. "OK, so this new animal can mimic with much higher precision than a parrot. Where was this footage taken? I'm guessing either North or South Dakota since I can see a few red scoria caps in the background."

"Very perceptive," the first man said. "The video was captured near Theodore Roosevelt Park in North Dakota."

"Astonishing," Donaldson said. "What can I do for you?"

"Again, it goes back to your report, Doctor. We believe several new species have emerged in northwestern Montana, in the Apex Valley. Perhaps you've heard of it."

"Can't say that I have," Donaldson said.

"Most people haven't," the first man said.

"What's this second animal, the one on the jumble of trees?" Donaldson asked.

"This one is a real zinger. It has the ability to construct large dams from forest materials. It has a tail made of keratin which can cut down trees. It's also put a few of our finest in the hospital."

"How?"

"Frequency blasts to the central nervous system," the first man said. "Nasty things."

Donaldson leaned forward and met the first man's eyes. "So both of these species are predators," he mused. "Predators need large territories to maintain adequate food supplies. Usually, juvenile males will strike out great distances to find new territory. My colleague wasn't able to determine the age of the specimen, but that process means that these species could start radiating out quickly depending on their rate of reproduction."

"In your report, you concluded that the spread of raccoons into new habitats was hastened by warmer temperatures. While we haven't proven it yet, we believe these new species may have spread because of warming temperatures, specifically the removal of glaciers from the ecosystem. Same process, different players, Dr. Donaldson."

"Perhaps," Donaldson said, nodding. "But they had to come from somewhere. There has to be a source."

The first man glanced to his feet and then back up. "Yes...a source. We're working on that."

"Let's be clear here," Donaldson said. "It's obvious these new species did not originate on this planet. Do you have any idea how many there are? My colleague speculated that this new predator was able to establish itself on our planet because the protein molecules it is ingesting must be similar to its original food source. Plants contain many potentially toxic substances, which the herbivores on our planet have co-evolved to digest, making it potentially more difficult for an alien herbivore to become established here. If there are more than one species out there then that would imply that perhaps an entire "ark" so to speak may have been sent here. I don't know if you are familiar with the concept of convergent evolution, but this discovery confirms that it applies to any planet. Particular types of body plans are more adaptive in similar environments, so even in different lineages similar forms will evolve with similar strategies. What strikes me is not how different these animals are, but how similar they might be. Species are only able to become invasive when they are both able to adapt to a new environment and can out-compete the native species. I'm sure Homeland Security is most concerned about these large predators, but in the long run, smaller species and plants can be the most difficult to eradicate and have increased rates of reproduction, allowing each successive generation to become more adapted to their new environment. Once a species becomes established, it can rapidly take over. Do you know exactly where the point of origin is?"

"The Apex Valley."

"I certainly hope you came here to take me there."

"The Department of Homeland Security has the paperwork in order for your temporary absence. We have men at the base of several of the dams now, taking samples and gathering evidence."

"I'm in," Donaldson said. "But I would like to know if there will be an opportunity to conduct research, or if you are only interested in containment?"

The second man spoke for the first time. "You will be able to perform research, Dr. Donaldson," he said.

"When do we leave?"

"Tonight. We'll have a car pick you up at nine p.m."

When the men left his office, Donaldson picked up the phone and dialed his wife.

He listened to the hollow rings. Already he felt a thousand miles away.

"Hello," Sarah Donaldson said.

"Hey, hon, how was your day?"

"Ugh," she said. "Ben hit his head on the slide. We have an ice pack on it now. Suzy is holding it for him. It seems the only time they get along is when the other one is injured."

"That's good," Donaldson said. "Family instinct."

"I suppose. When will you be home?"

"I'll be home at five, and then I need to pack."

"Pack? For where?"

"The Apex Valley."

"Where the hell is that?" she asked.

"They say it's in Montana," he said.

ELMORE

"So I guess this is goodbye," Angela said to a rough-haired Colbrick in the driveway.

"Yup."

Angela went to hug him, and he tried to turn away, but she caught him, tucking her head against his chest.

"Thank you for saving our lives," she said, squeezing him.

"Not a problem," Colbrick said.

Angela pulled away, leaving a clear path between Bishop and Colbrick.

Bishop went to shake his hand, but Colbrick turned, keeping his head down and walking into the lodge.

"It ain't no goodbye yet," Colbrick said, slamming the door behind him.

Bishop watched his tall, shadowy figure disappear through the frosted side windows.

"That guy's responsible for us even being here," Bishop said. He reached for his cheek and wiped away a tear.

Angela blinked her moist, reddening eyes. Then she reached for Bishop and embraced him.

*

Although Bishop hated the idea of leaving Colbrick, he trusted Angela. They needed to know more. Sitting back at Big J and waiting for whatever crept or flew along was not what he wanted to do for the rest of however many days he had. Someone was out there—someone who knew at least a *tiny* bit about current events. And it was their duty to find out.

They checked the truck for ambushers, got in, and sped down the road, leaving an expanding, roiling cloud of dust between them and Colbrick.

No secapods sunbathed on haystacks, and no wacky bird teetered in the grass. Things looked as they should.

Except for the road dam to the north.

Angela glassed the highway, checking both routes. "It's still there," she groaned.

"I wish we could do something about it," Bishop said. "Imagine what it's doing to the land. How many lives is it trapping? How many people have been killed?"

"It's probably best not to think about it right now," Angela said. "There's nothing we can do."

Bishop gripped the wheel hard enough to whiten his knuckles. "Just letting something like that rape our world..."

He pulled onto Highway 18 and headed south, grinding his teeth. Then he checked the rearview mirror and the hazy road dam.

"I'm not done with you yet," he muttered.

*

The summer day was bright and clear—as they are in the Rockies—with pleasing contrast between rock, vegetation, and sky. But there were no birds singing, or deer feeding, or bears thundering through the understory. For all intents and purposes, Apex Country was dead.

The truck sped down Highway 18, back towards their vacation rental in the heart of the Apex Valley.

"I wish we had sunglasses," Angela said, wincing.

"You'd think there'd be some lying around," Bishop said with a light chuckle.

"Why's that?"

"Because in disaster movies, everyone seems to have a nice pair of sunglasses. You'd think with everything fucked up, that...I dunno...maybe the sunglasses wouldn't be in the best shape."

Angela laughed. "I suppose. Unblemished designer sunglasses would seem to be in short supply during apocalyptic times."

They let out a rip-roaring laugh and the pain of leaving Colbrick receded. Silence filled the truck as they thought of the hard-as-nails man back at the lodge. Bishop pictured the stubborn bugger fighting off legions of secapods and pigras, taking them out like they were nothing, then cooking them up for a barbecue.

The road changed, as Bishop expected it would. He reduced speed and rolled to a stop. Their mouths hung open as their eyes canvassed the devastation.

For hundreds of yards on either side of the highway, the trees lay like toothpicks. Jagged half stumps with bright, raw wood gleamed in the sun. Millions of broken branches jabbed up from the tangle like the arms of pleading, injured people. A creeping mist shrouded certain portions of the blasted heath, and Bishop wondered what obscured creatures lingered there. He knew what lay ahead in the murk: the road dam they'd approached earlier. The carcasses of moose, elk, deer, and other animals littered the stained ground. The air reeked of feces and a strange glittering lingered about the area. Bishop wondered if it might be a leftover pheromone from the frequency seal workers.

"Holy shit," Angela said.

"I don't think there's anything holy about it," he said.

"Do you think this was built by the same things as the one north of Big J?"

"I have no doubt," Bishop said. He gazed northeast to an impossibly wide swath of cut and slashed forest. Bishop pointed to the carnage. "They probably cut a path through the woods and then came back up on the highway north of Big J. They seem smart enough not to destroy a route that brings food."

"What about the jets you saw? Couldn't one of those kill them?"

"Sure, but not all of them. Also—"

Bishop paused and looked into the footwell.

"What?"

"The jets could have flown into the fliers we saw the other night. I only heard one pass, Angela, one pass—and they were going north. The smaller fliers could've fouled the jet intakes."

Angela turned away and said nothing.

"We've got to get around this," Bishop said. "There was a gravel road a mile back, it might take us around this thing. But I sure can't see that well from this position."

Angela's eyes sparked.

"I'll go on the roof," she said.

"What the fuck are you talking about?"

"I'll go on the roof and scout while you drive. Keep your window open so you can hear me."

"I'm not letting you on the roof. The fliers could pick you off, or who knows what else."

"I don't think there's anything here," Angela said, turning her head to examine the landscape. "Come on, Bishop, how else are we going to get around this dam?"

Bishop gazed out the windshield at the rough terrain.

"Fine. But you hold onto the roof racks when we go over some of this shit, do you understand?"

"Of course."

She hugged him, the warmth soothing his nerves.

After driving back a mile, Bishop found the gravel road and turned right. Angela lowered her window, opened the door, climbed onto the hood, and accessed the roof via the windshield. Bishop leaned over and closed her door. He left the window down so she at least had some kind of quick entrance if any of the creatures showed themselves. Bishop took a deep breath, reached into the backseat, and grabbed the shotgun, resting it in-between Angela's seat and the center console.

"Ready?" he asked.

Angela tapped the roof with the heel of her sneaker, both of which were visible at the top of the windshield.

Bishop inched the truck up the dirt road.

"Go left," Angela said, her hands gripping the roof rack as the truck lurched.

Ahead of them lay a combination of chopped trees, animal skeletons caught in unspeakable poses, drying pools of slime and Stinson Creek, a feeder for Cooke's Creek. Bishop thought of his father casting his fly rod and shouting with joy when one of the small cutthroat trout took the fly. He hoped the cutthroats had moved downstream.

"More left!"

"OK, baby. How you doing up there?"

"Good, good. This is fun. Maybe a little like surfing."

"Don't just focus on the route," Bishop said. "Please keep an eye on the sky and woods as well."

"I know. I've been doing both."

Bishop steered around a living room-sized log with its roots pointed upwards. A putrefied mass of bones, hair, and flesh hung off the right side of the gangly roots. Bishop thought it might be a moose, or what used to be a moose. He found it strange and uplifting that he didn't see any carcasses of mountain lion, wolf, or bear. Maybe they caught scent of something they didn't like and avoided the road dams.

"More left again!"

Bishop followed her advice, and the truck lurched to the side.

"Woah!"

"Hang on!"

He jerked the wheel to the right, avoiding a nasty hole.

"When you clear the hole, make another hard left."

The back wheels slipped on the mud and slime as the truck lurched. Bishop advanced a little too fast, and he smashed the front end into an uprooted tree.

"Shit!" Angela shouted as she tumbled down the windshield.

Bishop's heart thumped out of rhythm for several beats, then settled back.

Angela recovered well before the uprooted tree and kneeled on the hood. She looked at Bishop with a mischievous grin and mock wiped her forehead while pursing her lips. Bishop watched the bottom of her sneakers on the windshield as she ascended to her guide position.

"Close one!" she shouted.

"Too close."

"OK, keep angling left. There's more grass there, and the creek is running through it but it looks much better than the other options."

Bishop turned left and the truck angled down, but it held ground and progressed through the flooding water of Stinson Creek. Bishop poked his head out of the window and studied the silted water. The creek had created channels through the mud and grass and ran downhill into the woods. Below them, the trunks of aspen and spruce were flooded like mangroves. Numerous animal tracks dotted what was left of the muddy road, most of them patterns Bishop had never seen.

Something flashed in the trees.

"Get in the truck," Bishop said.

"What?"

"Get your ass in the truck now!"

"OK, coming."

As Angela's steps thumped the roof, the flooded ferns pushed aside, and a peculiar splashing came from the shadows. Bishop reached for the shotgun, rested it on the window frame and flicked off the safety. Angela shimmied through the window and into her seat.

The thing sprang forth from the trees.

Bishop moved his finger from the trigger.

Angela broke out laughing.

The uncoordinated bird stumbled a few steps towards them, splashing across the flood water and ruffling its vibrant plumage. The bird tilted its head and gazed at them. Then it ruffled its plumage and performed a strange in-place dance by raising one leg as high as it could, then the other.

"What is wrong with that thing?" Bishop asked.

"Maybe it's thinking the same about you?" Angela said.

"I came close to shooting it," Bishop said. He pulled the shotgun back in.

"I'm going back up."

Angela clomped onto the roof and secured herself, and they watched the bird as it clumsily worked the flood, looking for who knows what.

"Onward!" she shouted on one knee, thrusting her arm toward the south. "Onward to Elmore."

Bishop maneuvered through the last several miles of quasi-road and pumped his fist in the air when they reached Highway 18, well south of the original road dam. Then he parked on the first section of intact highway so Angela could get in.

Bishop raised the binoculars and glassed to the south.

"All clear," he said. "Although—"

"—yes?"

"There appears to be a dark cloud over where Elmore would be," Bishop said.

"Probably just a storm," Angela said. "This place has been in a drought. Some rain might be nice."

"I suppose," he said.

Soon, they passed the yellow Subaru with its unfortunate former passenger.

"What happened there?" Angela asked, turning as she caught a glimpse of the half-consumed corpse.

"Secapod," Bishop said.

"How do you know?"

"I was sitting right there with you when it happened," Bishop said, pointing to a patch of roadside fern.

"You didn't do anything to help?"

"I made a choice," he said. "I had to protect you, and the place was thick with bad things."

"Thank you," she said, staring at the blurring trees and grasses. "Should we go back to the rental?"

Bishop shook his head. "That place was crawling with them. I think Colbrick was right when he said they liked lower elevation."

Highway 18 curved downhill to Elmore, the forest now thicker and more verdant due to higher moisture levels. Cedars became prominent and shadows lingered, the light of day seeming to lose some of its power.

"Ow," Angela said.

"What's wrong?"

"My ears hurt."

Angela moved her jaw side to side, trying to pop her ears.

"From the elevation change?"

"I think so…"

Then Bishop's mouth twitched and his ears started to ring.

"That's no elevation change," he said as the left side of his mouth pulled upwards. His left eye soon followed.

"No," Angela said, shaking her head. "Please no."

As they turned a blind corner, a gnawing frequency seal appeared in the middle of the road, its chunky torso rippling as it bellowed. Its grabbing, scrubbing mouth contorted like a spastic hand puppet and four of its limbs clawed the air.

"It's hurting me," Angela said, right before the rest of her words became garbled nonsense. A thick string of drool trickled from her lips.

Bishop tried to yell, but nothing made sense. He focused on the road with one good eye and one good arm, aiming the truck at the frequency seal. Then Bishop's arms dropped from the wheel as his legs flailed in the footwell. The frequencies created intense, colorful flashes in their minds, accompanied by pounding cacophonies which rhythmically triggered shifting and oozing greens, blues, and reds. The centers of the colorful flashes revealed a star-like body shimmering with the light of a thousand suns.

Bishop heard and felt a sickening crunch.

Slowly, his vision returned. *Come on, you idiot,* he thought. *Come on, hit the fucking brake*s. Despite the numb sensation in his foot, he found the brake pedal and stomped it.

The harsh smell of burning rubber wafted into the truck, rising from the front bumper in intermittent clouds while the throaty V8 idled. Bishop turned to Angela. Her eyelids fluttered.

"Angela...you OK? Angela?"

He reached for her shoulder with a numb and sweaty arm. Angela responded to his touch, her eye spasms receding. She licked her lips as if waking from a long slumber.

"...are we alive?"

"Yes," he said.

"It's dead, isn't it?" she asked, her voice uneven.

"Yes."

Bishop's strength returned in waves, his vision thawing from icy blurriness.

Chummy slime coated the truck hood. He looked into the woods, and his nerves pricked. He didn't like the way this section of road felt. And to confirm his beliefs, an unidentifiable insect landed on his left arm and dug its saw-snout into his flesh, the tiny, leathery wings buzzing and slapping. Bishop went to swat the thing, and as he brought his palm down, the insect's curiously devious eyes locked onto him. Then it sprung and latched onto the skin just under his eye, and Bishop used his left hand to pull the buzzing menace off.

He held the helpless bug out in front of him. "Look," he said. "I saw these by our rental. Horrible little fucks, aren't they?"

"What an awful thing," Angela said.

They stared at it, and it stared back with psychotic, bulging eyes.

"I think they like this lower elevation," Bishop said. "I didn't see any at Big J."

He went to smash the creature with his other hand.

"Don't," Angela said.

"What?"

"I don't know. There's something about it."

"Yes, there is something about it. It's annoying and painful as hell when it saws into you."

"I'd just let it go," Angela said.

"Why?"

The insect buzzed and sawed at the air with its snout.

"Karma."

"OK, Gandhi," Bishop said, holding the insect out the window and letting go. He rolled up the window so the insect couldn't enter the vehicle again. It hovered near the glass, its leathery wings a blur, its mad eyes gawking.

Angela rubbed her temples and gazed out the windshield.

"I hate those freaking seals," she said.

"Well, there are now three less of them," he said, pressing the accelerator.

The wheels rolled over the dead frequency seal and Bishop's stomach turned. He observed the lump of guts in the rearview mirror, and the queasiness turned into satisfaction.

"How about that for karma?" he asked.

"It tried to kill us," Angela said.

"And if it could, that insect would too," he said.

"We don't know that. Maybe it just wanted a small piece."

"I think the frequency seals might have damaged your brain."

"Oh I think we're way beyond that," Angela said.

*

The shadows grew deeper between the trees and ferns, attaining an impenetrable quality. Darkened clouds blocked the sun, and the air cooled as if near a lake or river. Bishop turned on the headlights. Dense patches of fog birthed and died and birthed on the road, rising to meet the truck, separating when penetrated and then coalescing behind it.

Angela crossed her arms over her chest and shivered.

"Isn't this supposed to be summer?" she asked.

"You know how it can get in the mountains," he said. "Hell, it's snowed here in July."

Angela reached into the pack behind her and took a sweater.

"I wonder what happened to everyone at Big J," she said.

"I think we found two of them."

"That couldn't have been all. Where did they go?"

"They probably thought the same thing you did—they wanted to know more, or as Colbrick said, they may have spooked by the burrowers."

The road descended and the trees grew stouter, the plants and branches glistening from fog. A family of the small mammal-like animals skittered across the road to the embankment and stared back at them with wary eyes. The pup's fur was a mix of red and brown while the adults showed solid red. One of them was wearing a flashing device. Bishop thought it was blinking faster now. He turned to Angela and saw a soft look on her face as she watched them.

To the west, the Apex Mountains carried more trees along the slopes. Although this end of the range was lesser in elevation than the north, the mountains were more foreboding with striking precipices and ever-present, low clouds that hid rocky peaks.

The fog dissipated for a moment, and the small town of Elmore came into view far down in the valley.

"I see about four lights," Angela said, frowning.

"They don't have power at all," Bishop said.

Bishop caught the unpleasant scent of burning timber and paint. Flames licked the horizon at the southern end of town, and a black, billowing smudge rose into the sky.

"Elmore's on fire," Angela said.

"Not all of it," Bishop said.

As they descended into the lowest portion of Apex Valley, fog blended with smoke, the acrid smell of burning wood and chemicals intensifying. They passed a few ramshackle businesses, and Bishop slowed down to get a better look.

"There's Brownies," Angela said.

Brownies was their favorite pastry shop. They'd purchased baked goods and other items there for the last five summers. Angela had even become friends with Sue Grafferton, the incredibly nice store owner. Bishop had numerous conversations with Sue's husband, Bill, often relating to fly fishing and nature photography. Good guy. Damn good guy.

"Slow down a bit, honey," Angela said, riveted to the window. "Damn it, I don't see any sign of them. Pull over."

"Do you really want to risk it—?"

"—please pull over, Bishop. What if they're inside waiting for help?"

"I don't see Sue's van," Bishop said. "They probably left."

"Where would they go? Their kids are in New England."

"OK, OK."

Bishop pulled into the small gravel lot and cut the engine. The truck was down to a quarter tank.

"Maybe we can get some fuel here," he said.

They exited the truck and crept to the wood-sided building. The storefront windows were wide, not high, and a squat second story with a log beam balcony shaded the walkway. Old growth cedars reached into the sky behind the shop, and the pleasant scent of baked goods and sweet grass filled their noses. An orange newspaper dispenser stood next to the door, with a July 2nd edition of the Elmore Standard.

Bishop took notice of the headline: *Streamwood residents complain of strange animal activity.*

"Look," he said, fetching a copy and holding it up for Angela.

"So the new arrivals trickled in, it didn't just happen all at once. If people were reporting it on July 1st—"

"—and Streamwood Resort is west of here, which means..."

"....it started there, towards the mountains," Angela said.

Bishop set the paper on the dispenser and checked his shotgun to make sure it was loaded.

"You got yours?" he asked.

Angela held her .357 in the air and smiled wickedly. "I don't leave home without it."

The sight of Angela smirking and holding such a dangerous weapon turned him on, and he had to wonder why in such extraordinary circumstances he felt that way. They could die at any moment, yet here he was, horny as a teenager. *Get a grip on yourself*, he thought. A voice from a corner of his mind uttered "you wish." Bishop chuckled, wondering if he wasn't going mad while Angela gleamed at him with those dangerous eyes.

"Stop," he said.

"Stop what?" she said, continuing to stare.

"That look. You know."

"I don't know anything," she said, smirking and continuing to stare at him while biting her lower lip.

"Fuck, let's look inside."

"Why you read my mind."

"Are you serious?"

They peered into the windows, and although the windows contained dark, tinted elements, they could see enough. The mini-grocery store was intact. The outdated desktop computer that Sue charged one dollar an hour for internet access sat between the wall coolers. To the right was the old-fashioned glass display case that contained the baked goods. Varnished log beams supported the second story at strategic intervals, and woven rugs with animal patterns covered portions of the hardwood floor in-between rows of snacks.

"No one's in there," Angela said.

"Good," Bishop said, licking his lips. "Because I'm really hungry and I don't have any cash on me."

They opened the white, creaky door and shuffled inside towards the glass display. The scent of baked goods owned them.

"Sue, you here?" Angela shouted as she stepped behind the counter. "Sue, it's Angela." She waited for a response, but it never came.

The wall coolers were silent.

"No power," Bishop said, opening a glass door and reaching his hand inside just to be sure. He closed the cooler door and grabbed the cordless phone from its cradle behind the register. Nothing, not even a click or hiss.

Angela reached into the glass display and retrieved two brownies that looked to be a touch stale. She handed one to Bishop and they devoured them, wiping chocolate from their mouths.

"Oh my God," Angela said as she tasted the delicious creation.

"Best fucking brownie ever," Bishop said.

"You have fucking on the brain."

"What?"

Angela pushed up against him, and for a moment, he thought he might pass out. The danger it seemed was heightening all their senses in every possible way. There was nothing selective about it.

Angela undid her pants and then Bishop's. Next, she placed her palms flat on the counter and spread her legs. In a second, Bishop was inside her. He didn't last long, for more than one reason. When it was over, they dressed quickly and business-like, then went about as if nothing had happened.

Bishop reached into the display, seized a hunk of Sue's famous huckleberry pie and devoured it like a wild animal.

"Wow, manners much?" Angela laughed.

"No one cares about manners in the apocalypse."

"Speak for yourself."

The slice of pie disappeared, and Bishop reached in and took another brownie.

"So good," he said between lip smacking.

"I feel bad eating these," Angela said. "Sue worked her ass off."

"I don't think Sue's around," he said. "And I'd feel worse about getting fucked on her counter than I would about eating her baked goods."

Angela laughed. "I'm going to check the computer," she said, moving to the beaten-up wooden stand. Above the computer, attached to a log beam via push-pin was a note in Sue's artsy handwriting: *Internet down, sorry!* Angela reached behind the computer and flipped the switch anyway. Nothing.

"No power, no computer," Bishop said from behind.

"I'm going to check upstairs."

"Let me go first," Bishop said, wiping his hands on his pants.

They entered a saloon style door on the far wall in-between the coolers, and headed to the back of the shop, through the kitchen to a set of wooden stairs. Bishop moved up the steps in a way that allowed him to peer into the second story with only the top of his head exposed. The second floor was dim, but he could ascertain certain details. Pieces of furniture were strewn about, and a wheeled file organizer lay upturned, the papers sweeping down like lava from a volcanic cone. A splotch of blood defaced a plaid couch, and a cheap color TV with a cracked screen sat on an antique stand in the corner. Bishop could see his reflection in the TV screen as well as the afternoon light shining down the hallway that led to the rooms Sue rented out to backpackers.

Bishop noticed something else in that cracked screen, something gaseous, growing as it slunk down the hallway towards him.

Then they heard a sound they had wished they would never hear again.

The eel emitted a pressurizing noise when its multitasking pupils observed enough movement near the stairs to comprehend the presence of an intruder.

"Stay below," Bishop whispered as he waved his hand at her.

Angela retreated down the steps and raised the .357 with a shaky arm.

The eel floated towards the stairwell, its independent pupils now all working in unison. Bishop waited, gripping the shotgun until his fingers hurt. The eel inched closer in the monochrome TV reflection. It was a big one.

The hissing grew louder.

Bishop sprinted up the stairs, shotgun pointed down the hallway.

Bam!

The once dim room flashed yellow and orange, and the thunderous blast rang Bishop's ears. Angela ran up the stairs to his side, and they watched the eel contort and hiss in a twisted and painful display. The struggling eel followed the light at the end of the hallway and rammed itself through the glass.

"Shoot it again!" Angela shouted.

"No."

"Why the heck not?"

"We don't want loud noises. Remember the fliers? How they keyed in on us from the nail gun?"

"OK, good point. *Good* point."

"Besides, I think it's just running off to die," Bishop said.

"I hope so."

A breeze rustled the white-laced curtains at the end of the hallway. Angela and Bishop crept along the carpet, guns aimed at the window. When they neared Sue's bedroom at the end of the hall, they smelled something putrid.

"Wait here," Bishop said.

He peeked into Sue's room, exposing a minimal portion of his frame so he was not a target. What he saw laying upon the bed was something he never imagined he would see, for Sue lay there face down, her arms and legs missing chunks of flesh. It appeared the eels preferred the meat of the calves and triceps. Bishop gagged, almost heaving the sugary bulging mess in his stomach. Sue's hair was wild and torn, as if the creature had latched onto it to flip her over so it could feast on the meat it preferred.

"Don't look in there," he said.

"She's dead, isn't she?"

"Sue is gone. I'm sorry."

Angela trembled as her eyes pooled with moisture, and soon her cheeks were dripping. She ran to the window and flung back the curtains, gazing out to the parking lot and the highway. Then she pointed her gun out the window.

"Come on fuckers! *COME AND GET ME!*"

Bishop pulled her away from the window and wrestled her into his arms.

"She was such a good person," Angela said, sobbing. "What did she do to deserve this?"

Bishop held her tighter, feeling her lurching sobs upon his chest. But he did not stop scanning the building, for there were enemies all around them.

*

They searched the rustic, cedar-paneled rooms for useful items and came up with a foldable knife, a daypack, spare AAA batteries for their headlamps, and even a quarter ounce of weed. Bishop held up the baggie in the light.

"I haven't seen that since college," Angela said.

"Me neither."

"So why are we keeping it?"

"It's pain medicine. You never know when you're going to need it." *And you never know when you don't need it either*, he thought.

Bishop remembered the bottle of Vicodin in the truck's glove box, of how the pills sang to him as if alive. When they headed downstairs, Bishop checked their rear, making sure nothing entered the hallway window. The curtain blew gently in the breeze, but nothing came.

Angela filled the backpack with Gatorade and other items from the coolers, laughing in-between sobs. "Poor Sue. She worked so hard, and here we are pilfering her life's work."

"Sue would want us to take this stuff," Bishop said.

"Where do you think Bill went?" Angela asked.

Bishop sighed. "I don't know. I hope that wherever he is, he's OK." But Bishop had a feeling Bill was scattered across a patch of gooseberry back in the woods. If he was lucky, it was quick—real quick. Bill often picked wild berries for Sue's pies. The creatures probably hit him at once, long before they crept into the shop to get Sue.

They took packets of beef jerky, plastic spoons, stove fuel, a single burner stove, bug spray, all the baked goods they could fit inside a cardboard box, and packs of gum.

"What's the gum for?" Bishop asked.

"It's scientifically proven that gum lifts your spirits," Angela said.

When Bishop went outside to load their cache, Angela maneuvered behind the glass display and took a tape recorder off a wooden shelf. Sue had used it for her famous recipes.

With the truck fully loaded, Angela got inside and shut the door quietly.

"I'm going to check the garage," Bishop said to her while standing outside the passenger side window. He walked over to the dilapidated structure, ever aware of what might pop out at him from the forest. Rays of light brimming with plankton-like motes shone between the warped slats. One of Bill's fly rods leaned against a rickety wall. On a work bench comprised of two saw horses and a slab of wood sat an aluminum gasoline can. Bishop carried it to the truck, then extended the wonky spout and inserted it into the gas tank. The viscous glugging was louder than he liked, so he raised the angle to hurry things along. When the can finally emptied, Bishop placed it into the back seat.

The gas needle ticked above half a tank as they pulled out of their friend's bakery and hostel.

"Goodbye, Sue," Angela said, taking Bishop's hand with trembling fingers.

*

Heading south on Highway 18, they approached Wilkin's Bait and Tackle. There were no signs of the cantankerous son of a bitch owner. Bishop had his run-ins with the old man over the years, and Wilkins once even accused Bishop of not spending enough money at his shop. Bishop never understood Wilkin's hate for tourists since they were the bulk of his business. Wilkins would even give bad information to those who "didn't spend enough," or send them to spots known to locals as fishless. In the taverns, these jerks would joke about the hapless tourists wandering off into the woods, sometimes with children in tow. It wasn't all pretty scenery in Elmore. There were some ugly, ugly people.

"I hope they got him," Bishop said.

"You don't mean that. Take it back," Angela said.

"I mean, come on. They took Sue, so it's only fair they got that son of a bitch."

"The bad ones never seem to die early," she said.

"Or maybe the good ones just haven't lived long enough to do bad."

"I'm checking it out," Bishop said, turning into the gravel lot.

"Do we keep it running?" she asked.

"Not sure. I can't remember if it saves more gas to keep it running or to start it again."

"Turn it off, I think," Angela said.

They got out, weapons in hand, and approached the wooden building with its small pitched roof and large display window. Fish smell permeated the air, like the moments after a heavy spring rain. When they opened the creaky shop door, a little silver bell jangled. Bishop froze, then cupped the bell in his hand and yanked it off the piece of yarn it was tied to.

Nothing seemed out of place. Wilkins was nothing if not neat. A row of spinning tackle and a row of fly fishing gear split the middle of the store. Several plastic basins were set against the left wall with tubes entering each one. The basins bubbled with fresh incoming water, and schools of darting minnows occupied each one. Bishop peered over a basin edge, and the minnows swarmed to the far side, tiny eyes locking onto him from behind.

"All clear," Bishop said.

Angela walked over to the cash register and picked up the phone next to it.

"Dead," she said. Then she turned to examine the wall behind the register. "Look at this, hon."

She handed him a brand new Beretta 92fs pistol and a box of ammunition.

"Hell yes," he said.

Then Angela took two expensive Rambo style knives that contained a compass in the handle and a hollow place for matches.

"You're on fire," Bishop said.

They loaded their winnings into the truck and got in, careful how they shut the doors.

"Wait," Angela said. "We can't do that."

"Do what?" Bishop asked.

"We can't just leave the minnows like that."

"Oh yes we can."

"No, we really can't."

"I'm not wasting my time with that."

"Fine, wait here then."

"You can't be serious?"

"I am."

"Are you insane?"

Angela turned to him with hurt eyes.

She's seen enough death, Bishop thought. He understood that something inside her would not let those minnows die flopping about in the soon-to-be dry basins.

"We're the better species," she said. "We do the right thing. That's what makes us different from the others."

Her eyes pleaded.

Bishop's incredulity receded, and his shoulders relaxed.

"OK, I'll help."

Angela cracked a smile, and they went into the asshole's shop, grabbing aquarium nets from the damp wall and fishing out minnows of various shapes and sizes. The minnows flopped and slithered in the nets, the tiny, fleshy sides making mealy noises as they rubbed together. Bishop opened the back door and they headed to the bait pond Wilkins had tended over the years. The last batch of rescued minnows plopped into the water and streaked to shadier portions of the pond. The minnows wanted to hide, too.

"There," she said. "I feel better now."

In a strange way, Bishop did too. In a world that was out of control, this was something they could control. They did good.

Bishop put his arm around Angela, and they proceeded around the fishing shop rather than going back in. They were learning.

Angela tried the walkie-talkie from the truck, but no luck. Lots of static, but at least the jarring frequency sweeps were gone. Bishop hated the radio and the way Angela spoke into the ether, as if they were the last people on earth. The empty static crushed morale. He wished he could toss the radio onto the gravel lot and run it over. If it wasn't for Colbrick...he gripped the wheel, not wanting to think about it.

Back on the highway, they passed Blanton's Car Repair, Denson's General Store, and Apex Crafts. All seemed deserted. Highway 18 turned into Main Street, a point where many confused tourists didn't realize they were still on the correct route. There were a couple right turns, a couple left turns, and signs to follow—although the positioning of the signs was questionable.

Main Street wasn't much. There was the tiny movie theater (Stanton's) with the wheeled popcorn maker out front, a deluxe candy shop, several clothing stores, and a souvenir shop that sold all kinds of tourist crap. The owner, Bob Higgins, had once been charged with selling knives to kids under the age of sixteen. The Lynyrd Skynyrd cocaine mirrors probably weren't a good choice either. It was your standard small town hub, except this one had views of the tremendous Apex Mountains with their unusual, mangled precipices. The scenery drew people to Elmore, but you can't eat the scenery, and many dreams of permanent residence in this beautiful place faded like fall leaves on the aspen. The locals clung to whatever was here, often inherited. They were not all that different from the ragged trees clinging to the high, rocky slopes.

Towards the southern end of Main Street, they saw the source of the flames and smoke—Jenson's Hardware. Bishop wondered how much propane Jenson had stored and if it had blown already. Flames tore through the flat roof and reached for the sky like orange weeds. Bishop stopped the truck and watched through the windshield. Angela coughed as smoke billowed down Main Street, skulking through the alleys like clouds between mountain peaks.

They jumped in their seats as a projectile rocketed through the store's front window, trailing eye-searing, rippling flames. The object screamed across Main Street, knocked bricks loose on the opposite building, then exploded.

"There goes a propane tank," Bishop said.

"Jesus, do you think we should move a bit—"

Pow!

Another tank shot through the hardware store window, dripping bright fire and smashing into an apartment window across the street. Fresh flames licked and teased the window frame from inside the apartment building.

"There goes that building," Bishop said.

"Do you think anyone is in there?"

"I doubt it."

"Maybe we should go look."

"You want to enter a building that's on fire while exploding propane tanks are launching into it?"

"We can go around back."

A burst of flame ripped through the apartment building roof, a final answer to their foolish thoughts.

"Never mind," Angela said.

Then they heard the barking.

From a second story window in the apartment building, a small, white head bobbed up and down, ears flopping above the windowsill, then disappearing. Bishop saw the occasional flash of teeth and a snout.

Ruff! Ruff!

"Bishop, a dog's trapped up there!"

He stomped the gas pedal, shoved Angela's head below the window frame and accelerated past the fiery hardware store. "Keep your head down!" he shouted. Then he made a hard left onto Trout Road and zipped into the gravel alley behind the apartments.

"Wait here and keep it running," he said.

"Be careful," Angela said, cupping her hand to her mouth.

Bishop opened a heavy door and entered a dimly lit, yellow-painted hall that reeked of mold and carpet cleaner. He found the stairs, smoke already creeping down each step. Bishop stretched his shirt over his mouth, and in the haze and sick stench, he followed the desperate barks to the second story. Each bark sent his heart into the pit of his stomach, making him hate the world even more. This was reality. Things fucking die, and die a lot. This dog may be just another gnat-like punctuation mark in the brutal chapter of life. *Fuck you,* he thought, not sure who he was even addressing the insult to.

The barking came from a door with thick coils of smoke streaming out the cracks. Bishop began to sweat from the heat, and a harsh cough forced him to drop his shirt from his mouth. He held his breath and reached for the brass door handle which was hot, but he wasn't fazed. When he flung the door open, huge plumes of smoke billowed into the hallway, followed by attacking flames that ignited the crusty yellow ceiling.

Bishop turned and ran.

This was the end of the line. He could do no more.

He reached the stairwell and looked back. A weak dog pulled itself along the carpet from the doorway, crawling below the pouring smoke. The dog managed to get a few feet down the hallway, its eyes narrowing from asphyxiation.

"Don't you fucking die!"

Bishop took off his shirt, wrapped it around his mouth and sprinted down the moldy, burning hallway. His arm hairs singed and his vision wavered. He saw a blur of white on the floor and reached for it blindly, feeling like his hand had been placed into an oven. His fingers grasped fur, and he yanked as hard as he could while turning away at the same time, dragging the pooch down the smoke-filled hallway.

"Gotcha," he said.

He placed the dog over his shoulder and teetered down the stairs. When he exited the rear door, Angela sprinted towards him, her eyes wild with worry. There he stood, shirtless and sooty, a mutt slumped over his shoulder. Then Bishop collapsed. His head slammed onto gravel, and swirling stars filled his darkening mind.

*

"Bishop, wake up, wake up honey, please, please wake up!"

A hand slapped his numb face. His eyelids opened and closed.

Slap!

His eyelids rose again as he emerged from the darkness. His mouth tasted like burnt paper, and his eyes stung.

"Thank God!" Angela said.

She took Bishop in her arms and hugged him, and he coughed.

"Where's the dog?" he asked, lips and throat sticking from dryness.

"Right here at your side," she said, smiling through a stream of tears. "He's right here."

The medium-sized, sooty mutt with floppy ears and long snout barked at Bishop. The dog even wagged his tail.

"You saved it, hon!"

"Help me up," Bishop said. "We need to get out of here before the fire grows."

Angela reached for him and pulled, and they heard another explosion.

A propane tank screamed across the sky above them into a residential area. The dog watched, a blazing trail reflecting in his eyes.

Angela helped Bishop into the passenger seat and opened the back door for the pooch.

"Come on, boy," she said. "Do you want to come with us?"

The funny-looking dog tilted his head, his wary eyes shifting to eagerness, and he leaped into the back of the vehicle.

"Good boy," Angela said.

"Get us out of here," Bishop said.

Angela hit the gas and sped back onto Main Street, heading south on Highway 18.

"Where to?" she asked.

"The hell out of this valley," Bishop said.

The dog spun around in the back seat, sniffing everything.

"I think he's hungry," Angela said. She pulled to the side of the road and grabbed a box of crackers, tossing a few at the desperate pooch. The dog gobbled them and licked his chops. Angela poured bottled water into one of the plastic bowls they took from Sue's. The dog lapped for at least a minute.

"Wow," Bishop said, starting to feel a tad better. "Poor fella needed nourishment."

They drove south along the twisting highway, and the southernmost portion of the Apex Valley appeared ahead. Once on the other side of the hill, the highway would take them out of the valley to the windy plains and Great Prairie Air Force Base. Visions of shiny bunkers with men in laboratory coats who had all the answers swirled in Bishop's mind like candy to a child. They might find their way out of this mess after all. The first thing they would do after making contact would be to return and find Colbrick, that's for certain. Surely this incident was contained within the Apex Valley? One could hope. The thought of the new arrivals spreading across the U.S. was not something to entertain.

Bishop turned to Angela and took her hand.

"I think we're on our way out of this," he said.

The hum of the wheels lulled their exhausted minds into reduced alertness, the ever-present forest blurred and verdant.

Then Bishop bolted upright in his seat and jabbed his finger at the windshield.

"Stop!" he shouted. "Stop now!"

The truck screeched to a halt, and the poor dog slammed into the backseat with a grunt, then recovered as if nothing happened the way dogs do. The pooch maneuvered himself between Angela and Bishop so he too could observe the action in front of them.

"No," Bishop said. "Please no."

Angela stared out the windshield, craning her neck.

A hundred yards down the road loomed a wall of haze, with numerous dangling roots and branches emerging from the top.

"Road dam," Bishop said.

Jammed up in front of the re-arranged landscape was a tangle of vehicles—an ambulance with flashing lights, a police car, several SUV's. Four officers discharged their firearms at a group of pigras that shambled from the tree line.

Bishop raised the binoculars for a closer look.

Muzzle flash lit the roadway and the officers scrambled.

A breeze shifted a cloud of silt, and the officers tried to find their sight lines in the partial murk. The pigras paid no mind as they crept along on their worn, bloody knuckles. Their matted fur blossomed grotesque red medallions as the pistol rounds found their targets. More pigras lurched out of the woods, replacing the fallen and injured. One of the pigras had a pulsing rectangle on its backside. Bishop counted forty-four beats per minute.

"We need to help them," Angela said.

"I don't think there's anything we can do," Bishop said, turning to Angela and putting a hand on her knee. "If we go up there, we're dead meat."

*

Angela bit her nails as her mind flashed with choices that made her feel cold and uncomfortable. She wanted to run out there and kill the monkeys—as many as she could. She wanted them all dead. She couldn't just sit back and let those men die. That wasn't her. But she couldn't help but think of Sue, her unseen body rotting on the other side of that wall. And the smell—she didn't want to be that smell.

The lead pigra succumbed to the bullets, and Bishop pumped his fist.

A dust cloud swirled towards the truck, carrying with it the scent of moist wood and pungent soil.

"We can help them, "Angela said. "We have to."

A sneaking shadow glided across the road next to them, as if the sun was being eclipsed by the moon. The shadow elongated across the dashboard and then over the hood.

More shadows followed.

Another shadow blocked what was left of the sun and then another. The air filled with whooshing gusts, looped gunfire, and the rhythmic beat of wings.

The day went from milky afternoon translucence to thunderstorm dusk. Glowing eyes dotted the sky, followed by smaller eyes attached to the backs of the giant fliers, like penguins waiting to dive-bomb in formation to targets of their choosing.

The pooch tilted his head and whimpered, for he had seen these things from the apartment window at night.

"Shhh," Bishop whispered. "Not a sound."

"Oh my God," Angela said. "The officers, Bishop."

There was nothing they could do unless they wanted to experience the wrath of the fliers.

The looping gunfire mimicry spooked the officers, and they turned to fire at the truck. "Idiots!" Bishop said, moving with lightning reflexes and jamming Angela's head down with his left hand. Bullets peppered the windshield and hood, the safety glass crackling like thin ice. They cowered in the footwells, listening to the looped mimicry of the small fliers and the fading reports.

"Stay down," Bishop said. "No need to see this."

Real shots rang out into the sky, mixing with the leathery flapping of a thousand wings and shrieks. Air whistled through the bullet holes in the windshield, propelled by the army of wings. The real gunfire receded into sporadic bursts, and finally into one meek and desperate shot. The officer's screamed, piercing the frenetic mimicry like a psychedelic trumpet in the center of a wide stereo spectrum.

Bishop didn't want to look, but they needed information. Maybe he could find a weakness.

He raised his head above the dashboard.

The small fliers buzzed around the gigantic ones, which appeared to be at least thirty feet long with a wingspan of eighty feet. They were not at all dragon-like, as the darkness at Big J suggested, instead leaning more towards a pterodactyl. Their wicked eyes revealed intelligence beyond the average bird. Two of the giant birds had flashing tags on their long necks.

Bishop counted forty-eight beats per minute.

Four huge fliers each gripped an officer in their immense talons, the yellowish hooks dismembering the men where they were held. Gushes of blood and organs slithered out as they tried to remove themselves from their impaler like worms on a hook. It was pointless. The flier's monolithic, oblong heads and sharp beaks jabbed down to the men, causing mortal injuries with every stab. The faces of the officers contorted in ways Bishop had never seen.

"What do you see?" Angela whispered from the footwell.

"Things you never want to see."

The screams of the four officers dissipated until they were nothing more than mumbles and air-sucking gasps. Then they were hoisted into the sky amidst the rhythmic thunder of wings. The small fliers maneuvered atop the backs of the large ones, and at once, their looped mimicry ceased. But their eyes still glowed, and the legion glared back down the road at the idling truck. Away they went, beating higher into the sky, the glowing eyes fading, the last scream of a man rendered silent under a beat of wing. Bishop watched as the fliers became shadows, soaring and flapping towards the mangled precipices and ever-present clouds of the southern Apex Mountains.

He waited until the fliers were specs and then sat up all the way. A group of pigras lapped at the pools of blood and innards, two of the foul things even pulling on a section of intestine like a game of tug-o-war. As the pigras huddled in front of the road dam, the tiny primate creatures emerged between cracks in the vegetation, and they too joined in the unsavory feast, pawing and shrieking at the other pigras. One of them sat up and used it forelimbs to wipe the blood from its face.

"Can I come up now?" Angela asked.

"Yes. And please drive us the hell out of here."

Angela sat up, her eyes glistening as she witnessed the scene.

"Don't look," Bishop said.

The movement of Angela's head caught the attention of a pigra, and the gathering shambled towards the truck on crooked limbs. The tiny primate creatures—which Bishop thought must be baby pigras—followed their parents, their crimson eyes shining, their fur stained with blood and other slop, which the adults licked off. The young emitted harsh, chirping vocalizations. The older pigras remained silent.

"Great," Bishop said. "So those things are pigra babies."

"They're all having babies," Angela said. "Not a surprise."

"Unbelievable," Bishop said, pointing to the eastern side of the road about fifty yards from their truck.

A dozen small, chubby creatures appeared from a patch of ferns. They had six limbs, four of which grasped sticks and branches. Five of the creatures worked in unison to carry a rather hefty branch towards the road dam. Two pigras appeared behind the seals, also holding sticks.

"Baby frequency seals," Bishop said. "Get us out of here."

Angela turned the truck around and headed back to Elmore, leaving the new arrivals in a state of disappointment, if they could even feel such a thing. Bishop doubted it.

"Where to?" she asked.

"We take a left on Trout Road and head away from the mountains, that's where fucking to."

"Why?"

"Because that's not where the fliers went."

"So now we know," Angela said. "The paper was right."

The dog whimpered behind them, and Bishop tossed the pooch a few crackers.

*

The burning hardware store appeared through the battered windshield, although the intensity of the flames had diminished. The apartment building across the street where they rescued the dog produced billowing, dense smoke. Flames rippled out of the windows and blackened the bricks.

Angela turned left onto Trout Road and followed the winding asphalt past mossy cedars and tamarack. After climbing a steep hill, they swooshed down towards Trout Creek and its famous, picturesque bridge.

What they saw churned their stomachs.

The affable dog looked on with brown, curious eyes.

Trucks and cars crowded the narrow bridge, and it seemed disjointed from the weight. The truck rolled to a quiet stop before the pileup, and the cause of the jumble became clear. A fuel tanker had jack-knifed on the eastern side of the bridge, blocking passage in both directions. Vehicles that fled the chaos of Elmore piled up on the western side, but there were no vehicles on the eastern half. An abject unease washed over Bishop as he pondered the absence of eastbound vehicles.

Fifty feet below them, Trout Creek tumbled down slick boulder falls. Moist canyon walls rose on both sides of the clear stream. Patches of moss and abandoned, twiggy nests adorned the nooks where uneven rocks formed ledges.

"I'd say this is a dead end," Bishop said. He got out of the vehicle, and Angela followed. The dog stayed in the truck and watched them through the glass. They approached a red Subaru Outback that had smashed into a king-size pickup, which in turn buckled under the tanker.

"Hear that?" Bishop asked.

"All I hear is the creek," Angela said.

"Yes, there's that. But there's something else. I think it's the tanker."

"I can smell fuel," Angela said. "But I can't tell if it's from the tanker or one of the smaller trucks."

"Oh shit," Bishop said, staring at several haphazard streaks of blood that trailed from the jumble to the grassy embankment. "Bodies were dragged from here into the woods. Stay on your toes, sweetheart."

The pooch watched them from the truck, head tilting, mouth agape, tongue lolling.

Bishop studied a blood trail that lead up the grassy slope into the cedars and bracken ferns. He aimed his gun at the forest shadows, daring one of them to come out. None did.

Angela backed away from the bridge, her eyes scanning the tree line and her arms shaking.

"Uh… I don't like this place," she said.

"Neither do I. But we might be able to get gas."

The dog put his paws on the driver's window and stared, trying to understand what the humans were doing the ways dogs sometimes do.

"Whatever fed on these people is gone," he said. "I think this was a day or two ago."

"Can we drive the tanker out of the way?"

Bishop went back to the bridge. Both ends of the tanker were smashed in place against the north and south rails.

"It's not going anywhere," he said. "We're not getting across unless we want to walk."

Angela crossed her feet. "Bishop?"

"Yeah?"

"Why aren't there any cars on the other side of the tanker?"

"Good question," he said, staring down into Trout Creek. A chilly breeze rose up to him.

Angela started snuffling behind him. He turned and embraced her.

"Is the whole world like this? Did they get it all?"

"I don't know, sweetheart. All I know is that you and I are alive, and we're going to stay alive. And so is that nutty dog in the truck."

"I don't think Nutty Dog is a very good name," she said, snuffling.

"What's wrong with Nutty?"

"OK, maybe he's a little nuts. But let's think of something better." Angela used her sleeve to wipe tears from her cheeks. "He's a survivor. He's tough. And he's quite handsome." She looked back at the truck and saw the goofy dog gazing at her with his floppy ears and protruding tongue.

"How about…how about Yutu?" Angela asked.

"What's Yutu?"

"It's Miwok Indian for *coyote on the hunt*."

"I like it," he said.

They hugged once more, high above the tumbling, cool river that Bishop had fished with his father as a child.

*

They opened the truck doors quietly and reached in to pet the dog.

"Hey Yutu," Angela said, her eyes sparkling.

Bishop pet Yutu on the scruff. "I don't know what your name was before, buddy, or if you even had one, but you have one now. I hope you like it."

The dog looked up with appreciative eyes, then licked his chops. Angela got the hint and tossed him a few more crackers.

"We need to get Yutu some real food," Bishop said. "But first, we need to see if there are any goodies in those vehicles. You got my back?"

"Always. How about it, Yutu? Do you want to come out and get *my* back?"

The scrappy dog reluctantly climbed out of the vehicle and pattered along the pavement.

Bishop searched the bloodstained interior of the Subaru, finding loose change and fishing gear that was piled in the back. He took the fishing gear and stashed it in the truck. His spirits grew dim when he realized he had no idea what sort of thing a fishermen might pull out of these waters. He had to assume everything was tainted, for their safety.

The Cadillac Escalade with the smashed front-end contained a switchblade in the glove box. He winced when he found two bloody teeth on the driver's seat along with chunks of scalp and hair. He pictured one of the pigras reaching in to grab the driver by the hair and knocking the unfortunate soul into unconsciousness with those disjointed arms.

The Escalade also contained a designer purse, a small baggie of cocaine, and a newfangled sugar-free sports drink. Bishop tossed the cocaine into the street.

"Doesn't that have some sort of use?" Angela asked from behind.

"No."

Bishop checked the other cars and noticed deep scratches and dents on the roofs, without question the work of fliers. Then Bishop crawled under the tanker to the eastern side of the bridge. "Be right back," he said. "Just going to look around the bend."

There has to be a car or two on the other side, he thought. Why would there be no traffic this way? He knew the answer, but was too stubborn and afraid to accept it. Bishop jogged along the roadside, trying to get a better eastbound view. Ahead was nothing but empty roadway framed by the dominant cedar, maidenhair ferns, and roadside grasses. But far ahead, he glimpsed a cloud of haze topped by a dark, jagged line.

Road dam.

Bishop sighed. He returned to the tanker and climbed into the cab. There was no blood and no signs of struggle inside the cab at least. Bishop figured the driver fled into the woods, and as they had all figured out, the woods are not where you want to be in the Apex Valley, oh not at all. He pictured the lost and confused driver stumbling in the brush, and all the scenarios ended with a battered and half-eaten body covered by wet leaves in some musty glade.

Angela screamed.

Bishop leaped out of the cab, the shotgun stock slamming into the ground and ripping from his hand. He recovered the gun and sprinted towards Angela who was tending to a yelping Yutu.

"What's going on?"

Angela pointed a shaking finger at Yutu. A rotten leaf clung to the right side of Yutu's face, and the poor dog shook his head in an effort to detach the creature.

"We saw one of these back at the cabin," Bishop said, stepping towards Yutu. "Come on boy, be still, OK?"

Yutu inched backward, still jerking his head about.

"I'm trying to help you. Stay still, boy, you hear? Stay still."

They heard a crunch, and Yutu whimpered.

"Jesus, it's biting him," Angela said.

The leaf squealed, and Bishop noticed a faint whistling as the squeal subsided.

Yutu yelped. Angela leaped at Yutu and pried the rotten leaf off the dog's face. Yutu yipped again, paws clacking on the asphalt. He tucked behind Angela and peered around her legs as the leaf flopped on the ground.

"Holy hell, I hate these fucking things," Bishop said. "I swear they're calling out to their buddies." He wanted to blow it to pieces, but firing the shotgun onto the asphalt wouldn't be the brightest move—especially with the nagging odor of gasoline that permeated the area.

The leaf lifted off the road using tiny, industrial legs and scuttled off to the grassy embankment. As soon as it reached the grass, Bishop aimed the shotgun.

"Wait," Angela said. "Is killing *this* worth attracting the fliers?"

"Yes."

The leaf emitted a high-pitched whistle that tingled the hairs on the back of Bishop's neck. Yutu tilted his head at an obscene angle and stuck his tongue out.

The shotgun roared, shredding the rotten leaf into dozens of fragments.

"Gotcha," he said.

"Good job," Angela said. "And good riddance."

Full of themselves, they high-fived like basketball teammates who just completed an alley-oop.

Yutu barked, for the pooch was happier than anyone to see that awful leaf no more.

"Let's get out of here," Bishop said, looking into the canyon, remembering his father working a fine fourteen-inch cutthroat in the pool below. He missed him so much. But in a way, he was glad his father wasn't around to see what was happening to his beloved valley. Bishop thought of an old Townes Van Zandt song and hummed the sober melody as if a second funeral hymn for his father.

"Are you humming?" Angela asked.

"Yes."

"What song?"

"My Proud Mountains."

"Good one."

Behind tree line, on the northern side of the road, came a cacophonic symphony that clashed with his humming. Bishop shuddered. "Get in the truck," he said.

The whistle symphony arose once more, like unbalanced and irritated crickets. But instead of the semi-unison of crickets, each voice shrieked with its own frequency and tone.

"Uh...not good," Angela said, pointing out the window. "Bishop, the slope."

Crawling down the embankment were dozens of rotten leaves.

"I've had enough of this shit," Bishop said. He jammed the gas and yanked the wheel, turning the truck onto the embankment. The tires slipped on the grass but the truck ran true, squishing the rotten leaves, each one dying with a squeal. One of the rotten leaves managed to cling to the windshield. Bishop's stomach churned when he saw the stingray mouth, razor teeth, and pink tongue with a spoon-like formation at the tip. He flipped the wipers, and the leaf flew off to the side. Yutu barked.

"I hope we killed them all," Angela said.

"You know what? I think we did," he said, erupting in laughter.

"You did good, hon."

"*We* did good."

They swerved onto the road, tires screeching as they transitioned from grass to asphalt. Back to Highway 18 it was, passing the endless cedars and ferns, and who knew what lurked in the shady hollows and glades. For now, the road was free of such things, and that meant they were free, however fleeting.

*

Main Street, Trout Road, and smoke.

"Now where?"

"Not the mountains. And we can't go east. The northern and southern routes are blocked. We could head back north—"

"Colbrick," Angela said. "I miss him."

"So do I," Bishop said. "I hope he's alright."

"We could try him on the radio."

"Nah. The range is too far."

"We need to find a place to spend the night."

"What about Sue's?"

"No freaking way."

"OK, bad idea."

"What about Fulton's Clothing?"

Bishop looked north down Main Street at the two-level department store with brick façade.

"Sure, why not. We've got good elevated sightlines to the west, north, and south, and we can watch the street through the storefront."

They parked behind the department store in a gravel alley with a green dumpster. A brown metal door with no external handle was the sole means of entrance.

Bishop grasped the edge of the door with his fingertips and pried it open.

The Fultons must have left in a hurry, he thought. He waved to Angela who was secure inside the truck with Yutu. She smiled a rare smile and then the love of his life greeted him at the door with the second love of his life, Yutu. He patted the dog on the head, and for a beaming moment, he was prouder than a mountain.

*

The bottom level of Fultons consisted of mannequins, racks of clothing, and shelving piled with shoe boxes. It wasn't at all like your modern, clinical clothing store. There was a dim mustiness to the structure. Leather belts hung from an antique coat rack, and two large windows framed the glass door. A dusty cash register and glass counter occupied the southeast corner, and next to this, a row of stairs ascended to darker portions of the building.

Bishop and Angela tiptoed, only the creaky floorboards giving them away. They held their weapons out, waiting for the inevitable.

Yutu followed.

"We need to check upstairs," Bishop whispered.

Angela nodded.

Bishop turned to Angela and pointed to his head. Then he returned to the truck and retrieved the headlamp they'd stashed in the glove box. He also took two Vicodin and swallowed them dry.

He met Angela back in the store, looking like an apocalyptic fashion victim with his garish headlamp and shotgun. Bishop inched towards the stairs and poked his head up into the darkness. The violet-tinted light caught the flimsy-looking railing and a brick wall on the second floor. He paused, waiting for rustling or movement, but there was none. Then he worked his way up the stairs to a narrow hallway with one door on the eastern side and two doors on the western. At the end of the hallway was a window with murky glass. This pleased him. Bishop waved for Angela to follow, and she did, with Yutu right behind.

"I'm going to check each room," he whispered, putting a finger to his lips.

The storage room on the left was clear, and since it was windowless, nothing could have entered, waiting to ambush them. They turned near the discolored window, and Bishop grabbed the doorknob to the first street-facing room. Locked. They crept to the next door and Bishop slowly turned the knob.

Yutu watched him, head tilting.

With the door two-thirds open, Bishop reached his arm across and pushed it all the way, stepping into the frame, allowing one eye to scan the room with his right arm angled in with the shotgun. The room smelled of junk food and alcohol. A disheveled bed, an Xbox, and a computer monitor occupied the southern wall. A few books were strewn about, and a sink and countertop held dirty dishes. The windows were shut and there was no sign of broken glass. To the right was a small bathroom, complete with shower.

"This looks as good as anything," he said.

They entered, with Yutu pattering behind.

Bishop shut the door and locked it.

"Home sweet home," he said.

Angela laid upon the bed and dozed off—the .357 dropping out of her hands onto the blue bedspread. Yutu tilted his head and joined her, curling up at her thigh.

Bishop raised the cheap window shades and scouted Main Street and the peaks of the southern Apex Range. This was an excellent vantage point and a good place for defensive purposes. He was never in the military, but in some ways, he'd become a soldier. He walked into the bathroom and flushed the toilet, shocked that it worked. He tried the shower. It worked, even producing warm water. *Must be a power source in the basement,* he thought. *Angela will love this.* The showers at Big J were unmercifully cold and intermittent.

As Bishop showered, he thought of the curmudgeon back at Big J. His skin broke out in goosebumps when he remembered Colbrick picking them up in his truck, saving their lives again by knowing the route to Big J, and saving them yet again by killing the frequency seals. He wished Colbrick wasn't such a stubborn asshole and that he'd come with.

Bishop took one of the grungy towels from the wall rack and walked downstairs with his shotgun. The new pair of jeans, underwear, and long-sleeved shirt were leagues more comfortable than his old, crusty clothes. He sort of felt human again.

The apartment grew dark as the sun set behind the mountains, and he laid in bed with Angela and Yutu, smashing himself against the wall so as not to disturb them. He placed his left hand upon her waist and his chin on her neck. Her hair tickled his nose the way it always did, and he scratched it.

*

Bishop woke to a fuzzy haze, punctuated with the cadence of dripping water. Steam drifted from the bathroom and he realized Angela was taking a shower.

Yutu sat on the edge of the bed, staring at him. Behind the pooch, dark sky.

Angela stepped out in a skimpy towel that barely covered her curves, wiping her wet hair and pulling it back.

"How long was I out?" he asked.

"A couple hours," she said. "We should get food from the truck."

"There has to be some here."

"I didn't find any. I think the tenant got lots of take out."

Bishop went to the sink and washed his face with cool water, then headed to the truck, shotgun in hand. Yutu watched him walk down the dark stairway, then trotted back to Angela and the safety of the room.

Bishop only used the headlamp inside the store, not wanting to send any beams into the woods that bordered the once popular tourist town.

Dinner consisted of peanut butter and bread, with Yutu scarfing down the crusts. They tried to give Yutu peanut butter, but he seemed to hate it, sneezing and backing away from the can.

Movement caught Bishop's eye, and he went to the windows.

"Shit."

"What?"

"Come look."

Angela hesitated, then crept towards the windows.

What they saw made them shiver. The sky around the mangled precipices was peppered with numerous green orbs. The haphazard collection merged into formation, the big, green orbs followed by smaller ones. Here and there tiny red lights blinked.

"They're heading north," Angela said. "What if they're going to Big J?"

"I doubt it. They have so much other ground to cover. Plus, there have to be targets here. We can't be the only ones alive in the valley."

"What makes you so sure?"

"It's not possible. This place fills with tourists and part-time residents in the summer. They can't all be dead."

"How many people have we seen?"

"The policemen. And I saw a person before Colbrick, who I told you was killed by the secapod."

"OK, so counting Colbrick, that's six other people."

"Yes."

"That's pathetic. There's no reason to believe there's anyone else left at this point."

"That's a terrible outlook," Bishop said.

"Look at the facts, hon. The northern and southern exits are blocked by dams. The woods are teeming with pigras, seals, and other creatures and the fliers pluck humans like pigeons to bread crumbs. Don't you see what's going on? Those creatures are hungry and their young are even hungrier. Now that the easy pickings are gone, they're going to get more aggressive. There's no one here, Bishop. No one. If there were people, this is where they'd be."

Bishop looked down to the street and grimaced.

"These animals know how to work with each other. I do think the leaf creatures are letting the others know where a meal is, so they can scavenge the leftovers," Angela said. "The frequency seals are doing what they do by design and building their nurseries with the pigras. These creatures aren't entirely stupid, and are at least intelligent enough to wipe out most of this valley, and who knows where else."

"Different species working together."

Bishop reached down and patted Yutu on the head.

"Well, you're working with us, aren't you, boy," he said.

*

They sat on the bed, crunching on Doritos. Angela tossed a few Yutu's way and he relished the zesty chips.

"I wonder where all these things came from," he said. "Every creature has a mother. You, I, even Colbrick."

Angela chuckled.

"Even these monsters have to come from somewhere. And how did they appear so fast like they did?"

"Someone must have sent the first ones," Angela said, wiping her hair from her face with a svelte hand. "Also, this is a remote valley, Bishop. These new arrivals could have been living for who knows how long in the forest, especially if they came from the wilderness area."

"Right. With that in mind, what if they were always here, buried in this valley somewhere and all it took to trigger the invasion or outbreak was a small change in the environment?

"You mean climate change."

"Maybe."

"Doesn't there have to be some actual place where it all started, where the ship or however they came here is located?"

"That would explain why only some have the flashing tags. Because they came straight from the source, while the others without the tags are their offspring. It's just like those shows you love to watch on National Geographic and Animal Planet where the researchers tag animals so they can monitor their every move. Remember the one where they tagged a great white shark? The scientists didn't even need to be anywhere near the animal after it was tagged as long as the signal was being sent. There's either someone or something putting on the tags and keeping track of them."

Bishop looked out the window and sighed. "That is the million dollar question," he said.

Angela caressed Yutu's head. "Well, I'm not going to let them get Yutu," she said, sniffling.

Bishop reached out and embraced her. "I won't let them get you two."

"Why are you laughing?"

"Because I meant you two, as in y-o-u t-w-o, not Yutu singular as in the dog."

Angela chuckled and eased her shoulders.

Bishop tossed Yutu more of the spicy chips.

"How do we fight them?" Angela asked. "We can't wait them out forever."

"Remember what we talked about back at Big J and which you stated so clearly? We accomplished that goal. We needed to find more information, and we have. I believe it's been and will be valuable to us."

Bishop patted Yutu and grabbed a handful of chips. "Now we know where the fliers come from. We know that Main Street is a ghost town, and there are few, if any survivors. And we absolutely know that the worst fucking place to be is in the woods without shelter."

"Colbrick should be OK," she said.

"I think so. I'm sure he's got that place more fortified than most bunkers at this point."

"We also know one more thing," Angela said.

"What?"

"Loud noise is not good. Not good at all."

"Oh yes."

They tossed more chips Yutu's way and he gobbled them down.

"Geeze," Bishop said. "You'd think he hadn't eaten in weeks."

They dumped the rest of the bag on the floor and watched the frenetic dog scoop up and crunch every last chip.

"I hope he's full now," Angela said.

Yutu jumped on the bed, curled in a ball and licked the cheesy flavoring from his snout.

Angela's eyes met Bishop's.

"We're going back to get Colbrick tomorrow, aren't we?"

"Absolutely fucking right," he said.

She hugged him again and smiled. "I hope he's OK."

"Is a rock OK?"

"Of course. A rock is always OK. You can't do anything to it."

"Well, there you go."

MEDORA, NORTH DAKOTA TEXT FEED

Stormchazer Michael Clemens
@PaulFreeze Dude Come out to I-90 at Ranch8 exit ASAP

PaulFreeze NDakota Native
@Stormchazer Now what have you gotten into

Stormchazer Michael Clemens
@PaulFreeze Weird birds, dude. No storm. All over the telephone wires. They mimic everything like parrots. Getting video.

PaulFreeze NDakota Native
@Stormchazer So what? Just birds, man.

PAULFREEZE, YOU HAVE PHOTO MESSAGE. DOWNLOAD?
DOWNLOAD PROCEEDING….
DOWNLOAD COMPLETE

PaulFreeze NDakota Native
@Stormchazer WTF?????

Stormchazer Michael Clemens
@PaulFreeze Do not come. Birds aggressive. Leaving now.

UNWELCOME TENANTS

Mornings felt different. Before the attack, they contained a nurturing magic that fed the spirit. They were always a wonder in the country. Now they felt like someone pointing a flashlight into a dark basement where things of unknown origin crept just out of light's reach. Night was almost a relief in the Apex Valley, for sometimes the light was best left off. Denial was comfort, and procrastination was ideal. Every corner, every turn could be the end.

*

Morning brought strange light.

Angela yawned and stretched, and her teeth chattered when she noticed a green tint to her hands and the blanket. She raised her eyes from the blanket to the windows. The glowing eye of an enormous flier pressed against the glass, its lethal beak pointed towards the roof. The eye glared into their room, and the beast opened and closed its colossal beak, letting out a steamy breath into the cold morning air. Angela gripped the blanket and a whimper escaped her throat when she realized the flier was standing on the sidewalk. It balanced against the building with wings that covered the upper two-thirds of both windows like gothic drapes. Yutu huddled next to Angela and kept quiet.

"What's wrong, baby?" Bishop asked as he massaged his temples with his eyes still closed.

"Don't move," she whispered.

Bishop stopped rubbing his temples and looked up.

"Holy—"

"I don't think it sees us," Angela whispered.

The flier folded back a rough, leathery wing, momentarily allowing sunlight into the room, then thrust it forward, releasing a rotten note from deep within its elephantine lungs. Glass shattered, and a discolored vestigial claw on the center of the wing groped the room.

Angela screamed.

"Out! Get out now!" Bishop shouted. He grabbed the shotgun and pulled Angela towards the door.

"My gun!" she shouted.

Bishop dove towards the bed and reached for the pistol, and the three-foot claw scraped his arm. He retreated and they left the room, slamming the door behind them as the flier wailed. Yutu was waiting in the hallway, growling.

"We'll get it later," he said, chest heaving.

Thump.

"Behind the door," Angela said, digging her nails into Bishop's hand.

Yutu glared at the apartment door and released a deep, slow growl.

Thump. Thump.

Wings fluttered against the door, and the looped mimicry of a shotgun blast filled the top level of Fultons.

"You're kidding me?" Angela asked, backing away. "From yesterday?"

"Probably," Bishop said, escorting her down the hallway and checking the dark stairwell.

The thumping was relentless, the muffled shrieks nauseating. The door rattled on its hinges, and flashes of green shone through the cracks.

They ran downstairs—Yutu taking the lead—and ducked behind racks of clothing. From crouching positions, they peered between dresses and slacks at the storefront window. Bishop's stomach knotted when the defined, tree trunk legs of the big flier appeared and the turbulent cloud of small fliers on Main Street. The big flier's tusk-sized talons scraped along the sidewalk, sending up chalky clouds of keratin and concrete. A small rectangle on its leg pulsated red. Bishop counted it for fifteen seconds and calculated fifty-six beats per minute. The towering flier backed up across Main Street, revealing its complete form and folded its wings. Then it jerked its head upwards and let out a distorted wail that hinted at vague, alien notes. Its wings flattened parking meters and ripped down the awning over M.B. Real Estate. One of the small fliers zipped near its prodigious beak, and it followed the buzzing object with three pupils, then snapped its beak upon the thing, swallowing it whole. The looping shotgun mimicry faded as the small flier traveled down its gullet.

"Great," Angela said. "They eat their own."

"Works for me," Bishop said.

The big flier smashed into the building across the street, angled towards the alley next to Fultons and charged, opening its wings and lifting from the pavement. It disappeared from view, only the rhythmic beat of thunderous wings revealing its presence. The small fliers were right behind, their shotgun mimicry growing faint as they joined the big one somewhere over the valley.

Yutu stopped growling.

"The gun," Angela whispered.

They went upstairs, and Bishop cracked open the door to their temporary apartment. He went to the bed and retrieved Angela's .357. He also took the backpack and the headlamp.

Bishop shut the door, and they stood in the hallway. Yutu sniffed the daypack and sneezed while backing away Angela glanced down the hall to the locked door.

"Don't you want to know?" she asked.

"The door? No, not really."

"It's bugging me," she said.

"It'll make too much noise."

"Not if we're careful. Besides, there may be things we need."

Bishop looked down the hall, focusing on the dark stairwell.

"You hear that?" he asked.

Angela paused, her cochlea twitching, always expecting the worst.

"I don't hear anything," she whispered.

"Oh, well I do. It's the sound of you being stupid."

She hit him with a right fist square on the shoulder.

Bishop shook his head and went to the locked door. He retrieved the multi-tool Colbrick had stashed in the backpack and jammed the saw blade between the door and frame, pushing against the steel bolt. The metal clicked, and he turned the knob. A chemical odor emitted from the room, similar to Windex. On the north wall hung newspaper clippings and photographs. A lone, army-style cot rested along the southern wall, with a single burner camp stove and several camping propane tanks on the hardwood floor. A laptop sat on a faded desk in the corner, along with USB card readers.

They studied the pinned photos and articles, Yutu sniffing the room behind them. Angela pulled down one of the newspaper clippings, her mouth agape as she read.

"What?" he asked.

"This was from two weeks ago," she said, grasping the paper. "And it mentions people seeing unidentified flying objects—especially at night."

Bishop pulled down another article. It featured a hysterical Elmore resident complaining of something in the leaves biting her the day before.

Gee, what could that have been? Bishop thought.

The photographs were blurry and unprofessional. They showed wooded areas and unidentifiable blurs of some creature, and Bishop guessed them to be pigras or frequency seals.

"Someone was paying attention," she said.

"Yes, and it wasn't us. We were clueless."

"What do you expect? We were on vacation."

Yutu found a morsel on the floor and wolfed it down.

"I wonder what they were doing?" he asked

"Maybe they were one of those paranormal investigative units like you see on TV."

"Possibly. Or maybe they know much more than that."

"Like the scientists in the pristine bunker you and Colbrick joke about?"

Bishop chuckled. "Yeah I see your point."

Angela turned away from the newspaper clippings and photos. "Jesus, Bishop. How could we be so freaking stupid? Laptop? The internet? Hello?"

Bishop turned on the silver laptop, his hand trembling. A white cord ran from the computer to the wall, and he guessed it to be a DSL line, which was the only kind of high-speed they had in the Valley, if you could call DSL high-speed.

A third of the battery remained—more than enough. He opened the web browser and tried several sites, but there was no connection. The network icon on the taskbar flashed in perpetuity. He clicked the arrow in the browser URL box to view the website history. The top address was *strangeoccurences.com.*

"The phones are dead, so it makes sense that the DSL is dead too," Angela said. "Did you get the name of the last site viewed?"

"Yep…strangeoccurrences.com."

"Sounds like a paranormal website," she said.

"No doubt about it. Probably just a clever kid who rented this place for the summer and happened to be in the right place at the right time. Whoever it is has a nice single burner camp stove, too. A backpacker for sure."

"We should search the laptop for more info," Angela said.

"Yeah but not here."

Bishop took the laptop and a USB card reader.

"Do you think they will miss them?"

"I don't think they're even alive," Bishop said.

*

Angela cracked the back door to Fultons and peered outside, sunlight stinging her eyes. She felt like a rodent peeking out of its burrow in rattlesnake country. Strange how their lives had changed.

Yutu watched from behind her legs.

"It's clear."

They loaded the truck, and Yutu hopped into the backseat.

"Wait," she said. "I want some new clothes."

Angela sauntered about the store, smelling the fresh, new clothing and holding it to her face. She folded pants, belts, blouses, and other niceties upon her forearms and entered the vintage dressing room. "If I'm going to die soon, I'm going to have some freaking fun," she said to herself.

When she opened the back door, Bishop couldn't believe it. She was dolled up, even wearing an extra glamorous application of makeup.

She got in, reeking of sexuality and verve.

"Woah," Bishop said.

"You like?" she teased.

"Hell yes," he said.

"Back to Big J?" she asked.

"Nope."

"Bishop, that was the plan."

"The plan temporarily changed since finding the laptop."

"Why?"

"Because, sweetheart, there's one other way to get internet service in the valley."

"Satellite."

"Bingo."

"And where would the best place be for satellite?"

"Streamwood Resort. They have the money."

"I thought you didn't want to go west?" Angela asked.

"Streamwood isn't too far in. Plus, this is as important as it gets. It's worth the risk."

They headed north on Main Street which soon morphed into Highway 18. Then they turned right onto Elk Drive and wound their way west amid cedars and tamarack. Mailbox clusters poked out of the woods, marking wide gravel drives that led to groupings of trophy cabins that may or may not have satellites on the roof.

"We need to look for two things," Angela said. "Satellites *and* a generator."

"Big J has a generator," he said. "We can grab a satellite and bring it back there if need be, but I'm hoping we can find both here."

"The Big J generator also needs gas," Angela said.

Bishop looked at the gas gauge and frowned. "That's one thing we have to find before we head back to Big J. We don't have a choice, actually."

The truck passed enormous specimens of old growth hemlock. Soon, the dim outlines of gaudy log cabins loomed between the trunks and over the tops of ferns and huckleberry.

Yutu watched the dark woods flash by, as if searching for something.

*

Streamwood was known for its wealth, and Bishop wouldn't be surprised if every cabin had satellite. They pulled into an overdeveloped and obsessively maintained property with a bulging log cabin, and sure enough perched on the roof was a satellite dish.

"Bingo," Bishop said. "What do you think? Clear? Good to go?"

Angela turned, checking every last patch of fern and shade.

"Good to go."

They got out of the truck, and a glistening leg swiped at Bishop's face, cutting into his cheek. He fell backward onto the ground, blood streaming down his face and onto his shirt.

"Bishop!" Angela cried.

Yutu barked and scraped his paws high on the side of the truck. Angela followed Yutu's point to the truck roof and saw a secapod in an aggressive stance. The lone eye bulged above the pancake midsection, the roaming pupils observing her and Bishop as it rotated. It raised two legs, preparing to jump on Bishop as he lay on the other side of the truck.

"No!" Angela shouted, running to the driver's side and aiming the .357.

The grotesque secapod grunted and clicked, then leaped into the air with the intention of landing on Bishop's bleeding face. Angela closed her eyes and fired in the secapod's direction. The .357 kicked hard, stinging her shoulder. She opened her eyes after the last bullet, expecting the worst.

The secapod lay upside down next to the front tire, its squid-like beak grinding as if sand was caught in its hinges. Bishop picked himself up off the ground and stomped on its soft, glistening underbelly, and all four of its legs clamped onto his right leg like a bear trap.

"Shit, wrong move," he said.

Yutu whimpered and clawed at the ground near the secapod.

Still groggy from the shock, Angela trudged over, bent down, and pried each moist, hairy leg from Bishop.

"You're free," she said in a far-off voice.

Yutu wagged his tail and pawed at Bishop, but something wasn't right. Angela turned her hands palm sides up and screamed when she realized they were sliced open as if she had grabbed a knife by the business end. Thick, wiry clumps that resembled pubic hair poked into the wounds, irritating the damaged flesh.

"Jesus!"

Bishop's first thoughts were to mash the dead secapod with his heel, and then to grab a weapon and run through the woods shooting every damn one of the things he could find. But he stifled that, and instead went right for the first-aid kit in the glove box. The largest clear pouch contained handy wipes. He ripped them open with his teeth, then applied the wet fabric to Angela's hands.

She grimaced.

He dabbed another packet.

More screams.

Bishop carefully wiped away the blood and hair, then held her.

She tried to embrace him, but her hands were in so much pain from the cuts and the treatment that they just lay there like hooked claws against his back.

"Rule number one, baby," he said, rubbing her back.

"We never talked about any rules," she sobbed.

"We are now. Rule number one is never touch them."

"Understood."

"And that goes for me too. This was my fault. Stepping on it got me caught, and you injured."

Bishop pulled away and wiped his bloody face with one of the handy wipes. When he finished, the material was soaked in blood.

"It's not that bad," Angela said, doing everything not to clench her hands.

He looked at the cabin and sighed. "We need to do this."

"My shots probably alerted the fliers," Angela said.

"Maybe."

Bishop took the gauze from the first-aid kit and wrapped it around her hands as she winced.

"You OK?"

"I'll be fine," she said, her tears smearing her eyeliner which she had so proudly shown off earlier.

"Can you still hold the pistol?"

"I don't think so. This hurts."

"You have to carry it."

"I don't think I can."

He finished bandaging her hands and snipped the material with the cheap pair of scissors included in the kit. He took one of the Vicodin and placed it in her mouth, then held a water bottle to her lips.

"I'm going to be comfortably numb, aren't I?"

"Just like two balloons," he said.

She smiled through the pain.

"I'll carry the gun until you heal," he said.

She looked at Bishop's face and shivered. He pretended like everything was perfectly normal.

"Let's go surf the internet," he said. "There's a commemorative plate on Ebay that I want."

Angela laughed.

They followed a manicured trail to the back door of the cabin, Yutu sniffing the ground behind them. To the north, in-between regal hemlocks, the cool waters of Lake Gallatin reflected sunlight. There were no boats on the picturesque lake today.

The backdoor was framed by an awning and porch, with a carved chair on either side. The door was locked, and Bishop kicked it open on four tries, the final effort splintering trim and revealing fresh, bright wood underneath the varnish. The cabin was immaculate, not a single item out of place. A heavy layer of dust indicated the owners did not live here full-time and that they hadn't been out for the warm season yet. An intertwining antler chandelier hung from the ceiling above a cherry wood dining table. Each chair had a set of outdoor-themed placemats. The north wall was all windows with a view of the lake in-between stout tree trunks. The east wall of the cabin held a spotless kitchen with marble countertops. The west wall contained an open door that led to a bathroom, and to the right of the bathroom, half-log stairs ascended to the second story.

"I guess this is what they call an open design," Angela said.

"Yeah. Great place," Bishop said.

He went to the kitchen and tried the phone. Nothing.

Yutu trotted to the pantry and scratched at the door.

In the corner, near the lake view window was a desktop computer, with several cables running out of it along the hardwood floor.

"Found it," Angela said.

She pressed the power button, but the computer did not turn on.

"I thought I saw a shed outside," Bishop said. "If they have a generator, that's where it would be. Are you OK here for a few?"

"Yes. Don't you see Yutu over there guarding me fiercely?" Angela asked.

Bishop chuckled. "Yeah, he's a real pitbull."

*

The forest was always quiet, and the changes made it even more so, and this frightened him. The short walk to the shed was unpleasant, and for the first time, he wondered what it would be like to be alone in this nightmare. He was lucky to have Angela and Yutu. Of this there was no doubt, and the reality of his love for them punched him in the chest, radiating goodness and light. This he could control, this was important. It gave him power, enough to smash the locked shed door with a force that he'd never tapped into before.

He was changing.

"Found you," he said to the generator, and pulled its lawnmower-like starter. He shut the door, manipulating it with pine cones and other forest litter to keep it closed. The generator shed had been insulated with foam, and the motor purred as he walked back to the cabin.

Something flickered on the lake.

Curiosity led him through the hemlocks and down the wooden landing until he reached the pier. All three hundred acres of beautiful Lake Gallatin stretched out before him, ponderosa pine blending with hemlock along the shore. Several cabins poked out of the old growth trees, breaking the cohesive texture of the scene.

Bishop stopped where pier met shore. The blue flashed again, and he realized it was a

frog just under the surface, except this wasn't like any frog he'd seen before. The frog was close to a foot long and kicked the water with six limbs. The back limbs forked into a shape that almost resembled a tail when the limbs drew together. Its sides were pudgy like earth's frogs, but it had unique, colorful markings down the length of its glistening back. The frog's mouth appeared too wide for its head, and when it opened its jaws, an elastic tongue shot forth. Bishop watched as the tongue stretched at least four feet and latched onto one of the buzzing mosquito-like creatures he didn't care for. Before the insect could escape, it was stuck to the frog's tongue. As the elastic tongue rolled back into the frog's mouth, the mosquito cut into it with its saw snout and flew away. A chunk of the tongue flopped into the water, but the frog let its tongue loll there. Bishop watched in awe as the tip of the frog's tongue slowly grew back. Satisfied with the regeneration, the frog recovered its tongue and scrutinized the shoreline vegetation with hungry eyes. A moment later, another invasive mosquito buzzed along the shore and the frog nailed it, this time lurching forward to meet its captured prey halfway before it had time to cut through the tongue. Bishop shivered as he watched the frog swallow the insect. He couldn't shake the creeping sensation that these things were making their home here. They were behaving as they would in their native ecosystem. Bishop shuddered and turned away from the frog. As he did, he caught a glimpse of a flashing tag under the surface. A minuscule wake rolled from the disturbance as it moved towards him.

Run.

Ruff! Ruff!

Yutu barked from halfway up the landing steps, startling Bishop. His first thought was how easy it would be for the hungry eel to drag Yutu into the water. He ran up the stairs and shielded Yutu. From behind came a tremendous splash as two huge eels leaped out of the water at the portion of the pier where Bishop had been standing. He heard rustling in the underbrush, the pressurized hiss, and a throaty death squeal. Then he turned to see one of the eels with the frog in its jaws. The first, bigger eel brought the limp frog to the other. After several seconds, they returned to the lake where they submerged near a fanned out area of sand. Bishop thought he saw a nest of eggs, but the light changed and the image disappeared.

Too close.

Yutu ceased his barking and crawled under the railing. From the safety of the high bank, they watched the eels glide back into deeper water.

You really need to pull your head out of your ass, he thought.

Yutu stared up at him with grateful, brown eyes, wagging his tail as if he agreed.

One thing was certain—he and his father had never caught fish like these on Lake Gallatin.

*

"What was all that about?" Angela asked, back inside the cabin.

"Don't go near the lake," Bishop said. "Promise?"

"Yes."

Bishop took two Vicodin from his pants pocket and went for the bottle of Seagram's on the counter. He was never much of a whiskey and firearms guy, but this was starting to become the wild west so why not.

"What's the latest viral video?" Bishop asked. He chugged the whiskey, saloon style.

"Uh...is that a good idea?" Angela asked.

"Do you have any better ones?" he asked.

"Jesus, Bishop. What's gotten into you?"

"Take a look around, sweetheart. That's what's fucking gotten into me."

"Do you think you can vent somewhere where I don't have to see it?"

"Ninety-nine percent of the time."

"Ninety-nine percent of the time what?"

"That's the amount of time I'm your nice, levelheaded, Regular Joe. Eventually, things do piss me off, and well here we are."

"Can you vent away from Yutu? I don't want you to scare him off."

Bishop cleared his throat and studied the cabin. He unclenched his fists and took a deep breath. "Sorry. I'm fine." And in reality, that wasn't a lie. The whiskey calmed his nerves in a few seconds. He felt the cut on his face, noticing it had grown puffy. He burped a raw breath of whiskey and reveled in the warmth that soothed his body.

"How do your hands feel?" he asked.

"What hands?" she said.

"Good, now we're both wasted," he said, looking into Angela's pretty eyes.

Angela laughed and smirked at him.

"The connection is password protected," she said. "So much for getting online. How about the TV?"

Bishop clicked the remote and the flat screen sprang to life. He leaned back on the leather sofa as Angela curled into his arms. Yutu watched them and then rested his head on Bishop's lap. As he channel surfed, it became apparent that the 24-hour cable news networks were on a high. At last, they had something really spectacular to report on.

CNN broadcasted a video labeled "North Dakota Unknown." It showed a dreary sky over the prairie. Tiny green eyes bobbed above telephone poles amidst a flurry of wings.

The small fliers.

Voices with a rural accent whispered and then shouted in the video as the flock of fliers swarmed to the camera. Then the video ended.

Bishop turned and flung a pillow across the cabin. "They got out," he said.

"Only to North Dakota," Angela said.

"We don't know that."

"At least we didn't see the big ones in that clip," Angela said.

They gathered from the various shows that Apex Valley was indeed the source and had been put under quarantine and a no-fly zone. By the time Homeland Security had put up a perimeter, there hadn't been any survivors left to get through to them. There was a repeating clip of some official pleading with any survivors to stay indoors and wait to be rescued without any mention of when exactly that would be. It became obvious that various government departments, along with foreign governments and even the UN, were fighting to get into the act. Conservative senators wanted to nuke the valley. Alien animal activists protested the killing of the fliers. Conspiracy theorists claimed the fliers were not aliens, but because they looked somewhat like pterosaurs, were really a secret genetic project gone astray. Many demanded that the government reveal the intelligent aliens who must be here too and hidden in a bunker somewhere. The haggard presidential spokesman kept saying there was no sign of any advanced aliens on the planet.

"Well, there we go," Bishop said, drinking more whiskey. "Screwed by our government. And the world's about to be screwed, too. *Say hello to mah leetle fliers,*" Bishop said in his best Scarface voice.

Angela grabbed the whiskey bottle from Bishop and took a chug, feeling a trickle ooze out the corner of her mouth.

"We have to fight," he said.

"That's what we've been doing."

"No, we've been surviving."

"They government's probably organizing in Billings, as it's the largest city in Montana and closer to the military bases." Bishop stretched and patted Yutu on the head. "Did you know that the reason Katrina was such a disaster was because the state and federal governments couldn't decide on who would be in charge? They're out there jerking around, while the valley is being completely taken over. They don't care about this place, but I do."

"We could try to make it to Billings."

Bishop looked down at Yutu and patted him on the head.

"I'm not going to fucking Billings," he said out the corner of his mouth.

"And why not?"

Bishop burped.

"Because I love the Apex Mountains, and I'm not going to let these things take that from me or my father. I grew up summers here. This is in my blood."

"Listen to yourself, Bishop. You think you're some mountain man now? What do you owe these woods? They almost killed me and will probably end up killing both of us and Yutu. And who knows what the hell happened to Colbrick. He could be inside some monster's stomach right now."

"Stop it," he said.

"We're going to find Homeland Security and they will get us out of here, maybe even escort us to Billings."

"No we're not," he said. "You want to risk crossing how many road dams? We know the situation here. We know where to go and where not to go, what to do and what not to do. We have Colbrick, too."

"Oh wow, we've got Colbrick. You hear that everyone? Bishop says we got Colbrick! Look, the creatures are retreating from the mighty Colbrick! See how the fliers whimper at the sight of him!"

"Stop it!"

"No!"

Angela went to punch him in the shoulder and he caught it. Then Bishop seized her wrists with one hand. He looked into her frightened eyes with the smeared mascara from the emotions of the day. They embraced, and Angela sobbed into his chest, her damaged hands dangling from his back. Bishop waited until she finished sobbing and kissed her forehead.

*

They woke two hours later, Bishop on the floor and Angela on the couch. Lake Gallatin shimmered through the window, sending a chill along the back of Bishop's neck. The whole lake could be filled with eel babies as far as he could tell.

Poison.

It was all poison.

Yutu trotted over from the corner where he'd been curled up.

"You hungry, boy?"

Yutu spun in circles.

Bishop found some old Saltines in the pantry and Yutu snatched them up. He spooned an expired jar of peanut butter into two bowls and brought it to Angela.

"Dinner time," he said.

She sat up, reaching for the bowl of peanut butter with her bandaged hands, wincing.

"Mmm...nothing like peanut butter for dinner."

"Better than nothing," he said. "Plus, it's loaded with calories."

"True. It doesn't taste bad either."

Bishop went to the kitchen and tried the tap. He filled two cups and brought one to Angela.

"Bishop...do you think the water's OK?"

"I think the wells are OK, maybe not the lake water...especially after what I saw in it."

"You never told me about it."

"Eel eggs."

"Oh.

"From now on, we only use creeks to get water."

Bishop nodded and choked on the peanut butter, needing all the water in the glass before he could talk again.

"Geeze, eat much?"

"Funny," he said, forcing the peanut butter down. "Sure, as long as the creeks aren't hot spots for the others. On the way to Big J, we saw pigras down low."

"Yes?"

"They were following a creek."

"And what about the fliers?"

"What about?"

"You said you saw them going up to the higher peaks."

"Yes, I did."

Angela licked her spoon and placed it into the bowl.

"I don't know. I feel like we could do something good here, you know?"

"You're not trying to pass off some sort of destiny mantra, are you?"

"I guess I am."

"You're convinced?"

"Yes."

"Bishop, turn on the TV again."

"Why? We know more than they do."

"Maybe we can find out what the white-coated scientists and all their lab equipment know. Turn on the science channels."

Yutu jumped onto the couch between them and put his snout on Angela's leg. They watched Discovery, The Science Channel, NOVA, Animal Planet, and National Geographic. Even History International had a special report. All the biologists confirmed the fliers could not have evolved on this planet or even been genetically engineered here. The scientists agreed they must have hatched here in the wilderness of the Apex Valley, although some did feel the need to point out that another means of transportation could be the cause. The question of why an animal and not an advanced alien was addressed while stock footage of the dogs, chimps, and other animals humans had launched into space played in the background. Les Johnson of NASA's Advanced Propulsion Laboratory explained the difficulties of interstellar travel. He became excited at the prospect of egg-containing probes being sent out to various planets with potential for colonization as a test. How the senders of the probes could know the test was successful and that the eggs had hatched put him at a loss. If such an object had entered U.S. airspace, why didn't we detect it? Bishop turned off the TV.

"I have a feeling about my dad. It sounds crazy, but I feel his spirit here, even in all this shit. It's in every breeze, in every fiber of this place. Hell, I know I'm not really superstitious or even religious. But I believe he wants us to stay and fight for the valley."

"Jesus, Bishop."

"Yeah, I know."

"We should go back and tell Colbrick."

"If he's still there."

Angela stood and walked to the big window, peering out at the lake.

The sun was losing its verve, dusk nudging aside the brightness.

"My God," she said. "They don't know anything about the tracking devices or even the other new arrivals."

Yutu trotted up behind her and sat in a handsome pose, and the two of them became silhouetted against the trees and water.

"Bishop?"

"Yes?"

"You said you wanted to fight for the valley?"

"You know I did."

"Well here's your chance."

"What are you talking about?"

Angela gazed at her husband and marveled at how fiery he looked, coiled for action.

"We can't send a message to tell anyone what's going on," she said. "I'm getting this strange feeling we need to do something soon. You keep looking at those tags."

"I'm counting the flashes. They're getting faster."

"What does that mean?"

"Nothing good, I'm betting."

The mellow hues of sunset disappeared, and evening shrouded the land. Owls did not hoot from snags, nor did the haunting call of loons echo across the lake. These native birds had moved on.

*

Bishop made a mean cake. A real mean cake.

Chocolate with stale frosting. Vegetable oil was used in place of eggs. He served it to Angela on fancy dinner plates with a glass of water.

"So Miss, what are your plans tonight?"

"To survive."

"Anything else?"

"To get wasted?"

"After the cake," Bishop said. "I'm declaring tonight a continuation of our anniversary celebration. The fliers did not hear us, and we also killed a secapod. Talk about a great fucking day."

"After dessert," she said with a mouthful of chocolate cake.

Bishop laughed and opened a box of Triscuits for Yutu, who ravaged them across the hardwood floors.

"We deserve this cake," she said, working the fork so it didn't hurt her hands.

"I wonder what Colbrick is eating?" Bishop asked.

"He probably cooked up some frequency seals."

Bishop looked down at Yutu. "You'd like Colbrick, buddy. He's a no-nonsense guy, and you're a no-nonsense dog."

They finished the decadent cake, and Bishop brought out another bottle of whiskey.

"Happy anniversary," he said, smiling.

"Didn't you know they say drinking too much is bad for you?" Angela said, beaming.

"*They* are probably gone," he said.

"Are the doors locked?" she asked.

"Yes. I even counted to five as I held them."

"Your OCD is kicking in a bit?"

"I'm a little hyped up."

Angela took the whiskey bottle and chugged. A rivulet of the harsh elixir trickled out the corner of her mouth and moistened her lips. "Here's to the Apex Valley," she said.

Bishop took the bottle from her and drank.

They were new. Their softness had been replaced by taut sinewy muscles and minds as sharp as hunter's knives. Ancient reflexes and instinct inherited from distant ancestors awoke within them. Angela walked over to the first-floor bathroom. She turned on the shower. It worked. She undressed and stepped in, letting the warm water clean her of the day's violence. She held her bandaged hands high, letting the water do all the work. Yutu sat outside the bathroom door, glancing back at Bishop and panting.

*

Bishop looked upon the black lake and the tree tops silhouetted against the night sky. The first few stars shone on the horizon. Before the invasion, the stars had felt alien to him. He thought he was crazy, for whenever he would gaze into the Milky Way, he could feel turbulent rivers in ancient canyons not of this world, and then would see and hear the waters and mountains of this world, and somehow these two things met across the endless gulf, interconnected. But on this night, he did not receive that familiar feeling. Tonight, he felt that the stars were an escape, a lost prayer, and that the world he stood on had become the alien one.

"What are you looking at?" Angela asked, wrapped in a towel.

"Everything."

"It's still very pretty," she said.

"So are you," he said.

"Cheesy, baby."

"Maybe, but still true."

Angela sighed and rested her head on Bishop's chest. Her damp hair soaked through his shirt and cooled his skin.

"Could they *really* be from another planet?" Angela asked.

"I guess it's possible. But...they could've been here longer than we think. A lot longer."

Bishop stroked her hair and kissed the top of her head. Yutu pleaded up at them and licked his chops, and Bishop tossed another triscuit.

Bishop stared out at his beloved valley, put his arm around Angela, and drew her closer against his chest. "It's here," he said. "We just have to find it. Every living creature has a mother. These new arrivals do too. Somewhere in this valley lies their seed mother. If we're going to survive, we need offense."

"Now we're fighting!" she said.

Bishop grinned, but it was a nervous one.

They made love all night in the upstairs bedroom. In another world, in another time, this would have been the last night of their anniversary getaway.

*

"It's time," Bishop said, taking his shotgun and opening the front door.

Angela peered outside. Her vision had always been better than Bishop's. "Clear."

They trotted to the truck, all the while scanning their perimeter. Angela hustled inside the cab, and Bishop jogged to the generator and switched it off, then checked the fuel level. Not enough gas to make it worth the effort. He shut the shed door, and a sense of purpose tingled in his chest. The truck started without incident and they rolled along the crunching gravel.

"We need gas," she said, leaning over to look at the gauge.

"You're always like that," he said.

"Like what?"

"Paranoid about gas."

"No I'm not. You're just nonchalant about having the needle on a quarter tank."

"A quarter tank gets you a long way."

"Not in the apocalypse."

"This isn't just about the apocalypse, though. You were like this before."

"Shut up, Bishop."

Yutu whimpered from the backseat, and they let out a chuckle. It was good to be heading back to Colbrick.

Each gravel they encountered led to clusters of cabins. On a cul-de-sac, they found a Nissan sedan parked next to an older, modest cottage. The driver's door was ajar. Droplets of blood trailed from the driveway to the cottage, and Angela gagged when the trail lead her to the source. On the sandy ground were human remains, although that would be a kind description. Scattered bones lay tentatively connected by sinew and meaty strands, as if drawn and quartered, but stopped right before everything was ripped apart. Most of the meat and organs had been picked clean, and odd, hoofed tracks marked the scene along with foul stool and puddles of urine.

"Pigras," she said in a depressed tone.

Bishop held out his palm to Angela and paused. Chewing came from the dim cottage, just inside the door. Angela pointed her .357 towards the opening, preparing for a nightmare. Bishop followed by pointing the shotgun at the dark doorway.

Rattling metal, more chewing.

The chewing stopped, followed by pattering paws.

Bishop put his finger in the trigger slot.

The chewing thing darted out of the doorway towards them, clenching a bag of chips in its snout. The creature held low to the ground, trying to hide its narrow face that rounded off to a big rump and bushy tail. It chittered nervously.

"Jesus," Angela said. "It's a freaking raccoon!"

Bishop removed his finger from the trigger and laughed. Yutu, however, retreated.

"Go raccoon go!" Angela said as it grew smaller and smaller between the hemlocks.

"Almost killed a native," Bishop said.

"We need to be more careful. That's a survivor there," she said, pointing to the last hint of the raccoon's big rump and the bright, red bag of Doritos it held in its mouth.

"No different than us," he said.

They left the mangled remains and inspected the sedan.

"They keys are inside," Angela said.

"There's also a full tank of gas," he said.

"How would we get past the road dam?"

"Good question, I don't think this could make it."

"We don't have a hose to siphon the gas, either."

"Wilkin's Bait and Tackle had rubber tubes for the bait tanks," Bishop said. "And the minnows sure as hell don't need them anymore."

Angela laughed.

They rode out to Highway 18. Still no people. Wilkin's bait shop remained empty, so they borrowed a bait tank tube that stunk of algae and mold. Yutu sniffed the tube, as if it required his approval to enter the vehicle.

"Back to the car?" Bishop asked.

Angela put her hand on his and shook her head.

"No way," she said. "I was thinking about this last night. No going back to the same spots within twenty-four hours. The cabin was an outlier."

"You're much smarter than me," Bishop said.

"If we can randomize our behavior a bit, we can at least fool some of them."

Bishop gazed at the tackle store. Although he disliked Wilkins, the emptiness of the old crank's dream shop saddened him. "Yes, but how do you fool a flier?" he asked.

"I don't think it's possible."

They drove towards the center of Elmore, eyeing each and every garage or store for a vehicle. An old Chevy Malibu was parked along Main Street, near Yutu's smoldering apartment building. The Chevy contained half a tank of gas, and Bishop inserted the moldy hose, then put his lips onto it and sucked. Gasoline belched up from the Chevy, and Bishop inserted the hose into the fuel can he took from Sue's. When the can filled, he poured it into the truck's tank. This process was repeated until the Chevy was empty. When the last drop to be gotten was gotten, Bishop stood, wiped the remnants of algae and gasoline from his mouth and looked into the clouds. The heat beat upon him, and he noticed a heavy layer of humidity—unusual for the Rocky Mountains.

In a moment, they were back on Highway 18, heading away from Elmore.

"Goodbye, Elmore," Angela said.

What had once been a fertile hub of activity was dead and deserted—a Rocky Mountain tourist town flipped on its back like an empty, weathered tortoise shell.

Yutu looked back at the town and the scents he'd known all his life. He liked the people he was with now, but missed The Man who raised him as a pup. There was nothing Yutu could have done as The Man had locked him in the apartment. He had barked and barked until his throat shredded, but his favorite Man never came back.

"Look at Yutu," Angela said. "He's acting strange."

Bishop glanced into the rearview, and sadness filled his heart. "We never found out what happened to his owner," he said.

Angela tapped a finger on the window and stared at the passing roadside.

"You saved him from the fire," she said. "And for right now, that's good enough."

*

Elmore disappeared behind them as they rolled past cedar, aspen, and tamarack. Bishop approached the bends at slower speeds, ever aware of obstructions in the road, alive and not. Every few minutes, Angela checked the sky.

They were getting smarter.

Yutu stared out the back window, his tail motionless.

FLIGHT TIME

Dr. Ted Donaldson chomped his gum as he looked out over the rugged Montana landscape. The terrain was far different than the Wisconsin hill country he hiked on occasion. Perhaps most noticeable was the minimal development, how the endless montane forest and meadows lacked the telltale gaps that indicated paved or gravel roads.

The UH-60 Blackhawk's blade-vortex interaction thundered the air above him, and he thought of his son, Ben, how he'd hit a homerun last week during his little league game. Ben hadn't hit the ball over the fence, but he'd hit it far enough so he could reach home plate. His coach told him later that it was the longest home run of the season.

Yep, Ben definitely got that from his mother's side, Donaldson thought.

Four other men were in the aircraft, including the pilot, a co-pilot, a gunner, and some kind of intelligence official. *I've hit a homerun, too,* Donaldson thought. The other biologists would be envious when they found out he was chosen to examine these new species. He'd convinced the official to allow for closer air surveillance of the species than protocol allowed *and* to hopefully dart a live specimen with a tag to track behavior in the wild. Although Donaldson was certainly used to dangerous situations doing field work, he had always felt envious when attending Society for Conservation Biology meetings and listening to others go on about how they were suspended in the canopy and all the others like them with their adventures. First, his job was to take notes from the air as the helicopter approached various disturbances and nesting areas. He already had considerable knowledge of the Stunners, and how they used the barriers to collect food and raise their young. The primate creatures displayed these same characteristics, also using the dams and even helping build them. The official told him his top priority was to document the Harassers. Homeland Security had placed M2 machine guns, laser-guided SAMs, and M242 Bushmasters around the perimeter to shoot down any Harassers attempting to fly out of the valley. The Avenger platform was in place, as well as shoulder-fired rocket systems for maximum flexibility. Of upmost importance were the FLIR/laser rangefinders, which allowed Army personnel to track fleeing aliens in darkness and target them. But the fools had given no thought to the thick forested areas in-between. An animal the size of a dog or smaller could easily get out. He was actually hoping for more species. If he could get close, he'd be the first person to discover one or more of them. The thought caused him to squirm in his seat. "We're passing over Barrier 1 now," the pilot shouted.

The pilot maneuvered the Blackhawk closer to Barrier 1, and Donaldson made notes of the intricate layering of aspen, spruce, and ponderosa pine. In a way, he admired the Stunner's sharp saw-like tails. He wondered about the Stunner's native habitat and how they used their tails there. Here, they were utilized to take down large trees. There was very little forest litter at this elevation. Not with the fires that frequently cleared out the understory and the fuels reduction work the United States Forest Service engaged in.

The Blackhawk flew close enough to Barrier 1 that its blades blew away much of the haze and rustled the branches and dying leaves at the top. When Donaldson reached for his binoculars, a horde of Stunners scrambled to the top and clawed at the air. Donaldson felt a buzzing in his head and his thoughts clouded.

"Whoa...we're pulling back," the pilot said. "Feeling them pretty good at this altitude."

Their stomachs roiled as the Blackhawk jerked upwards, away from the sonic reach of the Stunners.

Donaldson looked below at the gathering animals.

Must be a hundred of them now, he thought. Around the perimeter of the Stunners, a group of primates collected, some groping forward as their babies clung to their chests with six limbs. Donaldson noted the color, hair, and other features in his iPad. Then his gaze turned from the creatures to the surrounding habitat. Numerous trails emanated from Barrier 1 into the Devastation Zone, which lasted for hundreds of yards on either side of the massive structure. The trails disappeared into intact forest at the perimeter, and this caught Donaldson's eye like a cat that watches a toy disappear around a corner.

"Can we head west?" he shouted to the pilot.

The pilot gave a thumbs up and maneuvered the Blackhawk past the Devastation Zone. The spectacular Apex Range loomed ahead of them, the granite peaks chiseled and defined below a deep blue sky.

Donaldson watched the landscape below, marveling at the outstanding ungulate and ursine habitat. He assumed the invasive species used those game trails, too. After all, why wouldn't they? It made no sense to create fresh trails except at the barriers. A non-native species can spread itself just fine using the traditional means of the native flora and fauna. Saving energy while expanding was a template for species survival.

As the Blackhawk thundered on, the forest rose to meet them. The trees changed from lower elevation species to whitebark pine, subalpine fir, subalpine larch, and Engelmann spruce. Huge rock formations split patches of trees, and soon, Donaldson stared into the vast alpine cirques and talus slopes of the high country. He thought of his son again, and his homerun, and how it had boosted Ben's confidence. Donaldson needed this home run, too. Oh, he had all sorts of theories spinning in his mind, such as how long these things had been here, what could've kept them hidden, and what sort of ecosystem shift might have triggered a spread across the landscape. As a biologist, he didn't have to look too far for surface disturbances responsible for such a move. There were two main types of disturbances in the Rockies the last hundred years, and these were fire and the melting of glaciers. Nothing approached either of these two in terms of impact.

He'd done a bit of research on the trip over and discovered that no major fires had occurred in the higher elevation forests of the Apex ecosystem in at least two decades. What was occurring was a record-setting melting of glaciers, and now only two glaciers remained, a puny eight percent of their original size. These were on the north side of Kilbrix Peak, and the north side of Onyx Peak. Nowhere else in the lower 48 had the glaciers disappeared so fast. Donaldson thought of the baseball rocketing off Ben's bat and gliding past the sun, two orbs in the sky, disproportionate. He chomped his grape-flavored Big League Chew and stared at the changing landscape below. He was starting to formulate a theory based on his ark idea that the species had perhaps been carried on vessels with sensors that fixated on planets with water and oxygen-rich atmospheres. He needed evidence of an entire ecosystem being released, even if many or most of the species hadn't made it on our planet. It made no sense to release only predators, unless they arrived here by accident. Donaldson knew all too well that there were basically two means for invasive species introduction: deliberate, a classic example being the now feral pigs wreaking havoc in Hawaii, and accidental, such as the invasive mussels released in bulge water. Although not impossible, he didn't really buy the idea of some alien zoo crash-landing here. Human colonists always brought species native to their homelands with them. White Europeans brought the pigs to Hawaii for food. At the time, they didn't think anything of it. Of course, now we see what they did as reckless and destructive. Did this other civilization consider what would happen to the native species of other planets? Did they care? Or did they think other planets would not have life on them?

Did they think that a planet inhabited by an advanced civilization would just shoot their vessel out of the sky or capture it so it wouldn't be a problem? Donaldson did admit that if a civilization was to go about colonizing the universe, it would be a great idea to see if their native ecosystem took hold before risking coming themselves. For all Donaldson knew, there could be who knows how many probes scattered around the galaxy.

The country was beautiful, maybe the prettiest he'd ever seen, and without question a rich ecosystem that was far beyond anything in Illinois, invasive species or not.

The sun warmed his skin and his face itched from mild sunburn. As he went to scratch his cheek, he saw movement below.

"Nine o'clock" he shouted to the pilot.

The pilot gave a thumbs up and turned the Blackhawk.

Donaldson glassed the rocky terrain and couldn't believe it. Seven eel-like creatures ghosted across the rocks. Their skin was see-through, like the *Kryptopterus bicirrhis,* or glass catfish he used to have in his aquarium as a child.

The eel creatures seemed to slow down, and everyone aboard the Blackhawk stared down in disbelief. The blades kicked up sand and dust, and the pilot gained elevation so as not to disturb the creatures.

When the dust cleared, the eels were gone.

Donaldson gripped the dart gun and scanned the terrain for the evasive eels. A moment later, an eel darted out from cover with a smaller six-limbed creature in its mouth. *That's it,* he thought with a gleam in his eye. Now if he could just tag one of them…

Through the gun's sight, he saw a red flashing tag on the eel. *That's really it,* he thought. *Conclusive evidence of deliberate monitoring.* Then Donaldson heard another helicopter. *Couldn't be,* he thought.

Something pummeled the Blackhawk, knocking it to the side. The blades stuttered and whined, and blood sprayed across the windshield.

"What the fuck!" the pilot shouted.

The gunner next to Donaldson fired again and again as the helicopter was flung about. The pilot shouted as the windshield darkened, then grew light as whatever had been attached to it blew away in pieces from the blade. The helicopter entered a dangerous pitch and Donaldson spit up his Big League Chew. "For fuck's sake, fly this thing!" he shouted at the pilot. More Blackhawks thundered around them as the sky darkened and time slowed. When he looked out his observation window, he realized how wrong he was. A cloud of fliers surrounded the Blackhawk, all of them mimicking it. Some of the small fliers were diced by the blades and whipped away. He'd seen this species of bird before. What he hadn't seen before was the monstrous version at the perimeter of the chopper blades. His first response was to marvel at its impressive form, a true flying machine designed as an elite predator with sensational auditory capabilities. It was a work of art. Deadly art, but art nonetheless. Donaldson fired his dart gun at the beast, but missed wide left in all the commotion.

The Blackhawks engines whined and stuttered.

"We're going down!" the pilot said.

"I love you, Ben," Donaldson said, bracing himself.

The machine gunner fired wildly as dozens of small fliers swarmed into the cabin.

"Love you, Sarah," Donaldson said.

The inconsistent whirring of blades clashed with the consistent, maddening tone of the mimicry.

"I love you, Suzy," he said.

Sporadic machine-gun fire filled his ears. Dismembered wings and wild eyes illuminated in the muzzle flash. Dozens of deformed and blood-spurting fliers rushed the cockpit, screeching and spraying blood everywhere. And yet more and more came, being forced through the gunfire and whirling blades as if ordered to do so by the vague, monstrous shapes at the blade's periphery.

Something enormous gripped the Blackhawk's skids, and for the first time, Donaldson saw the big flier's triplicate pupil eyes and deep into its gullet. The enormous flier glared at him and cried out as it twisted the helicopter upside down, careful to avoid the blades.

Thwap Thwap Thwap.

A patch of jagged mountain raced towards his observation window as the screaming fliers tore away his face.

DRY COUNTRY

They maneuvered along the dirt road bypass back through the woods, Angela commanding from the rooftop—an apocalyptic, angelic surfer. Bishop stopped the truck and looked to the west. Far off in an unnatural clearing, he saw a jumble of trees and vegetation sloping to the fern-covered forest floor, and assumed it to be the start of the road dam. Bishop guessed the seals and pigras moved on from the ends of the dam after construction and instead concentrated on feeding, reproduction, and maintenance at the middle structure.

There were no signs of the wacky bird. Bishop was hoping they'd see it again, and he knew Angela was too. When they reached Highway 18, Angela got back inside the truck.

"Something isn't right," she said.

"Well no shit, nothing's right."

"It's too humid. And the trees look sick."

Bishop glanced to the tree line and noticed a reddening of the branches and a malnourished aspect to the trunks. "They're sick."

Angela reached into the glove box and plucked a Vicodin from the bottle. Bishop winced.

"Your hand still hurting?" he asked.

"Everything hurts."

Then she reached into a backpack and took the yellow walkie-talkie Colbrick had given them. She gingerly held the device to her mouth and pressed the communicate button. Bishop was blown away with how much she'd changed. Angela peered out the windshield with dirty, narrow eyes, hand bandages curling against the yellow Walkie-talkie, her hair put up in a ponytail. Sure, part of her was afraid, but damn if she also didn't look like a *warrior*.

"Colbrick, can you hear me?" she asked into the device. She waited thirty seconds, the dead crackling and offensive frequency sweeps filling the truck.

"Colbrick, this is Angela. Can you hear me?"

Nothing.

"The range is too far," Bishop said. "Didn't he say two miles?"

"Yeah."

"We're still ten miles out. Give it a few minutes, OK?"

Angela put the radio in the glove box and stiffened her posture. As they drove on, they gained altitude. The once dominant cedars were replaced by spruce and aspen. Meadows began to appear amidst the deep woods—a welcome change from the hemmed-in and gloomy Elmore.

"Where did that come from?" Bishop asked, slowing down and pointing to the western side of the road.

"Oh my God, a motorcycle! Someone else is alive!" Angela kicked her feet and slammed her bandaged hands onto the dashboard. "Pull over!"

"What do you think I'm doing?"

They idled next to the beater motorcycle and stared at it as if they'd never seen such a vehicle. The bike wasn't in the best of shape, and was propped up by a rusting kickstand. Angela cracked open the door for a better look. A door closed faster than a window in case of attack.

"Anyone there?" she shouted out to the grassy embankment and tree line. "Anyone?"

A breeze answered, tousling her hair.

The truck vibrated, and Bishop wondered if the engine was out of balance. He depressed the gas pedal while in park. The engine was fine.

The truck vibrated again.

Something across the road caught his eye, and he turned to look. Two mature aspen parted like mere weeds, and what he saw he couldn't explain, for he wasn't sure he was seeing it. There stood a creature twelve feet high, with the rough, grey skin of a rhinoceros and six bulging legs capped off with discolored toenails. At first, he thought it was an elephant, but there were no tusks or trunk. The triple-pupil eyes boiled with rage. The mouth was an elongated extrusion seven feet long, containing numerous teeth the size of dollar bills. The mouth attached to a wrinkled, baggy face and hung open bizarrely as if unhinged. Two flush nostrils with no visible nose or snout steamed and gushed snot with each tortured breath. The elephantine creature swung its gaping mouth side to side, stomping its feet in place. A rectangular tag flashed on its neck, and Bishop guessed it at eighty beats per minute. It seemed sick or in pain as it thrashed.

Bishop went to shift the truck into gear, and Angela slammed her hand onto his. Apparently, she'd been paying attention to the other embankment and the motorcycle.

"Where are you going?"

"Angela, no! Get off—"

The creature rammed into the truck and the elongated mouth ripped into the back window. Yutu yipped and jumped onto Angela's lap and then out the opening in the passenger side door. A stench of bile and shit besieged them, and long slobbers of drool coated their gear as the creature's grotesque tongue curled, unfurled, and groped.

"Jesus! Drive, drive!"

The creature pulled its mouth out of the truck, generated incensed rumblings from deep within its lungs, and slammed into it again, using the side of its head and temporarily knocking the truck up onto two wheels.

"Bishop, Go!"

"I can't—"

It walloped them again, cratering the driver's side panels and covering the truck with foul-smelling slobber. Then the creature reared back and led with its mouth through the driver's side window, crunching through the glass like it were tissue paper. Bishop tried to duck and protect his face, but it was too late. He saw the gunk-encrusted wrinkles on its mouth and its purple gums that were sprinkled with glinting particles of glass. The mouth hit him like a garbage can filled with concrete. He was losing consciousness. Angela's screams, Yutu's vicious barking, and the excited, guttural breathing of the creature were dreamlike, awash in trippy reverb.

Where was he? What happened?

Bam!

Was that a shotgun blast? Whose dog is barking? Where am I?

That was a shotgun blast.

Bam!

And another.

His head throbbed. He went to touch it, and felt slickness he was sure was blood. Angela was crying. He wanted to open his eyes, but they fluttered. No energy. The scent of gun smoke stung his nostrils.

Yutu growled.

Bam!

Bam!

Something huge grunted on the road next to him and then thundered off, bellowing. A flood of light inundated his mind and stung his eyes. He looked out the driver's side door frame and saw the aspens shaking and then looked to his right to see Angela crying. A nasty cut streaked up her arm and her left eyelid was the color of a prune.

"Baby," she said, reaching for him with open and careful hands, her eyes darting to a spot above his brow. "Don't move, baby, OK?"

She offered a half-smile, but betrayed the smile with watering eyes. He felt horrible for her as she did her best not to show him how bad his knock was.

Bishop heard movement outside the truck, perhaps the final monster, the one that would end this insanity. They would be shit in the woods, no different than most of the valley's residents. As the shuffling and limping inched closer, Bishop saw it was a man with a serious-as-hell face.

"Long time no see," the man said through shattered glass, slime, and moist chunks of creature skin. "I do believe we've met."

Angela sobbed, and Yutu barked from somewhere out of sight.

"Hey," Bishop said weakly. "I do believe we have."

Bishop's eyes fluttered and he faded to black. He welcomed it.

*

When Bishop's eyes opened again, a familiar skylight loomed overhead, and he felt the supple texture of leather underneath his body. His head hurt so fucking bad, each throb sending white flashes across his visual periphery. Still, he couldn't figure out where he was.

"Bishop?" Angela asked, her voice shaky.

"That's me...I think," he said, grimacing.

Angela wrapped her arms around him, placed her head on his chest, and squeezed. "I'm so glad you're back," she said, crying.

"Where am I?"

"You're at Big J," she said, wiping at tears and smiling. Her left brow was swollen black.

"Ah...good ole Big J," he said. "It's nice to be back."

"Colbrick kept this place in tip-top shape," she said.

"Where is he?"

"Kitchen table."

"How did he get out to the road?"

Angela put a finger to his lips and reached for a water bottle. "Too many questions," she said. "You need to rest."

"I've had plenty," he said. Finally, Big J's living room dialed into focus, and the clarity that had eluded him since the battering creature returned. "How did Colbrick get to the road?"

"He used that old motorcycle," she said. "We left it on Highway 18 and took the truck back."

Colbrick walked over to the couch.

"Hey slick, you seen better days, eh?"

"Just a scratch," Bishop said, reaching his hand out to Colbrick, who shook it heartily.

"I found that bike behind some plywood in the garage. Had some gas so I decided to do some scouting of my own."

"What the hell was that thing on the road?" Bishop asked.

"I call 'em Rammers."

"Rammers, as in they *ram* you?"

"Yup."

"That's pretty weak, dude."

"No worse than *Frequency Seal*," Colbrick said, chuckling. "I saw it gunning through the meadow yesterday morning. Damn thing shook the ground. I thought a bunch of those monkeys were headed this way, or maybe a pack of seals."

"How did you find the one on the road?" Bishop asked.

"Just driving along, minding my own P's and Q's, taking a look around and it ran across the road in front of me. I parked the bike and headed into the forest on the opposite side of the road."

"Wait—why did you do that?" Angela asked, her brow furrowing.

"Because when the bastard ran across the road, I saw that it was well aware of me, and that it wasn't exactly on the up and up."

"You mean it was playing with you," Bishop said.

"Yup. I knew if I continued down the road, it would bolt back out and kill me. These things aren't stupid, folks. I could see the deceit in its eyes."

"Why didn't you just turn around?" Angela asked.

"In the time it took to get that bike around, it would have been on me. I was already too close, and on a bike you have no safety structure. So I parked and decided to play its game, and do something it wasn't expecting. I guess most people just run from it, so I did the opposite."

"And that's when we came along," Bishop said.

"Yup."

"Thanks for scaring it away," Angela said.

"Not a thing. I just wish I could have killed the bastard. No shotgun will kill that God damned thing unless it has slugs."

"We haven't seen that one before," Bishop said. "It seems more suited to open country. But I don't think there's much of a chance for it to get to the prairie."

"What are you talking about?" Colbrick asked.

Angela looked to the floor and spoke in a somber tone. "We couldn't get on the internet, but we found a working television with satellite, Colbrick."

"Go on."

"...I don't want to..."

"Colbrick, we're quarantined," Bishop said.

Colbrick frowned and spit hard. "What in God's name are you talking about?"

"Homeland Security has created a perimeter around the Valley, but there are at least two or three road dams between us and them. No one from Elmore or anywhere in the valley made it there that we know of. I don't think Homeland Security believes there are any survivors left, but we're supposed to wait it out until someone comes to rescue us."

Colbrick walked away and gazed between the window reinforcements, out into the big sky country he'd known all his life. He gripped the stock of the sawed-off enough to whiten his knuckles.

"We figure the government is converging in Billings thanks to its numerous resources and military bases. I also wouldn't be surprised if they're telling people near the valley to temporarily relocate there."

"Billings?" Colbrick asked. "I ain't going to God damned Billings."

Bishop chuckled.

Angela shot him a look.

"Military base or not, we put our asses on the line making the trip out there. So, that leaves waiting it out here," Colbrick said.

"Not exactly," Bishop said.

Angela let out a deep breath and patted him on the shoulder.

"It seems the outside world only knows about the fliers and doesn't know anything about the tags," Bishop said. "They have their heads up their asses trying to figure out what's going on. Another thing, Colbrick—they're taking their sweet time about it. Time we don't have."

"Before we're eaten?"

"Before they send a message," Angela said.

"The white-coated scientists with their billion-dollar labs figured out the fliers are aliens and the source must be near here. Some think an alien civilization sent these animals to see if this is a good place for them to live," Bishop said. "They don't know what we know yet. But they must think they have all the time in the world because they can't see that the tags are flashing faster."

Yutu pattered into the living room and jumped onto the couch at Bishop's feet.

"You met Yutu, Colbrick?" Bishop asked.

"You're not making sense, slick."

"Yutu, the dog. We found him trapped in a fire in Elmore."

"Oh yes, the dog. He's a mighty fine animal." Colbrick whistled with an authoritarian tone and Yutu sprinted to his side.

"Hey...what the heck?" Angela said.

"Used to train dogs," Colbrick said. "Old hobby."

Colbrick found a box of dog bones in the pantry and gave one of them to Yutu. Yutu bounded away with glee, wanting to relish the wonderful treat all by himself.

"I don't know about any of this shit, but I know I ain't going to Billings," Colbrick said. "Also, I got a surprise for you folks."

Colbrick disappeared down the hallway and they could hear him opening a locked door. When he came back, he was holding a large mason jar. In-between the thick, clear glass quivered a rotten leaf.

"You did not," Angela said.

"Yup."

He set the jar down on the coffee table and Bishop grimaced.

"I hate those things," he said.

"Agree with you there, slick. But I've been thinking about the tags, too. See this here tiny tag. It's really going now. Getting faster every time I look at it. I captured another leaf and the tag went dark when I took it off to look at it better, so I'm keeping this one alive to watch it. I'm thinking it means that something's going to happen, something I'm not going to like."

"I noticed that too and came to the same conclusion," Bishop said. "I think some device or ship or whatever is in the mountains, maybe waiting to be set off when the flashes get to a certain point. But I don't know how we'd find it."

"What about your new friend?" Colbrick asked. "I been hunting with dogs my whole life."

"OK..."

"Give Yutu the scent of the tag and let him lead us to the source."

Bishop and Angela's mouths hung agape.

"You folks up for a little trip to the Apex Range?"

Bishop pulled himself up, and Angela flashed him a look of concern, holding her bandaged hands near him in case he fell.

"Slow down, Colbrick, what the heck are you talking about?" she asked. "I'm all for contributing to the cause, but I don't want to embark on a suicide mission. Do you have any idea how big this mountain range is? How long it would take to find this thing? And all that time we'd be exposing ourselves."

Bishop leaped up and paced the room, shaking off his headache. Sometimes you just had to get your blood flowing to feel better. "Honey, I love you, but this is the one chance I have to lay my life on the line for something I believe in. Colbrick understands. He's not a pussy. His father gave his life for this country, and I'm willing to give mine for the Apex Valley and my father."

Angela watched Bishop pace with that wild look in his eyes and stepped towards him .

"Well, I have a pussy and my pussy is telling me that my husband has gone off the deep end and I need to bring him back."

"Whoa, you two," Colbrick said. "Never a good idea to get in the middle of a marital spat, but I need you to calm down and think this through. You're both right. We can't wait for Homeland Security but getting killed won't save the valley either. We need to plan this out."

Bishop and Angela looked at Colbrick and sat back down. Bishop brought a hand to his bandaged head and groaned. "The fliers," he said, wincing. "I saw them heading to the southern end of the range, near Elmore. I get the feeling the seed mother will be near there."

"Good work, slick." Colbrick turned and spit on the floor. "And not a bad name this time either."

Angela cracked a smile.

"Thanks," Bishop said. "I'm not sure which exact peak it was, you know how they're always obscured by clouds."

"Yup."

"We need a topo map," Bishop said.

"Already done, partner."

Colbrick went to one of the hallway rooms and came back with two folded maps, one lavender and the other green to distinguish the national forest districts.

"This one here, now this is the northern half of the forest," Colbrick said, pointing to the green map.

"That's us," Angela said.

"Now, this purple one, this is the southern half, near Elmore."

A wave of uneasiness hit Bishop at the mention of that town. The dead shops and impenetrable cedars flashed in his mind.

"Now, these aren't the closest type of maps, and I'd like a 1:24,000 level, but they do offer the names of the peaks, lakes, and even show trails. They're damn well good enough for what we need to do."

Colbrick spread the maps onto the table before them, and they gazed at the huge swaths of green and the flowing, bending contour lines that rose sharply to patches of brown and grey. "Here's us," he said, pointing a finger to a white square hemmed in by a sea of green. "Big J is surrounded by national forest. There are trails leading up into the mountains from this very ranch, mostly horse trails."

Angela frowned. "If the fliers are coming from the southern range, why would we start at the northern half? Why not just drive towards Elmore and head west into that portion of the range?"

"She's got a point," Bishop said.

"Because you run a motor into whatever drainage these things are coming out of, and you may as well dip yourself in barbecue sauce and shout 'eat me,'" Colbrick said. "They find us by noise, remember? And you want to run a V8 up into their nest? Shit, you two are crazier than I thought."

"So we're going to hike atop the range for thirty miles until Yutu picks up the scent?"

"You got a better idea?" Colbrick asked.

"Yes. We have other options. We can wait this out. We can also prepare for a trip to Billings."

"I ain't fucking going to Billings," Colbrick said.

Bishop grinned, and as Angela whipped her head, shook it loose.

*

Angela hated the idea of hiking into the mountains exposed. But she also liked the idea of killing the invaders. Still, Billings was a community, and damn did she miss being part of a societal fabric. She missed the people, the smiles. That's why she lived in the city, to reap the rewards of a diverse culture—the shops, the languages, the eateries that were not chains like the strip-mall-ridden suburbs. The unique bookstores and her book club...

"So I'm outvoted I guess," she said.

"Colbrick has a good point, sweetheart. If we drive too close to the fliers, we're screwed. We have to find a quiet route."

"OK...so let's say we figure out a route. What the hell are we going to do once we find this source?" Angela asked.

"We're going to shoot it," Colbrick said.

"You're going to have to do better than that," she said.

"I'm afraid we don't have better," Colbrick said.

"Oh yes we do," she said. "We have the gas in the truck, gas in your motorcycle, and I'm sure there's more fuel around this ranch somewhere. I'm not going up there with these pea shooters. Colbrick's right, we need a real plan."

Bishop grabbed the edge of the map and pointed to an area of narrow peaks bunched together. The contour lines on this section bent perversely, forming acrobatic rises and falls of solid rock.

"That's where I saw them go," Bishop said, tapping a finger on the spot.

"The Hoodoos," Colbrick said with a sense of awe.

"Great. Sounds so inviting," Angela said.

"The Hoodoos are mostly covered by glaciers," Colbrick said.

Yutu whimpered from the other side of the room, and Angela went over to investigate.

"What's wrong, boy? You OK?" she asked.

She approached Yutu, and he backed up, growling, showing his teeth.

"What's gotten into you?" she asked. She turned to Bishop. "What's wrong with your dog?"

"Uh...that's *your* dog," Bishop joked.

"Seriously, Bishop." Angela rubbed the back of her neck as the hairs tingled. Yutu backed up further and then ran down the hall.

"Bishop—" Angela turned her head, thinking she saw a pair of eyes staring at them between the living room window reinforcements. "Did you—?"

Thump.

"What the hell?" Colbrick asked.

Thump. Thump.

"Not good," Bishop said, staggering from the couch. "You guys feel that?"

Angela ran over to Bishop and helped him up. "Yeah, the hairs on my arms are all standing up," she said.

Colbrick moved to the windows and peered out. A pair of wild, crimson eyes stared back, the pupils dilating, eyeing them with contempt and hunger. Colbrick ducked.

"Get down," he whispered, contorting his lips. "Get down now!"

The creatures banged on the boarded windows and doors.

"What are they?" Bishop asked, checking the windows.

"Monkeys," Colbrick said. "The God damned monkeys have found us."

The pigras shook the walls with their incessant pounding. The front storm door shattered, and a pigra shrieked in pain. Angela heard liquid splattering on the patio. The yard resounded with dragging knuckles and the mewling of the pathetic creatures.

"This is it," Colbrick said. "This is the one."

Angela thought to cry, but that was the old Angela. The new Angela grabbed her .357 Colt Python and aimed it around the lodge like an assassin.

Bishop turned towards the rattling front door and noticed the rotten leaf acting even more repulsive than usual. It was glowing red, almost humming, changing hues and brightness as it zigzagged inside the jar. It let out a series of high-pitched sounds, some barely audible.

"Holy hell," Bishop said. "I think this is how they found us. It's whistling."

"God damn it," Colbrick said.

"Take it out," Angela demanded. "Take it out now."

Bishop tilted the jar onto the Santa Fe style rug and the leaf clung to the jar as if it knew what was coming next. Bishop shook it out. The leaf flew onto the rug and Bishop raised his foot to smash it. As he did, the leaf protracted its many legs and recoiled, then changed what it was projecting and ceased the high-pitched whistling.

The pigras halted their pounding.

"Uh …what the hell?" Bishop said, his foot holding in the air above the leaf.

The leaf squeaked and moved further away.

"Did I just see that?" Angela asked, shaking her head.

"What are you two doing over there?" Colbrick asked.

The pigra clan shambled around the lodge, the dragging knuckles and disgusting noises coming from every direction. The sound of scraping gravel came from the driveway, indicating a possible inter-pigra scuffle.

"It just sold out to save its life," Bishop said, shaking his head in disbelief.

"That's exactly what it did," Angela said. She bent down to the leaf and pointed the tip of her .357 an inch from it. "And you're not going to let them know we're here again, are you? Otherwise, you're going to meet my little friend here, you understand?"

The rotten leaf did nothing.

"What the hell do we do with it?" Bishop asked.

"I don't know. It could rat us out again."

"Put it back in the jar," Colbrick said. He reached for the jar and the leaf arched and flashed hints of red.

"Don't!" Angela said.

Colbrick moved away with the jar and the leaf relaxed, revealing nothing on its surface other than the moist, pockmarked skin with offensive moles. Then it let out a mocking chortle.

"Well I'll be," Colbrick said. "Sneaky little bastard, ain't ya?"

The leaf remained still.

"If we didn't need it, I'd step on it now," Bishop said.

"God damn it," Colbrick said, peering between the window reinforcements. "The damn things are hanging around like teens at a kegger."

"At least they aren't trying to bust in," Bishop said.

"They seem confused," Colbrick said.

The rotten leaf relaxed.

"They're starting to leave," Colbrick said. "There must be dozens of the bastards. I can smell 'em through the glass."

"Awful creatures," Bishop said, limping across the room and holding his head.

Angela fished into her pocket and found two Vicodin. She handed them to Bishop.

"Thanks," he said, swallowing them dry. "How many left?"

"Ten," she said.

"Save those for when we really need them," he said, studying her bruised and swollen eye.

She brought a bandaged hand to the wound and winced.

"You look great," he said, kissing her brow.

A thousand pounds lifted from their shoulders. Bishop turned and watched the pigra clan shamble towards tree line. He scanned the sky for fliers, but didn't see any.

Angela turned towards the leaf and gasped. "Uh...guys, where's the leaf?"

"Shit on a stick," Colbrick said, half-limping, half-running to the living room.

The leaf was not in the living room.

Angela threw the cushions around, digging into the couches. Bishop joined the search and headed down the hallway. He stopped and stared well ahead of the door to the master bedroom. He didn't know if he truly saw his father in that room, or if it was his imagination. All he knew was that he did feel *something*, even now, looking down the dim hallway. He moved closer to the master bedroom door, and the sensation filled him again, as if there was something in that room sucking him in. Each step down the hallway was a thousand reaching, splaying hands beckoning him.

The spell broke, and he retreated to the living room.

"Found ya," Angela said, shaking her head. "Guys, you won't believe this."

Colbrick and Bishop limped to the pantry.

The leaf was eating a Ritz cracker that had fallen to the floor. It crunched the tasty morsel with its hidden stingray mouth. Colbrick approached, and the leaf arched its back and let out a faint whistle.

"You son of a bitch," Colbrick said, moving back.

The leaf chortled.

"I guess it's hungry," Angela said. "May as well let it eat."

"What's worse? Dealing with this rogue leaf or a full attack on Big J?" Bishop asked in a weary tone.

"Easy one," Angela said. "We deal with this brat."

Colbrick grimaced at the leaf and left the pantry.

"Don't touch the damn pop tarts!" he shouted back at it.

*

Dinner consisted of stale bread and water. Pop tarts were dessert.

The leaf was happy with the crumbs on the pantry floor. Yutu was not happy with the leaf and gave it a wide berth. The leaf didn't seem so thrilled either, sometimes arching and turning green when the pooch approached. Colbrick had a time getting it back into the jar.

"I guess we're heading out tomorrow," Bishop said.

"Yup."

"Are we healed enough?" Bishop asked.

"We ain't ever gonna heal," Colbrick said.

"My hands should be fine," Angela said, holding them up and wiggling her fingers.

"I feel great," Bishop said. "At least physically."

A moment of silence consumed the room as they pondered their plans.

"More weapons," Bishop said. "Wilkin's has some back in Elmore. We picked up a nice pistol there."

Colbrick nodded. "We got two shotguns, a .357, a Beretta, plus whatever gas we can get our hands on. The garage had storage cans, and we can use paper towels for the wicks. These woods are sick, folks, and it's my duty to right a wrong."

"You're preaching to the converted," Bishop said. "Running isn't going to get the job done. We need to fight."

"We only have two overnight packs," Angela said.

"Make that three," Colbrick said. "I found a stash of gear in one of the bedrooms. When you include the gear in the packs we brought, we got down sleeping bags, pads, camp stoves, you name it."

"Outstanding," Angela said, flashing a smile.

Colbrick looked at them, his eyes as serious as ever. "It's up to us to do the right thing," he said. "I believe God allowed us to live so we could carry out this deed. I'll be glad to be at your side as we climb those mountains tomorrow."

"We have to climb mountains?" Angela asked, blinking.

The two men glared at her, and she laughed.

"Just kidding. Hello? Apex freaking Mountains to our left?"

Night came to the ranch, and the pigras shambled along the trailed, lower country the way pigras tend to do. From high up on the slope, where trees give way to rock, a great horned owl hooted, then flew off, its silhouette undulating across the Milky Way.

OFFENSE

Morning brought the familiar, aching stiffness. The three survivors prepared their gear, utilizing the high-end backpacks. They stuffed in down sleeping bags, ponchos, heavier layers, headlamps, water filters, a supply of pasta, canned goods, dog biscuits, and the ammunition. Bishop tried on his pack and was surprised by the weight.

"Damn I'm out of shape," he said.

"We'll bulk up before we leave," Colbrick said. "No sense in letting all this food rot if we ain't coming back."

Angela looked up from her pack. "We plan to come back," she said. "Speak for yourself, grumpy."

"I hope you two have come to grips with reality. The mountain itself could kill us before any of those damned creatures do," Colbrick said.

"Maybe," Angela said, tearing up. "But I'm not going to drown myself in pity."

Bishop put his arm around her as she kept packing, pretending not to cry.

"It's OK, we'll be fine," he said, lying to her, but believing the lie. If he didn't, why would he take two steps up that mountain?

*

They finished packing and gathered what fuel they could. Some of this came in the form of lighter fluid and from power tools in the sheds. They siphoned half the gas from the truck. Angela didn't have the heart to use it all. Something inside her still wanted to escape to Billings—to see people again, to be part of a community. What gas they managed to salvage was placed in aluminum cans they strapped to their packs.

Colbrick held something in a clenched fist, beaming, as if a child at show and tell.

"You see this?" he asked, unclenching. "This is the match that will light the fire. Remember that."

Yutu watched Colbrick and wagged his tail, even though Colbrick had managed to secure a harness and plastic bottles filled with gas for the pooch to carry.

"We'll, I'm glad someone is paying attention," Colbrick said, patting Yutu on the head and grunting at the burden of the pack as he bent over. Then he took his sawed-off from the counter and limped to the front door. Yutu followed.

"We'll, you comin' or what?" Colbrick asked them. "Ever cook yourself some pumpkin seeds? Mighty fine with a generous helping of salt."

"He's insane," Angela whispered to Bishop.

"At least he's on our side."

"He's our Dennis Rodman."

Bishop laughed, but the smile turned to a frown when a shadow caught his eye in the narrow, dim hallway. "You two go ahead," he said. "I need to use the bathroom."

Bishop stepped into the hallway, the familiar, reaching hands pulling at him. He stopped at the wooden door that was raw enough to deliver splinters. He thought he saw faces in the organic fibers, and beyond the faces, medieval forests and interconnected scenes of animals and Native Americans. He reached out a hand and opened the door. The air was stale and tinted with a whiff of cologne. The boarded-up windows barely let in light, and what light there was felt pointless. He stood in front of the mirror, shocked at how much he'd aged in such a short time. But he looked stronger, his face more defined having lost a layer of plumpness. Bishop swung the mirror and checked for more Vicodin. Another full bottle. A Big J resident either had back pain or just liked to get high. He swung the mirror back and popped two of the pills, then slipped out of his pack and drank from the faucet like a cat.

He went to the plush chair in the corner and sat. It was all too much. And the chair was so comfortable on his sore bones. His eyelids fluttered and he nodded off.

A figure came to him.

It couldn't be.

He gathered all the courage he could and tried to speak. "Dad?" he asked.

"Yes, it's me, Bishop."

A great sense of sorrow overcame him and he wept.

"Dad...I'm so sorry. They took your valley. They took it all."

"Yes, I know, son. We had some good times here, didn't we?"

"Dad...Cooke's Creek is destroyed. The people are all gone. They even got Wilkins. Elmore is dead. And I haven't seen any of the wildlife we used to watch. It all changed, and I couldn't do a single thing about it."

"You're doing the right thing."

His father's words produced a calming effect.

"How did you get here?"

"I've always been here, Bishop. The Apex Mountains are my home. They're where my heart is."

"Did you know Big J?" Bishop asked, sniffing.

"I worked here as a teenager one summer, long before I met your mother when I was still chasing girls and when more grizzly bears roamed these mountains."

A wave of emotion crashed into Bishop, but the revelation did not cause sadness, only joy. "Dad, you helped us find Big J, and you helped me find Colbrick, didn't you?"

"Remember when I put the worms on the hook for you over at Lake Gallatin?"

"Yes."

"And remember when you caught those trout?"

"Yes, Dad."

"Just because someone baits your hook doesn't mean they caught the fish. You did all this, son. I don't really know if I did anything to help you. I don't control a lot of things now. What happens, happens."

"You knew that Colbrick knew about Big J, and that somehow you would help us here, help us to keep safe."

"I can't answer that, my boy. What I can say is that I love you very much and your mother."

"Mom...she's hurt, isn't she?"

"I don't know."

Bishop's chest heaved, and he swiped at his moist face with the sleeve of his shirt.

"I love you too, Dad."

"There's one more thing," his father said, the kindness on his face hardening to steel eyes and a rigid jawline. "It's up there. Free the valley."

The opacity of his father's figure grew fainter and he disappeared.

"Dad, wait, please don't go."

Angela burst into the room, holding her .357 like she had done it all her life. Bishop jarred awake.

"Jesus, you OK?" she asked. "I heard you talking. Is something in here with you?"

Bishop reached for her and embraced her.

"I saw him, Angela."

"You saw who?"

"My father. He came to me in my dream."

"What? Bishop—"

"He said he worked here as a teenager," Bishop said through sobs. "I think he set all this up."

"Oh my God," she said, crying. "Oh my God, Bishop."

"It's going to be OK," he said, and for the first time, he truly believed it.

*

They headed west into the national forest via an old horse trail, and where the horses had gone was anyone's guess, although Bishop imagined the fliers taking them away like bleating, helpless sheep.

The daylight faded in the understory of golden currant and western snowberry. To the northwest, a creek trickled downhill, becoming blocked by a beaver dam and forming a narrow pond. The gangly, soaked sticks wound together, the water seeping through weak points with a soothing hush. Layers of grass draped over the bank, interspersed with white angelica. Pointed, gnawed aspen trunks thrust up in the surrounding woods. There was no sign of the beaver. But there were human remains, picked clean to the bone. Only the leather boots and work gloves remained, concealing hunks of intact, rotting flesh. Yutu sniffed the skeleton, then trotted to the pond for a drink.

"Awful," Angela said, putting a hand over her mouth.

Bishop checked their perimeter.

"Eels," Colbrick said, spitting. "Didn't know what hit him."

Colbrick walked past the skeleton and picked up a rectangular metal box near a glove. The lid squeaked as he opened it, and his eyes flashed. "Winner, winner chicken dinner," he said. "Folks, we've just been given a hell of a gift." He turned to Angela and Bishop and held the box open so they could see, his huge fingers dwarfing it.

Bishop couldn't believe it.

"Are you kidding me?" Angela asked, her facial muscles straining as she peered into the box.

Inside the thin metal box lay eight sticks of dynamite.

"What we got here is a ranch hand coming to blow the beaver damn. Common practice out here, slicks. The wicks are long, probably waterproof too."

"Why would anyone blow up a beaver dam?" Angela asked.

"Some folks believe they can flood pastureland, and in this case, the Big J meadow, although this little pond doesn't pose much threat."

Colbrick sighed. "But sometimes out here, folks kill things just to kill things."

"Do you know how to use them?" Angela asked.

"Sure as hell do. Light the wick and run!"

Bishop chuckled, trying to hide the nausea. What had they gotten into? Hanging with a maniac who carried a sawed-off and dynamite. They'd be lucky to make it up the mountain without killing themselves.

Angela bent down to Yutu, unhooked his harness, and he wagged his tail. "I'm not having him carry flammable liquid if we have dynamite."

*

They wound through tiers of aspen, ponderosa pine, and spruce. Muscular boulders and delicate ferns appeared in the understory. As they climbed in elevation, the smaller trees turned ragged, their branches pointing east due to wind blasts from the peaks. The boulders increased in number and became swollen—a few eclipsing school busses in size. Enormous trunks of old growth hemlock and red pine crisscrossed the mossy forest floor. A palpable quiet leveled the surroundings, their footfalls absorbed by spongy, damp moss.

Soon, they came across the gurgling creek again, light reflecting off the water in-between boulders and fallen timber.

"This looks good for a break," Bishop said, dropping his pack.

"Not good at all," Colbrick said. "We shouldn't rest on the trail. The damn monkeys are trail happy."

"He's right," Angela said, hands on her hips as she tried to catch her breath.

Yutu sat and wagged his tail, happy to be amongst them.

"Let's head up the creek a bit," Bishop said, bending and swaying into his pack.

After several minutes, Bishop and Angela set their gear down and rested on a moss-covered ponderosa pine. Yutu nestled in-between them. Colbrick did not rest.

"Why don't you pull up a seat?" Angela asked.

"I'll rest when I'm dead," Colbrick said.

"You're limping pretty bad. Why don't you cut yourself some slack?" Angela asked.

"I'll take a vacation when we kill these bastards." He turned from them and grumbled.

A creature called out upstream. They reached for their weapons.

Peee peee pijur pijur.

The flittering of small wings drew closer, and they dropped to the ground.

Peee peee pijur pijur.

It flashed in front of them, following the stream and dipping along its course, disappearing from view within a second.

"Wow," Angela said. "It's a water ouzel."

Bishop thought of his father. *There's still something left.*

"Bishop, did you see it?" Angela asked.

"I sure as hell did."

"It's a miracle," Colbrick said. "Native wildlife, God bless it."

After the ouzel disappeared, they huddled around the boulder-filled creek, splashing cool water on their faces. Bishop observed two young cutthroats finning in a pocket of water six inches deep. This was still cutthroat country.

"If we weren't marching to our deaths, this would make a mighty fine camping spot," Colbrick said, killing whatever sense of peace they managed to absorb from the tranquil nook.

Angela frowned and shouldered her pack. "Break's over," she said.

Yutu trotted behind her, putting his snout on her calves, sniffing the wounds and then running in front of her.

"What are you doing?" she asked.

Yutu rolled over, his paws in the air, tongue hanging out of his mouth.

Angela laughed, went to one knee and scratched his belly.

Jarring, ancient peaks revealed themselves between curves in the trail where the canopy failed to intertwine. Each breathtaking glimpse managed to infuse significance to their mission, but also seemed to mock them.

The trail leveled as it spilled into a ten-acre meadow. Tall, golden grasses swayed and thick aspen commanded the edges. Behind the aspen rolled the last of the pine-covered foothills below the craggy, defiant mountains. The day brought few clouds, and the tallest of the peaks shone with a biting definition unseen at lower elevations.

"That's Onyx Peak," Colbrick said, spitting up phlegm. "The highest in the northern range."

"It's taken quite a few climbers over the years," Bishop said.

"Mostly by lightning," Colbrick said.

Angela cringed at the word. She didn't much care for lightning. Well, that was putting it lightly. It was a certified phobia of hers, and the thought of it induced a hard-to-shake panic. Bishop knew this, and she noticed him watching her after Colbrick's comment.

"Colbrick, how long of a hike are we looking at here?" Bishop asked.

"Well, the good news is that the Hoodoos are at the northern edge of the southern range. The bad news is that we're still in the northern range if that makes any sense to ya." Colbrick ran a hand through his hair. "We've got the gear to do this."

Bishop turned to Angela. "We've done overnights before, sweetheart."

"Those were ten-mile hikes, round trip," she said. "I think this is thirty…one way."

"Like any big project, you have to break it up into chunks," Bishop said. "Building a house seems impossible, but not when you do it brick by brick each day over a period of months. Look at this hike as three separate ten-mile hikes spread out over a period of days."

Angela smiled at him and eased her shoulders.

Yutu bounded ahead on the trail, tongue wagging.

They paused in the tranquil meadow, wind bending the grasses and eliciting comforting rustling from the aspen leaves. The blue sky gleamed above them, the metamorphic rock of the peaks reflecting light and piercing their eyes. Water gurgled and splashed over boulders from an unseen forest glade.

Bishop gazed at the slopes below the crags. The last few stunted and wind-ravaged pines clung to the hostile rock like mountain climbers frozen in time. The wind gained momentum, whipping through the meadow grass and knocking them back on their feet.

"Jesus," Angela said, holding her arms out for balance, her bandages rippling.

Bishop reached out and grabbed her forearm.

"These mountains have many surprises," Colbrick said through the punishing wind, as if he was admiring the brutal nature of the place. "Best be on your toes, slicks. Up in the Apex, you could be enjoyin' a beauty of a day, and next thing you know, you're blown off the rock. This range holds many secrets and hazards, folks. Do not be lulled by the beauty. Danger lurks at every turn in the trail and the not-so-trails."

*

They pushed through the windy meadow, each step more difficult at the higher altitude. Yutu benefited from his streamlined figure. The wind to him was a vehicle for smells. Exciting, puzzling smells.

"Do you guys notice anything?" Angela asked.

"We're hiking," Colbrick said.

"Seriously. Look over there," Angela said.

Yutu was way ahead of her, sniffing at a sun-bleached skeleton. It had four long limbs and two shorter limbs near the chest cavity. From the skull protruded what looked like deer antlers. A dead tag had fallen into the rib cage.

"Never seen one of these alive," Colbrick said. "Guess that's what the others ate before they found the deer...and us. Must've not made it off the mountain."

"We must be on the right track," Bishop said. "Let's check the leaf."

Colbrick took the jar out of his pack. He gave the leaf a cracker, while Bishop counted the tag pulses. After counting, he had a sudden urge to sprint up the mountain. What if they were taking too long?

Bishop examined the peaks that dominated their view, wind stinging his eyes. "If the cause of all this is up here, make no mistake we're headed directly into a high concentration of creatures, including ones we've never seen."

Yutu advanced far up trail, his soft fur rippling in the wind.

"Back in school, I had a friend who worked for the Forest Service during summers," Angela said. "She told me something which may or may not be useful. Apparently, there are these beetles which invade healthy pine trees. They burrow into the trees—enough to kill them with their numerous larvae. The freaky thing is that these beetles release a pheromone all over that infected tree once they've taken it over that tells other flying beetles to move on to an unoccupied target."

"Interesting," Bishop said. "The new arrivals *could* be doing the same thing. They could be trying to create their own ecosystem, and when established, move on to other locations."

"My friend also told me about these pouches scientists would make, full of a synthetic copy of that pheromone, and they would tack these to the trees to save them."

"So the beetles would move from healthy tree to healthy tree, completely fooled," Bishop said.

"Maybe we can come up with a device...a technology to keep these things away from us," Angela said.

"Yeah, and maybe I'll sprout wings and sing the national anthem in three-part harmony," Colbrick said. "You know what the trigger scent is for them damn things to leave? No more humans and native wildlife to eat."

Angela frowned.

"If they leave for greener pastures, then that gives us a better chance," Bishop said.

Angela watched Yutu. "And these flashing tags...they're beating faster. I hope we aren't too late."

Angela gripped her gun and glanced behind her. "Let's say these tags were put there by a civilization that wants to track their wildlife like a biologist would collar and study a pack of wolves. They want to get to a point where they know that a large number of animals of all kinds have lived long enough to assume that they've become established. That's why the tags go dead when the animal dies. We're assuming the faster flashing means they're getting closer to sending the OK signal. We're hoping that the tags are sending their signals to some central device here that we could destroy. Otherwise, we'd have to pick off the tagged animals individually, right?"

"Right," Bishop said.

"Makes sense," Colbrick said. "Daddy's pets hang out long enough, live long enough, then zap the word back to Papa that everything's all peachy in the Apex Valley. Then bam, Papa shows up."

"To a planet all ready to live on," Angela said. "Why risk yourself and your own species until you know for certain the best planets to live?"

"Bingo," Colbrick said.

Angela stopped and regarded the wilderness all around them.

"How in the hell are we going to find this place?" she asked, holding her arms out. "We have thirty miles of mountains to cover. And we have no idea what it looks like or how big it is."

"Well, I guess I got more faith in Yutu than you do. Here, boy," Colbrick called.

Yutu trotted towards him with eager eyes. Colbrick carefully removed the leaf from its jar. Covering as much of the creature as he could to show only the tag, he held it near Yutu's nose. Yutu backed away at first, but then understood. The Man had shown him objects to sniff and then Yutu had followed the scent. The Man had praised Yutu with pettings and treats, but that wasn't as necessary as the Man thought. Yutu enjoyed having a mission and being needed. He took several deep sniffs from the tag's surface.

A blast of wind unfurled from the peaks and pushed them onto their heels, and they struggled to regain composure. But instead of blowing back, the stealthy Yutu streaked ahead into the wind, his streamlined body cutting through the force.

"Good boy," Colbrick said.

Yutu zipped ahead on the trail. When the pooch reached the edge of the meadow, his head poked above the grass. He stopped, looked back at them, and barked twice.

Bishop and Angela turned to each other, stunned.

"That's how we find it," Bishop said, goosebumps springing up all over his skin.

"Yutu has found himself a scent."

"God Bless that dog," Colbrick said.

Yutu continued up trail, checking behind every so often to make sure they were following. The pooch exhibited a newfound confidence, although he still missed The Man.

The meadow segued into an area of jagged, loose rock. Squatting here and there amongst the sheared rock were slabs of house-sized stone. Masochistic pine trees clung where they could.

"This place ain't no good," Colbrick said, wincing at the terrain. "Something don't feel right."

Angela raised her .357.

"Feels like we're being watched," Colbrick said.

Bishop noticed a deep patch of shade between two big slabs. He peered into the shade and listened. In the gloom, two sinister eyes glowed, each containing three pupils. Before he could aim the gun, a pressurized burst emitted from the crevice and the eel charged from its hiding place at a speed they'd never witnessed in previous encounters.

The eel's eyes narrowed and focused on the old timer.

"Colbrick!" Angela shouted.

Yutu yipped and ran towards Colbrick, leaping through the air and biting onto the eel's tail. Then Yutu whimpered and flopped to the ground, stunned and unconscious. The eel glared back to make sure Yutu was incapacitated, then returned to its intended target.

But Colbrick was no fool. Yutu had bought him enough time, and the sawed-off was aimed right at the eel's head. Before Colbrick could pull the trigger, another eel bit into his arm, forcing him to drop the sawed-off. He fell to the ground, cursing.

"Get down!" Bishop said, aiming his shotgun.

Angela dropped and Bishop fired, illuminating the rock slabs with muzzle flash, the silhouettes of the eels dancing around them. The blast roared off the stone, ringing their ears and violating the stillness of the alpine environment. The buckshot caught the first eel in its gaseous midsection, sending it into a tailspin. The second, ambushing eel aimed for Colbrick's throat, intent on finishing the kill.

Angela raised her weapon a few inches off the ground and fired six rounds at the attacker's head. One of the bullets found its mark, and the eel collapsed to the ground where it proceeded to convulse and hiss.

The first eel, now injured and observing the fate of its hunting partner, hesitated and veered towards Bishop. Bishop held the shotgun steady, and as the thing seesawed towards him, he squeezed the trigger, sending a full spray of buckshot into the eel's face. The snake's eyes disengaged from its head, and the independently functioning pupils disintegrated. Then the eel nosedived to the ground, biting into the rock with its disfigured face, trying to burrow away from them. Sparks of blue electricity emanated from its whipping tail as static charges revved and receded.

"Finish it!" Angela said.

From out of nowhere came a thunderous blast, and the eel slumped to the ground.

"Gotcha," Colbrick said from behind a curl of smoke.

"Oh my God, Yutu!" Angela screamed. She ran to the motionless pooch's side.

"No, just no," Bishop cried, kneeling beside him.

Angela ran her hand through his fur, crying. "I'm so sorry, Yutu."

Colbrick limped over to Yutu and examined him. Some of the fur around his neck was singed and smoking, and the smell of burnt hair wafted into the air. Colbrick slipped off his pack and reached into the front pocket, pulling out an object that he obscured in his fist.

"Sleeping dogs ain't always dead, slick," he said as he held the fist in front of Yutu's nose.

Angela and Bishop held each other and watched, expecting the worst.

Always expecting the worst.

The wind seemed to hold its breath, and the murmuring creeks hesitated, as if this moment held monumental importance and what was left of the valley waited for its conclusion.

Colbrick continued to hold his fist in front of Yutu's nose.

The nose twitched.

And twitched again.

"Yutu?" Angela cried.

The soft, gentle eyes of the dog slowly opened, and the snout twitched even more so, and soon Yutu's neck and head were off the ground and craning for the concealed object inside Colbrick's fist. Yutu's wet and curious nose sniffed Colbrick's hand, and Colbrick opened it, revealing a dog treat. Yutu's eyes grew wide, and the pooch grasped the treat in his flashy, white teeth and crunched down.

"Yutu!" Angela cried.

A tear stung the cuts on Bishop's face.

"They say dogs can come back from the dead for a milk bone," Colbrick said, grinning.

Yutu pulled himself up and groaned. When he got to all fours, he stretched his back legs. Then he shook his head as his goofy ears flopped about. Angela hugged him, and the sore pooch backed away from her grip, then licked her face. Bishop patted Yutu on the head.

"You did real good, boy," Bishop said, caressing his fur.

Colbrick tossed Yutu another treat, and Yutu gingerly trotted towards the milk bone, then snapped it up with zeal. In seconds, he crunched it down to nothing and looking back at them with appreciative eyes.

"I owe you one," Colbrick said to Yutu.

"It's about time you were the one who had their life saved," Angela said, wiping away salty tears.

"I guess so," Colbrick said, staring at the mountains that loomed above them. "But my time will come soon enough, folks. You can bet on that."

"Don't be so morbid," Angela said.

"Look around. I'm nothing more than a reflection of reality."

"I see mountains and a couple of dead eels," Angela said. "And we're going to clean all this up, somehow."

"Maybe. But that don't mean ole Colbrick's going to be around for the awards ceremony."

Angela rolled her eyes. "You aren't that old, Colbrick. You have just as good a chance as us."

"We'll see."

Bishop cleared his throat. "We should get moving. The last thing we need is the fliers honing in on those gunshots—"

Out of the corner of Bishop's eye, a shadow blocked the sun, and a moment later, the sky filled with ominous, black shapes and the rhythmic beat of taut wings.

"To the cave," Bishop said, trying to express urgency without shouting.

They scurried to the darkness like rodents from an owl and peered out with nervous, darting eyes. Yutu, still groggy from shock was the last to enter, his wispy tail swallowed by the blackness.

The throbbing of beating wings surrounded them like a tribal death march.

A swarm of small fliers zoomed about the slabs in blackening numbers, their soulless eyes glowing green. The looped mimicry of their gunshots emanated from the fliers paunchy midsections, echoing off the rocks in a psychotic cacophony.

The survivors backed into the cave until they could back no more, the last of their fearful eyes disappearing in the gloom. They remained silent, for even the slightest whisper meant certain death. Daylight turned into a black fog of wings, and the wretched things hovered and zinged like infuriated mosquitoes for an hour—a hell of a long time to keep quiet.

Finally, the small fliers gathered onto the backs of the large ones, their looped mimicry ceasing. Behemoth wings pounded up dust swirls. Shadows gave way to sunlight, and the wing beats faded down mountain.

The survivors stepped out of the cave, grains of sand from the settling dust grinding against their teeth.

Angela looked to the sky and shivered. Bishop put his arm around her.

"Never seen anything like it," Colbrick said, spitting. "Bats…bats can ping radar across the sky, and when it's blocked by an insect, they know right where to find it. But this? Never heard it or seen it before."

"Each shot up here, each loud noise could be death," Bishop said. "Unbelievable how fast they reacted."

"Yup."

"We're getting closer," Bishop said. "The fliers perch here on the mountains, listening to the valley which of course is where the humans are—"

"You mean were," Colbrick said.

"Yes, were."

"Great. So we're entering their territory?" Angela asked.

"I do believe so," Colbrick said, looking to the sky and shading his eyes. "If they get out of the valley, that's how they'll get the big cities. Sitting on all those buildings, swooping down and taking people like they were nothin' but ants."

"Why not just shoot the fucking things off the rooftops?" Bishop asked.

"Shooting them down would bring new fliers right to the shooter's location," Angela said, examining one of the dead eels. "I bet they could kill a bunch. But this would likely bring on even more, and soon the fliers would overwhelm the shooters, like an ant colony overtaking a spider. Sure, the spider is bigger and a tough predator, but when too many ants come upon one, they're in trouble."

"Sheer numbers," Bishop said, watching the sky.

Angela reached down to tousle Yutu's hair, and the pooch wagged his tail. "You know, in certain Amazonian tribes, it is alleged that elders can listen to the land, literally," Angela said. "Bishop, you've been coming here for decades, well before we even met. Your father was here long before that. And how long have you been here Colbrick?"

"All my life, miss.'"

"So maybe you're tuned into the land, too. Defenders of the natives, we seek to wipe out the invaders."

"Like Tuco Ramirez said, 'we go kill them all,'" Bishop said.

"Yep. Just like good ole Tuco," Colbrick said.

"Who's Tuco?" Angela asked.

"From the movie the Good, the Bad, and the Ugly," Bishop said.

Angela blinked. "Is that the '*wa wa wa*' music I always hear in the living room?"

Bishop grinned at her.

"It's a Clint Eastwood," Colbrick said.

"The greatest film ever made," Bishop said.

"No doubt about that," Colbrick said.

Angela rolled her eyes.

Yutu headed up trail, preferring to follow the scent than to listen to the babble. They followed him while whispering to each other.

The mountain peaks loomed closer and the air thinned, forcing them to take harder, more frequent breaths. This was particularly true for Angela and Bishop who were flatlanders, living full-time at a whopping seven hundred feet in Chicago. On this hike, they'd be traversing to twelve thousand feet. Bishop thought they were lucky to not be displaying the symptoms of altitude sickness.

The slabs and boulders of metamorphic schist bloated into steroidal proportions, and some of them resembled eerie, behemoth fossils. The air chilled, and Bishop thought he could see his breath even though it was sunny and the middle of the afternoon. And why was it sunny? Nothing bad ever happens when it's sunny. Right? Yet here they were, the valley crushed by invaders from who knows where, and if one were not cursed with this information, one would think it a perfect, bluebird day in the Apex Mountains.

Yutu paused, lifted his snout into the air, and twitched it.

"He's got a new scent," Colbrick said, raising his sawed-off.

Angela and Bishop took cover behind a slab and peered at the sky. Bishop noticed the scent too—an all too familiar one. Gasoline.

"You folks smell that?" Colbrick asked.

"You bet," Bishop said. "Gasoline, maybe some leaked oil too." It reminded Bishop of when he used to work with his father on the family car in Chicago. His father had taught him the basics of car maintenance. He'd enjoyed those moments—the smell of motor oil, greasy, marked hands, ball games on the cheap radio dad kept in the garage, the bond they formed.

"There could be other people up here," Colbrick said. "Maybe a few of the outfitters retreated to these parts. Proceed with caution, folks. If there are people here, they must have an awful bad trigger finger by now."

They weaved around the misshapen boulders and slabs, each turn bringing a special flavor of anxiety. The rocks were riddled with cracks and scrapes, and here and there a fossil from the Cretaceous period was etched into the rock, as if screaming for release.

The smell of gasoline grew stronger, and as they rounded a huge, warped slab, they came upon a theater-sized opening surrounded by shale slides. What they gazed upon made no sense at all, at least for a few seconds. Before them lay an alpine junkyard strewn with numerous motorcycle parts, leather jackets, and human remains.

"Dear God Almighty," Colbrick said, holding out his left arm to stop the progress of Angela and Bishop. Yutu sat at Colbrick's feet and stuck his snout in the air, the breeze rustling his fur.

"Unreal," Angela said, grabbing onto Bishop with a bandaged hand.

"You two stay here," Colbrick said, stepping into the shale bowl. "No sense in all of us getting killed."

Bishop watched Colbrick pick through the junk, and Angela peered into the sky, shielding her eyes with her hand.

Colbrick held up a bulky leather jacket and dropped it to the ground. He bent down several times for a closer look, spit a few times, and shook his head on multiple occasions. Then he met them back at the slab.

"What we have here folks is a Harley Davidson group which was picked up, bikes and all, and dropped into this bowl. Angela, do yourself a favor—don't look at the bigger pieces of slab."

"I'm not a kid," Angela said.

"Suit yourself," Colbrick said. "We should stay spread about twenty feet apart. No sense in letting one of those things grab us all at once."

Colbrick had put it nicely. Harley Davidson parts were strewn in every nook from monumental drops. Scattered amongst the bike parts were pieces of clothing and chunks and strips of humans. Thick ropes of intestine, like rolled dough covered in spaghetti sauce trailed off one of the horizontal, jutting slabs. Chrome bike parts half-slathered in blood reflected the sun into their wincing eyes. Ahead, a misshapen pair of leather bike pants lay on the ground with the legs still inside.

The rest of the body was missing.

Strings of tough sinew and flesh glistened from where the body had been sliced in half, and the ground was discolored with blood. The leather pants and legs were twisted in a way which was inconceivable to the human mind, caused by the tremendous fall from the grip of the fliers. Chrome, blood, and chunks of humans were everywhere. The air stank of gasoline, coolant, oil, and the nose-stinging scent of exposed flesh.

"I guess they don't like Harley noise," Bishop said.

"Who does?" Angela asked.

*

They left the last few desperate trees behind, entering the barren world which only the cruel winds and now the creatures called home. Perhaps there were still a few wolverines, maybe a few mountain goats and grizzly bears—the only animals of size that called this barren environment home. Of winged, native life, there might be a few surviving golden eagles and peregrine falcons.

Sweeping patches of snow and ice carpeted the shady crevices and gullies while metamorphic schist rock loomed into the royal blue sky, creating a striking contrast that suggested alien terrain. This portion of the Apex Range raced upwards in sharp, jagged edges. Geologists considered it an old range compared to much of the Rockies, but according to what Bishop had read, this is the opposite of how an old range would appear. Younger ranges were steeper and sharper in appearance. He did, however, remember reading in the Mapleton College library that some geologists were split on the exact age of the range, and the contradictions contained in several rock samples and the overall appearance were a source of controversy. Those days spent in the library seemed so long ago—back when he would read anything he could get his hands on concerning nature, always desperate for a fix while in the sprawl and turmoil of Chicago. He pictured the view from his office and wondered where the peregrine falcons went, and if the towering fortresses of the Magnificent Mile were now empty, the streets filled with a haunting peacefulness they had never known, the gargoyles replaced with real ones in some cruel joke only the cosmos could understand.

As they worked up mountain, the Apex Valley spread out below them. Lush stands of aspen, fir, and lodgepole stretched on as far as they could see. Meadows rich with forbs and grasses punctuated the sea of trees. Bishop thought he saw Big J's meadow, but he couldn't be sure under the sideways sun that dangled at the tip of the peaks, daring to fall and usher darkness upon them.

"We better make camp," Colbrick said. "I ain't hiking around this place blind."

Angela nodded and released her pack, then lowered it to the ground. Yutu paused on the trail and stared ahead, then turned to face them, as if saying *come on, I know it will be dark soon, but I'll lead the way!* Instead, he sneezed and trotted back.

A flat piece of ground on the west side of an enormous boulder made an acceptable location to set camp.

They drank from the water bottles, and their stomachs rumbled. Bishop reached into his pack for the tent.

"No stakes," Angela said. "We pound those in, we're doomed."

"I'll try to push them in with my foot," Bishop said. "If we're not staked in, we could lose it."

"Don't go clanking the poles either," Colbrick said, carefully spreading his poles and stakes on the dusty ground.

The tents went up with ease, for Colbrick and Bishop had seen their fair share over the years. Bishop had always been a tent geek, and Angela teased him on their camping trips for his weird fascination. He couldn't help it. He always saw them as tiny, important forms of portable housing—maybe even the future of housing in a growing world. His father had told him never to go cheap on a tent or sleeping bag. You could on other gear, but never on those. As usual, his father had nailed it. The tents they'd just erected were of high quality and this gave him a sense of confidence in regards to their mission. They would need gear they could rely on—a shelter from howling winds, freezing temperatures, and even the sun which threatened dehydration in the afternoons.

With the last stake in the stubborn ground, the sun—as if waiting for them—dipped behind Kilbrix Peak. The air cooled. The fading light ushered in a blast of wind, threatening to blow their tent sacks off the mountain. Yutu chased after the tumbling, colorful sacks.

"Put the sacks in the tent," Colbrick said. "The wind can't get 'em that way."

A single burner camp stove boiled plain pasta which they devoured like cavemen, the blue flame hissing and glowing as they chewed. Colbrick reached into his pack and tossed Yutu several milk bones, and rather than running off, Yutu joined them during their meal, crunching away like a maniac.

"Jesus, Yutu," Angela said. "You might alert the fliers with that chomping."

Bishop laughed.

"That's a damned good dog," Colbrick said, his mouth full of pasta.

Bishop's mind retreated to that moldy, hot hallway, and how Yutu's barks shattered his soul, and how he had to push through that smoke— not only because he wanted to save the dog, but because an unexplainable feeling compelled him to do so. The entire sequence— from entry to exit—had felt like slow motion, and he'd played everything perfectly. It was Yutu's desperate barks that drew their attention on Main Street, and it is now Yutu's sense of smell which may lead them to the source.

Too many coincidences.

He was never a big believer in destiny, or in preordained existence, but damn, sometimes he wondered. And the dream with his father at Big J, how do you deny that? Or his words?

The first stars appeared over the horizon, setting upon the darkness with a subtle, pristine beauty across the eerie void. Yutu gazed upon the stars and tilted his head in awe. He whimpered, and the stars blinked down to him in some form of communication no man could understand, for only the truly wild and pure of soul can communicate with the stars.

"You know animals, they ain't as dumb as people think," Colbrick said, ever watchful.

"Of course," Angela said. "The problem with what we think we know about them is that we've never *been* them. Until we experience that, all of our supposed understanding about their consciousness is speculation."

Bishop patted Yutu on the head, and Yutu looked at him with grateful, star-reflecting eyes. Venus was in there too.

"I use to watch peregrine falcons out my office window," Bishop said, studying the galaxy. "After several weeks of observing them, I realized that maybe I wasn't the superior species. There I was, walled into a self-made prison, while these supposedly dumb birds dove and swooped about me, free as can be."

Colbrick nodded. "You were the trapped one, slick. You were an animal in a zoo to them."

"I don't know," Angela said, forking the last of her well-earned pasta. "Did we really build a prison for ourselves? While I do agree the nine to five rut is a trap of sorts, I don't think our structures were."

Bishop watched her eat, pained by her bandaged hands and black eye. He brushed her hair out of her eyes. "You doing OK, sweetheart?"

"As good as I can be," she said, frowning.

He reached over and hugged her.

Colbrick turned away and moved towards the eastern rim.

Far below them, something shimmered in bright oranges and reds.

"God damn," Colbrick said, spitting into the night. "I think one of the road dams is on fire."

Bishop, Angela, and Yutu met Colbrick on the rim.

To the east, out past Big J, huge, silent flames licked the sky where Highway 18 cut through the sea of green.

"I hope that doesn't spread," Angela said. "I want these things gone, but wiping out the valley isn't the way to do it."

Yutu growled as he watched the flames.

"Even if by some miracle we stop this signal, how are we going to get rid of the ones already here?" Bishop asked. "It's impossible."

"Yup," Colbrick said. "Let's worry about that for another day, partner."

"I want them gone," Bishop said, kicking the ground with a swollen foot. Pain shot up his leg, but he didn't care, not one bit.

"Well, folks, I've enjoyed today's competition for the Boy Scout Doom patch, but I'm beat," Colbrick said. "I'd put out the fire but since we don't have one, I won't."

"Are you a fire hawk?" Angela asked him.

"What's that?" Colbrick asked.

"One of those people at a campground who have huge fires day and night."

"Nope. I just need a fire to keep me warm, not to play with."

"Glad to hear that," Angela said. "Those people get on my nerves."

Colbrick chuckled and crawled into his tent, then zippers and a light cough in the empty night.

*

An ice-cold wind tumbled down the dim peaks while Bishop huddled with Angela in the glow of millions of stars.

"All the lights," she said, looking down at the valley. "They're gone."

Bishop put his hand under her chin and gently tilted her gaze to the sky.

"They've always been on," he said.

She smiled and her heart warmed. He always had a knack for saying the right things when it counted. Heck, that was how he seduced her to begin with. His charm had receded a bit over the years as time sometimes rubs off the shine, but she was glad to see it emerge once more. It was still there, deep inside him, just like there were still a few native animals in the Apex Mountains. And as long as something was left, it could be built upon. That much she knew.

"Who needs those fake lights when we have these," Bishop said, gesturing his hand out before them.

Angela rested her head on Bishop's chest.

"What are the chances we make it?" she asked, more for comfort than for an honest answer.

Bishop paused. "Our chances are as good as anyone's," he said, taking her hand. "With Yutu and Colbrick, we're a lethal, unstoppable squad."

Angela smiled. "It's just us up in these mountains, isn't it? The valley...it's in our hands."

"I don't think we can expect an army to come up here and save us," Bishop said. Then he lowered his voice and gave it a crusty inflection. "Shit don't work like that, slick."

Angela put a hand to her mouth and busted with laughter. "Shhh...you're going to wake him up."

"I heard that," Colbrick said from his tent. "You should look into doing some stand-up."

"Goodnight, Colbrick," Angela said. "Get some rest."

"Yeah I guess. 'night."

Yutu laid his muzzle upon Angela's right leg and glanced up at her with his soft eyes. She patted him on the head and scratched his scruff, and Yutu thumped his tail.

"You're such a good boy," she said in baby talk. "You don't deserve any of this mess. I'm so glad we found you."

"Here, here," Bishop said, framed by glittering eternity and the atrophic woods below.

The three of them sat there, making contact with each other in one way or another, silhouetted on the mountain in front of the universe. To the west, a shooting star streaked across the brilliance.

Angela made a wish. She kept it to herself.

There was still hope.

IDEA MAN

Pvt. Lance Berkman was getting sick of the fuckers—sick of their scurrying and building, sick of how they put his buddies in the infirmary. The hospitalization of his good friend, Robertson, was the tipping point. Sure, they'd approached Barrier 1 when they weren't supposed to and that had triggered the attack, but who gives a shit? They should've shot the things to begin with and not bothered studying them. All the creatures wanted to do was build and eat, and any available human seemed to be the preferred meat.

Berkman's platoon had strategic placement four hundred yards from Barrier 1. Their job was to maintain the status quo and escort civilian scientists to retrieve samples when applicable. These civilians studied Barrier 1 and its inhabitants with a range of expensive monitoring gear such as 800 millimeter Canon image-stabilized telephoto lenses with HD video-enabled camera bodies, thermal imaging scopes, and night vision optics. Of course, most of the time they couldn't see the Stunners and their monkey pals unless the wind shifted. Something in the barriers created haze, and Berkman had overheard one of the civilians telling another that it might be caused by excretions from the Stunners, but couldn't be sure. They did know that the Stunners kept their disgusting babies in the tangle of trees and vegetation, along with the babies of their monkey pals. Anyone who approached these nesting areas in daylight was immediately attacked by the Stunners, and the monkeys, too, if they were in range.

Eight klicks to the north of Barrier 1 was the second platoon, and they were responsible for making sure no civilians approached Barrier 1. Two point five klicks to the north of Barrier 1 was another platoon.

Pvt. Berkman spit. The time for waiting was over. Yesterday afternoon, the Stunners had incapacitated Robertson and then swarmed on him, taking out a chunk of his abdomen. The dual, sandbagged M240's on either embankment had saved him. But that wasn't enough, at least not for Berkman. He wanted Barrier 1 gone. It had to be gone, for Robertson was unconscious with tubes sticking out of him and fed by IV. Robertson was a smart guy. He'd joined the Army to help pay for college, as had Berkman. They were going to both major in business and start an online recreational equipment store. Robertson was the numbers man. Berkman was the idea man. He always had that role, it seemed.

At dark, Pvt. Berkman removed the crucifix necklace from under his shirt and kissed it. Earlier in the day, he'd stashed a gasoline can on the eastern side of the road, back in the tree line. He'd also observed a game trail that must've been used by deer that ran parallel along the road to the eastern side of Barrier 1. He'd informed Olson and Louris, the platoon's M240 operators of his plan, and they agreed to look the other way. Had he not gained permission, there's no way he'd pull this off. A few snapping twigs inside the tree line, and they'd have lit him up, or at least spotlighted him.

Berkman hoisted his M16A2 rifle, hunched over, and trotted into the woods. In a few steps, the forest swallowed him. Sure he was clear of outpost sightlines, he approached the downed tree where he'd hidden the can of fuel. Still there. Berkman grabbed the can and followed the trail east, the stars bright above him, offering just enough light to reveal obstacles in his path. After a hundred yards, he entered the Devastation Zone, the area where the Stunners had cleared huge portions of forest for the construction of Barrier 1. Stumps and forest litter surrounded him. Here and there a few trees remained, unsought by the Stunners for whatever reason. Each tree in the darkness was like a human figure, and he swore he saw his mother in one, and his sister in another, the tree limbs like their arms reaching out to him. Berkman's heart raced. Sure this was dangerous, but he had a good idea he'd figured these things out by now. They weren't as active at night, like humans. He'd also heard the civilians mentioning no sign of other creatures in Quadrant Five, meaning the Stunners and their monkey friends were the only things here. That increased his odds. The monkeys didn't show up all that often. When they did, it was to help the Stunners carry sticks and trees to Barrier 1, and in one instance, to assist them in an attack.

Two hundred yards from Barrier 1 now.

Berkman paused and kissed the crucifix again. He picked up speed, ghosting past the few remaining spruce and aspen, lone sentinels under the Milky Way. Soon, the jagged outline of Barrier 1 appeared in the sky before him, blocking out the bottom third of the southern horizon. Berkman paused every twenty yards and listened. He thought he heard chittering from one of the baby things coming from Barrier 1, but that was OK as long as it wasn't coming up the game trail he was on. As Berkman ran, the fuel sloshed in the can. He tried to keep it as quiet as possible.

Twenty yards now from Barrier 1.

Ten.

The Stunner babies chittered to the west, deep in the nooks and crannies of Barrier 1.

At last, he stood at its base, where it sloped to the east into what was left of the forest like a lumbering dinosaur.

"For you, Robertson," he whispered to the structure. Berkman put his rifle down and popped the lid on the can, making a loud *thock!*

Something rustled to his west.

Berkman climbed Barrier 1 and emptied the can as he went. His boot caught in a snag and he jerked it out, sending a stick to the ground.

A series of dull cries emitted from the west, some of the cries deadened by woody debris. They'd been alerted to his presence.

Fuck, he thought.

Berkman thought of Robertson and of his own mother and father, but most of all his sister, how they'd learned the monkey bars together, how she'd given him money for college after she'd married a doctor. He wanted to see her again so bad, tell her thanks for all she'd done. He knew he would. He was the *idea man*, and he'd come up with a plan out of this mess, too.

With the can emptied, Berkman set it down carefully in a cradle of branches so it wouldn't make noise. Then Berkman climbed down and reached into his pocket and took out the box of Strike Tip Matches he and the boys used for their smokes and cigars. Lighters were not cool enough, not when *The Man with No Name* in the Spaghetti Westerns used matches for his smokes. He held the match in his hand and listened. The cries stopped. Maybe the things went back to sleep, or whatever they did at night.

Berkman lit the match, and the orange flame revealed a dozen eyeless faces, all of them encircling him in the penumbra. The Stunners gnawed at the air and clenched and unclenched the claws on their six limbs.

"Shit," Berkman said.

The left side of his mouth twitched up to his cheek, and his left eyeball tried to pull to his forehead. He collapsed to the ground and dropped the match. Flames purred along the fuel route and climbed Barrier 1. The Stunners retreated into the darkness, away from the flames. Berkman rose to his feet, then realized his right pant leg was on fire. Before he could swat it out, one of the Stunners returned and shocked him with the frequencies. Then another Stunner came back. And another. They blasted him, and he convulsed like a beached dolphin as the flames seared his legs. A moment later, the convulsing stopped, and the Stunners retreated into the darkness as their eyes brightened with flame. Berkman staggered to his feet and swatted at his pants while running west along the front of Barrier 1. As he ran, the flames grew, and soon they gravitated to his shirt. Berkman screamed, hoping his platoon would hear him.

The flames reached his hair, causing excruciating scalp pain. Flames dried out his right eye, and then a harsh pop as he lost vision there. He slumped in the fog in front of Barrier 1 as spotlights from his platoon penetrated the haze. He screamed again.

On his knees and swatting at his head, Berkman noticed several of the Stunner babies approaching him as the bigger ones stayed behind and watched. The baby Stunners squealed and aimed their bulbous heads at him, and he felt the pinprick shocks of their weak sonic blasts.

Squeaaaaaaal!

One of the baby stunners chewed at his burnt and smoking boot. In one last surge, Berkman got to his feet and dove into a burrow. The last thing he saw in the wooded rookery was a horde of vicious baby Stunners squealing and crying at him, and then their mouths gnawing at his loosening skin.

Louris and Olson aimed their M240's across Barrier 1 as the spotlights lit it up. A flash of orange came from the eastern portion of the Devastation Zone.

"Fire!" Olson shouted. "It's on fire!"

Numerous blazing objects emerged from the haze, and then many more.

"What the hell," Louris said, reaching for his radio.

He wanted to get the message to his platoon commander, but the burning Stunners were too close. The M240's roared across the night, muzzle flash illuminating the six-limbed monstrosities within meters of their sandbag bunkers. From behind the burning freaks came unburned animals, kinds Olson had never seen before. One of them was the size of a God damned elephant, and behind it came what he could only describe as floating snakes. These were a hundred yards away. He kept his finger on the trigger, relishing each instance of a bullet finding its mark. Then Olson heard four other M240's. *Impossible*, he thought. There were just two here. Before he could ponder the source, a gush of air beat upon him and he was taken into the air. He looked down and saw Louris convulsing on his machine gun as a horde of Stunners moved in on him. As Olson was carried into the night sky, he saw rippling flames consuming the eastern portion of Barrier 1. Furious blasts from the M240's came from somewhere above him, interrupted by the beat of impossible wings.

NO QUARTER

The early morning storm rained down from the peaks like a furious God. Gust after gust slammed into them as snake-tongued lightning slithered across the sky. Fat, cold drops of rain battered their tents—the first rain they'd seen since the invasion.

"Stay in the tents!" Colbrick shouted from his, the words almost like a song. "You're the only thing keeping them from flying away!"

Yutu paced in Angela and Bishop's two-man tent, a growl preceding each turn.

"It's OK, boy," Angela said, petting him.

"The scent," Bishop said. "The storm could scrub it clean."

Yutu clawed at the tent zipper.

"No, boy," Angela said. "You'll blow away out there."

"I think he's worried about the scent," Bishop said.

"We can't let him out," Angela said. "We'll lose him."

"Come on, Yutu,'" Bishop said, grabbing at his scruff.

Yutu gave in and calmed, but continued staring at the tent flap and tilting his head, waiting for someone to open the damn thing so he could get that scent again—the big, red, flashing trail which only he could see. Yutu turned to Bishop, pleading, whimpering.

The frightening gusts whipped into dangerous gusts, hammering the tents without mercy. Bishop thought he heard unusual utterances from certain howls, like prophetic old men who'd been disturbed in their sleep speaking in raspy tones. In one particular gust, Bishop thought he heard his name. His nerves tightened, and he looked to Angela for comfort. That was a mistake.

"Bring it on," Angela said, her teeth clenched. She glanced at Bishop, then at Yutu's manic eyes and the relentless, flapping tent. She was tired of waiting, tired of detours and these vile creatures. "Is that all you got, cruel bitch?" she shouted back at the gusts, a nasty jab of wind shaking the tent as she spoke. "Is that it?" she asked, punching the tent wall. "That all you got? You already fucked us over, and now you want to kill us with a storm? Well, I have news for you, you aren't shit."

Bishop backed away, mouth open.

Her nostrils flared, and her eyes turned glassy like a spooky doll.

Another blast of wind shellacked the left side of the tent.

"That's it?" she asked, almost growling.

Even Yutu looked on with bewilderment, taking a few steps back.

"You call yourself mother nature? You're nothing but a two-bit whore!"

Another blast of wind rattled the tent. Streaks of lightning illuminated the blue fabric and were followed by unusually long rolls of thunder, as if the earth was cleansing itself, retching to get out poison.

"You can't wash us away!" Angela said.

Something was trying to scrub them off the mountain, like a camper cleaning the last sticky parts of a pan.

"We're not done here yet! Do you hear me?" Angela shouted, turning to Bishop with watery, bloodshot eyes.

Bishop went to grab her, but pulled his hand back. Sometimes people needed to vent. Beats hitting the bottle every night.

Angela collapsed into a corner of the tent and punched the stony ground with her bony fists. "I'm so sick of this," she said.

"It's OK," Bishop said, speaking in a soothing tone but still careful not to touch her. "Maybe this was all a mistake. Maybe this wasn't supposed to happen."

"Is anything supposed to happen? You never believed in that."

The tent walls flexed, creating their own turbulence. The western wall was the worst, playing principle victim to the storm's violence.

"I don't know what to think anymore," he said. "After that dream with my father, my perspective has been thrown into chaos."

"What happened in that room, Bishop?"

"That room—"

An earsplitting barrage of thunder shook the mountain, and the rocks they were camped upon prickled with a discombobulating electrical sensation.

"—is calling to me," Bishop said. "The first day there, I thought I saw my father standing behind me in the sink mirror. The room pulled at me, sort of beckoning me to go back there, like I was supposed to. And when I finally went back into the room and fell asleep, he spoke to me in my dream."

Angela blinked and said nothing. She knew Bishop was no tale-teller. Perhaps, when he would return from a fishing trip to Apex country, he would exaggerate the size of a trout. She'd learned to knock it down by about two inches—a rule that applied to other men things, too.

"He told me we were meant to do this, and that in his own bizarre way, he helped us."

Yutu rested his muzzle on Angela's lap.

"And he told me the source of the creatures was in these mountains," Bishop said.

A surge of wind rattled the tent, and the walls became concave and convex in a fast, repetitive pattern. Unsettling tones swirled in the gusts, as if the groaning and mumbling of ancient and all-knowing sentinels. Angela's arms and backside lit afire with the actual sensation of electricity underneath them, and the electricity of fear.

"What gets me about that encounter was not seeing my father in my dream as if he were real," Bishop said. "But this feeling that saving the valley would save him as well. I know he's dead, but he told me that he lives on here. I guess he meant his spirit lives here."

"And then?"

"He was gone."

"And then I showed up."

"Yes."

"I wish I could see my mother."

"I'm sorry," Bishop said.

"I wonder if she knows your father, wherever he came from."

"Maybe."

"And my father, Bishop. We weren't close, but I hope these things don't spread and hurt him."

"I bet he's fine," Bishop said.

"I hope," she said. "We saw the video of the small fliers in North Dakota. I don't see why the large ones couldn't go farther."

"Only guesses," he said. "Your father's fine, and so is my mother. Chicago is a long way away."

"Maybe," Angela said. She put her hand on the billowing tent wall and gently slid her fingertips down the shifting material.

Yutu whimpered. Although he could not understand language, he understood tone and inflection.

"You folks doing alright?" Colbrick asked from his tent.

"We're fine," Bishop said, taking Angela's bandaged hand in his and squeezing.

"How's your tent holding up?" Colbrick asked.

"Just fine," Bishop said. "These aren't dime-store specials."

"Yup."

Lightning slithered across the sky, illuminating the tent walls with a surreal glow.

The wind. It sounded like the peaks were shooting tornados from their caves, one after the other. The tent walls vibrated with an intensity Angela had never seen despite years of camping with Bishop. She went to speak, and then shut her mouth. There was no need to add to the anxiety by asking Bishop how bad it was. She watched him, and he went to speak, but thought better of it himself.

Yutu sat in the corner and placed his muzzle upon his paws, his soft eyes gazing around the tent. Every few seconds, he let escape a soft growl. *Not okay, not okay.*

*

"What time is it?" Angela asked.

Bishop checked his watch. "One p.m."

The winds receded, as if the storm needed to wind down rather than end abruptly, a testament to its overwhelming and unusual power.

"This son of a bitch is closing shop," Colbrick muttered from his tent.

A sense of relief overcame all of them, even forcing Angela to smile. She unzipped the tent flap and observed the cool rain, how it glistened in the alpine air like diamonds. Everything smelled of ozone, the terrain lush with moisture.

Yutu darted out of the tent and paced the campsite, searching for the scent. Colbrick, Bishop, and Angela watched the precocious dog.

"You can do it, boy!" Angela said.

Yutu ran back to her and tilted his head, then ran away once more with his nose held high in the air. He moved to the north, paused, and then moved north again—this time a few yards. He shook his head and let out a yip, then trotted up the trail along the shale and boulders.

"That dog's got a fine nose," Colbrick said.

"We were lucky to find him," Angela said.

"And he was even luckier to find us," Bishop said.

Angela went to laugh, and then stopped herself when she pictured the desperate dog barking behind the window of the burning apartment. "Very lucky indeed," she said instead.

*

"Guys, I think I agree with you about the killing," Angela said, her breath heavy from the hiking.

"What about the killing?" Colbrick asked.

"What that Tuco guy said. I go kill them all and be right back!"

Colbrick and Bishop erupted in laughter.

189

"You got that right, Miss," Colbrick said, grinning from ear to ear.

Bishop put his hand in Angela's for the brief moment he could. The rugged terrain forced them to use both hands along the pass, and Bishop winced when he watched Angela grip the jagged rocks with the flappy bandages.

"How are your hands?" Bishop asked.

"They're getting better," she said, putting her .357 down and holding her hands out, palms up. "The bandages may look stupid but they help prevent blisters. I guess I've gotten used to them."

"Why don't we rewrap those suckers?" Bishop asked.

"No need. Save whatever we have for someone who really needs it. And Bishop—I get the horrible feeling that someone is going to need it soon."

Bishop said nothing.

"Did you know when I was little my mother told me deja vu ran in our family?" Angela said. "*I* never believed it, but every once in a while, a specific scene in my life felt so dang familiar, like I had been in that exact scene before or dreamt it. And guess what? That awful storm—I'd seen that exact situation before, down to the color of the tent, the people I was with, the specific noises and even the color of Yutu's fur. Now, when I thought of that or dreamt it many years ago, I didn't know the who's and why's. All I knew was the single image, frozen like a vivid painting."

Bishop nodded. He'd never been a psychic kind of person, but recent events and the startling dream with his father were spinning that viewpoint on its ass. Funny how experience had a way of setting you straight.

The air had taken on an angelic, diffused quality, lighting each mark and cut in the rocks with acute detail. Yutu scrambled up the vibrant rocks ahead of them, and they noticed his movement becoming more difficult. Sometimes, he had to leap from rock to rock, and none of this terrain must have felt good on his paws. This was not territory meant for dogs, for not even the wolves went this high in the Apex Range.

Bishop wondered what had become of the magnificent Kilmeister wolf pack which called these mountains home. They were gone with everything else save for the lone grizzly bear at Big J and a few birds.

The Apex Mountains were a cruel, twisted sort. From the valley, they induced a warming flood of wonder. But when upon their rugged, omnipresent peaks, they mocked mortality. Bishop glanced up an imposing cliff and noticed something that sent his heart into his throat. Halfway up the cliff on an unreachable ledge rested a circular intertwining of branches and other woody debris. And for a moment,

Bishop thought he saw a slight movement inside the bulging nest. He squinted in the half-sun, and a tiny, ruffled head poked above the nest. The creature wailed, its powerful call echoing off the cliff sides of the isolated cirque.

A golden eagle fledgling.

Bishop pointed to the nest, and Angela and Colbrick let out whoops of joy upon seeing the clumsy fledgling.

"Oh my gosh," Angela said. "Where's momma?"

"She has to be around," Bishop said, putting an arm around her.

Colbrick spit and held out his hand towards the fledgling, giving it a thumbs-up. "You can bet your teeth momma's around," Colbrick said. "This eaglet couldn't survive a couple days without her."

"I hope so," Angela said.

An answer came in the form of a gliding shadow that rippled across the rocks.

This time, it was a native.

The great bird did not cry.

They turned their heads to follow the dark shape, and when the sun lit upon its brown and golden feathers, they let out an inspired sigh. The eagle's shiny, hooked beak reflected the vitality in the air, and its talons gripped something that made their jaws drop. Clutched and impaled on the mother eagle's talons, was a winged creature with bright, green eyes. The faint, looped mimicry of an eagle cry emitted from its puffy midsection.

The eagle studied them with keen eyes and pulled higher so she could loft down upon the nest. Her black talons dug into the small flier, and green ooze dripped from its bloated midsection onto the shale with a sickening plop. The looping mimicry ceased, and the green eyes faded.

The great bird lofted into the nest, laid the meaty morsel in front of the fledgling, then nudged the meat with her beak.

"Well I'll be," Colbrick said, shaking his head. "She figured out how to hunt the fliers."

"The small ones at least," Angela said. "I'd prefer her to kill the big ones."

"And I'd prefer to snap my fingers and have all these bastards gone," Colbrick said. "But shit don't work like that. Any time one of these bastards dies, it's a victory."

Angela gazed up at the nest and nodded. "You're right."

"Did you guys notice the looping cry?" Bishop asked.

"Yup."

"I wonder if she figured out how to lay a trap," Bishop said. "Maybe she just perched in a dark corner, cried out a few times and waited for them to come."

"I doubt it," Colbrick said. "Golden's ambush from above their prey. I'm guessin' this golden soared above the fliers and picked this small one off the back of the carrier at great velocity. Maybe she cried as she dove, and the small flier tried to mimic her before she caught hold. There might be a squadron of fliers out there who are mimicking this golden right now, unaware of what happened to this small one."

"Plausible," Angela said, staring up at the nest as the fledgling poked at and then tore into the bloated flier. "This is all great, but it raises more questions. Like...how many golden eagles does the U.S. have?"

"Not many," Colbrick said.

"What about bald eagles?" Angela asked.

"I know what you're getting at, but no good," Colbrick said. "Bald's are scavengers. A lot different from goldens. Goldens live in remote, western areas. Their numbers dropped because of poaching and pesticides, but they hung on pretty good in the Rockies and in the arid lands between here and the Pacific."

Bishop nodded. As an avid wildlife enthusiast, he knew all of this, but didn't want to irk Colbrick. Most locals didn't care for tourists to one-up them.

"It could be that the goldens have learned to prey on the small fliers. So could red-tails," Bishop said.

"Red-tails?" Angela asked. "As in the hawk?"

"Yes," Bishop said. "Very populous across the U.S. You've seen them."

"Red-tails aren't nearly the size of goldens," Colbrick said.

"True," Bishop said.

"They still might take a small flier, though, but I doubt anything bigger," Colbrick said. "Now the golden—they're known to take young deer and mountain goats, maybe even a bear cub—"

"Which means they could take out other new arrivals," Angela said.

"Yup."

High above them, the mother golden eagle cried out as she looked upon her fledgling. The mother angled her massive head, opened her wings and cried again while hopping in place.

"What's she doing?" Angela asked.

"She's not happy," Bishop said.

A puzzling scraping and clacking came from down mountain.

"Dear God, look below us," Colbrick said.

They did, and whatever triumph they'd felt from the golden faded to dismay as they witnessed a legion of secapods crawling and clicking a hundred yards below. The ground seethed with glistening secapods, going as far back to the tree line in some spots, like an undulating carpet of maggots seizing the countryside.

"Move," Bishop said. "Move now."

"Where's Yutu?" Angela asked, panicking. "Yutu?"

Yutu trotted to Angela from his wide advantage on the trail.

"Stay by my side, OK, boy?" she said.

They scrambled up the jumble, cutting their hands and ankles. "Something tipped them off," Angela said. "Did the leaf squeal?"

"Shit, I forgot to feed it,'" Colbrick said, huffing as he looked for a foothold. He stopped, opened the pack, took out the jar, and threw it.

"Bishop, the eagles," Angela said, pointing to the nest.

"They'll be fine," Bishop said. "The secapods have no way of getting to them."

The swelling carpet of secapods crept up the mountain, the clicking and garbling resonating to the survivors in random waves. Baby secapods struggled to keep up with the adults, disappearing and reappearing in large crevices that their parents groped over. Some of the babies rode the flat midsections like tourists on a bus. Many of the adult secapods had the flashing tags, and they all pulsed in unison. Bishop counted ninety-four beats per minute.

The talus and bus-sized boulders made for slow passage. When they reached a massive rock face with a wide ledge, they realized they could go no further, and would have to retrace their steps a hundred yards in order to find a workable route. Yutu went to make his way back down the mountain, and Angela grabbed him by the scruff and yanked him back.

"Uh-uh," she said. "You're not going near those secapods. See these bandages?"

Yutu panted and paced, anxious to continue on the scent trail.

Below them, the mass of secapods crept closer, their sandy grunting echoing in the stillness.

The golden eagle shrieked.

"Well, this is it, folks," Colbrick said, spitting and taking off his pack, an unsavory gleam in his eyes. "We don't have enough bullets for this, not even close." He carefully grasped the sticks of dynamite. "Four for the secapods and four for us."

"Stop it," Angela said.

The carpet of secapods poked and prodded their way up the jumble, some of the disgusting things falling into the cracks between boulders and getting impaled by their sibling's legs. Their bulbous eyes rotated gleefully, and rivulets of milky liquid dripped from their moist underbellies.

Angela held out her .357 and clenched her teeth. Yutu looked below while pacing the ledge. Bishop watched the golden eagle, for something was in the air, an intangible quality he detected which the others had not. It wasn't all that different from the sensation he got while watching the diving peregrine falcons from his office window.

The giant golden hopped in place and spread its wings, releasing a chilling cry that pierced louder than before. The secapods groped closer. Bishop could hit them with a rock if he tried. The baby secapods squealed and grew frenetic as they closed in.

Colbrick intertwined the dynamite wicks and held a match between thumb and forefinger.

Angela grabbed Bishop's hand.

"I love you. You know that, right?" she asked, her voice cracking.

"I love you too, more than anything," he said, meeting her eyes.

The eagle cried again, louder.

The secapod clacking grew maddening as they groped to within thirty yards. Their single eyes rotated atop their flounder midsections as they searched for the best kill approach.

Bishop squeezed Angela's hand.

Manic whooshing came from the cliffs.

Dark, blurry projectiles screamed down from the highest crags, plumage flattened by speed, their keen, vengeful eyes riveted to the secapods. The feathered missiles let out the echoing cry of the nesting golden eagle.

Down they came, zipping through the air like organic missiles, zinging into the cirque, feathers rippling from the velocity.

The cries, the cries.

The vengeful cries.

Bishop looked up through a watery prism of tears as the air force of golden eagles shone down from the heavens, talons outstretched and ten-foot wingspans unfurled as they slammed into the glistening secapods, popping the bulbous eyes in fantastical, violent bursts that splattered goo in all directions.

The secapods reached up with their hairy legs and claws, but the goldens were too fast and went for the eyes, their beaks eviscerating the ocular pudding like a fork into sunny-side up eggs. Each puncture of eye triggered a shrill scream from the secapods and accelerated clacking. When the secapods grew too numerous, the eagles retreated to the air and soared over the creatures, their shadows creating uneven light on the glistening backs and eyes. The secapods gazed wearily to the sky, growing quiet, waiting for the next assault. Once the secapods were blinded, the goldens would dig their talons into the flat midsections and stab their beaks down with the force of a hammer swung by a gorilla.

The survivors watched, awestruck by the swarming concoction of feathers, claws, and flesh. The constant beating of wings and breath ushered hot air up the mountain and the scent of raw, exposed flesh—the kind of scent which offends the nostrils in bright, eye-watering flashes. The goldens thrashed the mountainside with the timing and bombast of an orchestra on speed, moving methodically from one secapod to the next, shrieking, flapping, ripping.

Yutu leaped from the dead-end ledge and trotted down towards the fray in an attempt to find a different path to the scent.

"Well, let's get to it," Colbrick said, repacking the dynamite and following Yutu.

Angela and Bishop did the same.

The group moved to within feet of the seething mass, and the spectacle became all the more gruesome. Above the mass of golden eagles soared the magnificent nesting golden, surveying the battlefield like a general. Above her, the fledgling also watched, taking in the battle as an important life lesson.

The group retraced their steps to a fork in the path they'd seen earlier, and chose what had seemed to be the incorrect route before. They scrambled up the jumble, following Yutu and his sensitive nose. When they reached the top of a dominant incline on the new path, Angela and Bishop looked back to the battle. Most of the secapods were dead, and many were maimed beyond repair—some crawling in circles with soup dripping from where an eye used to be and others limping along with missing legs. One lethal, hopping eagle remained, making sure to jab its hooked beak into a nerve core in the maimed survivors, letting out a cry for each secapod killed. Then the eagles beat their majestic wings and rocketed to the cliffs, many carrying secapod parts to feed their young which were hidden away in dark nooks in this last haven for the rare predator birds. Up and up they flew, disappearing into the sky like zigzagging fireworks, their silhouettes swallowed by the hot light of the sun.

All that remained was the first mother golden eagle, and she lofted into the nest with a chunky piece of secapod. She dropped the chunk into the nest and nudged it towards her big-eyed fledgling, which in turn ripped into the meat with a hearty relish. The great bird watched them with weary but keen eyes, for humans had not been kind to them, not at all.

"I don't even know what to say," Angela said.

Bishop shook his head, stunned. "For whatever reason, they helped us."

"Or they were hungry," Colbrick said, gripping his sawed-off.

"Don't you think the timing—?"

"Timing schmiming," Colbrick said. "Just some hungry birds."

"Always have to play devil's advocate, don't you?" Angela asked.

Colbrick smiled. "Gotcha. You're damn right that was something special. They saved our behinds."

Angela smiled.

Bishop looked back to the nest. He couldn't make out much of it thanks to the gleaming sun, but what he did see made him feel almost human again. The great bird fed her fledgling, passing on survival skills to ensure the continuation of the species. Bishop stood straight and strong, then saluted the bird.

Yutu panted and bolted up the trail, anxious to follow the scent.

The new path was better, leading to a narrow and disorienting notch that allowed access to the northern side of Kilbrix Peak. They shimmied through, their packs catching on sharp extrusions. When they crossed the mountain, a clear view to the north opened up to them for the first time.

Wickedly, the Hoodoos rose, the place where Bishop had watched the big fliers travel to from the apartment window on Main Street. There were eight separate peaks, but peaks would be too kind a word. These were twisted and mangled spires, seeming to violate all rules of physics, each one bent and lightning-blasted into a narrow tower of rock, all the while reaching for the sky as if the gnarled hands of some disfigured entity begging for forgiveness.

Colbrick unfolded the map and tapped it with a scarred finger, indicating a sheltered cirque between the eight warped spires.

"There we are," Colbrick said, frowning. "This used to be all ice."

Although the Apex Range was bathed in sunlight, an unexplainable, dense vapor clung to the Hoodoos, like their own private weather. The vapor wafted in-between the twisted peaks, and for a moment, Bishop thought he saw the flash of a blue lightning bolt.

At least two miles of uneven and dangerous saddle separated them from the Hoodoos.

"Jesus," Angela said, grabbing Bishop's hand with her own trembling one. "We have to go down to go up?"

"Yup."

Yutu slowed, analyzing the scene and holding his nose into the fur-ruffling breeze. Yutu's eyes crackled with curiosity and confidence. He did not want to enter the land he saw, but he felt a sense of duty to the people, even though he missed The Man. Yutu was beginning to sense that these people were the New Man and New Woman. He liked that very much, and the thought caused him to wag his tail.

"Funny pooch," Bishop said, bending down to pat Yutu on the head. Yutu looked up with loving eyes.

"There lies our end," Colbrick said, pointing to the Hoodoos.

"Come on," Angela said. "Don't you think we're all thinking that? Any need to vocalize it?"

"No, suppose not."

"Let's do this," Bishop said, following Yutu.

The group headed north down Kilbrix Peak to the rough saddle stretching out before them, and towards the imposing Hoodoos.

Bishop thought he saw another flash of blue light behind the swirling vapor.

There was no turning back. Back there lie monsters. Ahead lie monsters as well, but mixed in there somewhere was a chance—one they had to reach for not unlike the gnarled spires of the Hoodoos.

THE SADDLE

The saddle connecting the mangled southern portion of the range to the uniform northern portion was ravaged with boulders and daunting maze-like sections where an unlucky person could disappear. The group huddled inside one of the stone mazes, peering into a crevice that could easily swallow them into its promise of pain and blackness.

Angela flipped on her headlamp, revealing moist rock walls and intermittent lichen. Water trickled far below.

"There's water down there," she said.

Yutu peered into the crevice and titled his head.

"No way to get it," Colbrick said. "And we're not too far from Hoodoo Creek."

"Not sure I want to drink anything from that area," Bishop said.

"Good point," Angela said. "Please hand me your sleeping bag sack."

Bishop rustled around in his pack and handed the black nylon sack to her, and Angela placed several rocks inside it.

"Colbrick, the rope please?" Angela asked, gesturing with an open palm.

Colbrick unhitched the rope from a hook on his pack and handed it to her. Angela tied the stuff sack drawstring around the rope, placed two rocks inside and lowered the device into the crevice. Bishop and Angela watched the sack sink into the ether while Colbrick remained on guard. A splash came from below, and the rope grew taut. Angela waited until the pressure grew, then pulled the rope up.

"Get your bottles ready," she said.

Yutu circled them. He was thirsty too.

The stuff sack rose from the depths bloated and leaking water. Angela kept it in the air by the rope as Bishop held a cooking pot underneath. Yutu went to his hind legs, almost dancing, and caught the leaking drops in his mouth.

"Ta-da," Angela said, beaming.

"Where'd you learn how to do this?" Bishop asked.

"I thought of it in the tent," she said. "I wanted to leave out pans and bottles during the storm, but there's no way they wouldn't have blown off the mountain. So this was plan B."

"Nice work, miss," Colbrick said.

"Thank you."

Soon, they were enjoying the fresh, cool water. So was Yutu, as he lapped at the bowl Angela set out for him. She went down to pet him, and her headlamp caught a glint in the abyss. She stared into the black. A pair of eyes with triplicate pupils blinked back. She gasped and grabbed Bishop's arm, then pointed at the eyes.

Bishop recognized the eyes quite well, unfortunately. "Time to move on," he said.

"What is it?" Angela asked, trembling.

"Burrowers," Bishop said. "Like the ones in the bunker at Big J."

Colbrick aimed his shotgun and then pulled it back. "I ain't wasting a bullet on those God damned things," he said. "They can't get us here anyway."

The eyes disappeared, and a faint chittering rose up to them.

"Disgusting," Angela said, putting a hand to her stomach.

"We'll just run the water through the filters," Colbrick said. "Up this high, you don't normally need to do that—the filters protect against Giardia, and not many things shit or die in the streams up here."

They collected what water they could from the pans and moved on, leaving the slab maze behind.

The path was a joke, and they followed the punch line, for they had no choice. Yutu traveled as best he could, his nose pointing at the Hoodoos the entire time, using his front legs like arms to pull onto rocks. Things were going as planned. They were making progress.

Then, surprisingly, Yutu stopped.

He curled into a ball next to a protruding slab. Angela gave him a milk bone and some water, but the pooch did not eat or drink.

"He's exhausted," Bishop said, unhooking his pack and laying it on the ground.

"That's four of us," Angela said.

The Hoodoos reared up before them, closer than ever, the scarred spires reaching and twisting through the vapor.

"A mile," Colbrick said.

"That's nothing," Bishop said.

Angela patted Yutu, but he did not wag his tail, his slumber was too deep.

Bishop, Angela, and Colbrick waited for their lovable and trustworthy trail leader. For however long it took.

Clouds passed overhead, taking on shades of pink and red as the sun dipped behind the horizon.

When the vivid sunset reached its peak, Yutu woke, yawning. The pooch rose, ate his milk bone and lapped at the water. He trotted over to Angela and Bishop, placed his muzzle upon their laps, wagged his tail and whimpered great, gushing whimpers of joy and love.

And then Yutu sprinted away from them.

He did not want to, but he had to. This much he understood.

"Yutu, boy, where you going?" Bishop said.

"Yutu, come back!" Angela shouted, her brow furrowing, her face reddening.

Yutu continued to sprint, never looking behind, his fur ruffling in the wind, his ears flopping.

"Bishop, do something!" Angela shouted through tears.

Bishop dropped his pack and ran after the pooch as fast as he could, but Yutu sprinted on, for dogs have much higher endurance and speed than humans. It was pointless.

Bishop fell to his knees amid the crumbling talus and put his hands over his face. "Yutu, come back, buddy!" he said through sobs, rocking on his knees, furious at the world and wondering what had prompted Yutu to run away from them after they had saved his life and cared for him. He thought they were a team, thought they would finish this together.

As Angela and Bishop cried, Colbrick let loose a masterful dog whistle, and the intentions of Yutu became clear: the pooch was not abandoning them. Yutu barked and snarled, unleashing a tone and harshness that rivaled his desperate vocalizations at the burning apartment, each bark reverberating off the rugged saddle and up towards the Hoodoos.

Bishop watched helplessly, the talus cutting into his knees. His nerves were inundated with dread, and when he looked to the Hoodoos, he knew that whatever was squatted in the cirque would hear those desperate barks.

Yutu continued to sprint away from them, heading down the saddle to the valley and forest. The brave Yutu never let up, barking until his vocal chords strained. Bishop felt his heart rip out of his chest and all the sadness of the world fill the empty space. He watched the beloved dog he rescued from certain death run off into what could only be a torturous end in one final act of courage. Bishop wept from sadness, but also because he was grateful and proud. Yutu was attracting the fliers so the group could get to the seed mother. This will be his legacy.

A hero.

Bishop ran back to Angela and Colbrick, stumbling over the shale.

"Seek shelter now!" he said, ushering them behind the vertical slab where Yutu had slept earlier.

Angela and Colbrick dropped their packs in case they needed to run and hunkered behind the slab. Bishop peeked around the slab at the Hoodoos and gripped his shotgun. Billowing puffs separated from the spire-impaled vapor, and his jaw dropped when the puffs roiled and were consumed by a nauseating green. Vapor curled off enormous wings and uncurled. A deadly beak framed by swirling mist opened wide, releasing a call that caused healthy men to plead for deafness. The massive wings flapped, and the last of the Hoodoo vapor streamed off the tips, passing over dozens of green-eyed devils on the giant flier's back like fiendish headlights upon a foggy road. The giant flier's eyes scanned the saddle, searching for the barking source. Its shadow ghosted over the boulders and slabs like a jetliner too close to a city.

Yutu continued barking, his voice growing hoarse.

The giant flier maneuvered to the sound, pounding the air, gawking with its plate-sized eyes, turning in a way it shouldn't be able to turn. After correcting course, it zeroed in on poor Yutu who was having trouble scrambling down the saddle to the forestland.

Bishop sat, clenching rocks and sand in his fists. There was nothing he could do, nothing that anyone could do. If he fired a shot, the fliers would focus on them, and they were as good as dead. Besides, firing a shot wouldn't have the slightest effect on such a large creature. Pointless. But Yutu's likely death needn't be. They needed to take full advantage.

"Let's go," Bishop said, fighting off tears. "Yutu's death will not be in vain."

Angela hugged him and sobbed against his chest. Bishop pried her off, and they shimmied into their packs, then moved towards the Hoodoos as fast as the terrain would allow.

They could still hear barking as they hiked, and Bishop couldn't help but glance towards the east, and in the dimming light, he made out a faint, white figure sprinting into the valley. Fifty feet behind the pooch was a seething cloud of small fliers, their green eyes like fireflies, the looped mimicry of Yutu's barks bouncing off the talus. The giant flier thundered down the slope behind them, its beak held open.

Then at once, the real barking stopped, and Yutu disappeared.

Only the looped mimicry and glowing eyes remained.

Darkness swallowed the land and their hearts.

"Goodbye my friend," Bishop said. "Goodbye."

*

Angela and Bishop held hands as they worked along the saddle. With the sun gone, the Hoodoos emitted an unsettling, blue luminance that cast eerily across the terrain, inferring alien landscape. With each strengthening shade of peripheral darkness, the light between the gnarled spires intensified, each droplet of vapor holding luminance. The air near the spires was humid, like back home in Chicago. The temperature also increased, and as the vapor engulfed them, vague noises floated down from the Hoodoo cirque.

"This is it," Colbrick said, spitting. "We need to find a low point in-between the spires, drop down and kill this bastard." Colbrick looked to the ground and grew quiet.

A rivulet of magenta fluid seeped into a fissure.

"Hold up a second, folks," he said, holding out his hand.

Colbrick worked his way downslope for twenty yards and then waved to Angela and Bishop, who shuffled to him.

"What is it?" Bishop asked.

"Looks like a graveyard."

Scattered bones of numerous creatures littered the rocks. Dead tags were swept into the crevasses. One skeleton looked like a six-limbed fish, but it had unusual fins, like the Coelacanth fish of the Colcomo Islands in the Indian Ocean. Its mouth was uneven, with an elongated lower jaw beset by sharp teeth. Bishop couldn't take his eyes off it. *If that had gotten into the rivers and streams...*

They heard whooshing as something rained down on them. Small creatures leaped from hiding places, bounced around, caught whatever it was with sticky tongues, and then disappeared.

"What was that?" Bishop asked.

Colbrick picked up one of the small objects and examined it.

"Looks to me like a seed," he said. "Harsh terrain for plants up here."

The uneaten seeds lay on the barren soil, and Bishop kicked at them. "Good, we don't want any alien plants either. But, we must be getting closer."

Colbrick moved one slow step at a time ahead of them and then put his hand up again. "We got something else," he said, bending towards the ground for a closer look.

"Now what?" Bishop asked, taking Angela's hand and moving towards Colbrick.

"It's like an inverted groundhog burrow," Colbrick said, examining the bulging rock and dirt with fervor. He took a jagged rock and dug into the structure, and an oil-like substance slathered out.

A squeal came from inside the mound. After a minute of digging, the structure was exposed, and they backed away. Synthetic matter filled the burrow. There appeared to be a skinless, oversized elephant trunk laid inside it. Inky fluid in pulsating veins trickled downhill. Colbrick took his knife and stabbed it, punching through tough, muscular fiber before easily passing through the middle of the elongated object. The wound belched a rotten stench.

"It's hollow," Colbrick said, twisting the knife out. As he did, a wail erupted from their side of the Hoodoo cirque.

Bishop checked to see if anything was coming.

"What do you mean it's hollow?" Angela asked, her face lit by the unusual twilight.

"Hollow like a straw," Colbrick said. "It's also made out of some kind of synthetic material. It's not muscle and guts as far as I can tell."

Another wail.

As they observed the grotesque tube, it glistened and produced more fluid. Their eyes grew wide when a bulging object squelched down the tube like a rat being worked down the midsection of a snake. The bulge passed out of view under dirt and rock, heading downhill.

"Come on," Colbrick said, ushering them. "Let's see where this comes out."

They didn't have to go far. Forty yards down mountain, the burrow emptied onto a ledge that overlooked the valley. Fluid dripped from the gaping hole and a tangled mess of membranes and tenuous fibers dangled from the opening. Muffled squealing emanated from the tube exit, which opened and closed in an involuntary manner like a urethra orifice. Below the mess was a mat of unknown plant material. It almost looked like cabbage leaves, but much darker. Gold and red flecked the broad leaves which seemed to form a cushion.

"Ever seen a plant like that up here?" Bishop asked.

"Hell no," Colbrick said, kicking at it with his boot.

"Do you smell that?" Bishop asked, holding a hand over his mouth and nose.

"It smells like them," Colbrick said, spitting at the hole.

A gurgling slime piped down the tube, and they waited with staring eyes.

"Jesus," Angela said, preparing to fire her pistol and run at the same time.

"Clear away," Colbrick said.

They moved to the sides of the ledge, watching with the eyes of pigs that see the farmer coming with the ax. The sloppy cadence grew steadier, louder, panicking them when it began to hum and sling through the tube.

"It's coming faster!" Angela said, gripping her .357 and backing away.

The tube quivered and spat out a bucketful of slop, and without warning, the object exited from the hole and shot into the valley, shimmering with a blue radiance.

"A freaking seed," Angela said. "Like the *Pilea microphylla*."

"The what?" Colbrick asked.

"The artillery plant," Angela said. "It shoots its seeds like projectiles."

They watched the gelatinous ball tumble out of sight.

"Where the hell do you think it landed?" Bishop asked.

Colbrick turned to him. "Who says it landed?"

The tube sputtered and dripped, and a winding noise came from deep within its dank passageway, although the noise was less intense.

"Uh, guys, another one is coming," Angela said, her voice uneven, her forehead flecked with sweat.

"There ain't shit coming," Colbrick said. He took a softball-sized rock and plugged it into the hole, triggering the membranes and fibers to instinctively grab his hand. "Son of a bitch!" he shouted, yanking his hand back.

"You OK?" Angela asked.

Bishop examined Colbrick's fingers and noticed numerous bumps popping up like extreme mosquito bites. There were also mild burns.

Colbrick cursed and tried to shake the pain away, his good hand grabbing the burned one by the wrist.

Bishop checked the tube exit. The rock was in place.

Although the noises were now muffled, they still came, and with them another object.

"Get ready!" Angela said

They reared back, expecting the worst.

The rock didn't do its job. It fell from the tube and a small life form plopped onto the leafy cabbage below.

"Stomp it," Colbrick said, holding his injured hand.

Bishop raised his boot.

"Not yet," Angela said, pointing her revolver at it. "Let's find out what it is. We could use this."

The small life form clawed with six limbs through a thin wrap of gelatinous material and cried out.

Bishop aimed his shotgun at it.

"No, it's not," Angela said. "It can't be. There's no freaking way."

"The hell it ain't," Colbrick said, aiming his sawed-off at the thing.

The animal removed all of the coating and tried to stand. It had a small, slug tail tipped with saw-like protrusions and irregular, brown markings on its chest.

"I'm gonna shoot it," Colbrick said, grimacing as he held the sawed-off with his injured hand.

"No gunfire," Bishop said. "We'll draw the fliers." He took out the survival knife they got from Wilkin's Bait and Tackle and unsheathed it.

The frequency seal tried to stand again and cried. Bishop moved towards it with his knife and Angela followed.

"This ends now," he said, preparing to make the cut.

Before he could finish the gruesome task, Bishop noticed a tingling on the left side of his head, and the left side of his mouth quivered and reached for his spasming eyeball. He tried to speak, but gibberish came forth. He gazed at Angela, powerless.

"Shoot—" Angela shouted, the last few letters swallowed by the paralysis. She convulsed, helpless. Her right eye met Bishop's right eye, pleading.

The frequency seal finally stood from its sheath, a perfect specimen with grabbing, sandpaper mouth and clawing limbs.

Colbrick, who was farther away from the creature would have none of it. With the quickness of a mountain lion, he leaped through the air, taking out his survival knife, timing the jump so that the only possible place he could land was on the head of the damned thing. Bishop and Angela watched with one eye through their unshakable tremors.

Colbrick seemed frozen in the ether, back-lit by the Hoodoo twilight, the knife glinting along with his determined eyes. Colbrick came down hard upon the thing, and the knife penetrated the top of its head with a sickening crunch. He used both hands to drive the ten-inch blade further than what seemed possible. The frequency seal gibbered, and a magenta liquid oozed out its flapping mouth, forming bubbles.

Bishop and Angela collapsed to the ground. Colbrick, still wincing from the damage to his hand ran over to them, survival knife dripping slime and bone particles.

"You OK?" he asked, concern wrinkling his normally stoic face.

"I think so," Angela said, shaking her hand, feeling the left side of her face and cracking her jaw.

Bishop did not get up.

"You OK, slick?" Colbrick asked.

Bishop could hear, but didn't want to answer. He didn't care about the frequency seal, he didn't care that it hurt him. All he could think about was the look in Yutu's eyes when he raced through that moldy, burning hallway to save the pooch's life. He missed him so much.

"Bishop?" Angela said, getting to her feet and brushing off the dust.

"I'm fine," Bishop said, groaning as he returned to his feet.

Angela went to hug him and he hugged her back. When he opened his eyes, he was looking directly at the blue, phosphorescent vapor of the Hoodoos.

Silence overcame them as they absorbed what they just witnessed. They'd been seeking answers for a long time, or at least what felt like a long time. And here on this ridge, they finally found one.

A big one.

"That's how they did it," Bishop said in a faraway voice. "Tubes like this one lead off the mountain, and each tube carries a seed or creature. The seeds get shot into the air, but the creatures get birthed onto soft mats of plant material."

"Yup."

"That's how they hit us so fast," Angela said. "And I bet there are other tubes like this one. It would make no sense at all to have only one exit from the craft. Any good colonization pod would have multiple exits that could withstand harsh climates, and these exits would be similar to plant roots, dug in and protected. They could even grow over time to complete their purpose. If life forms can't get out, there's no point. And it looks like these exits may have been blocked by glaciers for quite some time if Colbrick is right. My question is, are there more on our planet?"

"This here is our own special Apex Valley bastard factory," Colbrick said. He reached into his pack and took a gasoline-filled bottle. He emptied it onto the garbling tube exit, the pungent fluid trickling over the membranes and fibers as they reached to grab the drops in vain. Colbrick struck a hissing match to the mess and watched it with gleaming eyes. The corned beef-like fibers squealed, and the smell of burning plastic filled the night as the flames sizzled and popped. Colbrick picked up a hefty rock and smashed it into the smoking mess, then another, and another—filling the tube and maiming it with the will of a madman.

"This one's out of order," he said, walking away.

Bishop and Angela glanced at each other in mutual admiration of the man and then followed him up the slope to the southern flank of the Hoodoo cirque.

"Come on, folks, time to get a move on," Colbrick said, his headlamp glittering through the blue vapor.

Something scraped along the rocks ahead, and the group stopped. Colbrick aimed his shotgun.

"What in the hell?" he said.

Before them, trying to bury its head into a crevasse, was a four-foot-long green worm. Bishop marveled at all the segments. Some species of earthworms had a hundred or so segments. This giant specimen had at least two hundred, and every ten segments or so was a single dark segment. Bishop could only guess at the purpose for such coloring. As the worm jerked on the metamorphic rock, it left behind a thick trail of clear slime.

Before they could speculate on what to do, the worm found a suitable crevasse and disappeared.

"Damn, I was looking forward to worm-chops," Colbrick said.

Angela grimaced. "I'm starving, and not even I was thinking about that as food."

After twisting through stone mazes and boulders with ancient markings, they reached the base of the Hoodoo cirque. The vapor turned so dense they had trouble seeing each other. Bishop called out to Angela and Colbrick in the disorienting gloom, relieved to see their figures reappear.

There was no wind to speak of. Odd for such high elevation. Patches of unknown plant life sprouted from various crevices. The plants didn't seem so healthy. One particular plant resembled an enormous Goldie's Fern and withered and shrunk as Angela approached it. When she turned away, it crept back to its original size. Another plant that looked like a dark red sunflower secreted fat drops of clear liquid from its stigma.

"Better Homes and Gardens my ass," Colbrick said.

The gnarled spires before them soared to a thousand feet, punching out of the vapor and into the brilliant array of stars. In-between the spires were mini-saddles made of talus—their access to the cirque. There were eight spires in all, their weathered bases creepily illuminated by the blue phosphorescence.

Bishop paused and listened. A gentle gurgling came from the cirque, not all that different from the geothermal features of Yellowstone Park, some five hundred miles south of the Apex Range.

Colbrick stopped below the mini-saddle, looked back at them, and then out to the Apex Valley.

He grinned.

"I just want to say, before we go in there, that it's been mighty fine working with you folks."

"Cheers to that," Angela said, walking to the impressive figure who stood before them, his demeanor mot much different than the coarse and sturdy rock of the Apex Range. She hugged him hard and laid her head upon his chest.

Bishop joined in the hug. Colbrick held his arms at his sides, refusing to hug back.

"Come on, Colbrick, you can do it," Angela said, sniffling and meeting his eyes.

Colbrick wrapped his NBA-length arms around them and squeezed. "Alright, I guess I sorta like you guys," he said.

Bishop felt Colbrick's powerful squeeze, and knew it was much more than *sort of.*

The vapor crowded them. The cirque gurgled and spluttered.

The hug continued.

Before the group pulled apart, Bishop looked to the valley, thinking he heard a faint barking from the cedars and ferns far below. *Probably just my imagination,* he thought, his heart sinking once more into the rotten place it had gone to when Yutu left.

Up here in the Hoodoos, there was no Yutu, there was no army. It was just them and whatever this seed-mother turned out to be, and Bishop had a pretty damn good idea what it was after the run-in with the birth tube.

A moment later, they passed in-between the two northernmost spires and into the cirque. The virus-like dread hit Bishop again when he took in their new surroundings. In the middle of the eight spires, the blue-tinted vapor was even thicker, and billowing curls shifted about the cirque, sometimes revealing strange, red-fleshed lacerations in the rock. Trailing out from the center of the cirque like an eight-pointed star were more of the burrow structures, and these traveled past each spire, likely ending at a cliff similar to the first tube they'd encountered. The air was musty and reminded Bishop of how northern Wisconsin smelled after a good rain—a pungent combination of moist soil, earthworms, and fish.

"God damn," Colbrick said. "What have they done to my mountains?"

"Eight spires and eight tubes?" Angela asked.

"Eight sticks of dynamite," Colbrick said.

Bishop noticed movement at his visual periphery. He blinked, focused, and blinked again, peering down the talus into the cirque. *What the heck?*

Fifty yards below, what appeared to be a ten-foot snake slithered on the rocks. Upon closer inspection, Bishop realized the snake had a mane, like the frill-necked lizard in Australia. He watched the snake slither around the perimeter of the cirque without hesitation or interruption. Its skin was almost garish, with bright yellow and black patterns.

Bishop tapped Colbrick on the shoulder. "You see that?" he asked.
"What?"

"Twelve o'clock," Bishop said.

Colbrick squinted. "Yup. Don't like it."

"There's not much to like lately," Angela said, staring at the thing.

"It's flesh," Bishop said. "But I don't see any eyes, or a way for it to make visual contact."

"Just 'cause you can't see eyes don't mean it can't see you," Colbrick said. "Different rules up here in the Hoodoos."

"I think it's a dangerous one," Angela whispered.

"Flip a coin on that," Colbrick said. "But it seems to like to hang out up here. And call me crazy, but this appears to be a good meeting place for the tubes. They connect to a center somewhere, probably the source we've been talking about."

"And that would be smack dab in the middle of the cirque," Angela said, pointing.

"Yup."

"Maybe," Bishop said.

The snake crept by them on the northern cirque perimeter, appearing in-between swaths of blue vapor and staying true to course, never hesitating. Its neck frill opened and closed as its forked tongue tasted the air.

"Time to take that thing out," Colbrick said.

"We need to get to the center where the eight burrows meet," Bishop said. "There has to be a transmitter—something which will send out a signal once all these species live long enough. If we can kill the transmitter, maybe we'll save the valley, and do something no one else here could."

"We might not save ourselves," Colbrick said, "but we just might save the Apex country, God bless it."

They gazed at the spectacle before them, vapor clearing from the cirque center and revealing substantial lacerations, as if some gigantic form was pushing up against the rock floor from below.

Colbrick sighed, and turned to Bishop and Angela with surprisingly jittery eyes. "This is where we go our separate ways," he said.

"What the fuck are you talking about?" Bishop asked.

"Your work is done here, folks. You two need to head back to Big J."

"You're crazy," Angela said. "We're coming with you."

"Nope."

"Stop it," she said, moving towards him.

Colbrick aimed his sawed-off at her, forcing Bishop to leap in front of the gun.

"Jesus Colbrick!" she said.

"I ain't joking. You two get back now."

"You won't shoot," Bishop said. "Knock it off. You don't always need to be the hero."

"Ain't nothin' heroic about it," Colbrick said. "I'm just doing the right thing. You need to survive to tell our story. That's your job. My job is to kill 'em."

Angela moved towards Colbrick, and raised the sawed-off into the air. A tremendous blast ripped through the cirque, echoing sadistically off the spires.

"Colbrick, no!" Bishop shouted, his ears ringing.

"I said get back. Go! Run from here, city slickers! This is cowboy country! Get gone!"

Colbrick fired again, shocking both of them.

"What have you done?" Bishop cried. "The fliers will be here in minutes, and who knows what else."

"I'm doing what I have to do. Now get gone. Go!"

"No!" Angela screamed.

"Then you'll watch me die."

Colbrick aimed the sawed-off at them and retreated down into the cirque, checking his footing and then glancing back.

For the first time, the snake veered off course, slithering over the lacerations and bubbling red foam. Then it angled towards Colbrick.

"Run!" Bishop shouted to him. "Run!"

"I ain't afraid of no God damned snake," Colbrick said, turning his back to them and facing it. Colbrick and the creature disappeared in a cloud of vapor and gun smoke. Another shot rang out, illuminating the vapor with muzzle flash and outlining Colbrick's tall frame.

The vapor and smoke cleared.

The snake kept coming, even though its narrow form was now missing chunks of flesh where the shotgun pellets had ripped through. There was no panic or hurry. It moved deliberately, same as before.

Angela screamed and aimed her pistol. She fired three shots, each one missing the snake as it sought Colbrick. The reverberation of gunfire volleyed off the spires in discombobulating waves.

"Get out of there now!" Bishop shouted, trying to shoot the creature but blocked by Colbrick's frame.

The snake approached to within ten feet of Colbrick and changed. It contorted half its length into a strike position and throbbed. Then it darted forth, opened its neck frill, and spit a substance at Colbrick. Colbrick screamed and held his left arm, then reached down with his survival knife and slashed at the snake, but the knife would not catch onto the scaly flesh.

"It's got him!" Angela cried. "Bishop, do something, please!"

Colbrick reached a hand out to grab its tail, but missed. The snake spit again and the substance fizzled into a rock next to Colbrick.

Bishop realized the snake had the ability to spit boiling acid, similar to the Bombardier beetle. This corrosive chemical had the potential to kill insects and other small creatures. His stomach churned when he knew a direct hit could eat right through Colbrick.

"Make sure you get the dynamite, partner!" Colbrick shouted, gazing at him with a mixture of appreciation and fear.

Bishop ran to him over the sharp talus. Movement flickered along the eastern cirque entrance, and a clumsy form also scrambled down to Colbrick. *No, no, not another one*, Bishop thought. But as the fast moving object materialized, Bishop saw it was the awkward bird they'd encountered near Big J in what felt like a thousand years ago. The fast but clumsy bird whirled towards Colbrick with its skinny neck and head inches off the ground, bits of dust and rock flying up behind it. Before Bishop could blink, the bird was upon Colbrick.

Cheeekooo Cheeekooo!

"Don't shoot!" Angela said. "Don't shoot!"

"Get away!" Colbrick shouted to the wobbly bird, trying to swat it.

The bird ripped at the snake with its beak, able to grasp it with considerable force. When the bird realized its grip was secure, it stopped, dug its homely feet into the ground and yanked the snake away from Colbrick. The snake coiled around the bird's rough legs and spit repeatedly into its face and plumage. The bird let out a heckling call and snatched the head of the snake with its powerful beak. Then the snake opened its barbed frill as copious amount of boiling acid erupted from its mouth. The bird dropped the snake and teetered.

Cheeekooo Cheeekooo!

Bishop winced, not wanting to see the torture and death of the poor bird. But instead of dying or collapsing in agony, the bird let out its uncanny call and clamped down on the snake's head as if gobbling the world's longest piece of spaghetti. The bird's midsection distended as it chewed and ate—to the point where Bishop was sure it would explode.

"What the heck is going on?" Angela asked, trembling.

Bishop shook his head, dazed.

To their shock, the bird regained a healthy form. It wobbled off, up over the eastern lip of the cirque, disappearing between two spires. Bishop wondered if its robust digestive system made up for its awkward movements. It was obvious the bird could digest things other creatures couldn't. Maybe on its home planet it ate anything it could catch, from strange plants to poisonous snakes.

The entire northeastern sky flashed white, brighter than any fireworks show Bishop had ever seen. It came from the direction of Big J. Shivers prickled down his spine as the air crackled with electricity. He tasted it on his tongue, like Pop Rocks candy.

Bishop turned his attention to Colbrick, but Colbrick was no longer there. Instead, he was running to the center of the cirque, taking great care as to where he stepped, for the lacerations and mudpots were numerous.

"Let's go," Bishop said.

Angela stumbled down the talus to meet him, and hand in hand, they moved over the questionable surface of the cirque. Random patches of seething organic matter squelched below them, and a stench of biological decay filled the air. Embedded and sometimes exposed amongst the rocks and pebbles was a thin, silvery material that looked like the emergency hiking blankets he and his father used to use. Large swaths of the material were connected by taut wire-like lengths. A pang of familiarity hit Bishop.

"Where have we seen that before?" Bishop asked Angela, pointing at the ground.

Angela scoured the ground and touched the material with a bandaged hand. "Science Channel," she said. "They were talking about these things called solar sails. The illustrations and videos looked similar to this."

"This is the seed-mother," Bishop said. "I can feel it."

"My God," Angela said as they maneuvered to the center. "How long has it been here?"

"A long time," Bishop said. "Way before our meteorite tracking systems were in place."

"We have no chance of destroying it," she said, turning to him.

Bishop thought of Yutu pulling himself out of the burning apartment. "No one is ever really powerless."

The vaporous air flickered with energy, and they saw something shoot across the sky—one of the projectile seeds. A second later, another projectile zipped across the sky, landing who knows where. The closer they got to the cirque's center, the more frequent the projectiles became. Phosphorescent, blue spheres whipped into the sky in all directions like rotten, popped corn kernels.

The dense vapor cleared, and they stumbled upon Colbrick who was kneeling and peering into a crevasse the size of a small car.

"I can see it," he whispered, motioning to them with his hand. "A big opening—about twenty feet down."

Bishop gazed into the hole with his headlamp and stumbled back when he saw the interior of the seed-mother. An opening with synthetic, smooth and grey walls at least fifty yards long tunneled back into the ground, which must have formed over the seed-mother as it rested here during the Gelasian period of the Pleistocene. Numerous coiled tubes emanated from what looked to be stalls housing invasive creatures in various stages of development. *A nursery*, Bishop thought. Some of the larger creatures inside apparent birthing pods were encased in a kind of placenta, similar to the one they'd seen the frequency seal claw out of earlier. Smaller tubes connected to big ones and disappeared into holes in the flooring. Surrounding the nursery area was a foamy red substance three feet thick. Bishop guessed this to be some sort of sterilization foam meant to protect the nursery from rogue microbes and other contaminants. They'd seen this on the surface, too. Placed in various locations were dark vats of water. Above some of these vats mosquito-like insects buzzed and swarmed. Bishop assumed the vats must be full of eggs. His attention turned to the stalls, where animals shifted inside placentas that were hooked to artificial nipples that protruded from the wall. Inside one placenta, Bishop caught a flash of red. A tag. In another stall, a robotic arm holding a flashing tag poked into a viscous placenta and then pulled out. The next stall looked to be an incubator, and it held massive eggs off the floor on sturdy-looking pedestals. All along the walls of the dimly lit interior were telescoping and retracting robotic arms. Some of them carried frozen embryos from one container to another, passing them along the wall like prison inmates passing contraband through the bars. A larger robotic arm secured to a track on the ceiling pushed a bulging placenta into one of the tube openings on the floor.

"Oh my God," Angela said. "I can't believe what I'm seeing. This is life, guys. Sure, it's not *our* life, but it is life."

To the right of the stalls, closer to their location stood an armoire-sized silver panel full of circular red lights, the same color as the flashing tags. Bishop noticed only two unlit spaces left. They were running out of time.

Bishop turned to Angela as she watched the surreal scene before them.

Angela felt a chill, but also a sense of discovery as a puzzling creature broke free of a placenta, exited the birthing pod, stood, and started nursing from an artificial nipple on the wall. When it finished, it turned and stared right at her. Conflicting emotions and thoughts hit her in rapid succession. The animal stood on four long limbs ending in paws, making her think of the pictures she'd seen of the extinct dawn horse. Its long, upright torso with two forelimbs made her think of a centaur. Was it gesturing to her? *My God, I'm the first creature it has ever seen, does it think I'm its mother?* A robotic arm came out of the wall and attached a tag to its rump. The tag started flashing rapidly.

Bishop and Colbrick both spoke: "The panel has another light."

The creature's large silver eyes and bright red coat made her think of Christmas and Christmas made her think of reindeer. "It's like a deer," she whispered.

"We have our own God damned deer, thank you very much," Colbrick said.

Angela looked around, a feeling of panic growing. "What if we could just dismantle it, capture the animals and study them?"

"Not interested," Bishop said, his eyes hard. "Colbrick, do you need help with the dynamite?"

The head-high vapor shifted again, obscuring the crevasse.

"God damn it, get this fog out of here," Colbrick said as he disappeared only four feet in front of them.

"Whatever we need to do, let's do it," Angela said. "The fliers—"

A prowling stillness swept over them, like a warm lull before a violent spring storm. Their cochlea's twitched, catching the faint beating of wings.

Puffs of vapor breezed to the west in unison, and pointed shadows ghosted across the twisted, eastern spires.

Drumbeats of wings. Pounding, piping, searching.

The blue vapor smeared with green luminance.

A psychotic mocking blared off the spires in surround sound. It pierced their ears, distracting and irritating.

The looped mimicry of Colbrick's shotgun blasts.

"They're here," Angela whispered, her eyes wide like a nervous rabbit.

"Get down," Bishop said. "Move with the fog. Take your shoes off so you don't make noise."

They removed their shoes and their packs, moving about the rock with socks, only their breathing potentially giving them away. The vapor bobbed around the cirque like organisms caught in an eddy. Above them, the beating of wings grew louder, and without looking up, Bishop guessed there were at least five big fliers. A flurry of wings and looping gun blasts dove towards them, and they crouched, trying to predict which way the vapor would move. If they guessed wrong, the fliers would be on them in no time.

The vapor shifted, exposing Angela's cotton sock to the fliers, causing several of the small fliers to dart in her direction, then fly away again as she yanked her foot inside the fog.

The vapor squeezed between them, prying them apart.

They were now all separated in the gloom, each working the changing density the best they could.

Humongous, leathery wings circled above, casting elongated shadows and green phosphorescence. Countless wings buzzed their heads, the looped mimicry searing them and then pulling away, only to come back again.

They know we're here, Bishop thought. If the fog cleared they were done—done as in eaten alive.

Impaled.

Chewed.

Shit out.

If he was going to die, at least it was going to be with Angela.

The vapor thinned, exposing Bishop's right leg, and he stepped to a denser patch. *Nice recovery.* He exhaled. Then he bumped into something and needed every ounce of energy he had to stop from screaming.

It was Angela.

He reached for her and held her in the zero visibility, and she cried onto his chest. He squeezed her, cherishing her body, her love, her soul.

"I love you," he whispered to her.

She squeezed him with great verve, her bandaged hands at last gripping his back.

A shadow passed over them, followed by a hint of green and then another shadow.

They waited for what seemed like an eternity, stepping and ducking in the uneven vapor, dancing the dance of the doomed and hopeless.

A long time ago, Bishop had seen a wildlife documentary on television in which killer whales would poke their heads rhythmically out of the ocean in an unusual, vertical posture in order to observe a seal that was stranded on an ice flow. It had horrified him as a child, and now he knew what it was like to be that seal. The seal never made it, slipping off the ice flow and exposing a flipper. A killer whale that had been under the flow grabbed the flipper and bit it off, and the seal bled to death on the ice.

Fuck all that, Bishop thought.

After another sidestep, he gazed upon the ground and realized he was inches from the crevasse. And he almost gasped when he saw Colbrick halfway down it, one hand and one leg pushed against the wall, the other hand full of dynamite. Bishop tossed a pebble into the hole to get Colbrick's attention. Colbrick looked up, his eyes pooling moisture.

"What are you doing?" Bishop mouthed.

Colbrick answered with a determined glare and a jerk of his head towards the red, pulsating floor only feet below him.

In an act of friendship and respect, hard, tough Colbrick looked up and saluted Bishop. When Colbrick pulled his hand away from his forehead, the ground shook with a power Bishop had never felt before, knocking debris into the hole. Crackling, blue light flashed through the vapor, stunning all of them with an electrical surge.

They fell to the ground, more concerned about making noise than what pain the rocks would bring. The rocks brought pain. Bishop forced his mouth shut as his ribs slammed into stone.

Colbrick grunted from inside the crevasse.

A patch of vapor cleared, revealing the eastern sky. Bursts of light rippled across the sky, watering their eyes. The ground rumbled and heaved, buckling their knees and chattering their teeth. The sky flashed again in a shocking display of explosions and colors. Eye-welting swaths of orange and white engulfed the world and then retreated.

This is it, Bishop thought as his eyes burned and his skull rattled. *This is it.*

CHICAGO TEXT FEED

JanineWolf Janine R. Wolf
@ShellyC What the hell is this outside my window

ShellyC, YOU HAVE PHOTO MESSAGE, DOWNLOAD?
DOWNLOAD PROCEEDING...
DOWNLOAD COMPLETE

ShellyC Shelly Caffareli
@JanineWolf Call animal control ASAP

JanineWolf Janine R. Wolf
@ShellyC They're covering the entire window now. Monsters I saw on TV

ShellyC Shelley Caffareli
@JanineWolf Call AC!

JanineWolf Janine R. Wolf
@ShellyC They pushing on glass, making construction noises, mimicking the L, buses.

ShellyC Shelly Caffareli
@JanineWolf get out NOW

URSUS ARCTOS HORRIBILIS

After the three hundred and twentieth U.S. Armed Forces casualty, all barriers came under assault by the United States Army and Air Force. The initial blasts of rocket-propelled grenades and incendiary bombs ignited the barriers and sent the new arrivals out into the night like a swarming colony of wasps.

The plan was to burn and crash the barriers and then disassemble them using construction cranes, bulldozers, and strategically-placed explosives. But half of the devices meant for the barriers reached the uncut forest, and in turn, created devastating explosions and fires.

A few cutting-edge, spinning incendiary bombs known as A-T4's went berserk, shooting past the barriers and into the night sky in blinding streaks of light. A group of pigras which had arrived at Barrier 2 in search of prey were ignited by the device. One unlucky pigra crawled from the black cloud of debris with its legs broken, gibbering out to its dead clan. The calls were answered by a blast of boiling chemicals that drowned the pigra as it screamed, its hairy head arched back and the ridged roof of its mouth exposed.

The bombs continued to fall, destroying meadows and trees.

Streams became polluted. Unlucky forests were set ablaze, and these roaring tempests added to the unholy light that illuminated the Apex Valley. The air filled with smoke, and in the haze, heat, and maddening light creatures of the invasion darted—from pigras to eels to secapods.

And still the bombs fell.

Frenetic energy rippled out from below AH-64 Apache helicopters and A-10 Thunderbolt II jets and ignited the trees like the world's biggest blow torch. A gang of frequency seals below one of the trees received the brunt, and they panicked into the night ablaze like stunt men, waving their burning limbs in front of their screaming mouths and melting faces. Their cries rang into the chaotic night, mixing with the cries of secapods, eels, and machine gun fire. The eels had it the worst, for the flames ignited their gaseous forms—the biological electrical systems a dangerous flame attractant. The blazing eels zipped through the ferns and trees, their trailing firelight eerily consumed by shadows. The panicking eels set the understory on fire as they sought company with others in their packs. Before they could escape, many of the eels were ensnared by a seventy-thousand-acre fire, the tallest flames rising to six hundred feet.

Amidst the spreading fires, the ground trembled from the explosions, sending four-hundred-year-old burning cedars crashing to the ground. Upon impact, millions of embers flew into the air, and the smoldering, white-hot wood incinerated a gathering of rotten leaves.

And still the bombs fell, maiming the valley. The bombardment sent hundreds of skeletons and other fleshy matter out into the nightmarish landscape, the bones and branches at first dark, then lit in unwanted detail as they were thrown into the massive wall of flames that consumed the barriers.

Subsequent blasts knocked over flaming old growth trees like they were bowling pins and sent uncountable sparks and debris into the night sky. Jets and helicopters roared above the maelstrom. An errant bomb exploded in Mission Lake, creating a huge wake that sloshed over Mission Dam, sending a flood of water east towards lower elevation towns and woodlands which happened to be geographically unlucky.

*

Corporal Erickson didn't sign up for this. He thought he'd be shooting foreigners in some desert, not battling these freak animals in the forests of Montana. But as his mother always told him, life's an adventure. *Yeah, some fucking adventure,* he thought as he sat tight against a tree just outside the devastation zone of Barrier 2. The creatures had breached Barrier 2 after the air assault. He'd lost his platoon and saw his commander carried off by some Godforsaken thing with green eyes. He heard them still, hovering overhead, echoing the sound of crisp, burning trees and gunfire. Some of the things in the sky even echoed the rotors of the Apaches. He'd run to the sound of the rotors once, and had to double back to a mess of fallen trees as it wasn't what he thought. Oh no, it wasn't even close. Luckily for him, the canopy had caught the thing's wings, allowing him to escape.

Erickson wiped his eyes and turned to the north. The woods were darker there, and he wouldn't be exposed. His night vision optics gave him an advantage, but who knew how many more of the things were out there.

Erickson turned to the south, the firelight reflecting in his eyes. He put a hand to his mouth to muffle a cough. Back through the flames and dead bodies was Outpost 2, and possible salvation if he could reach Outpost 3. But the smoke was too much. Asphyxiation was a real possibility. And if he ran into any of those things in the light, all he had was a single clip.

Erickson reached into his pocket and pulled out a photo of his daughter, Abby. He smiled as he studied her short blonde hair and tiny nose. The background was that fuzzy blue marble color all the mall photo stores used. His mind drifted to the soothing music and air-conditioned sterility of Rexford Mall. He wished he was there with his family, having a slice of Sbarro's, and talking about shit that was inconsequential. He scrunched his eyes closed and kissed the photo. North it was.

He put on his night vision goggles and sprinted uphill, branches and leaves brushing against his uniform. His priority now was to clear the smoke. He wasn't equipped to outlast that, and his survival depended on finding a clear route away from the fire.

The contrast of what was behind him and what lay ahead was remarkable. He felt the heat on his back, and was sure he was visible at least for a few more dozen yards from the south. Ahead was nothing but darkness, with the occasional flash in the sky. Erickson knew for certain that as his backside cooled, he was sinking into the darkness and becoming less of a beacon for the creatures. After five more minutes, he disappeared into the Rocky Mountain night, the crackling of burning trees now behind him. He stopped to catch his breath and checked his M16. All good. His face was sweaty from the night vision goggles, so he removed them. After wearing the damn things for so long, he wanted his eyes to feel the cool air. He blinked and squinted at the sky and the display of stars. Abby loved the night sky. She'd always ask questions about the moon, the planets, and the stars. He'd even researched the solar system so he wouldn't seem ignorant when she asked him the questions. He thought he'd be the teacher when they had her, but in many ways, Abby was teaching him. And that was OK. He'd rather learn new things and spend time with his daughter than hang out with his friends who'd begun to drink too much. The weekend benders they'd enjoyed since high school had turned into every day partaking, and the spark of it all had been replaced by a slow, throbbing fade. Abby was a light in the darkness, that much he knew. He also knew he needed to get his damn goggles on ASAP or risk ambush by the creatures. Erickson stretched the optics over his head and proceeded uphill into the bigger trees. The air cooled again, and his lungs cleared.

Ten minutes up trail, Erickson reached a rock outcropping with a clear view of the lowlands he'd just crossed. Barrier 2 was engulfed by flames, and so was the forest for a mile around it. The flames reached hundreds of feet into the air, and numerous explosions emitted from the core fire—probably the munitions of Outpost 2 and maybe even Outpost 3. In-between explosions, he heard something rustling on the trail below and turned to look. One of the humongous elephant-like things bellowed fifty yards to his south and disappeared behind the trees.

Shit, he thought. He put his goggles back on and sprinted up the mountain, desperate to lose his tail. Five minutes into the run he stopped and listened. The noises behind him were gone. He took a drink from his canteen, and as he swallowed the water, a new noise thundered above him. It was the sound of helicopter blades.

Thwap Thwap Thwap.

Erickson raced to another outcropping thirty yards uphill and prepared his flare.

Thwap Thwap Thwap.

He reached the outcropping, gazed into the sky with his night optics and saw a shape hurtling towards him. Erickson pocketed his flare and dashed into a short clump of trees, the branches and needles rough on this face. He watched from a hole in the vegetation as one of the huge fliers swooped over the outcropping and into the valley, its eyes reflecting the hellfire below.

Erickson watched the burning valley and listened. The option of waiting this out was starting to appeal to him. Maybe the fire would remain low and not creep up the mountainside. Maybe it was best if he remained in place, reducing the odds of running into one of the creatures.

The green eyes of the flying thing disappeared into the night, and he remained in his hiding spot. As he gazed into the valley, he swore he saw the edges of the fire expanding, and in a way that seemed too fast. Erickson snapped a twig off the tree. Way too easy. These woods were dry as tinder. If he remained in this location, the flames would arrive sooner or later.

Erickson proceeded west up the trail, into a forest and occasional meadows. Slabs of rock punctuated the forest openings, and the air was colder than anything below. Eric thought of his wife, Cindy, of her gentle brown eyes and smile. Things hadn't been as good as they could be with them, and when he got back, he was going to fix that. Oh hell yes he was. Roses, attention, showering her with praise, whatever was necessary, he'd do it.

Erickson stopped and listened. A branch cracked to the south. He turned and scanned the woods. The night vision goggles revealed movement to the south. The head of a creature.

Shit!

He tried to run, but his balance was poor, and he hobbled instead. His left eye twitched towards his forehead and so did the left side of his mouth. He drooled for the first time since kindergarten as his left leg trembled and gave way. He fell to his knees and dropped his weapon, the shapes closing in on him in the periphery of his night vision optics. He screamed, and as he did, one of the frequency seals screamed too—a baby mocking him in its delight. The parent of the baby followed with its own scream, overjoyed that its precious baby was helping cripple their dinner.

Erickson tried to move, but was only able to watch as his legs and arms shook. The seals closed in on him, their screams joyous at a fresh meal.

He screamed at the top of his lung. "F-f-fucking h-h-help me!" His teeth chattered and he bit his tongue, moistening his twitching lips with coppery crimson. One of the baby frequency seals clamped onto his boot and tore at it, and its parent gripped his arm and pulled away a patch of skin in one bite. Erickson screamed again.

The creatures wailed and bit him.

Erickson tried to reach for his sidearm, but it was no use. As he tried to look away from the seals, movement came from behind vegetation uphill. A massive head emerged from the ferns, and two big glowing eyes stared back at him.

Then another head emerged, similar to the other.

And then another. Round ears. Dished face. Powerful jaws and gnashing teeth.

Two smaller heads emerged below the bigger ones. Babies. *No, not babies*, he thought. *Cubs.*

Erickson screamed again as a frequency seal gnawed on his hand.

In the blink of an eye, the creatures stormed downhill, the ground shaking under their paws. The frequency seals turned to the attackers—who were running at forty-five miles per hour—and were immediately pummeled to the ground, the incredible paws of one gargantuan grizzly knocking a frequency seal's head clear off, sending it tumbling downhill. One of the bear cubs chomped onto a baby frequency seal and thrashed it as it squealed and shook. Erickson moved his limbs as the effects of the frequencies abated, but thought better about running as he'd read that it was best to play dead this close to grizzly bears. Oh how badly he wanted to scream, wanted to flee as the carnage unfolded around him. The noises emitting from the fight were beyond anything he'd ever heard, or wanted to hear again. The grizzlies' fur ruffled and quaked as their powerful forelegs pinned the frequency seals and tore at their innards. Every time a seal tried to fend off a bear with a limb, the bear would rip it off and maim their face. All of the frequency effects vacated Erickson's body, but there was no way in hell he was moving an inch as the grizzlies and their cubs decimated the hapless frequency seals. Erickson wondered if the seals never had time to engage the grizzlies as they were so fast, and maybe panicked as they were overtaken with such brute force. The grizzly cubs picked off the babies like a wolf to chickens. The cubs swallowed the babies in big chunks, their appetite so voracious they gagged from eating too fast. Some of the bears stumbled, no doubt affected by the frequencies, but not incapacitated by them. The growling and squealing turned into the slapping of paws on dirt, huffing, and the tearing of meat as the grizzlies feasted.

Erickson waited, still, silent.

Deep, slow breaths.

He watched the stars above him, letting deep space calm him, get his mind right.

What star is that, Daddy? Abby had asked him last week, pointing to the north. He wasn't able to provide a correct answer, and after he put her to bed, he'd researched it online.

"That's Alkaid, honey," he whispered. "And it's part of the Big Dipper."

More slow, deep breaths as the grizzlies ate.

He heard the shuffling of paws near his head and felt the hot stink of breath as a mother grizzly studied him. It took every ounce of energy he had not to get up and run. The sow's two playful cubs approached him, but the mother nudged them away from Erickson and to their dinner.

The constellations shifted in the night sky and explosions rocked the land far below. Erickson heard digging and scratching to his right. The grizzlies were burying their meat and sniffing the air.

The largest of the bears stood on hind legs and gazed at the burning valley, then ran off to tree line, for this animal did not care to be seen in the open, not after years of persecution by humans. Another grizzly followed, and this one's belly was swollen and its fur bloody from nonstop feeding. They all ran into the shadows and disappeared, making their way towards the alpine realms and high meadows where man did not care to roam and where the strong winds had their backs. And as they ran one by one, grunting and huffing through the eerily-lit night, the stars from a certain northeast constellation blinked down to them in a form of communication no man could understand, for only the truly wild can understand the stars.

*

Bishop and Angela watched as the sky spasmed with light. The ground quaked and lurched, knocking them off balance. The mega-explosions and fire shimmered in the valley below.

"Fucking government is torching the valley," Bishop said.

The fliers weaved and bobbed in confusion, not sure whether to focus on the paltry group hidden in the fog or to investigate the mayhem that thundered below them from the east.

Seeing an opening, Bishop took Angela by the hand and led her to the crevasse. When they looked down, Colbrick was sinking into the pulsating, red foam at the pod entrance. Colbrick's face was contorted and sweaty, and he was trying not to scream. The scent of burning human hair wafted up the hole.

What was left of Bishop's heart blew into a thousand pieces. "You alright, buddy?" Bishop asked, his voice trembling.

Angela gripped his hand and let out a heaving sob.

Their talking went unnoticed by the confused fliers, some of which flew to the edge of the cirque, ogling down into the chaotic valley.

"I'm fine, slick," Colbrick lied from below, wincing as his feet sunk deeper into the foam. "I'm just going to hang out a bit with our seed friend here."

"Hold on," Bishop said. "I'm coming down to get you."

The vapor condensed and swirled above them, shielding them from the fliers.

"Like hell you're coming down!" Colbrick snapped back. "Like I said before, get gone! You and the misses need to work on helping the valley. Ole' Colbrick will be just fine."

"Stop being so stubborn and get back up here now," Angela said, sobbing.

"And then what?" Colbrick asked, his steel blue eyes flickering and wincing. "I need to make sure this here seed gets a proper serving of explosives."

"Stop it, Colbrick. Please, please stop it...get up here now," she said, crying.

Colbrick gasped and sunk to his knees in the burning foam. "I'm afraid I won't be doing much walking," he said sarcastically in that Colbrick kind of way. His contorted face and grimace betrayed the sarcasm.

"No!" Angela cried, reaching for Bishop and weeping onto his chest. "Don't let him do it! Don't you dare let him!"

Bishop embraced her and gazed upon his good friend—the one who plucked them from certain death on Highway 18 on that fateful day, the man who'd saved their lives numerous times since the invasion. "Please don't do this. Get up here now!"

"I'm afraid I can't feel my feet, slick," he said, turning a shade of red. Colbrick sunk even further into the foam and let out another hoarse gasp. Grimacing in pain, he still managed to hold the eight sticks of dynamite that he'd bundled with a bungee cord from his pack, interweaving the wicks so they could be lit with one match.

"Not yet!" Angela screamed. "Don't you freaking do it, Colbrick! Don't you freaking do it. Get out of there first!"

Colbrick met the long, waterproof wick with the match he'd shown them earlier at Big J. Then he ignited the match with his thumbnail and grinned at the flame, sweat pouring from his face. He sunk further into the foam, and fizzing arose from the portion of the seed-mother Colbrick was mired in. The earth rumbled, knocking flecks of mica and granite from the rocks into the pod, almost throwing them off balance. Colbrick's hands trembled as he tried to meet flame to wick. He teetered in place and at last joined the two elements. A white-hot spark consumed the end, burning with the intensity of a police dog on a suspect.

"I'll see you guys in another life," Colbrick said, grinning up at his dear friends and saluting them. "I ain't had much luck with friends—too stubborn I suppose." The wick crackled and spit sparks near his face. "I'm doing this for you, for the valley—"

Before Colbrick could finish his farewell speech, Bishop started working his way down the hole with the assistance of Angela who'd tied the rope around a boulder at the crevasse entrance.

"What are you doing?" he shouted back at them. "We'll all die. The Apex Valley needs you fools!"

As sparks reflected in Colbrick's eyes, Bishop rappelled down the damp hole with the rope around his waist.

"Go back, go back! God damn it! You'll die, Bishop! Let me alone! Let me die a hero like my father and his father before him! I seen this coming for a long time!"

Bishop grunted his way down the hole towards the pod, careful not to step on the foam. He stuck his hand out and reached for his injured friend, grabbing onto his shirt.

"Shit don't work like that," Bishop said

His strong hand now gripping the even stronger Colbrick, he nodded to Angela, and she assisted in pulling them up as he worked the crevasse walls with his feet and free arm.

Speechless, Colbrick dropped the dynamite onto the pod floor. He used his feet and arms to push and climb. Free of the burning foam, his legs exhibited red lacerations.

"Hang in there, buddy," Bishop said, concentrating everything he had on removing them from the hole.

The dynamite sunk into the foam, and a gleam appeared in Colbrick's eyes when he saw the fuse was still sparking, the white-hot light reaching ever closer to the final meeting place of dangerous, packed powder. Colbrick used his hands to push and grasp along the walls while Bishop pulled, and the two of them collapsed in a heap at the entrance. The dense vapor swirled above them as explosions lingered in the valley.

"Thank you," Colbrick said, turning to them.

"Consider us even," Bishop said, patting the old timer on the back.

"My legs. I can't feel 'em," Colbrick said.

"Ever go swimming in real cold water?" Angela asked, whispering. "Well, imagine this is the same thing—that your legs are there, they're just real cold right now, and if you move enough, the feeling will come back."

The earth heaved again, and the vapor lit with vibrant reds, greens, and oranges. Explosions pounded the valley, sending up collages of sound that ricocheted off the spires. Heat and light filled the sky.

The survivors crouched and scrambled through the fog.

"Keep going," Bishop whispered.

"Hold up," Angela whispered. "I forgot to do something."

"Are you kidding?"

"Just hold up."

Angela took something out of her pocket, turned it on, placed it next to the nursery crevasse, and ran back to them in the swirling mists.

"Go," she mouthed to them. "Go."

They scrambled through the fog across the cirque, and an amplified voice came from behind them in the haze.

It was Sue Grafferton's voice.

HALF CUP SUGAR...TWO TABLESPOONS OF BUTTER...FOUR CUPS OF HUCKLEBERRIES...ONE-THIRD CUP OF FLOUR...NINE INCH CRUST PASTRY.

"What the hell did you do?" Bishop asked, trudging along with Colbrick, keeping his head down.

"Something I've been planning since back at Big J," Angela said. "A diversion tactic."

"A what?" Bishop asked.

"A recording with my voice in case we needed a diversion from the fliers."

HALF TEASPOON OF CINNAMON...

Suddenly, the world became still again, the tremors ceasing. The last assault of light faded to the horizon like a dying campfire.

The voice changed from Sue's to Angela's.

They scurried through the haze, their shoeless feet whisper-quiet on the punishing surface. Behind them, Angela's recorded voice rang across the foggy cirque. The recorder was pushed to its limits, the speech clipping, distorting.

No longer confused by the mayhem in the valley, the fliers turned their full attention to the tape recorder, their mimicry now playing back Angela's voice. Her booming voice was everywhere as they worked their way to the northern spires, hunched over and gasping.

MY NAME IS ANGELA. I HAVE SURVIVED THE ATTACK, AND I AM HERE TO TELL YOU THAT YOU WILL NOT WIN. YOU KILLED MY FRIEND SUE AND MOST OF THE APEX VALLEY. I AM HERE TO TELL YOU THAT YOU WILL NOT WIN.

DESPITE NUMEROUS OBSTACLES SINCE THE FIRST DAY OF THE ATTACK, WE SURVIVE AND ACT AS A DECENT SPECIES. WE WILL SURVIVE, WE WILL OUTLAST YOU. MARK MY WORDS. AND IN CASE YOU NEED TO KNOW, THIS IS A RECORDING.

SEE, I CAN RECORD JUST LIKE YOU DO. BUT THE FUNNY THING ABOUT A NOISE IS THAT YOU HAVE TO BE SMART ENOUGH TO KNOW IF IT'S REAL. AND I'M BETTING THAT YOU FLIERS CAN'T TELL THE FREAKING DIFFERENCE. IN FACT, I'M BETTING EVERYTHING ON IT BECAUSE I JUST DON'T THINK YOU'RE VERY SMART. HOW'S THAT FOR MIMICRY? HOW'S THAT FOR A PLAYBACK DEVICE? I DON'T KNOW WHEN I WILL USE THIS TAPE, OR EVEN IF I EVER WILL. BUT YOU CAN BE SURE THAT IF IT IS USED, IT WILL BE A VERY BAD DAY FOR YOU. THERE ISN'T ROOM ENOUGH FOR BOTH OF US.

The fliers swarmed the recorder, two of the huge ones following the horde of the smaller pests. They clouded over the recorder like a virus attacking a cell, wings beating away puffs of vapor. One of the big fliers landed clumsily, knocking the recorder into the nursery crevasse. Enraged by the retreating voice, the flier stuck its oblong head into the hole, knocking bits of debris from the walls. The recorder landed on a ledge, and as the flier opened its deadly beak, its searching, grotesque eye reflected the last spark from the dynamite, manufactured in Hobart, Indiana.

A blinding flash of yellow shot up to the sky. Through the disorienting rumble, the fliers shrieked and panicked.

"Keep going!" Bishop shouted.

"Colbrick, how you doing?" Angela asked, huffing.

"Better. I can feel my legs now, they hurt like hell but at least I can feel 'em."

"Good sign," she said. "Can you keep moving?"

"What God damned choice do I have?" he asked.

Angela said nothing.

They worked over the rugged terrain, wincing and grunting. The fliers wailed and thrashed behind them.

"Oh my God," Angela said, looking back. "Keep freaking going. Do not stop, do not stop!"

Bishop glanced behind and saw even more fliers gathering above the nursery crevasse. The swarm was so thick that smaller fliers were batted down by the wings of the larger ones as the birds panicked. A few of the giant fliers ghosted as high as the tips of the Hoodoo spires in the chilling night sky.

Colbrick looked back, eyes wide. "If they see us, we're fertilizer!"

"Thanks for the play-by-play," Angela shot back, panting. "Get moving!"

Colbrick stumbled and Angela and Bishop stopped to help him up.

"Keep moving!" Bishop shouted. "We have to get over the mini-saddle."

Bishop glanced back and noticed the fliers crying and weaving above the nursery crevasse like seabirds to whale guts, their frantic, glowing eyes darting and uncertain.

The survivors reached the northern mini-saddle and climbed over, assisted by an incline which they ran across like a ramp to safety. They collapsed on the other side of the northern Hoodoo spires, catching their breath and watching with anxious eyes.

"I can't move anymore," Angela said, her chest heaving.

"No choice," Bishop said. "Come on!"

They ran down the lengthy saddle, fearful of glancing back, always expecting the worst. But sometimes curiosity outweighs fear, and another wail was enough to force Bishop to see what the hell was going on behind them. He stopped, and so did the others.

They watched. They could not help but watch.

The fliers massed in the uneven light between the deformed Hoodoo spires, their eyes wild and their beaks opening and closing as if automated. Perhaps they realized the nursery was their mother.

Bishop noticed a sound down in the valley, one he'd become familiar with in Chicago during construction season. It was the sound of helicopters. Goosebumps rose on his limbs.

"Choppers," he said to Angela. "From the east!"

Angela turned as three Apache Gunships roared up the saddle, their 30-millimeter M230 chain guns and Hydra 70 rockets firing away at the fliers. Numerous Hydra 70's screamed through the night, emitting flames and trails of smoke. The swarm of fliers within the cirque dispersed as the rockets and bullets devastated them. Some of the fliers shrieked and fell to the ground, bullets ripping apart their wings while others imitated the death calls of their peers. Other fliers mimicked the helicopters and bolted towards them at full speed. The Apaches moved closer, and Bishop wondered why the hell they'd initiate such a maneuver. When the helicopters approached to within a quarter mile, they launched a coordinated round of Hydra 70's that traced across the night sky. Before the rockets could reach their targets, five gigantic fliers shot from the darkness above and attacked all three Apaches, fouling the main rotor blades as they were sliced apart. The Apache helicopters tried to turn away, but it was clear to Bishop they were in trouble. Then the roar of a jet engine pierced the night. An A10 Thunderbolt raced in from the north, firing its heavy-duty GAU-8 Avenger rotary canon. As it cut apart a group of fliers inside the cirque, its rear engine intakes sparked and smoked. Bishop watched in disgust as he realized the small fliers were being sucked into the intakes. The A10 Thunderbolt smashed into one of the Hoodoo Spires and exploded, illuminating the cirque with fire glow. As burning jet fuel dripped down the Hoodoo spire, countless shadows of small fliers ghosted past. Bishop turned to the Apaches and watched as one retreated to the valley. The other two Apaches spun in the sky as the rotors emitted grinding sounds. Flames burst from one Apache as it disappeared to the east. The last visible Apache spun to the alpine rock at speeds Bishop knew no man could recover from. The impact explosion irradiated their faces as they watched helplessly. In the orange glow, injured fliers shrieked and flopped to the rocks, while others swooped down into the valley where the other two choppers had gone.

Silence filled the Apex Mountains.

"Unbelievable," Angela whispered in awe.

"I have nothing to add," Bishop said, shaking his head.

Angela, Bishop, and Colbrick turned to the south, sore and almost broken. Before they could take a step, the sound of a helicopter came from the direction of the Hoodoo's. They stopped and turned.

Thwap thwap thwap.

Angela met Bishop's eyes. "I think one of the helicopters may have made—"

"Move!" Bishop shouted as he ushered Angela and Colbrick on.

The three survivors scrambled across the saddle, trying to outrun the thing behind them in the darkness.

Thwap thwap thwap.

Bishop turned and saw the green eyes of a big flier, and its pulsing red tag. The tag beat much slower now, almost as if it was about to stop altogether. The big flier streaked towards them, its long beak opening and closing, its eyes mirrors of rage and hunger.

Forty yards now.

"Keep going!" Bishop shouted.

"Jesus," Angela said, crying.

Bishop and Angela heard a thud and watched as Colbrick collapsed to the ground. Angela stopped and reached for him. Bishop stopped and turned. They were in this together. They would not leave their friend to the flier. Never.

Twenty yards now.

"I love you, Angela," he said.

"I love you too," she said, sobbing.

Ten yards.

Bishop felt the breath of the big flier on his face, the hot stink of it. He looked deep into its triplicate pupil eyes. The giant flier's body showed the scars and blackened, nonsensical writing of burning branches from the valley below.

Here lies their end. Colbrick was right. As Bishop prepared to sacrifice himself for Angela and Colbrick, the left side of his body was hit with a gust of wind. Something massive moved through the air to his left—something with wild, violent eyes. The thing in the air came down upon the big flier's neck, pinning it to the ground as the flier's enormous wings flapped above it. The four-legged animal flashed its dangerous teeth and bit into the flier's neck. The flier screamed and ceased its mimicry of the helicopters. It opened its beak and tried to jab at the animal on its neck, but the beast would not relent, and it used its powerful forelegs and sharp claws to keep the flier's vulnerable neck pinned to the ground. It bit again and again, and the flier's shrieks grew quiet, and its elephantine lungs relaxed and heaved no more. The gigantic grizzly bear stood on its hind legs, opened its jaws, and released a bone-chilling roar into the mountain night. Saliva dripped down its bloody muzzle. The great bear roared again and slammed its forelegs onto the dead flier. Once more, the bear stood on its hind legs, and Bishop saw only three toes on its right front paw.

Old Three Toes is a bear you don't mess with, his father had told him on one of their recent Apex trips. So the legend was true. Here stood mighty Three Toes, the evasive and cantankerous bear that haunted these rugged mountains. This was his home, his land.

The bear glared at them, huffed, and slammed his paws onto the flier again. They backed away slowly, and when they were seventy yards away, they turned and moved downhill, listening for any movement behind them.

*

Colbrick winced. "Let's go home," he said.

"Where's home?" Angela asked.

Colbrick stuck out a finger and made the shape of a "J" in the air.

Angela smiled.

"Colbrick, where's your pack? What are you doing in these rugged mountains so poorly equipped?" Angela teased.

Bishop laughed.

"Kick a guy when he's down, eh?" Colbrick asked.

They limped across the saddle into the glow of raging fires, and from the valley came the screams of dozens of strange creatures who had lost their way, who had lost their mother.

The survivors headed in the direction of Big J, gearless, but with the confidence of grizzly bears.

They walked towards home.

RETURN OF THE SONS OF NOTHING

Bishop, Colbrick, and Angela gasped and swore over every last step, limping down the trail.

"Nice shoes," Colbrick said to Angela, pointing at her silver-studded biker boots.

"Why thank you," she said. "I got them for twenty percent off at Talus Hell. Great store. Highly recommended."

The fires had spared Big J country, and a hint of dew gleamed about the meadow. Curling tails of smoke weaved in and out of tree line. So did something else.

"Look," Bishop said, pointing to the southeast corner of the meadow.

A white-tailed deer foraged on the lush grass. The deer lifted its head, and a small bird flew near it with a beautiful, orange breast.

"A robin *and* a deer," Angela said, her eyes watering. She hugged Bishop.

They hobbled towards Big J, trying not to swear or moan so as not to frighten the deer. The rare ungulate watched them approach the lodge and resumed feeding.

"I bet it hasn't seen humans in quite some time," Bishop said.

The battered front door had held its ground while they were gone, and Colbrick opened it with great care, almost caressing it. "It's good to be home," he said.

Angela smiled. Bishop put his arm around her.

Big J was Big J, and the warmly decorated lodge seemed to welcome them.

"Still lots of food in the pantry," Colbrick said.

Colbrick and Angela shuffled over to devour whatever they could find, but Bishop angled down the narrow hall to the master bedroom. He entered the room and no longer felt any strange sensations. It was now just a room.

He went to the medicine cabinet, then reached into his pocket and retrieved the bottle of Vicodin. "I don't need these," he said, setting the bottle on the shelf.

Bishop went into the bathroom closet for a towel to wash his face and discovered a framed picture resting upon the towels. The picture was black and white and showed a young ranch crew from who knows how many years ago. On the backside was a list of names written in cursive. Bishop stopped halfway through the list and took a deep breath. In the middle of the names was *John T. Gallatin*, his father. Bishop flipped the picture over and studied the faces. There in the back row, with the Apex Mountains behind him was his father, no more than eighteen years old.

"I did it, Dad," he said.

*

They sat at the kitchen table, pride and accomplishment beaming across their faces.

"So what are you going to do without your sawed-off?" Angela asked. "It's like you're naked without it."

"I dunno," Colbrick muttered. "I suppose I'll just take Bishop's and cut it down."

"I don't think so, buddy."

"Worth a try," Colbrick said.

The kitchen filled with the sound of chewing. Bishop took a hunk of stale bread and devoured it.

"Slick, Angela tells me your old man used to work at Big J?"

"Yes, he did, although I didn't know it until recently," Bishop said. "Funny coincidence, right?"

"Yeah. Funny how life sometimes throws you a surprise," Colbrick said. "But to tell you the truth, slick, I'm tired of surprises."

Angela laughed.

Bishop turned to Colbrick, admiring the man who'd saved their lives and risked his own at the Hoodoos. But there was something he wanted to ask.

"Colbrick...are we...are we really still 'slicks'? I thought 'slicks' meant idiots or fools?"

"I'm afraid you read me all wrong, partner. My old man called me slick, and me him. And my old man called his old man that, before he died in the first world war."

Bishop froze, his eyes watering. Angela grabbed his hand under the table and squeezed.

"Ah, OK, I didn't know—"

"That's alright," Colbrick said. "That's alright."

They feasted on the meager pantry items throughout the day and drank from the good Big J water. Outside, the sun streaked across the meadow, filtering through the smoke haze. The deer was joined by another.

*

"You coming, Colbrick?" Angela asked as they walked to the maimed truck in the driveway.

"Nah, you folks go on ahead. I'm wiped. But do please find me a shotgun, and do your best to get some chow."

"10-4," Angela said, saluting Colbrick with bandage-free hands and walking to the truck with verve.

Bishop emerged from the lodge, tan and fit and hopeful. Yet great sadness ate at the hope like a disease.

"Let's roll," he said, hopping in the driver's seat.

"Elmore?" Angela asked.

"Yes."

They reached Highway 18 in good time and parked. Angela glassed to the north. The road damn lay blackened and burned.

Towering flames and ethereal reds dominated the eastern horizon. Mushroom clouds the size of nuclear detonations filled the sky, casting a pall across the landscape, but also inferring cleansing.

Each mile towards Elmore brought a deeper sense of blackened sorrow that seized their hearts. *I should be happy,* Bishop thought. He took Angela's hand and she squeezed, and both of them held back tears as they remembered the frantic, helpless barks of Yutu coming from the burning apartment building.

"There's nothing we could have done," Angela said.

"I could've shot the fliers is what I could've done."

"I think you're suffering from Testosterone Overdose Syndrome. You shoot at that moment, and the seed-mother is still here, and this place is still under siege, and we're dead."

Bishop gripped the wheel. He wanted to punch something, anything.

"There it is," Angela said, pointing to Denson's General Store which preceded downtown Elmore by several miles.

They parked in the back. Bishop got out of the truck and noticed a bright-red piece of clothing laying twenty yards into the cedar forest. They approached the object, guns out.

It was a human. A man.

His right side had been chewed off, but the left portion of his frame was intact. He wore spectacles, a red rain jacket, and an Elmore Grizzlies football t-shirt. There was something about this body that intrigued Bishop, but he couldn't put a finger on it. He felt compelled to bury the man, exposed as he was, half-eaten. There were atrocious marks and cuts around his neck—likely the work of an eel.

"Watch my back," Bishop said. He bent down to search the man, thinking he may have the keys to a gun closet or maybe the General Store. Instead, Bishop's fingers touched upon a folded piece of paper in the man's breast jacket pocket. Bishop unfolded it.

"What does it say?" Angela asked, curious as ever.

Bishop cleared his throat. "To whom it may concern—if you are reading this, I am likely dead, and my plan did not work. I need to make a food run for both myself and my dog as we've been stuck in our apartment—"

Bishop paused. Angela looked at him, her eyes gushing, pleading.

"Keep going," she said, her lips quivering.

"I need to make a food run for both myself and my dog as we've been stuck in our apartment since the attacks began. The few neighbors I had went to their cars when the creatures pounded on the roof and windows. But my dog and I stayed put. I never saw my neighbors again."

"Oh no," Angela cried.

Bishop paused once more, his eyes dripping, his fingers gripping the note and shaking.

"My dog—his name is Vermillion—is at Geldon's apartments on Main Street, building address 2265, room 8. He likes milk bone biscuits, to be pet on his belly, and he loves to play Frisbee. He's a great dog and very smart. I told him how to do many tricks, and if you point your finger at him in the shape of a gun, he will lay on his side, paw his face and play dead. I think it's his favorite trick. Also, please do not let him eat lettuce, it upsets his stomach."

Bishop stopped reading when his sobs made his speech too erratic.

"Keep going," Angela said, placing a hand on his shoulder. "Please keep going."

Bishop wiped at his eyes and held the paper to his face.

"Although I have left out numerous bowls of water and some food, please retrieve him immediately from the apartment upon reading this note. I locked the door so those things could not harm him. I don't know what I would do if I lost him. Please tell Vermillion I love him, and please attach my class ring to his collar so he can still have my scent, which I know he will miss because he has the best nose I've ever seen on an animal. Please pat him on the belly for me and tell him I will see him again someday. Thank you for taking care of my beloved Vermillion. Sincerely, Robert Jenkins."

Bishop crumpled the paper and tossed it to the ground, then walked towards the store.

"What are you doing?" Angela asked, wiping her eyes and cheekbones.

"I'm going to get some food," Bishop muttered.

Angela reached down to the man and took his class ring from his finger, then put it in her pocket.

They gathered as many groceries as they could, loading the truck with colorful boxes of carbohydrates and silver cans of meaty stew, then started towards Big J. Angela had taken something else from the store, putting it in her pocket with the ring. She watched the countryside with wary eyes and took the ring from her pocket, rubbing a finger on it like it was magic.

"What if...what if things sort of repeat themselves sometimes?" she asked, turning to him.

"What do you mean?"

"What if Yutu is still alive?"

"Come on," Bishop said, punching his fist into the steering wheel, pain shooting up his arm.

"Jesus," Angela said, recoiling.

Stillness grew between them, and Angela snapped it in half.

"Go back," she said.

"What?"

"Go back to Elmore."

"Why?"

"I could use some clothes," she said.

"Yeah, OK, makes sense to get as much as we can in one trip."

Bishop turned the truck around.

Soon, they reached Fulton's on Main Street. Dense smoke wafted from the alleys.

"Keep going to the next intersection," Angela said, pointing with a shaking arm.

"Any reason why?" Bishop asked, his eyes darting. He did not want to go back there, ever. The scene haunted him, even worse than the creatures. You knew the creatures were evil. They did what they did. But what kind of God or creator allows a lovable dog to possibly burn in an apartment or get chewed apart by monsters?

"I want to see the building Yutu was in."

"Are you serious?"

"Yes. Please, Bishop?"

The apartment building was burnt to a crisp on top, but the brick seemed OK save for the black stains and broken windows. They entered through the burnt door frame, and the odor of charred, moldy wood fanned towards them. Waves of panic grasped Bishop, and his vision blurred.

"Are you coming?" Angela asked. "The note said apartment eight."

"Why are we doing this?"

"Because it's the only thing we can do."

They crept up the blackened stairs past the charcoaled woodwork, and Bishop flashed back to all that smoke and heat and the frantic barking which increased the panic and swirling vision. He reached out to a charred wall to ground himself.

"You OK?" Angela asked, looking back.

"I'll be fine," he said.

A moment later, they reached the hallway to the second story. He wanted to turn and run. The blackened beams mocked him, the torched yellow plaster leaping at him in twisted, haunting shapes.

Angela walked ahead of him, peering into each blackened room. Bishop wondered why in the hell she was doing this.

Then Angela stopped and put her hands to her mouth. Her eyes lit with the wonder of a child gazing upon a Christmas tree on the big morning.

She waved to Bishop frantically.

Why was she doing this? Did she hate him? Bishop swallowed and stumbled down the hallway, claustrophobic from the panic.

He followed Angela's pointing arm, and there inside the apartment of Robert Jenkins was a dog, curled up in the corner on a burned comforter. The dog was scratched and bloodied, but clearly alive.

Bishop bolted into the room screaming his lungs out with unbridled happiness, and Yutu shot up from his deep, healing slumber and wagged his tail. Then the pooch leaped into the arms of the man who had saved his life, whimpering and yipping.

Angela joined in, crying with complete disbelief. In a time of madness and death, here at Robert Jenkins apartment on Main Street, there was something for the world to behold.

Bishop held him in his arms, squeezing him. Yutu licked his face.

"You're such a good boy," Bishop said, burying his head into Yutu's neck. "Such a good boy."

The mangled, burnt apartment building was a million miles away. All Bishop felt was love.

"I missed you so much," Angela said with a huge grin, patting Yutu on the head as Bishop held him.

Bishop stared in wonder and happiness, a big, fresh grin stuck across his face. All the anxiety and death peeled away as he watched his beloved Yutu.

"I thought I lost you, boy, I'm so glad to see you again!"

"He came back to find Robert," Angela said.

Bishop nodded as Yutu licked his face. Then Yutu twirled in place and licked and bobbed at Angela.

"How did you do it, boy? How in the heck did you escape?" Bishop asked.

Yutu barked, for although he could not understand humans, he knew The Man was asking him a question, and a bark was the only way he could reply. And then Yutu smelled something on The Woman— something he'd known a long time. He sniffed her pocket and wagged his tail.

"The ring," Angela said. She took it out, let Yutu sniff it and then hooked it onto the metal ring of the collar she'd taken from Denson's General Store. She clipped the collar onto him, and Yutu puffed his chest out and raised his muzzle, proud of his prize.

They left the apartment of Robert Jenkins and piled into the truck.

In the front seat, Angela's serious eyes met Bishop's.

"We need to bury someone," she said.

Bishop nodded.

They parked back at Denson's and let Yutu out of the vehicle, and Yutu immediately raced towards the decayed body of The First Man.

Bishop and Angela allowed it because it's better to know than not to.

Yutu nuzzled and cuddled with The First Man, yipping and yowling.

In the late afternoon, Yutu moved away from Robert Jenkins and towards Bishop and Angela, and they knew it was time to bury the body. Tools were procured from the general store, and a proper grave was dug for a good man and good dog owner. They rolled Robert Jenkins into a blue plastic tarp and lowered him into the grave while Yutu looked on with his paws at the edge, tilting his head as the tarp was lowered.

Yutu remained until the last patch of dirt was thrown upon the good man and even until Bishop started the truck. It was only when Bishop gave the truck a bit of gas that Yutu bolted from the grave and to the vehicle, leaping inside as Angela opened the door.

The road was free of the terrible creatures.

"Like Colbrick said, sometimes life just throws a surprise at you," Bishop said.

"I like this surprise," Angela said, hugging Yutu as he sat on her in the front seat.

Bishop peered out over the land that his father loved and which he too had fallen in love with many years ago. But he had come to learn one thing as he marveled at the wonderful passengers in this ravaged truck—that no matter how beautiful a place may be, it's the people and living things you care about that really matter.

*

The damaged truck rumbled down Highway 18.

Behind it, out of the shadowy vegetation, a creature emerged that the hopeful passengers did not see. The animal walked with confidence and carried a muscular hump that connected to powerful claws and forelegs. The head was dish-shaped with a distinguished, blocky snout, and the native animal flashed its sharp teeth. It ambled, yellow claws clacking on the asphalt trail which it did not like, for man had not been kind to it. It was from the hot and dangerous roads that the bear sought shelter, heading west up towards the alpine meadows to seek hiding and food. Soon, it would look for a den, because winter waits for no one, especially in the Apex Mountains.

*

"What now?" Bishop asked as he watched Big J Meadow from one of the paddocks.

"We wait for the feds to show," Colbrick said. "I suppose they'll have lots of questions."

"Not a surprise," Angela said, gesturing with a bandage-free hand. "Not looking forward to that, *at all*."

Colbrick nodded.

As the three survivors gazed across the meadow at a pair of feeding white-tailed deer, Yutu bounded off to the tree line. The affable pooch growled and pulled something out of a shadowy patch of bracken ferns.

"Whatcha got, boy?" Angela asked.

Yutu trotted towards them, wagging his tail. Something squirmed in his jaws, and he dropped it at their feet. The little creature squeaked and limped away on six legs. Its tag did not flash.

THE END

Michael Hodges is an American speculative fiction writer located in Missoula, Montana. His short stories have appeared in over twenty magazines and anthologies, and his debut novel, The Puller, was released on April 24, 2015. The film rights for The Puller were purchased by Hollywood producer Sonny Mallhi, producer of the horror classic The Strangers. Foreign language rights were purchased by Luzifer Verlag, and The Puller was translated and released in Germany. Michael is also a member of SFWA and the HWA.

Michael is represented by Laura Wood of FinePrint Literary, NYC.

He also taught a writing panel with Game of Thrones editor Anne Groell ("How to Improve Your Novel's Ending", Missoula Con, 2015), and a panel with best-selling Eragon author Christopher Paolini.

https://www.facebook.com/MichaelHodgesAuthor/